DYNASTY

23

The Cause

Cynthia Harrod-Eagles

sphere

SPHERE

First published in Great Britain in 2000
by Little, Brown and Company

This edition published by Warner Books in 2001
Reprinted by Time Warner Paperbacks in 2004, 2006
Reprinted by Sphere in 2009, 2010

A CIP catalogue record for this book
is available from the British Library.

ISBN 978-0-7515-2538-0

Typeset by Palimpsest Book Production Limited,
Polmont, Sterlingshire
Printed and bound in Great Britain by
Clays Ltd, St Ives plc

Papers used by Sphere are natural, renewable and
recyclable products sourced from well-managed forests and certified
in accordance with the rules of the Forest Stewardship Council.

Mixed Sources
Product group from well-managed
forests and other controlled sources
www.fsc.org Cert no. SGS-COC-004081
© 1996 Forest Stewardship Council
FSC

Sphere
An imprint of
Little, Brown Book Group
100 Victoria Embankment
London EC4Y 0DY

An Hachette UK Company
www.hachette.co.uk

www.littlebrown.co.uk

Also in the *Dynasty* series:

SELECT BIBLIOGRAPHY

Burnett, John	*A Social History of Housing*
Carr, Raymond	*English Fox Hunting*
Chadwick, Owen	*The Victorian Church*
Chesney, Kellow	*The Victorian Underworld*
Clapham, J.H.	*Economic History of Great Britain*
Crow, Duncan	*The Victorian Woman*
Darley, Gillian	*Octavia Hill, A Life*
Ensor, Sir Robert	*England 1870–1914*
Ernle, Lord	*English Farming Past and Present*
Gretton, R.H.	*Modern History of the English People*
Hammond, Peter	*The Parson and the Victorian Parish*
Hobsbawm, Eric	*Labouring Men*
Huggett, Frank	*Life Below Stairs*
Manton, Jo	*Elizabeth Garrett Anderson*
McLaren, Angus	*Birth Control in 19th Century England*
Mingay, G.E.	*The Victorian Countryside*
Parsons, Maggy	*Every Girl's Duty*
Plumptre, George	*Edward VII*
Plumptre, George	*The Fast Set*
Rubinstein, David	*A Different World for Women*
Rubinstein, David	*Victorian Homes*
St Aubyn, Giles	*Queen Victoria, A Portrait*
Strachey, Ray	*Millicent Garrett Fawcett*
Strachey, Ray	*The Cause*
Todd, Margaret	*The Life of Sophia Jex-Blake*

THE MORLAND FAMILY

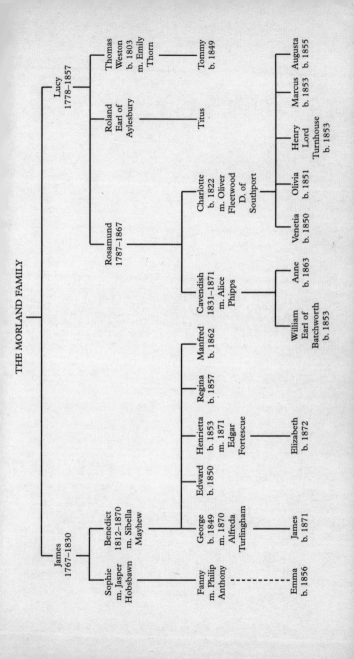

BOOK ONE

Starting Out

Unlike are we, unlike, O princely Heart!
Unlike our uses and our destinies.
Our ministering two angels look surprise
On one another, as they strike athwart
Their wings in passing.

Elizabeth Barrett Browning: *Sonnets from the Portuguese*

CHAPTER ONE

May 1874

Venetia Fleetwood came into the green drawing-room of Southport House in Pall Mall at her usual energetic pace, a clutch of stiff white envelopes in her hand. Her mother Charlotte, the duchess, was reclining on a sofa with a writing-case on her lap, composing a letter.

Venetia was a little too tall and thin for conventional beauty, and at twenty-four past girlhood, but she had a vivid, expressive face, and eyes that not a few young men had found fascinating. She paused to observe how slowly her mother was writing, and said, 'That looks laborious.'

Charlotte shrugged off the implied sympathy: she never made much of her ailments. 'Not nearly as laborious as when we had to use goose quills. I was quite an expert at cutting a nib when I was a girl: I made all my father's for him. You may thank progress that it's now a lost art. What's that in your hand?'

'More wedding replies,' Venetia said. 'I brought them up to save Ungar the stairs. You really ought to pension him off, Mama.'

'It would break his heart.'

'It's his heart I worry about. I can't think how old he is.'

'I wouldn't dare ask him. He's been my butler since before you were born, and he wasn't a young man then. But he was always terrifying.'

Venetia smiled at the idea of her mother being terrified of anyone. She waved the envelopes. 'Where would you like me to put these?'

'Oh, with the others,' Charlotte said, a touch wearily. 'I can't deal with them now.'

'Where is everyone?' Venetia asked. 'You aren't having to do everything alone, are you?' She crossed to the table to add the envelopes to the growing pile, sparing a surprised glance for a rather crude and brightly coloured figurine standing there, and returned to her mother. 'You look pale. Has the pain come back?'

'I'm just a little tired, that's all,' Charlotte said.

'If you have a headache you shouldn't be writing. What is it, anyway?' She craned her neck to look over her mother's shoulder. 'A thank-you note?' she said in surprise.

'Don't say "note", darling.'

'Letter, then. But you don't have to do those yourself. What do you have secretaries for?'

'Miss Scanlon's running messages for me, and Temple has quite enough to do. And besides, this is a special case – old Mrs Golding, who was your father's nurse, down at Ravendene.'

Venetia frowned. 'The old lady who lives in the cottage by the butcher's shop? The one Gussie calls "Mutton Chops" because she has more whiskers than Marcus?'

'Don't be cruel. She hasn't two farthings to rub together, poor thing, apart from the pension your father pays her, but she still sent a wedding present.'

'Don't tell me! That china figure on the table?'

'I'm afraid so. But it was very kind of her, and quite unlooked-for. She says it was given to her on her wedding day.'

'Not by Papa, I sincerely hope!' Venetia said. 'What on earth is it?'

'I think it's meant to be Lord Nelson. There was quite a craze for him in those days.'

'Oh, yes, I see now. I wondered why it only had one arm.'

4

'I expect it's had pride of place on her chimney-piece for the last fifty years,' Charlotte said, 'so please, darling, do say something kind when you see her next.'

'I'm always kind. It's Gussie who's tactless. But where is everybody?' Venetia reverted to her unanswered question.

'The girls are in the ballroom, laying out the presents that came this morning. And your father's gone to the House.'

'Again?' Venetia grinned. 'You know, Mama-duchess, I don't think Papa ever really meant to retire.'

'Oh, he meant it,' Charlotte said. 'But he found that he didn't like it as much as he expected.'

The Duke of Southport had retired from politics at the end of the 1871 session, worn out with his struggle to get Cardwell's army reforms through, against fierce opposition that had even included his own younger son, Marcus, who was a cavalry officer. The duke had given up his government position, closed up Southport House, and invited Charlotte to share a life of pastoral serenity with him down at Ravendene, his seat in Northamptonshire. Charlotte's health had been damaged while nursing in the Crimea; like many who had been at Balaclava, she had never been entirely well since. She suffered from intermittent bouts of severe pain, fever and debility, so the prospect of bucolic bliss had pleased her.

But it hadn't been long before Oliver had started to miss being at the centre of things: Charlotte noticed the ill-concealed eagerness with which he seized the London papers from the butler's hand every morning. Soon enough a day-trip to London 'on business' was casually mooted. This was by way of being the thin end of the wedge. The day trip was repeated, grew more frequent, and eventually was lengthened to an overnight stay so that the duke could 'catch old So-and-so at the club' or sit in on an important debate the next day.

By the time the decision had to be made whether Venetia should be married in London or from Ravendene, there was little doubt which Southport would choose.

'Your papa simply couldn't get used to not being consulted,' Charlotte said now to her eldest daughter.

'If he wanted to get back into government, he's missed his chance, poor Papa, now Mr Gladstone's gone out!' Venetia said.

In January of this year the general election had returned a Conservative majority. It was said that the brewers' vote was responsible: the Licensing Act of 1872 had been so unpopular that the brewing trade had turned *en masse* against the Liberals, and every public house had become a Conservative committee room. In February Disraeli had been invited to form a government, and it was only as a member of Her Majesty's Opposition that the Duke of Southport now spoke in the House of Lords.

'Oh, I dare say he'll still make himself useful,' Charlotte said.

'Not work for Mr Disraeli?' Venetia said in mock horror.

'Don't be silly, darling. It's not as if the Fleetwoods are an old Whig family. And in any case, there's good work to be done in opposition.'

'Devil's advocate, Mama-duchess!'

'Naturally I want Papa to be happy,' Charlotte said. 'There's no comfort for a wife in a discontented husband. Speaking of which, where's John? Didn't he come back with you?'

Venetia wrinkled her nose. 'John?'

'Your fiancé, had you forgotten?' Charlotte said drily.

'I can never think of him as "John". I don't know how you've mastered it so soon.'

'Not soon at all. You've been engaged for a year.'

'Yes, I know. But he'll always be Beauty Winchmore to me.'

'Beauty' had been Lord Hazelmere's sobriquet when he was Captain Winchmore, the most handsome and dashing of Blues officers. He had been the hardest rider and lightest dancer in the Heavy Brigade, pursued by ambitious mamas and their daughters alike, but never with a serious eye for anyone but Venetia.

Charlotte laughed, but she said, 'You must give the poor man a little dignity, now he's come into the title.'

'Beauty doesn't need dignity,' Venetia said carelessly. 'He has everything else – looks, charm, rank and fortune.'

Not so very much fortune, Charlotte reflected. The estate Winchmore had inherited from his father had been found to be much less healthy than supposed, emaciated by the extravagant lifestyle of both father and son. Hazelmere had been embarrassed but frank about it when closeted with Southport to discuss settlements – so Oliver had told Charlotte privately afterwards. Oliver had been obliged to agree to make a larger settlement on Venetia than he had anticipated, 'or they'll have nothing to live on,' he said. 'And whatever she thinks, Venetia won't be content with love in a cottage. She wasn't born my daughter for nothing.'

At that moment the door opened and three young women came in: the duchess's other daughters, Olivia and Augusta, and her ward, Emma.

'Oh, you're back!' Augusta exclaimed to Venetia. 'I say, that's a splendid hat!'

'I'd forgotten I was still wearing it,' Venetia said. She pulled out the long jet pins and removed it – a smart and rather mannish black glazed straw trimmed with cock's feathers.

'Where did you get it?' Augusta pursued. 'I must say, old Sissy, your clothes have taken a turn for the better since you became an engaged woman.'

'You're too kind. I always come to you to know what to wear, Gussie dear,' Venetia said, with an irony lost on her sister.

Augusta's self-confidence was impervious. 'We've been unpacking your wedding presents,' she informed her. 'Lots more came today – everyone in the country seems to be sending something. We've used up nearly one whole side of the ballroom, Mama. We'll need more trestles if anything else comes.'

'You have made a careful note of everything, haven't you?' Charlotte asked anxiously.

'Of course we have,' Augusta said. 'Olivia wrote down who sent what and so on – didn't you, Liv?'

'And we've put each person's card on display next to each present, Aunt Charlotte, just as you told us,' Emma added. 'Though, honestly, some of the things they've sent – you wouldn't think they'd want to own up to them! A pokerwork escritoire that looks like snakes writhing about in agony! The Milners sent that.'

'They should be made to sit and stare at it for an hour every day. That'd teach 'em!' Augusta snorted.

'And Lady Tonbridge only sent a photo-lith of the Queen in the most dreadful silver frame, which I call mean,' Emma said.

'And there was a pair of hideous Chinese vases from someone called Lady Pastry. Who on earth can *she* be?'

'Lady Paisley,' Olivia corrected patiently. 'I told you, Gussie. It was bad handwriting, Mama.'

'I don't think I know her,' Charlotte said, faintly puzzled. 'She must be someone of Hazelmere's.'

'Well, the vases were vile, and the fist was viler,' said Augusta, who picked up slang from her brother Harry, the heir, with whom she was a favourite. 'I don't know where you and Beauty are going to live, Ven, but you'll need a huge room just to put all the ugly things in. Or a better solution might be to have two houses – one for you and one for the wedding presents.'

'You mustn't call Lord Hazelmere "Beauty", darling,' Charlotte reproved.

'But *everybody* calls him that,' Augusta protested, opening her eyes wide. 'You can't really expect a person to call him John?'

'*You* are not to call him by his Christian name at all, you horrid infant,' Venetia said. 'He's Lord Hazelmere to you.'

'Oh, don't be stuffy! When I danced with him at

Lady Carmichael's last week he was as nice as can be. He dances divinely, you know. In fact, I rather think he's wasted on you. Everyone knows you don't like to dance.'

Charlotte intervened. 'Girls, do please sit down. It makes my head ache trying to look at you. Venetia, darling, draw the curtain across, will you? The sun's come round.'

Venetia went to obey her, and the others sat down on two of the green-silk-covered Louis Quinze settles that gave the room its name. Of the three sisters, only Olivia was a real beauty, with golden hair, regular features, and her father's violet eyes. She moved gracefully, and had a particularly lovely voice. Her years at Court as a maid-of-honour had given her both polish and a certain gravity; everything about her had a poise and restraint which made her seem older than her twenty-three years.

It had been no surprise to anyone when Olivia attracted the attention of one of the equerries, Charles Du Cane, ten years her senior and destined for great things in the Household; but the Queen disliked change, and maids-of-honour could not marry. It was typical of Olivia that she was quite content to leave things as they were for the time being. The large and static rhythms of Windsor and Balmoral, like the slow surgings of a full tide, had imprinted themselves on her quiet mind. At some point in the future she and Mr Du Cane would be married, but there was no hurry. She loved him, and could no more have doubted his intentions than God's goodness.

Augusta, the youngest of Charlotte's five children, was in a hurry for everything. Had she been in love, she would have been more likely to elope than wait for anyone's approval. She was always on the fidget, always talking, always ready for a new thought or a change of action. At nineteen she was a slender girl with thick sandy-gold hair and rather popping eyes, not a beauty, but with a smile, when she cared to use it, that would melt basalt. She never wasted it on her family, however: it was reserved for gentlemen, and not even all of *them*.

9

In her childhood she had lacked the personal attention the other children had received from parents and grandparents, and her education had been neglected. She had learned only what she wanted to learn, which was very little beyond reading and writing. Since her come-out she had read nothing but magazines and Burke's *Peerage*. She adored clothes and studied fashion with an almost religious devotion. Today she was wearing a gown of dark green tartan print and lilac silk, tight in the bodice over stays so fiercely laced that bending was an impossibility. The long sleeves, the panelled bodice, and the intricacies of the skirt were much trimmed with frill and self-coloured bows; the full, draped bustle and long train meant she could only sit sideways and had to have a settle all to herself. From this vantage point she bent a critical look on the other females in the room and sighingly deplored their entire lack of style. It was awful to have to live with such a pack of dowdies!

When finely dressed, Augusta liked to go visiting, to walk or drive where she would be seen, to go to parties, to dance and chat with 'the men'. Venetia was appalled by her ignorance, and called her an empty-headed little flirt; Augusta was equally appalled by Venetia's intellectual leanings, and called her a frightful blue-stocking. Charlotte, struggling with the awful lethargy of her illness, feared she had not done quite right by either of them. If they could have been blended together and then divided equally, she thought, they might have made two reasonable young women.

'So do tell,' Augusta said to Venetia, 'what *have* you done with Lord Hazelmere? I thought you were looking at houses today.'

'Only this morning,' Venetia said. 'The agent had two for us to inspect.'

'Did you like either of them?' Charlotte asked.

Venetia shook her head. 'The one in Henrietta Place was too small, and the other was in Kensington. We didn't even go and look at that. Beauty – *Hazelmere* spoke to

Griffin pretty sharply about wasting our time. He said – Griffin said – that there was something coming up in Bryanston Square or Bryanston Place, I can't remember which, that he thought might suit. But we can't see it until next week.'

'It couldn't have taken very long to look at one house,' Augusta said. 'What on earth have you been doing ever since?'

'I don't have to answer to you, miss,' Venetia said sharply.

'Of course not, darling,' Charlotte said quickly, 'but you were supposed to have a fitting this afternoon. I had to send round to Madame Bartoldy to cancel when you didn't come in.'

'Oh, Lord, I forgot! I'm sorry, Mama.'

'We quite thought you were going to bring John back for luncheon.'

'Instead of which,' Augusta finished, 'there we were without a man of any sort, staring at each other like four old cats.'

'Don't be vulgar, dear,' said Charlotte.

'You must have misunderstood me,' Venetia said. 'He couldn't have come to luncheon anyway. He had to see someone at his club, and then there's a debate on trades unions, or somesuch, in the House this afternoon. I suppose that's what Papa's gone in for?'

'Oh, never mind boring old politics,' Gussie said. 'What we want to know is where you've been all this time *without* Hazelmere. Did you lunch with someone nice?'

'I didn't *lunch* at all, if you must know, you horrid, nosy child,' Venetia said. 'I went to the New Hospital for Women to see Mrs Anderson. She was just going off to inspect some new premises, so I went too.' She turned to her mother, knowing where her best audience lay. 'You remember I told you they have to move somewhere larger because they're so overcrowded? Well, she's found two adjoining houses in the Marylebone Road with a fourteen-year lease. A group of us spent a couple of hours

11

going over them and making plans. It was so interesting! There'll be room for twenty-six beds when the alterations are finished.'

'The building work will be expensive,' Charlotte said, from experience.

'Yes, and there's all the equipment to buy – bedsteads, blankets, lockers, bedpans – absolutely everything! Mrs Anderson's started a fund, and she's going to write to everybody for donations.'

'I'm sure I can find a few guineas for a worthy cause,' Charlotte said.

'Thank you, Mama,' Venetia said. 'I knew I could depend on you.'

'I'm happy to help. Mrs Anderson's a remarkable woman,' said Charlotte.

'She is,' Venetia agreed. 'As well as running the hospital and planning the move, she operates, lectures, attends dozens of cases – sometimes in the middle of the night – and on top of all that she's pregnant again!'

Olivia protested. 'Oh, Venetia, must you use that word? It's so – unnecessary.'

'What *would* be unnecessary would be to wrap up a plain fact in fancy ribbons,' Venetia retorted.

'The Queen would dislike it so.'

'Luckily the Queen is never likely to hear me say it, or anything else, for which I am sure we're equally grateful,' Venetia said. Olivia looked a little hurt, but she disliked quarrels, and said nothing.

'If you didn't have any luncheon, darling, you must be hungry,' Charlotte said. 'Ring the bell, Emma, and we'll have five o'clock tea.'

Augusta reverted to the point that interested her. 'So, but who brought you home from your horrid hospital, then, Sissy?'

'Nobody brought me home,' Venetia said shortly.

'You didn't come in a cab *by yourself*?'

Venetia's brows drew down. 'If I'd wanted to, I would have, but I didn't. I took the omnibus.' She observed the general reaction with impatience. 'For heaven's sake,

12

there's nothing improper about the omnibus! All s̶
people ride on them.'

'Not *all* sorts,' Augusta said. 'Not people like us, just the lower orders – and the horrid do-goods that you meet at your dreary meetings and committees.'

'It's not "horrid" or "dreary" to try to improve the lot of the unfortunate,' Charlotte reproved. 'I've devoted a great deal of my own life to it.'

'It's different when you do it, Mama,' Augusta said kindly, then added with an exaggerated sigh, 'I'm sorry to have to say it, but Venetia's becoming awfully middle-classed.'

Charlotte roused herself to sternness. 'That's enough, Gussie. Your sister's not answerable to you; and until you have opinions worth listening to, you had better hold your tongue. All the same, darling,' she added to Venetia, after a pause, 'I'm not sure I like the idea of your travelling alone on an omnibus.'

'A contradiction in terms, surely?' Venetia said.

'Don't prevaricate. I can't quite think it right for a female to travel unaccompanied—'

Venetia burst out in exasperation, 'For heaven's sake! Can't a sensible, mature, educated woman travel on a public omnibus in broad daylight? Why is a woman alone assumed to be either feeble-minded or vicious? Really, I wonder I was able to hand over the fare without a man to tell me which coin was which and protect me from the conductor's advances!'

Augusta, having provoked an interesting reaction, was enjoying the outburst. 'Go it! Give 'em socks!' she urged her sister.

Charlotte said, '*Please* don't let your father hear you speak like that. I do sympathise with you, darling, but the world is what it is—'

'And it will never be any different if we don't try to change it,' Venetia snapped.

At that moment, fortunately, the door opened and Ungar, the butler, announced, 'Mr Weston, your grace. And would your grace desire the tea to be served now?'

...g it in, Ungar, and a cup for Mr Weston,

'I have already taken the liberty of providing one, your grace.' Ungar bowed and stepped back to admit Tommy Weston; behind him, two footmen waited with vast silver trays, one containing the kettle, pot, spirit lamp and other paraphernalia, the other with plates of thinnest bread-and-butter, small French-iced cakes, and a dish of the first strawberries.

Tommy Weston crossed the room to kiss the duchess's hand, and she greeted him with relief and warm affection. 'Now you will keep my turbulent brood at peace with each other,' she said.

'I'll do my best,' Tommy said, sitting down beside Emma. He was the adopted son of Charlotte's uncle, Thomas Weston, and had run tame about the Southports' houses most of his life. He was twenty-five, neither tall nor handsome, and with an indefinable look of fragility to his face; but a pleasant young man with a warm smile and easy manners. He was in blacks for his mother, who had died in November.

His father, who had been MP for Winchendon, had given up his seat at the last election, and had now retired to a small house in Brighton. Weston's considerable fortune would all be Tommy's when he died, in token of which – for he was a fair-minded man – he had settled a very large allowance on his son. 'No use in Tommy's scraping about, getting into debt and ending by wishing me dead,' he had said; to which Tommy replied hotly that of course he wouldn't do any such thing. But it was certainly nice to be independent and do as he pleased without worrying about money, especially as he had no turn for any kind of work.

Over tea, Tommy settled down to make himself agreeable to everyone. He enquired after the duchess's health, and then elicited from Venetia an account of her day. He had a snippet of his own to add when she had finished.

'Did you know that Mr and Mrs Anderson are about to

move house?' he said. 'Not very far, though, just further up Upper Berkeley Street to number four.'

Venetia laughed, beguiled out of her scowls. 'It's true after all,' she said. 'Tommy does know *everyone*!'

He talked to Olivia about the Queen's surprising fondness for her new Prime Minister: Mr Disraeli had even persuaded her to agree to meet the Tsar of Russia, which no-one had managed before. Then he drew Olivia out on the subject of Her Majesty's anxiety that the Prince and Princess of Wales were moving in a 'fast' set.

'I have heard that Marlborough House parties are so boisterous the noise can be heard at the other end of Pall Mall,' he said seriously.

'It's true,' Augusta broke in, 'because I heard it myself one night, hanging out of the window. They must be wonderful parties! I wish I might go,' she added wistfully.

Tommy suppressed a smile at the thought and asked her instead about the entirely respectable performance of Handel's *Messiah* she had attended the evening before. This seemed to have been notable not for any musical excellence but because a tall handsome man with 'the most killing blue eyes' had begged to be introduced to her, as Augusta was only too eager to tell.

'Mr Cornwallis came back to our box after the first interval and said, "By Jove, Lady Augusta, you've had a remarkable effect on the most unimpressionable man I've ever known!" I asked who it was, though I'd guessed, because I'd seen him looking up at us and whispering furiously to Mr Cornwallis down in the stalls. So Cornwallis pointed him out and said, "His name is Wentworth, and he has a very nice estate in the north and twenty thousand a year." They were up at Trinity together. So Cornwallis said, "He's a very good fellow, but by my head, he's as cold as ice and I never knew him to notice any woman before in my whole life."'

She paused to see the effect this was having on Tommy. He made encouraging noises, enjoying the show, for Augusta had quite a turn for mimicry, and the whole scene was quite clear to him. She went on, 'So I looked demure

– like this – and said, "Oh, really?" And Cornwallis said, "Yes, but he has been positively raving about you: 'Cornwallis, who is that lovely girl you've been talking to – I must meet her,' and so on." So then he begged me to allow him to present his friend, and I said very graciously he might, and in the second interval Mr Wentworth appeared in our box, and chatted most amiably – not a hint of coldness about him – though he didn't so much as *glance* at Anda Cornwallis, despite her looking ravishing last night, in white and with her hair done a different way which doesn't make her neck look quite so short. But he only had eyes for me – and such eyes! I never saw bluer. He asked if I was going to be at the Somersets' ball and of course I said yes, and he looked *very* significant and nodded a great deal but just then the interval ended and he was obliged to go away, otherwise I'm sure he'd have asked me to keep a dance for him. Afterwards Anda Cornwallis said she hoped I might not be smitten, but I told her it would take a great deal more than twenty thousand a year to smite me, even with such blue eyes.'

Tommy laughed and said, 'You must be sure to make a large number of men very unhappy before making *one* man happy.'

But Venetia had listened with impatience and contempt to all this, and said that Gussie was as vain as a monkey and a disgrace to her sex and that it was lucky for her that their mother had fallen asleep and not heard her talk, or she'd not be allowed to go to the Somersets' ball at all, even with Lord and Lady Cornwallis's chaperonage. Augusta retorted that *she* was a fine one to talk about chaperons, rushing about alone all over London like a hoyden. Then Olivia interrupted the exchange gently but firmly by asking Tommy how his father was.

Tommy shook his head sadly. 'Of course he's over seventy, and one shouldn't expect too much, but he took Mum's death very hard. I went to stay with him last Friday-to-Monday, and there was something about him . . .' He paused, remembering. 'We went for a walk along the sea front, and he walked so slowly, not like his old way. And then we sat down on one of those new seats for a while, and when I spoke to him, he looked at me quite vaguely, as if he didn't know who I was.'

'He will be coming up for the wedding, won't he?' Venetia asked.

'I'm sure he will, if he's well enough. He wouldn't miss it for worlds – he's very fond of you, you know.'

'As one black sheep of another,' Venetia said, smiling. She stood up. 'Well, if you'll excuse me, I have some letters to write.'

Her departure broke up the party. The duchess woke, and, feeling less well than she would admit, withdrew to her room. Olivia took Augusta away to make her practise – 'You've precious few accomplishments, Gussie, you can't afford to neglect your playing' – which left Tommy Weston alone with Emma.

For a while they sat silently, each absorbed in thought: as old friends, they did not feel the need to make conversation. Emma's thoughts were not happy ones. Like Tommy she was in black – for her mother, Charlotte's cousin Fanny, who had died the previous December. Her mourning and Venetia's impending wedding had been the excuse not to make any decision so far, but she was aware that when both were over she was going to have to think about what was to happen to her.

Her mother had been an invalid for almost as long as Emma could remember, and she had been brought up at Ravendene, sharing, through the kindness of 'Aunt Charlotte', a governess with Augusta. The girls had been 'best friends' through their childhood, but Augusta's come-out had emphasised the difference between them, and removed her to another world, one where Emma could not follow. For Emma was illegitimate: she could never enter Society, nor look for the kind of match that awaited a duke's daughter.

And when Augusta married – which surely would be soon – her own position in the duchess's household would be exposed as something to be questioned. Not that Aunt Charlotte would be unkind or cast her out, but there was no real place for her here, nothing for her to do. Thanks to the comfortable fortune she had inherited on her mother's death, Emma would not be destitute, but a girl could not live alone, and the prospect of spending her life in retirement and isolation down at Ravendene in the house of an elderly invalid, seemed, to an eighteen-year-old, hardly preferable.

She came back from her reverie to find Tommy looking at her intently. 'Poor little Em,' he said. 'Not happy thoughts, I guess?'

He had taken her hand, and Emma almost held her breath, for it was an unconscious gesture, and she didn't want to do anything to make him drop it. She had been in love with Tommy for years, but she was sure he thought of her only as a little sister. He had known her most of her life, and in any case, he had long nursed a hopeless passion for Venetia.

For a while Emma and Venetia had lived together, under chaperonage, in a house in Bedford Square. During that time Tommy had called most days and, in the absence of any encouragement from Venetia, had involved Emma in his liberal concerns. They had become very close, but – from Emma's point of view – not close in the right way.

'I hate to see you wearing crape,' he said. 'When do you leave it off?'

'For Venetia's wedding. I shall be in half-mourning by then. I'm having a gown made of grey twill with lavender trim.' She sought about for a subject to keep him talking. 'Tell me what's been happening to our Langham Place friends. Have there been any great victories for the Cause?'

'Great victories? You know that's not the way these things happen. We progress by painful creeping steps. Of course, it was rather a blow the Liberals going out.'

'Doesn't Mr Disraeli believe in Reform?'

'Yes, I think he does – but many of his party don't. However,' Tommy said, 'we soldier on.'

Oh, he had let go her hand; but at least he seemed disposed to chat.

'I met Miss Davies the other day,' he went on, 'and she said one of the young ladies at Girton has sat both the Mathematical and the Classical Tripos. That's a tremendous achievement – and all the signs are that she'll pass with high marks.'

'But she still won't be given a degree?' Emma asked.

'There's no question of that. She took the papers quite unofficially. They're being marked by a friendly professor. But it proves what women are capable of. Unfortunately there's yet another report being circulated about study being bad for women.'

'Oh dear, I thought that sort of thing was behind us.'

'They used to say higher education would damage a woman's mind, and *that*'s been disproved,' Tommy said. 'Now they're saying it will damage her physical health and prevent her from fulfilling her natural function – which means having babies, I suppose.'

'But that will be disproved too, in the end, won't it?'

Tommy shrugged. 'Women who are strong-minded enough to persevere against such fierce opposition tend to be the ones who don't get married.'

'Oh dear. It's all so complicated.'

'Needlessly so,' said Tommy.

'It makes me almost glad that I'm too stupid to study,' Emma said.

'I don't think you're stupid at all,' Tommy said warmly.

'Don't you?' She turned her face up to his hopefully.

There was a moment of silence, as Tommy suddenly became aware that little Emma was not a child any more, but a young woman of eighteen. He had been used to talking to her unguardedly, as to a sister; but there was something in her expression that warned him. It occurred to him that a man had better be careful how he behaved if he did not want to raise unjustified expectations in a woman.

And yet, he thought, were they so unjustified? He had

grown very fond of Emma over the time that they had met in London and gone to meetings together. She was not Venetia, but she was charming and a comfortable companion. Tommy had been in love with Venetia for as long as he remembered, without any hope of a return. Venetia had never had time for anything outside her own ambitions, while Emma had always entered eagerly into his concerns. Venetia, in any case, was about to marry Lord Hazelmere, a circumstance Tommy had helped to bring about.

And Emma had grown from a girl to a pretty woman – a woman, moreover, who was looking at him with definite tenderness. It occurred to him suddenly that he might ask Emma to marry him. She was alone in the world and needed a protector: he knew better than anyone the limited choices facing her. His own origins were as obscure and lowly as hers, but he had been legally adopted by a man of connections, given a name, family and fortune; and while there were some who would still turn up their noses at him, for all intents and purposes he was a normal member of society. It was different for Emma, and he thought with pity that while a person might do quite well without a mother, having no father was a very much more serious proposition.

There would be a sort of logic and symmetry in his marrying Emma; and she, knowing the worst about him, would never scorn him. Soon Venetia would be irrevocably out of reach as Lady Hazelmere. Why wait for that day? It would make no difference. She could never have been his. And, he thought, looking down into Emma's eager face, he probably would not have been happy with Venetia anyway. She was too different from him, too high, too proud, too ambitious, too hard. Whereas Emma shared his tastes and interests – and Emma was everything soft and feminine and yielding.

'Emma,' he said, 'you know that I am very fond of you?'

'Are you?' she said – almost whispered, so keenly was she listening for what she longed to hear, and hardly dared hope for. She had seen the change in his expression. Her hand crept into his again, she could not say by whose volition. 'I am too – of you.'

'Oh, Emma, you are so very sweet!' A warm rush of affection surged through him. He was not a vain man, but he could read her eyes and it touched him that anyone's happiness could hang so completely on his approval. 'We've had some happy times together, haven't we?'

'Oh, *yes*! Very happy!'

He saw with a sudden flash what it could be like: him and Emma, comfortable together, married companions, much as his father and mother had been. To give her pleasure, to see her smile, to have her loving company – all would enhance his life.

'Emma,' he began, and paused an instant on the brink of what he would not be able to take back. But she had changed physically in the year since Bedford Square, and he saw now the difference in her, a difference that was exciting.

'Yes?' she said.

Her lips were trembling – soft lips – warm, inviting, womanly lips. Because of his adoration for Venetia he had remained a virgin: he had never even kissed a woman before. He discovered now that he was ready for love, more than ready. Emma really was *very* pretty. How could he do better? He plunged over the edge.

'Emma, dearest, will you marry me?' he asked.

'Oh, yes, *please*,' she said. 'Oh, Tommy, I do love you so!'

And so he kissed her. It was the first time for Emma, too, but she had been thinking and dreaming about it for so long that she felt as if she knew all about it. Her eager response to the brush of Tommy's lips awoke a response in him. He kissed her on and on, and after a while his hand came up and cupped her soft, curly head to make the kissing easier.

CHAPTER TWO

Though Tommy had never spoken in public, he had worked for a time as secretary to an MP, and he knew how to present a case clearly. He felt he did himself reasonable credit before the duchess, and she listened without showing surprise or dislike of the idea.

At the end she said, 'Well, Tommy, it's not me you have to persuade. It's the duke who is her legal guardian.'

'Yes, ma'am, I know, but I thought – I hoped you might—'

'Do the asking for you?'

'Oh, not that. I know what's right. But perhaps you could give me the hint as to what his reaction might be.'

'I think he will see it as a very good offer for Emma,' Charlotte said. 'Better than might be looked for, given her circumstances. But will your father like it? Not that you actually need his consent.'

'I should hate to proceed without it,' Tommy said. 'I owe him everything. It would be horribly ungrateful to marry against his wishes.'

'But you would if you had to?'

He hesitated. To hurt and offend Dad? Ah, but then to hurt Emma, even to lose her? Faced with the question, he knew he very much did not want to lose Emma. The knowledge fortified him. And, anyway, why should Dad object? 'It won't come to that.'

Charlotte wondered. She knew how much Weston had always wanted the best for Tommy. Emma was no catch, and an illegitimate wife would be a grave disadvantage to a man who wanted to 'get on' – in politics, say, or with the *monde*. However, Tommy had no desire to 'get on' anywhere, being quite happy where he was. Weston was an intelligent man and ought to see that; but he was old, and old people could be contrary and stubborn.

'When will you go and see him?'

'As soon as possible. I only want to speak to the duke first, and then I'll go straight down to Brighton.'

'Southport's at the House and he dines out tonight, so you can't see him before tomorrow. Why don't you go to Brighton now? I'll explain to the duke. And I think I can speak for him, that he will give his consent.'

'You know that I can't bear to delay an instant!' Tommy said gratefully. 'You are very kind, ma'am.'

'Never let it be said that I stood in the way of true love,' she said, with a smile. 'Go on, off with you. I believe there's a train on the hour, isn't there? You'll just catch it.'

Emma could not have survived without telling someone, and it was natural for her to choose Venetia. Venetia's was not the world's most cosy bosom, but she was the person Emma knew best. She hurried along to Venetia's room and was admitted by the maid, who was laying out Venetia's evening clothes, while she sat at her desk, writing. Venetia looked up and, seeing the bursting expression on Emma's face, sent the maid away.

'Oh, Venetia, the most wonderful thing's happened!' Emma cried, before the door had even closed fully. The words were so inviting that it would have been more than could be expected of flesh and blood for the maid not to lay an ear against the panels to hear what the wonderful thing was.

Venetia put down her pen, got up and went to the window-seat, patting it and saying, 'Come and sit here and tell me. Is it Tommy?'

Emma blushed beautifully. 'Yes. How did you guess?'

'Well, he was here, and you were there, and I'd have to be more of a fool about people than I am not to know that you like him. All those months in Bedford Square when you were gazing at him moony-eyed—'

'I did not!' Emma said hotly. Then, 'Did I? Do you think he noticed?'

'*I* don't know, love. So what have you got to tell me about Tommy now?'

'He asked me to marry him. Just now, in the green drawing-room. Oh, Venetia, I'm so happy!'

'I'm very happy for you! It's splendid news.'

'But do you think it will be all right? Your father—'

'Will be pleased too, I'm sure. Why shouldn't he be?'

'Because I'm not good enough for Tommy.'

Venetia laughed. 'But, Em, that's not his concern. He's your guardian, not Tommy's, and he's bound to see it's a good match for you. Why on earth should he object to a young man with a good fortune taking you off his hands?'

Emma lowered her gaze. 'Well, I don't suppose he likes me. I know he didn't approve of Mama.'

'But he took her in – and you with her – and having accepted the responsibility he would never shirk it. Papa was never a piker.' This was not very flattering to Emma, she realised, so she added, 'I'm sure he's fond of you, really. Who wouldn't be?'

The big brown eyes were lifted, suddenly and frankly. 'Tommy was always in love with *you*.'

Venetia met the gaze steadily. 'Now, what is this? Are you too happy, so that you have to pick at yourself? Tommy just asked you to marry him, didn't he? Did he say he loved you?'

'Yes.'

'Well, then.'

'And he kissed me.' Emma blushed again.

'So I should hope.'

'You don't think it was wrong?'

'I should have thought him a very poor fish if he hadn't.'

'I kissed him back,' Emma admitted. 'It was *wonderful*!'

24

Venetia concealed a smile. She didn't remember ever having been as young as this; but, then, she had been educated both in advance of her years and her sex. For a moment she envied Emma her simple happiness; envied all those women who accepted a woman's lot without struggle, because it was all they knew and all they wanted. Tommy would involve Emma in the Women's Movement, but Emma would go along with it because it was Tommy's crusade, and still find her all in all in him.

'So I suppose it is to be kept a deep, dark secret for the time being?'

'Oh – yes,' Emma said, coming back from her reverie. 'Until your father's given his permission – and Tommy's father. You won't say anything, will you? But I had to tell someone, or I should have burst.'

Venetia leaned forward and kissed her. 'I'm glad you told me, and I'm very happy for you, and of course I won't say a word until it's announced officially.'

She didn't hold out much hope, however, for Emma's keeping it from Augusta. Even if she didn't feel driven to tell, Gussie would probably worm it out of her. Worming was Gussie's second greatest talent.

Tom Weston's house in Brighton was tall and narrow, one of a terrace of red brick with white copings. The stairs were not what one would have chosen for a frail elderly gentleman, and they took a heavy toll of servants, but Weston seemed to have been drawn to it – perhaps by the memory of the tall, narrow house in which he had lived with his mother for so many years.

With the way building had gone on in Brighton over the years, it no longer had any view, even from the top windows; and Brighton itself was no longer fashionable – or, at least, not with people of the *ton*. As he walked from the station through the warm, insect-laden evening, with swallows stooping and flickering over his head, Tommy wondered again why his father had chosen to retire here, rather than to one of the quieter towns, and concluded that it must be sheer perversity.

The door was opened by Weston's elderly manservant Billington, who looked as frail as his master and no better suited to a life of steep staircases.

'Hello, Billington. Is my father at home?'

'Yes, sir, indeed he is. Dining alone tonight, too, so I'm sure he'll be glad of the company,' Billington said, taking Tommy's hat and waiting for the gloves. 'You will be staying to dinner, sir?'

'If there's enough for me? I don't want to put anyone out.'

Billington looked stern. 'What a question, sir! As if there wouldn't be enough. And you'll be staying the night?'

'I didn't bring any things with me,' Tommy pointed out.

Billington allowed himself a pleasantry. 'Things there always are, sir. It would be a shame to cut the evening short for worry of trains and such like.'

'How is he?' Tommy asked abruptly.

'As well as can be expected,' said Billington calmly, but his eyes were naked. 'Mrs Weston is very much missed by everyone.'

'I'll go up. Where is he? In the drawing-room? No, don't you come – save your legs. Those stairs are the devil.'

'Better I announce you, sir,' Billington said firmly. 'Sometimes if the master's been asleep it takes him a minute to remember where he is. Better he sees my face first, being what he's used to.'

So it was that bad, was it? Tommy thought, as he trod at painfully slow pace up the stairs behind the creaking manservant. Well, the news should buck the old man up. In the drawing-room the curtains had been drawn and the gas-lamps lit, though it was not full dark outside, and there was a small fire, despite the warmth of the day. The room was furnished with pieces from Upper Grosvenor Street, favourite things which Tom and Emily had chosen to take with them when they left the house to go and live by the sea for Emily's health. For Tommy it gave the place a strange air, to see furniture he knew so well in a room he knew hardly at all.

His father was sitting by the fire in a high-winged chair, an open book under his hands, his chin sunk forward in a doze. He looked so frail, Tommy's heart misgave. In the six months since Mum died, he had gone with frightening speed from vigorous old age to senescence. Seventy was not so very old these days, not for people of their class. Gladstone was seventy, and Disraeli sixty-nine, and neither of them had come to nodding by the fire.

Billington went over to his master and bent to speak in his ear. 'Are you awake, sir? There's a visitor here for you.' He shook him gently by the forearm, and Weston stirred and grunted, lifted his chin from his chest, opened his eyes and looked blankly at the fire. 'A visitor, sir,' Billington repeated.

'Eh?' Weston shifted in his chair, sat up a little more. 'What did you say? I was dreaming,' he went on, without waiting for the answer. 'Damnedest dream – about Venice. Haven't been there since my Grand Tour, with my brother. We were in a gondola, and someone was singing . . .' He looked at his servant at last. 'Oh, it's you, Billington. I must have dozed off. Couldn't think for a moment where I was.'

'Brighton, sir,' Billington mentioned. 'Our house in Brighton. And there's a visitor to see you. It's Mr Tommy, sir, come down from London. I took the liberty of asking him to stay for dinner. I anticipated you would want a nice long chat.'

The eyes sharpened a little, and Weston said, with something like his old spirit, 'What a lot of information you manage to pack into one short speech, old friend. Now I know where I am and what time of day it is. How long until dinner?'

'Half an hour, sir.'

'No other guests?'

'No need to dress, sir.'

'Very good. Bring him in – and pour the sherry.'

Billington straightened up and moved aside, and Tommy took his cue. 'I'm here, Dad,' he said clearly, stepping forward to stand in front of his father.

'So I see,' said Weston. 'No need to talk as if I were deaf or mad.'

'Sorry.'

'I get a little confused when I doze off, that's all. You'll be the same when you're my age. Good to see you, my boy. Come and sit down. Billington, where's that sherry? Is the fire too hot for you? Sit over here, by me. I can't see the expressions on people's faces these days unless I'm close to them.'

Billington handed the sherry and left them.

'Here's to you, Dad,' Tommy said, lifting his glass. 'Excellent sherry. You always have the best.'

'It's the last of the cellar I inherited from Papa Danby. You don't remember him, do you?' Tommy shook his head. His grandmother's second husband, who had adopted Weston as his own son on their marriage, had died before Tommy had been brought into the family. 'Always had superb taste in wine. Left me some fine port and Madeira as well as the sherry. This was his chair, too. I remember him dozing off in it, just as I do now. Come to think of it, he died sitting in this chair.'

Tommy didn't like this turn of the conversation. He said quickly, 'I got a very good train down, Dad. Hardly stopped at all. Very quick journey.'

Weston nodded a little vaguely. 'My mother once raced a team of horses from London to Brighton. Beat the Prince of Wales's time by a good bit. Not *this* Prince of Wales, of course – George IV, I mean. It's on record somewhere. Crockford's, perhaps.' He sipped his sherry and looked at his son. 'Mind's wandering. How are you, my boy? What brings you down here?'

'I came to see you, sir.'

'Sir, is it?' Weston grinned suddenly. 'That sounds bad. You want money, I suppose. Outrun the tallyman? How much are they dunning you for?'

'No, it's nothing like that,' Tommy said. 'My allowance is very generous. I manage very well – although of course—' He remembered suddenly that a married man would have more expenses than a bachelor. 'That is, some adjustment will have to be made – I mean, I should hope that you would consider—'

'Spit it out! Have you got into trouble?'

'No, not trouble.' He was aware that he was not handling this well. 'The thing is, I want to get married.'

His father's eyes were bright with amusement. 'Is this a general ambition, or have you anyone particular in mind?'

'It's Emma, Dad. Emma Hobsbawn.'

The twinkle disappeared. 'Oh? And how long has this been going on?'

'Nothing's been going on. I mean, of course I've known Emma for ages, but then I suddenly—'

'Suddenly?'

'Not exactly suddenly. What I mean is that I've always been fond of her, but never realised quite—'

'You haven't proposed to her?'

'This afternoon,' Tommy said, wishing it didn't sound like an admission. 'We happened to be left alone together at Southport House, and—'

'She trapped you,' Weston said flatly.

Tommy blushed with vexation. 'Not at all. It's not like that. I *want* to marry her.'

'Then you're a damned fool,' Weston said, and the blackness of his tone struck Tommy to the heart. He had never been spoken to like that before and he was hurt and shocked. 'Are you bent on throwing yourself away? Do you want to be ruined?'

'I don't—'

'Is this what your mother and I loved and protected you all these years for? Is this your gratitude for all she did for you?'

Tommy was smarting now, and felt this use of his mother was unfair. He tried to defend himself. 'She liked Emma.'

He got no further. For a frail man, Weston was strong in words. 'Emma Hobsbawn is the illegitimate daughter of a disgraced woman. I had some sympathy with Fanny's predicament, and she had good qualities, but she was never a well-regulated woman, and the seeds of her destruction were in her own character. What is amusing liveliness in a young female becomes unforgivable lightness with mature years.'

'But why should Emma be punished for her mother's faults?' Tommy protested.

'I'm not concerned with Emma. My concern is – as it has always been – with your well-being. To marry a girl of her background—'

'You forget, sir, that my own background is questionable.'

Weston flared, 'Don't presume to tell me what I know! Your unfortunate origins ought to make you doubly careful how you ally yourself. You above all men have to be circumspect. I've given you a name, a family, respectability, and a fortune, and I won't stand by and see you throw it all away. You can't possibly love this chit. Did I rescue you from degradation for you to destroy yourself on the whim of a moment? If you have no gratitude towards me, you might at least show respect for the memory of your mother.'

'You can't think I'm not grateful to you and Mum,' Tommy said miserably.

'Very well, then,' Weston said. 'We'll say no more about it.'

'But, Dad—'

'We'll talk about something else now. The subject is upsetting me.' He pressed a fist against his breastbone. 'Giving me heartburn. Tell me what's been going on in Town. Have you been to any plays, my boy?'

The last question was put in a much more genial tone, and Tommy thought it best to drop the matter for the time being. When Billington came in to announce dinner, Tommy rose and went to help his father out of his chair. He came up like a cage of dried twigs between Tommy's hands, almost frightening him, for he still had not fully appreciated how fragile his father had become. Once on his feet, Weston refused an arm and walked under his own power to the dining table. Over dinner he talked much more like his old self, discussing the political state of affairs with acuity, enquiring after old friends in the House and at his clubs, and telling anecdotes of his former life. It did not quite conceal from Tommy the fact that he hardly ate anything. Billington served them, and though Weston took a portion of everything offered onto his plate, he merely tasted and left it.

After dinner they returned to the drawing-room fire where Billington brought them port and cigars. Weston accepted both, but after one sip put down the port and made a face. 'Damn this indigestion! One of the sadnesses of growing old is not being able to tolerate the good things of life. I keep hoping I can get back to port, but somehow it doesn't happen.'

They sat in silence for a while. Weston's cigar went out, and when Tommy offered to relight it, Weston shook his head. 'No, I shall go to bed.'

Tommy rose and helped him up. 'Dad, about this other matter,' he began tentatively.

Weston put up a hand to stop him. 'Not now,' he said, but more kindly. 'We'll talk in the morning. I can't bear the upset of it now. It makes me feel quite ill. So goodnight, my boy.'

'Goodnight, sir.'

Weston's brows arched. 'Have I killed all affection, then? I'm a heartless tyrant, I suppose?'

Tommy smiled unwillingly. 'Never that. Goodnight, Dad.'

'Goodnight, Tommy.' He laid a hand briefly on his forearm. 'I couldn't have loved you more if you had been the son of my own body, you know.' And he went slowly to the door, where Billington was waiting with his candle: the gas did not go as far as the bedrooms.

Tommy stayed by the fire drinking port and finishing his cigar, until Billington came back to say he had settled his master and Mr Tommy's room was ready now.

'I'll go up, then,' Tommy said. He waited while Billington lit his candle and said, 'Don't you come up. I can fend for myself.'

'Very good, sir. I've laid out a spare nightgown, and one of the master's shirts for the morning, and I'll send the boy round first thing to have the barber come and shave you.'

'Thank you, Billington. What time does my father get up?'

'Early, sir. But he still breakfasts at eight. Shall I call you at seven, sir?'

'Yes, thanks.' He hesitated, and then, 'I'm sorry I upset him earlier. I'm afraid he didn't make much of a dinner.'

'It couldn't be helped, sir,' Billington said philosophically. 'The master hasn't been himself since Mrs Weston died. It fair knocked the stuffing out of him, as you might say. He's got so he doesn't like changes, you see – they worry him. But I expect he'll come round, given time.'

Tommy did not sleep well. The room seemed stuffy, and when he got up and opened the window, the air that came in was hardly refreshing, warm and damp and smelling mostly of smoke and horses, and only faintly of the sea. The dawn chorus woke him from restless dreams and he could not get off again. Finally he went to open the curtains and look out. It was grey outside, partly because the sun was not yet up, and partly because a sea mist had come in, cloaking the roofs and making the pavements glisten with damp. The town was quiet, the streets empty. On top of the lamp-post outside the house a large seagull perched, shuffling its wings from time to time and turning its head from one sharp profile to the other. On the house opposite, the mist seemed to roll down the slope of the slate roof like the slow ghost of water.

Behind him the door opened, and he turned to see Billington, fully dressed. 'Is it seven already?' Tommy said in surprise.

'No, sir, it's only a quarter past five. I usually go in and see if the master wants anything. He's always awake from about four o'clock, and sometimes he likes a cup of tea at five or thereabouts. It's a long time until breakfast, you see. A cup of tea, and perhaps a piece of bread and butter.'

Billington's voice was perfectly normal, but Tommy could see now that he was shaken, his eyes unnaturally blank. 'What is it?' he said suddenly. 'Is my father ill?'

'No, sir, not ill.' Billington's face seemed to waver and collapse, like the façade of a house being demolished. He teetered a little and put his hands up defensively to his cheeks. 'He's dead, Mr Tommy. Must have died almost as soon as I left him last night. He's quite cold, and his candle's burnt right out. He didn't even have a chance to put it out.'

'Poor Tommy's absolutely devastated,' Venetia said to Lord Hazelmere, as their horses paced side by side along the tan in the Park. 'He blames himself for shocking his father, though the doctor said it was only a matter of time anyway.'

'People like to blame themselves,' Hazelmere said. 'It gives them relief from sorrow – a counter-irritant, if you like.'

'But Tommy feels he more or less murdered him. And it's left poor Emma in a confusion of guilt and fear that he might call the whole thing off. Really, I can't understand Uncle Tom objecting to her. It seems the ideal solution for them both. But old people get strange ideas. I suppose that's all one can say about it.'

'The question is, how does it affect us?' Hazelmere asked.

Venetia looked sideways at him from under the curly brim of her hat. He affected not to notice and let his eyes rove with casual interest around the other equestrians. They were riding early to avoid the crowds, and it was mostly grooms on exercise and riding-school parties of breathless, bumping girls.

Venetia laughed. 'Oh, poor Beauty! What an eventful course our affair has run. You must wish with all your heart you'd never met me.'

He turned to grin at her. 'Fishing, my dear Venetia? How could I ever wish anything so irrational? Don't you know that all men are born perverse and run the harder after anything they think might be denied them? An easy conquest would have killed my love for ever, but you have only to keep one step ahead of me to keep me following faithfully like an old hound, all the way to the grave.'

He had loved her a very long time, since her débutante days, and she had favoured him over other admirers, largely, he believed, because he did not weary her with mooning and fawning, but loved her lightly and made her laugh. She had always had her mind set on things beyond frivolity, wanting to do more with her life than dance, flirt and gossip; and a spell in Berlin during the war of 1870 had confirmed her in the desire to be a doctor.

An irrational and impossible desire, Hazelmere had thought it: the medical profession, like the law and the Church, were closed to women by the fiercest diehards in creation. But Mrs Anderson – Venetia's model and heroine – had managed somehow to wriggle through various loopholes, and now practised as a doctor and even ran her own hospital. So Venetia had persisted in trying.

When she finally managed to get herself accepted as a medical student, she had met the full force of her family's resistance: the duke furiously forbade her to do it, and Venetia responded by threatening to leave home, a course which would have ruined her, had not her 'aunt' Fanny (Emma's mother) saved Venetia's reputation by taking a house and living with her as her chaperon. Later, when Fanny's health failed, a distant cousin had been found to take over and live with Venetia and Emma in the house in Bedford Square.

Hazelmere, like Tommy Weston, had been a frequent caller in Bedford Square, both doing what they could to protect the girls, and give some variety to their days

34

by escorting them on expeditions of amusement. But Venetia's great adventure had ended in failure in the May of the previous year. First two of the lecturers had banned her from their classes, and then her studies had been terminated by a petition from the male medical students, who felt she was bringing ridicule on them and damaging their chances in the profession.

To add to her misery, there had been a terrible and tragic accident, when the rakish Lord Marwood, who had been forcing his attentions on her, fell to his death down the staircase before her horrified eyes. The most appalling scandal threatened. Simply appearing at the inquest would have been enough to expose Venetia to damaging gossip, even if no worse speculations were aired about what Marwood had been doing there, and why Venetia had been living away from home in the first place. It was then that Hazelmere had had his chance to shine. He had arranged everything, interviewed the coroner, bamboozled the press, squared the duke, and comforted the shocked and distraught Venetia, who tended to blame herself for everything.

That it had all happened in the middle of Augusta's first Season made it all the more imperative that there should be no scandal. Hazelmere told Venetia that he would be able to protect her so much better if he was her fiancé. He had almost held his breath, but Venetia had accepted his offer of marriage, and had allowed herself to relax gratefully into the safe embrace of his love.

The strain had taken its toll of her, however, and she had collapsed under a *crise de nerfs*. Since the duchess's health was also far from good, it had been decided that they should go abroad together for the summer, and that the wedding should take place in the autumn. But there had been a series of put-offs. First, the ladies had stayed abroad longer than envisaged. Then on their return the duchess had been too taken up with Fanny's last illness and death to think about weddings.

Venetia and Hazelmere had talked tentatively of a March wedding, but in January the duchess's cousin,

Lord Aylesbury, had been killed while out hunting at Wolvercote, the family seat in Oxford. Charlotte would be in blacks only for two months, but the death had been unexpected and the grief great, and it was unthinkable to have the wedding when so large and important a part of the family would be unable to attend. July was therefore the earliest that could be contemplated.

At least that allowed time to arrange a wedding grand enough for a duke's daughter. Southport had been angered by Venetia's rebellion, but it had not stopped him loving her, and now that she had been restored to his bosom, he wanted an occasion suitable to his consequence. It was also important that no-one should be able to suggest there was anything half-hearted or desperate about the business. Hazelmere had always been a popular and well-respected young man, so his comparatively minor rank and small fortune would not cause any surprise, as long as Venetia's family could be seen to be thoroughly in favour of the match.

So it was to be the grandest of grand affairs: St Margaret's, eight bridesmaids, twenty carriages, and a wedding-breakfast for two hundred at Southport House. The carriages alone, with four greys apiece, would be four guineas each to hire, not counting tips, and the cake came in at over a hundred and fifty. The amount of money it would all cost had risen to such a scale that it had passed beyond comprehension in Venetia's mind and she felt quite detached about it now. Her father's present to her was to be his grandmother's diamond tiara and matching earrings; Hazelmere was giving her a sapphire and diamond necklace.

Her present to him – which he did not know about yet – was a hunter. The one part of the wedding preparations she had really enjoyed had been finding and choosing a horse good enough for him, and doing it all in secret. She had managed it with the help of her cousin Thomas Chetwyn, the new Earl of Aylesbury's eldest son, who arranged to have various suitable animals brought to Wolvercote where Venetia could go down and inspect them.

All the preparations were well advanced, and the Aylesburys would be out of mourning at the end of the month. But now poor Beauty was wondering if Tom Weston's death would mean another put-off. She hastened to put him out of his misery.

'I've talked to Mama about it. She consulted Papa, of course, first thing, and the upshot is that things are too far along to postpone. Although we all called him Uncle Tom, he was only Mama's uncle, not mine. She says she will wear black gloves – I suppose Lord Aylesbury will too – but that we needn't. But, of course, poor Tommy will be in deep mourning and won't come to the wedding at all.'

'And what's to happen about him and Emma?' Hazelmere asked.

'Well, he's asked her now, and Papa's given consent, so he won't back out of it. Not that he wants to, but he feels very bad about it being the cause of his father's death – or so he thinks anyway,' she anticipated Hazelmere's objection. 'I suppose their wedding will be put off for quite a while. He won't want to marry while he's in deep mourning. Six months' crape for a parent.' She sighed. 'Sometimes I think this whole mourning business goes too far.'

He raised a quizzical eyebrow. 'What? You wouldn't have us honour the dead?'

'Of course I would. But life must go on, you know. Sometimes it seems as though every event is kept hanging in suspense, waiting for the one or two days – or even hours, sometimes – when everyone involved happens to be *not* in mourning.' He was laughing now. 'Really, it becomes quite a juggling act. You should be grateful,' she added sternly, 'that you've no close relatives hanging around waiting to queer us.'

'Lady Venetia, what slang! But don't speak too soon, my darling. I've a maternal grandmother still clinging to life up in Westmorland.'

'Hush! Don't tempt fate!'

'You'd mind, then, if it was put off again?'

'What a question! Of course I would.'

'It's just that I have wondered occasionally if I didn't bully you into agreeing at a time when you were down and almost out. You really do want to marry me?'

'You did bully me,' she said, putting a hand on his arm, 'but that doesn't mean I didn't want to be bullied. I can't wait to be married to you. I think it will be perfect bliss.'

He lifted her gloved hand and kissed it. 'I think so too,' he said.

CHAPTER THREE

At the beginning of July the London Season was still in full swing, and excitement about the Southport wedding had grown to the point where every hostess, great and small, wanted to be able to boast the engaged couple on her guest-list. Despite the duchess's known ill-health and state of mourning and the duke's general indifference to social functions, invitations poured in to Southport House for everything from picnics to country-house visits, from operas to race meetings.

All the young Fleetwoods came in for their share of the fun. Augusta, who was being chaperoned for her second Season by the Cornwallises, was invited everywhere for the purpose of being pumped for the details that could not be got from the inaccessible Southports. As she was already becoming known for a lack of discretion, she rarely disappointed. The Cornwallis daughters, Miranda and Alice, benefited from her sudden popularity, and had the most exciting Season, in the heat of which both received more proposals of marriage than they could have expected on their own merits.

Olivia went to one or two of the quieter affairs. Her next waiting began in mid-July, when the Queen went down to Osborne, and what she saw as her real life was in suspense until then. But she loved Venetia dearly, and was profoundly glad that she had turned from her previous ruinous course to the respectability and normality of marriage with Lord Hazelmere. The wedding preparations, including the fittings for her bridesmaid's dress (she and

Gussie would make the first pair of the eight) helped to pass the time for her.

Of Venetia's brothers, Marcus, the younger twin, confessed on one of his visits home that he had become the most popular officer in the mess, despite his assuring everyone it was not in his power to secure invitations to the Event of the Season. Henry, Lord Turnhouse – the heir – had no need to become more popular: since his majority that March he had been much sought after. His sister's wedding was only of passing interest to him. On a visit to Ascot in June he had met Charles Carrington, the Prince of Wales's closest friend, and the two had taken a great liking to each other. Carrington had invited him to stay at his father's place in Buckingham, a bachelor party at which Turnhouse had met the Prince. Now he only waited for the wedding to be over to become a full-fledged member of the Marlborough House set.

One day in early July, with only a fortnight to go before the wedding day, he met Lord Hazelmere coming up the steps at Southport House just as he was leaving it.

'What ho, Hazel! You're looking hot.'

'It's a hot day. But you're looking as cool as the proverbial,' Hazelmere replied. Lord Turnhouse was wearing his top hat on the back of his head and was twirling his silver-topped ebony cane in a manner that had taken lengthy practice to render casual.

'I'm off to luncheon with Carrington and Petersham, and then we're going to Tatt's. They want my opinion of a filly. What have you been up to?'

'Choosing the bridesmaids' presents. It was a case where I could have done with a woman's guidance, but with no sisters of my own . . .'

'Should have borrowed one of mine. I've all too many. Gussie's got good taste, though.'

'I'm hoping to borrow one now: an hour or two in Venetia's company will soothe my fevered brow.'

Henry grinned. 'You've a queer taste in females, I must say! I find Venetia about as soothing as a wire brush –

but I suppose she's different with you. Are you engaged tonight?'

'I'm having dinner with Baby Sutton.' Augustus 'Baby' Sutton, an old friend, was to be his groomsman.

'Why don't the two of you join us? Freshwater's booked a room at Rules – Carrington, Petersham, me, Francis Knollys, Georgie Hope – all friends. And probably HRH will drop in. Bags of room for two more. A topping dinner and perhaps the theatre afterwards. What do you say?'

'It's very kind of you. I'd have to see what Sutton feels. We have to discuss the wedding – batting order and so on.'

'Oh, you can do that any time,' Henry said airily. 'I'll take it as fixed, then. Well, I must toddle.' He touched his hat facetiously and strolled off down the road.

Hazelmere watched him go, then turned and trod up the steps. Young Turnhouse seemed to be moving in exalted company – not that the heir to a dukedom wasn't entitled to inhabit the top sphere, but all those named were older than him, and HRH ran with a frisky pack. Ah, well, it did a man good to be let off the leash occasionally. At the end of a very long engagement, Hazelmere was feeling quite an accumulation of friskiness himself; but this wasn't the moment to be acquiring the Prince's and Lord Carrington's taste for actresses. If he and Sutton did dine with them this evening, he would make sure he left the party before it got too naughty.

A footman admitted him to Southport House without surprise. Hazelmere enquired first, correctly, after the duchess.

'Her grace is not at home, my lord.'

'Lady Venetia?'

'Her ladyship returned not fifteen minutes ago, my lord. I believe she is still in her room. Was your lordship expected?'

'No. Perhaps you'd enquire if she will receive me.'

'Certainly, my lord.'

Hazelmere was shown into the library, and it was half an hour before the door opened and Venetia came in, looking fresh and lovely in a light, loose-fitting gown of harebell-coloured silk. 'I'm sorry to have kept you waiting, but I simply had to change. I've been baking all morning in a sober suit,' she said, with a smile. 'Have I forgotten something? I wasn't expecting you, was I?'

'No, I just called on the off-chance that you weren't engaged. I missed you,' said Hazelmere.

'Oh, how nice that is,' she said. She gave him both her hands and stepped close. 'Isn't it nice that engaged people are allowed to be alone in a room together?' she added, in a different voice.

For answer Hazelmere took her in his arms and kissed her. There was a long silence, at the end of which Venetia broke off and pulled herself away from him rather breathlessly, saying, 'No more of that, my love, or I shan't be able to answer for myself.'

'This has been a damned long engagement,' Hazelmere replied shortly, breathless himself.

Venetia's eyes were bright and soft. 'What a lot of nonsense a wedding is! Why shouldn't two adults just go off together, without all this fuss? I half wish we could run away.'

'*Would* you run away with me?'

'For anything! You don't know how I long to be with you properly, naturally – completely!'

'Oh, my darling!'

Venetia evaded his reaching hands. 'No, no more kisses, love. I can't be frivolous in this room, with all these dusty old scholarly works around me, breathing out must and disapproval. You must wait for our wedding night.'

Her boldness in approaching the subject made him tingle. 'You're not afraid of – of the physical side of marriage?'

Venetia laughed. 'No, why should I be? Girls who go in terror to their marriage beds are generally those who've been told nothing, or told lies. I know the facts perfectly well, and the human body holds no fears for me.' She saw a slight frown cross her lover's face, and realised that was not exactly complimentary to him. 'Besides,' she went on, 'how could I be afraid of you? I long for you so much that sometimes at night it makes me feel quite sick. And now,' she added lightly, before he could answer, 'tell me what you've been up to today.'

'Looking at more houses,' Hazelmere said shortly.

'Oh, yes, I'd forgotten. Have you had any luck?'

'Nothing. Griffin seems to be scraping the bottom of the barrel now.' He eyed her curiously. 'I must say, you seem to be taking our lack of progress very calmly.'

The fact of the matter was that the wedding was so huge and indigestible a lump in her future that she had difficulty in seeing past it, and the question of where she and Hazelmere would live was something she simply couldn't bring her mind to get to grips with. When she tried to think about it, her imagination failed her. In fact, it seemed to her quite unimportant: they would live somewhere, *ça se voit*. Still, it wasn't tactful to say so to him, especially as he was wearing what she thought of as his 'bruised' expression.

'Of course, darling. But I'm in your hands, you see! It's for the bridegroom to provide a home for his bride. She must simply submit to his choice.'

'Unexpectedly traditional of you,' he said drily. 'But I really think we ought to look again at Bryanston Square. It's the best of them so far, and if we don't settle on something soon, we shall come back from our wedding tour to find ourselves homeless. Did you dislike it very much?'

'Of course not,' Venetia said, trying to remember which one it was. 'I could be happy anywhere with you, my love.'

'Not very helpful,' he said shortly.

'Oh dear, you are cross! Are you hungry? I should have offered you some refreshments. Shall I ring?'

'I wish you would stop clowning, Venetia,' Hazelmere said, 'and tell me seriously.'

'Seriously?'

'And truthfully,' he added.

'Ah! That's more dangerous. Is the unvarnished truth

43

the best thing between a husband and wife? Very well: seriously, I should be happy to live with you anywhere convenient. I can't remember the Bryanston Square house in any great detail, but if you think it will do for you, I'm sure it will do for me. After all,' she added, seeing he was still not pleased with her answer, 'we can always move again, can't we?'

'Yes, you're right, of course. I'm sorry I was cross. I am hungry, now I come to think of it. You might give me luncheon, do you think? And tell me what you've been up to this morning.'

'Oh, such an interesting day!' Venetia said, crossing the room to ring. 'I went on an errand for Mama to Ettie's, and as I was coming out I bumped into Sir Frederick Friedman and Dr Anstie.'

The former was an eminent surgeon who had been Venetia's sponsor in securing her place at medical school; the latter a physician at the Westminster Hospital.

'I haven't seen Sir Frederick since I was thrown out of St Agatha's,' Venetia went on, 'so I was delighted to meet him, and he asked most kindly after my progress and said he'd heard about the wedding, of course, and wished me joy and so on. Anyway, the two of them asked if they could walk along with me, and we had the most delicious talk about medicine!'

'Delicious?' Hazelmere asked quizzically.

'Well, it was to me,' she said, laughing. 'We discussed the Cause—'

'Women doctors?'

'Naturally! And, as *you* must know, since the Liberals went out the Enabling Bill has had to be dropped and everything is at a standstill.'

'Even if the Scottish universities were "enabled" to admit women to study medicine, there's no guarantee they'd do so,' Hazelmere pointed out.

'I know – and in some opinions, no likelihood either! I never put too much faith in the Bill myself. Anyway, Dr Anstie said in his view the only way forward for women was to open their own medical school. He said

44

the Westminster wouldn't for an instant consider mixed classes, and Sir Frederick said the same thing went for his hospitals. But they both thought that if a group of women got together and found a suitable house, there would be no difficulty in finding people to teach them.'

Hazelmere nodded. 'That's the way the women have gone at Cambridge, isn't it? The Girton house.'

'Yes. The difficulty, of course, is the same for all of us – recognition. The Girton women do the work and pass the examinations, but they're not given the degrees, and it would be the same for us. Still, just to do the work would be a step in the right direction.'

'Wasn't there a debate in *The Times* last year about a medical school for women?' Hazelmere said.

'Yes, between Mrs Anderson and Miss Jex-Blake,' Venetia said. 'Mrs Anderson was against a separate school in case it led to lower teaching standards and a useless qualification. She was for women going abroad to study. But Miss Jex-Blake thought women shouldn't be driven out of their own country like that, and that in any case few women could afford it. I suppose,' she added thoughtfully, 'that provided the courses were absolutely rigorous and there was no compromise, a separate school would be the best option.'

'Well, Miss Jex-Blake would seem to be the right person to start the ball rolling,' Hazelmere said lightly. 'She never minds a fight.'

'That's what Sir Frederick said—'

Venetia broke off as the footman came in, and ordered a luncheon for them to be served in the Peacock Room. When he had gone, she resumed, 'Dr Anstie said he had already written to Miss Jex-Blake. And Sir Frederick said it was important to get Mrs Anderson to put her name to the scheme, and wondered if I might have a word with her, since we're acquainted.'

Hazelmere was not hugely interested in the subject, but put his mind to it for Venetia's sake. 'Do you think she will agree? If she's against a separate school for women . . .'

'Sir Frederick thinks she'll see the importance of a

united front. The trouble is, she queered it for the rest of us. Her success made the fossils of the GMA doubly determined no-one else shall succeed and they've closed all the loopholes. I don't think she realises how impossible she's made it for everyone else.'

'Perhaps you'll be able to persuade her. And I suppose, if the school comes about, you'll want to be one of its patrons?' he added, with a smile. 'Well, I don't mind my wife putting herself down for ten guineas to the fund.'

'Dear Beauty!' Venetia laughed. 'You're all generosity! I'll take your ten guineas gladly, but I shan't be a patron, my dear, I shall be a student!'

'What?'

'I should be the first to join. I've lost so much time already – a whole school year and more. If the school does come about, it will be the best chance – perhaps my only chance – of getting on. I see great difficulties in the scheme, but if that's the only way the teaching can be had, then—'

'Wait, wait! You're going too fast for me. Are you seriously telling me that you want to enrol in this school?'

'You're being painfully slow about it, my dear. Yes!'

'You want to become a medical student again?'

The light faded a little from her eyes. 'Why so surprised? Of course, the idea may come to nothing, but if it does come about . . .' She studied his face. 'You know that I want to be a doctor. You know that.'

'I knew you *wanted* to be. Naturally I thought that was all over.'

'*Naturally?*'

'We're going to be married. You will be my wife. Yes, it's *natural* to assume that that will take the central place in your life.'

'Did you assume that, when you asked me to marry you?' she asked, in a light, hard voice.

'Yes, I assumed it. I do assume it.'

'Then why did you tell me you would help me realise my ambition? Did you lie to me, Beauty?'

He flushed at the word. 'If I said anything of the sort—'

'You did say it! It was the condition on which I accepted you. I thought you were on my side – that you supported me!'

'Venetia, darling, I'm always on your side. But as my wife you'll have so many things to occupy you. You'll have a house to run, we'll entertain, there'll be children – you won't have time even to think about doctoring. You'll be a happy – and loved – wife and mother. Surely that's enough?'

She was almost in tears. 'If you didn't mean it, why did you *say* it?'

'Oh, darling, people say things in the heat of the moment. I suppose I meant it at the time, but on reflection, you must see that the thing's impossible.'

'Not impossible for Mrs Anderson!'

'You're not Mrs Anderson. You're the Duke of Southport's daughter. You'll be Lady Venetia Hazelmere Surely you can see how impossible it would be for my wife to examine patients and cut up bodies and do all those disgusting things. I'm hurt you should even want to. Isn't being married to me enough for you?'

'No, it's not,' she said. 'Would it be for you?'

'Yes,' he said, a little angrily. 'I'm a gentleman and a peer, and people of our class shouldn't usurp the place of others. We have privilege and influence and we don't need to work for our living. What would happen to the lower orders if we took all the jobs? They'd starve. I shall be content to run my estate, love my wife, and raise my children. If I want for occupation I can always go down to the House.'

She looked at him bitterly. 'A fine and rousing speech, Lord Hazelmere. Have you given it to their lordships? Your beloved wife, of course, hasn't your particular resource. She can't go down to the House when she's bored. She will have to challenge her intellect by giving tea to the tenantry or making an annual speech to the children at the local Board school.'

He was afraid of the anger in her voice, and tried to draw back. 'Oh, Venetia, don't let's quarrel. I'm sorry

47

you're upset. Perhaps I've been tactless – I should have chosen my words more carefully. And really, darling one, there's no need for all this, is there? For all we know, the school will never come about, and we'll have quarrelled for nothing.'

'For nothing?' She gave him a strange look. 'You really don't understand at all, do you, Beauty? Even if the school doesn't come about, I couldn't marry you now, not now I know how you really feel.' She heard her own words on the air and for a moment panicked and wished she could call them back.

Hazelmere paled. 'Don't say that. You can't mean that.'

It was the wrong thing to say to Venetia. 'I always mean what I say – unlike some people,' she said. 'You aren't the man I thought you. The marriage is not the bargain I thought we'd agreed on. You said you would help me to become a doctor and I took you at your word. So that's all finished with now.'

'But, Venetia, I love you!'

'I love you too. But I can't marry you.'

She turned abruptly and left him, surprising the footman who had just come in to announce that their luncheon was ready by running past him in the doorway, her hand to her mouth. The footman turned his head after her, then looked enquiringly at Lord Hazelmere. Hazelmere could not think of a single word to say, and after a moment merely waved him away with an abrupt gesture of the hand.

If a mortar shell had hit Southport House, it could hardly have caused more turmoil. The word spread like fire in a hold through the servants' regions, and they huddled together, whispering, moving quietly about their tasks and watching the bell indicator fearfully.

Upstairs, the duke raged. His anger at being defied was exacerbated by his concern for his eldest – and favourite – daughter's welfare: for what can be more infuriating than being balked from doing what's best for one's child?

Words poured from him in a torrent. 'How dare you take such a course of action without consulting me? Have you no respect for my authority? Are a father's wishes to be set at nothing by the daughter he raised?' He threw at her all those things she was jeopardising. 'Our good name . . . Your family's credit . . . Your sisters' fortunes . . . Your mother's health . . .' He lashed her with the daunting list of her sins. 'Ingratitude . . . Disobedience . . . Selfishness . . . Callous disregard for feelings . . . Wilful neglect of your own and others' welfare and credit . . .'

Venetia did not cry defiance, as she might have five years ago. She faced him in anguished silence, biting her lip, sometimes swallowing back tears. When at last he paused to draw breath, and demanded of her angrily if she had nothing to say for herself, she licked her lips and said faintly, 'Indeed, sir, I am very sorry to vex you—'

'*Vex* me?' For a moment words failed him. Venetia wisely kept silence as he paced about the room. In a moment or two he returned and stood before her, icy with self-control, which in its way was much more frightening than his pouring rage. She had never been so well aware that he was a duke, a prince of the realm.

'Have you the least idea how much has been done in the last year to recover your credit? Your mother's efforts and mine, not to mention Hazelmere's, to repair the damage your previous behaviour inflicted on you and your family.' He spread his hands in a little, spurting gesture. 'The *cost* of this wedding alone—' He broke off again, overcome by the consideration.

Venetia thought of it, the dresses, the carriages, the flowers, the caterers, the champagne, the stationery, the extra servants – the sheer exhausting effort of everyone involved, especially her mother – and she quailed. 'If I *could* do it, sir, oh, I wish I could!' she said, close to tears.

He softened a little, seeing her weaken. 'Come, child, these are emotional times. Any young woman approaching her wedding day is entitled to be a little nervous – and you are so capable in so many ways, we tend to forget that in some respects you are the merest girl. Whatever has happened between Hazelmere and you, it is a momentary misunderstanding, and the two of you are intelligent enough to get over it. You love him, don't you? And I know he loves you. Two people who are so well suited will not fall out for long. He will make an excellent husband and you will be very happy – I would not have consented to the match if I thought otherwise. You believe that, don't you?'

'Yes, Papa. I know you have my best interests at heart,' Venetia said, daring to raise her eyes to his face.

'Well, then,' he said, taking this for surrender, 'we'll say no more about this.'

'But, sir, you don't understand. Nothing has changed. I am very sorry to disobey your wishes, but I must. I can't marry Hazelmere.'

The brows snapped down again. 'What do you mean, can't?'

'I want to be a doctor. Hazelmere told me when he proposed to me that he would help me. Now he says he won't. I must go on with my studies, and I *will*. So I'm afraid,' she swallowed, 'there will be no wedding.'

For an incredulous moment the duke stared at her in silence, and then the storm broke again. Venetia bowed her head and endured it.

Over the next few days Venetia had plenty of time to ponder her decision. She loved Hazelmere, hated hurting him, missed him dreadfully, and quailed at the thought of never seeing him again. A life without the comfort of him seemed bleak indeed. But that was the heart: the head said otherwise. She could not sacrifice the integrity of her mind and spirit for the comfort of her sad, silly, womanish heart. That would be the worst betrayal. She wished often and often that she did not have a head at all, but wishing achieved nothing. It made her miserable, but she could not change her decision.

The rest of the family took every opportunity to attack her with their own arguments.

'If you do this to me, I shall never, never forgive you,'

Augusta cried. 'My beautiful bridesmaid's dress! The wedding breakfast! The ball! Everyone would have been looking at me, *everyone*! And what will happen to us if you jilt him? People will never forget. All our prospects will be ruined!'

Lord Turnhouse was furious. 'Do you mean to make a laughing-stock of the whole family? Bad enough to be jilting Hazelmere, who's as decent a fellow as ever lived, but what about all the guests – some of the most important people in the country? Making us look fools in their eyes – there'll be nobody who matters who won't know about it! I'll never be able to walk into any club again! I'll have to go abroad if you go on with this mad start!'

Olivia was tearful. 'Oh, darling Venetia, please do marry Hazelmere! You'll break his heart if you don't – and everyone will be so cross! Papa will be in a bad temper for ever, and no-one will speak to us any more. And what will the Queen say if you really do try to be a doctor? You know she doesn't approve of ladies doing such things. Everyone will blame you, and cut us, and we'll all be so miserable. Oh, do, do marry him!'

Even Marcus came home on purpose to corner Venetia and harangue her. 'It'll be all over the mess! The men will hear and laugh at us – my career will be dished, you know! Hazelmere's a decent sort, and it's far too late to be cancelling at this stage. Nobody pulls out of a wedding two weeks before. Dash it, the arrangements are all made, the invitations have been accepted, everyone's looking forward to it. You can't let 'em all down. And my new dress uniform's already finished and paid for!'

Only Venetia's mother kept silence, looking grave, unhappy and very tired. At the first breaking of the news she had turned pale as an instant realisation flooded into her mind of the work and worry that would follow a cancellation. To send back all the presents alone would be a colossal task! To have to write to everybody! The explanations, the looks, the false sympathy, the endless, endless speculation! Too, too exhausting and dreadful!

The next day she did not leave her room. Her maid,

Norton, who had emerged to announce reproachfully that her grace was not well enough to leave her bed at present, seared Venetia with a flaming look every time she passed her – which seemed to Venetia to be suspiciously often. Of all people, Venetia had expected her mother to understand, and of all people's, it was her disapproval she most feared.

When eventually Charlotte sent for her, she went in trembling. She could withstand her father's rage, but she was afraid she would give in to her mother's tears.

But Charlotte did not weep. She was sitting at the desk in her bedchamber, writing something, looking very pale and worn, her eyes shadowed and the deep marks of pain lining her face. She was dressed, but her hair was loose, covered only with a cap, and Venetia noticed with a pang how grey it was. She crossed the room and stood before her, clasping her hands behind.

Charlotte looked up and studied the intense young woman who seemed so like her at the same age. She, Charlotte, had done unconventional things, shocked propriety, given pain to those who loved her. The difference, of course, had been that Charlotte had had an independent fortune, had been a countess in her own right, had been entitled to choose for herself. There had been no duty of obedience on her, as there was on Venetia.

'Well,' she said at last, 'you've put us all in a fine uproar.'

Venetia swayed like a sapling with the intensity of her emotions. 'Oh, Mama, don't *you* rail at me! I can't bear your anger, not yours.'

'I'm not going to rail at you, child. I'm too tired and sad for that.'

'But that's worse!' Venetia cried. 'I depended on your understanding me. I don't want to make you unhappy.'

'Are you determined not to marry Hazelmere?'

Venetia bit her lip. 'Oh, I know it's awful of me, after all the arrangements have been made – I can't imagine how much you've spent!'

'A fortune,' Charlotte said simply. 'And the social cost

of cancelling is beyond computing. So tell me, is there no way to reconcile you and Hazelmere? Don't you care for him at all?'

'I do love him,' Venetia said. 'He's a dear, dear person, and so kind to me, and so amusing. I thought we could be very happy together – I wouldn't have accepted him otherwise – but it was all under false pretences. He says now that he will not allow me to go on with my medical studies, and I can't marry him on that condition.'

'I thought you'd given all that up,' Charlotte said wearily. 'This past year you've said nothing about it.'

'I never gave it up. After that awful Marwood business I felt tired to death, and unhappy and confused. I needed a holiday from it. And I didn't see any way forward. But I always meant to start up again after we were married, if there was any way it could be done. I thought Hazelmere would help me. With his influence and support, I thought I would get further. Now it seems he never meant it at all,' she finished bitterly.

'It was natural that he should think your ambition would be put aside when you were married. Any man would think so. I thought so myself, and if anyone can understand how you feel, it must be me.'

Venetia looked at her stonily. 'And now you don't want me to go on. But I must, I must! There's talk of opening a medical school for women, which would mean—'

Charlotte stirred and sighed. 'Venetia, I would not want you to marry any man against your will. But you say you do love Hazelmere, and I ask you to consider this: if you do not marry him, it will not bring you any closer to realising your other ambition. You are dependent on your father, and he will never, never allow you to study medicine after this. You have no means of supporting yourself, and there's no Aunt Fanny to help you; and you must know by now that even if you can find someone to teach you, you can't study medicine without a considerable income, for your maintenance and all the fees.'

'You might help me,' she said, in a small voice.

'After this,' Charlotte said, with another sigh, 'I would not even argue for you.'

Venetia was silent.

'For your own good, as well as ours,' Charlotte said, 'marry Hazelmere. It is your only chance of happiness. You can't want to remain a daughter at home all your life, knowing that you've disappointed your father – and you're not likely to receive another offer, after jilting Hazelmere.'

'So even you are against me,' Venetia said, in a low voice.

'For your own good.'

'My "own good" seems to involve my being miserable for ever, one way or the other,' Venetia said.

'Talk to Hazelmere. It's not too late. He still wants to marry you, and none of this is public knowledge yet. Who knows,' she forestalled her daughter's negative, 'he may change his mind about your studies. You may be able to come to an accommodation with him. But if you can't,' she concluded sternly, 'I still urge you to marry him – and be grateful.'

The interview with Hazelmere was painful in the extreme. He was hurt, wary, half angry, half conciliatory. When he spoke gently to her, and particularly when he laid his strong, warm hand on her forearm, Venetia's body yearned towards him. Her emotions wanted him to take her in his arms and to kiss, pet and caress her. Her desire for him was great, her affection strong, and above all he represented safety and shelter, which her frayed nerves and bruised mind longed for. It would be so easy to yield, to let him take care of her, to stop struggling against the current and be loved and approved instead of reviled and accused.

But he said firmly and unequivocally that he would not, could not, allow his wife to do anything so repugnant as to become a medical student, and when she asked him again why, in that case, he had misled her, they quarrelled again. She ended by declaring hotly that she *would* go on and *would* succeed; he told her that she would never do it – no woman could ever do it – without a man's support, and that no man would ever agree to such a thing.

'But there are men who agree with the women's cause,' she cried.

'For other people's women,' Hazelmere said, with uncomfortable acuity, 'not their own.'

So the wedding was cancelled. Charlotte composed a short letter of explanation, and she, Olivia and Venetia, together with her secretaries, spent every hour copying it out and addressing it to each of the guests, so that they could all be sent out simultaneously. But, of course, the story was out before the letters had been posted, and the door-knocker was never still. Paragraphs appeared in the social columns of various newspapers, letters of condolence, some sincere and many more malicious, came in by every post, endless streams of visitors and press reporters were denied by Ungar and his largest, most muscular footmen, and the duke learned to regret his decision to have a London rather than a country wedding.

The assistant clergy, the organist, the choir, the florists, the caterers, the livery stables, the stationers, the mantua-makers, the domestic exchange, the upholsterers, the musicians, the french polisher, the man who tuned the chandeliers, all had to be paid off. The wedding presents had to be packed up again and sent back. The servants drooped about the house wreathed in gloom, the cook became distressingly erratic, and Augusta alternately sulked and raged (sulking was easier to bear because it involved pointed silences) because she was missing all the events of the end of the Season and didn't see why *she* should be confined to the house because Venetia had behaved badly.

Hazelmere left Town immediately and went to the South of France to nurse his wounds and avoid the gossip and pitying eyes. Olivia went back into waiting, to the life that seemed to her much more real, and where she could put her family's unhappiness at a more comfortable distance. Lord Turnhouse accepted a long-standing invitation from Lord and Lady Londesborough to join a house party at their home in Scarborough, which he hoped would be far enough from the capital for him to be able to enjoy himself.

And when all the business of cancelling had been completed, Southport House was shut up and the rest of the family prepared to retire to Ravendene for the summer, where they hoped for a little more privacy. Venetia, however, begged hard to be excused.

'I know Papa won't want to have me there, reminding him all the time,' she said to her mother. 'And I'd rather be spared the continuous reproaches. Please, Mama, mightn't I go somewhere else? I think it would be best for everyone.'

While not necessarily wanting to spare Venetia the consequences of her action, Charlotte did think it would be better for her husband's temper not to have her around – especially as the sight of her tended to provoke Augusta into renewed complaint. So she discussed it with Oliver, and after a brief exchange of letters it was arranged that Venetia should go down to Wolvercote for the summer, to be under the eye of Lord and Lady Aylesbury.

The Chetwyn family was by then in half mourning, but still had little desire to be out and about in the world, so there were no parties and no visiting. But they were a warm-hearted, cheerful clan, and the atmosphere was not gloomy or depressing.

The late lord had been unmarried, and the title had passed to his brother Titus, who was married and had five children. As well as the Aylesburys, there were two unmarried brothers, Maurice and Clement, in residence for the summer, together with an older sister, Lady Lucilla Hendon, on leave from her husband with whom she did not get on. Another married sister, Emily, was there with her husband Lord Avens and their six children. In addition, Venetia's cousin Lady Anne Farraline –

daughter of her mother's late brother – was living there semi-permanently.

Venetia was welcomed with quiet cordiality, and no-one spoke to her about the painful affair, or vexed her with questions or lectures. There were horses to ride, a vast park to ride in, dogs to walk, conversation, music, and plenty of quiet, cheerful family fun. Venetia would not think about the future, not even about what would happen at the end of the summer. Sufficient unto the day, she told herself, when unwelcome thoughts importuned.

The closest anyone came to mentioning her wickedness was when twelve-year-old Lady Anne, who had long had a crush on her, squeezed her hand as they were going into dinner one day and said, '*I* was always on your side. I think you were very brave.'

Venetia looked down at her sadly. 'Oh, love,' she said, 'don't make me your model.'

'I won't,' Anne said. 'I mean to be my own model. But I still think you did the right thing. I say, after dinner, Louisa and I have got a topping new game we've thought of that we want to try out, but everybody has to join in. Will you help us make them? Otherwise I expect the grown-ups will just want to talk as usual, and what fun would that be?'

'None at all,' Venetia agreed, with a painful smile. 'I'm coming to the conclusion there's all together too much talk in the world.'

CHAPTER FOUR

The carrier's cart put Alice Bone down at the end of the drawbridge to Morland Place. The carrier lifted down her box with exaggerated grunts, climbed up again and shook the horse into a shambling trot. Alice's nervous goodbye was lost in the rumble of wheels and gritty swirl of dust. In a moment he had disappeared over the rise, and she was alone in what seemed like a very big world.

It was a little before six o'clock on a fine July morning. The sun was up and the pale sky was filled with shoals of small clouds like rosy fish, gilded along their spines. The dew glinted as if someone had spilled a treasure of diamonds in the grass, and the stones of the barbican were warmed to the colour of honeycomb. Alice was no lover of antiquities, and the first time she had seen that drawbridge and barbican she had thought it looked unpleasantly like a prison. Even now in the morning sunshine there was a cold smell from the moat, which made her think of dungeons. But she gave herself a little shake, reminding herself that this was her first day as under-housemaid, and she was lucky to get the place.

Life was far and away better for servants in country houses than in towns, her mother had told her – especially in a big country house with a large staff. Most other girls Alice knew couldn't wait to go off to Leeds or even London; but Mam had said they would end up as slaveys in some mean place, the only servant kept, having to do everything themselves – more than likely without even enough to eat.

'You get into Morland Place, my lass, that's my advice to you,' said Mam, her voice jerky as she scrubbed at the washing-board. 'And on your day off you'll be close enough to come home and see us all.'

This last was a big inducement to Alice, who at fourteen had never left home before. Girls went into service as young as ten, to their 'prentice place, where they worked part time to learn the ropes and save up for the uniform they would have to buy for their first real place. But Alice was the eldest and had nine little brothers and sisters, so she had always helped her mother at home; until this year, when her Dad, who was a horseman, had had an accident that left him unable to work for several months. So now Alice's wages were needed for the family budget. Morland Place, just outside York, was one of the most important houses hereabouts, and only five miles from home – less across the fields.

She picked up her box and hurried across the draw-bridge to find someone to report to. The gatekeeper, who popped out of his little damp room under the barbican, where he lived like a toad in a cave, agreed she was who she was, and sent her on up to the house. She remembered in a whirl of mental images the previous times she had come here. First she had been interviewed by Mrs Holicar – a large, handsome woman in a black dress with white collar and cuffs – in the housekeeper's room, which had cupboards, floor to ceiling, all round it. That, she learned, was where all the good things – jam and cake and fruit cordials – and the precious china and linen were kept locked up. Mrs Holicar had a great weight of keys on a big ring and chain attached to her waist, symbol of her great authority.

She had questioned Alice pretty stiffly, before saying, 'Well, you have no experience, it's true, but you seem a sensible girl, and you are pretty, which is an advantage. The mistress likes well-looking maids. If you are taken on, and do your duty, you may be promoted before too long.'

Alice had had to come back another day to be inspected

by the mistress. On that occasion she was taken to the sitting-room, a bright, modern apartment Alice admired much more than the grand, ancient marble hall she passed through to get to it. There were papered walls, carpeted floor, chintz-covered chairs and sofas, little tables, vases of flowers, a chimney glass, china ornaments and framed photographs everywhere, and a canary in a cage by the window. Mrs Morland was reclining on a sofa, in a much ruched and frilled gown of lavender silk. Alice had been too scared to take more than one peep at her, and got an impression of gaunt, aged beauty, eyes like bright blue stones, and golden hair elaborately dressed with the merest dab of lace on the top by way of a cap.

The mistress had asked Alice one or two questions – if she had been baptised, if she could read and write, how old she was – then surprised her by demanding to see her teeth, just as if, Alice thought afterwards, she was a horse. But the teeth seemed to have clinched it, for Mrs Morland had waved a hand and said she would do.

So here she was, starting her new life at twelve pounds per annum, paid quarterly, and all found; one day off a month and one half-day a week from two o'clock onwards. It was her first time away from home, and she felt small, nervous, and a bit tearful. Entering the house she was at once accosted by a tall young man with thick curly hair, who popped his head out of the small room opposite the door. He was wearing a black apron and had a gentleman's boot in one hand and a brush in the other. 'Hullo!' he said. 'What have we here? Who are you?'

'I'm the new housemaid,' Alice said, wondering if she should call him sir.

'Have you got a name, new housemaid?' he asked, looking her over in an embarrassing way.

'Alice.'

'That's a pretty name. Pretty name and a pretty face. I'm Thomas, fourth footman. When's your day off?'

'I don't know. I've only just got here,' she said, bewildered.

His insistent eyes wandered again over her face and

figure. 'Come you find out, let me know and I'll change mine and take you out walking. You're a tastier piece than the rest. The females in this house are old boiling hens!'

A maid appeared at the far end of the passage at that moment, attracted by the sound of his voice. 'Who's that? Is that t' new girl? Lord, you haven't got time to stand chatting, y' knaw!' Her voice was deep and rough with a strong accent. 'You leave her alone, Thomas, she's on'y a little kid. You've to watch out for Thomas, love, he's not nice to knaw. Eats little girls whole and spits out t' boots.'

'Aye, and tha'd love to 'ave me tek a bite, wouldn't tha?' Thomas laughed, imitating her, and gave Alice a wink.

'Cleanin' boot's all you're fit for,' the maid said, giving him a ripe look of contempt. 'Come on wi' me, love.' Alice hurried to her. 'I'm Katy,' she said. She was a strong-looking country girl with a big chin, red cheeks and red-rimmed eyes. Her hair was dark and greasy, and slipping down out of its pins from under her white cap. She looked about eighteen, and her figure was pillowy under the blue cotton dress and coarse apron – the same sort that Alice had been obliged to provide herself with.

Makepeace's, the drapers in York, had a servants' department and knew the uniform for all the gentry houses round about. Two dresses, four coarse aprons, four white aprons and four plain white caps, Alice had had to buy, together with boots and stockings. Four pounds, it had all cost – a large investment, which made it doubly important that she kept her job.

'What's y' name, love?' Katy asked.

'Alice. Alice Bone.'

'That's nice. We haven't got another Alice. The girl 'at left, the one what's job you've got, she were another Katy. Caused a lot o' confusion. Is that your box? Come on, then, I'll show you our bed, but you'll have to get a move on. We've a sight to do, and you're not even changed yet. I'd have thought you'd've had t' sense to come in your uniform.'

'I'm sorry, I didn't know.' Her eyes filled with tears.

'Oh, Lord, don't cry! I'm not Mrs Holicar, I'm just lowest o' th' low, like you! She's set me on to show you what to do, but she'll be after us both if we don't get t' work done, so I'm on'y hurrying you for your own good. Are you struggling wi' that box? Give it here, then. Lord, you've got arms like two sticks o' celery. Never mind, you'll soon build up some strength.'

She talked tirelessly as she escorted Alice along narrow corridors and round corners to the back stairs, up which she hoisted herself briskly, her broad blue-cotton behind wagging before Alice's face.

'Is it a nice place here?' Alice asked the bottom, a little breathlessly.

'Oh, it's not so bad as places go. I've been here eight month. I like a big house, me. There's more servants, more fun and variety, like. I don't reckon I'll stay, though. I never stay long in one place. I get bored wi' it. Ma last place I were six month, an' place before I were two year. That were a big house, bigger than this, an' servants' quarters were better. I liked it there; but th' butler drank, and when he were foxy, he used to chase us maids some'at shocking.'

'Does the butler here drink?'

'Mr Goole? No, better if he did, nearly. He's a terror, watch out for him. Mrs Holicar's all right if you do your work. But Mr Goole takes it out on us if he's in a bad temper, or the master's rated him. Still, even he's not as bad as that Hayter, t' master's valet. Mr Goole'll ignore you if he can, but that Hayter looks for some'at to blame you for. He's a sour man. No, I don't reckon I'll stop here long. I'm for goin' to Leeds as soon as I've a bit saved.'

'My mother says servants are better off in the country,' Alice said tentatively.

Katy reached the top of the stairs and turned to look at her. 'I'm not for stoppin' a servant all me days,' she said. 'Don't you knaw they're takin' on girls o' sixteen in t' factories at twenty-three pun a year? Hours are no worse, and if you've to find your own lodgin's, at least your life's your own once you've finished work. It's a daft game, bein' a servant. Here, you take your box now, I'll light t' candle. There's no windows up here.'

They were in the roof space, with shadowy beams rising into dusty darkness, bare boards underfoot, and only enough light filtering from God knew where to make out a table on which stood a collection of candles in various candlesticks and holders. Katy lit one and led the way through what seemed like a maze of narrow passages and finally opened a door onto a small bare room containing two iron bedsteads, two wooden chairs, and a table with a bowl and ewer standing on it. It seemed to have been created simply by erecting a lath-and-plaster partition between the floorboards and the roof beams, so that high overhead she could just make out the underside of the tiles. It seemed gloomy and comfortless, but Alice had no time to examine it in detail, for Katy patted the nearest bed and said, 'This is ours. Put your box down there, that's right. And now for pity's sake hurry up and change into your uniform. We're half an hour behind as it is. Halls and stairs is our job, and it's all to be done before the gentry's astir. There's 'ell to pay if they come down and catch us at it.'

Alice remembered the halls and stairs from her second interview. The staircase hall was a great room built for nothing, it seemed, but to house the staircase – and what a staircase! The treads were fully five feet wide and the wooden banisters were delicately carved into a lacework of fruit and flowers. The stairs marched round three sides of this room, up to the bedroom floor. On the walls were portraits of ladies in silk gowns and men on horseback, and the distant ceiling was all curly plasterwork like the icing on a wedding cake. There was a sort of window in the middle of the ceiling that Katy told her – surprised she should ask – was called a lantern. Alice had never seen anything like it in her life – imagine, all this space just for stairs!

The stairs were covered down the middle with drugget, and her and Katy's job was to brush the drugget and polish the exposed wood of the stairs on either side.

'Then polish the handrail. Then sweep the hall floor.'

'What about all this?' Alice asked, indicating the lacy banister carvings.

'Not our job, thank God,' Katy said abruptly. 'We've enough to get on with.'

When they had finished the staircase hall, they passed through into the great hall, which was another vast room going the whole height of the house, on one side of which was the main house door, twenty feet high and eight feet wide, solid mahogany with a brass lock the size of a lectern. There was a marble floor, which Alice and Katy had to scrub. There was also a massive fireplace – all carved marble – a chandelier about six feet across, and a few tables and hard chairs pushed back against the walls, no furniture in the middle at all.

'What do they want it for?' Alice asked in a whisper, as they knelt and scrubbed. She'd been warned they must not make a noise. 'This big empty room?'

'Oh, it's just for comin' and goin',' Katy said airily. 'The gentry likes everything big. But they have parties in here sometimes – dancin' an' everything. It's like a proper ballroom, then.'

'How many people live here?' Alice wanted to know.

'Just the master and mistress and their little boy – Master James. He's two and a half years old, and the sorriest scrap of a kid you ever saw, poor little mite.'

'Is that all?'

'Aye, but there's visitors come and go all the time. There's three lots stoppin' at the moment, though that was a—'

She broke off as Mrs Holicar appeared from the kitchen passage and crossed the hall as quickly and smoothly as if she was on wheels. She directed a sharp look at the kneeling maids and snapped, 'You haven't time to gossip. You're late as it is.'

Katy turned up her red face. 'This is t' new girl, Mrs Holicar. Alice. I'm learnin' her.'

'Teaching her,' Mrs Holicar corrected. 'And I've told you before, Katy, I won't be answered. Get on with your work, and don't teach Alice bad ways.'

She rolled on and disappeared into the staircase hall. Katy made a face at her back. 'Old cat,' she whispered, when it was safe. 'I won't stop here long, I can tell you.'

'Go on about the visitors,' Alice whispered. 'What you were saying.'

'Oh, aye,' Katy said gleefully. 'That were a piece o' work! Well, master and mistress have some 'portant relatives in London, a duke and duchess no less, what's daughter were gettin' married, and master and mistress were invited to t' weddin'. You never saw t' like o' the excitement! Bought new clothes. Told everyone about it. Mistress went out on purpose every day for a week to leave conjy cards.'

'Leave what?'

'It's what ladies leave at their friends' houses when they're going out o' town for a bit. They write on 'em, "poor prondra conjy". That's French for, "Ah'm off!"'

'Why do they write it in French?'

'Cos it's posher, o' course! Lord, you are soft! Anyroad, Mistress left cards with everybody to make sure they knew she were goin' to this duke's weddin' – swankin', tha knaws! And then right at last minute comes a note to say weddin's off. The girl's jilted her fee-ancy, and duke's family's all gone to t' country to hide from t' scandal!'

'Oh dear, how awful!' Alice whispered.

Katy's eyes sparkled with malicious enjoyment. 'You never saw such a fuss! Mistress were fit to be tied. All her plans o' hob-nobbin' wi' the greats done up, and after she'd told everyone an' all! I thought she'd go stark mad. Master had to send for t' doctor in the end to give her laudanum. Anyroad, next thing they've sent off invitations for people to come and stay, just so it doesn't look as if they've nothing to do! These three lots were all they could get at last minute – I don't reckon they even like 'em much! But from what I 'eard, there'll be house parties all through t' summer now, just to prove to everybody they can do wi'out dukes.' The sparkle died. 'Makes a sight more work for us, do house parties. Ah've a mind to give my warning and go and try ma luck in Leeds.'

After nearly two hours of the hardest work Alice had ever done, they finished the hall just as a maid in the same blue dress but with a fancy cap and apron came hurrying out of the kitchen passage with a tray in her hands.

'Haven't you finished yet? Tea trays are going up. Who's *this*?' she said, but she didn't wait for the answer. Alice got up off her knees and stared in amazement as the trim little figure dashed across the freshly scrubbed hall like a clockwork toy.

'Mildred, upper housemaid,' Katy informed Alice briefly. 'Snooty thing! That's the gentry's morning tea and bread-and-butter. Upper housemaids take it up to the guests, which is about all they're fit for, idle useless things. Mr Hayter and Mamzelle take the master and mistress's. And it means,' she added, brightening, 'that breakfast is ready. Come on, I'll show you where we empty buckets. Better wash us hands as well – Mr Goole inspects 'em sometimes.'

Alice was famished, and glad to hear the mention of food, even if it came with a terrifying butler attached. But it turned out that the butler wasn't breakfasting in the servants' hall that morning. The long, high-ceilinged room was dominated by the immense wooden table down the middle, flanked with what looked like a forest of chairs. As Katy and Alice entered, the first thing they heard was that Mr Atterwith, the steward – a very great man and only a small step below the master – had come up to the house to breakfast, so Mrs Holicar had invited all the upper servants to eat with her in the upper servants' parlour. That meant the butler, cook, lady's maid, valet and first footman, together with the personal servants of the house guests, would be absent from the long table.

'And they get a special breakfast,' said one of the

kitchen maids crossly, pushing past them with a covered silver dish, 'which I've to serve them, *and* try and get my own breakfast at the same time.'

'What's in there?' Katy called after her.

'Bacon in oatmeal. And there's fried eggs,' the voice drifted back.

'Never mind fried eggs,' said the second footman, a cheerful-looking, middle-aged man, now the senior servant present. 'Sit down, Katy, and try and keep your mouth shut for two minutes. Is this the new housemaid? What's your name?'

'Alice.'

'Right, Alice, sit ye down. I'm John, by the way. I'll give you all the names when we're assembled.'

Katy drew Alice to sit beside her at the middle of the table. Normally the butler sat one end and the cook the other, with the upper servants nearest them in order of seniority, women one end and men the other. 'So the lower you are, the nearer the middle,' Katy explained. 'That's us, the lowest of the low.'

'Except the scullery maids,' said a fresh-faced girl, who was still laying the table around the gathering hordes. 'Hullo, I'm Peggy, I'm a kitchen maid. We're all behind this morning. Mrs Pender didn't like having to do separate breakfast for the uppers, even if she is eating it herself!'

Gradually the seats filled. John, the second footman, took the butler's place, and the head housemaid, Lucy, took the cook's seat at the other end. When the scullery maids, who had the job of serving everybody else, had slipped into the last two places in the middle, John rapped the table, everyone bent their heads, and grace was said. Even before the amen had died away, hands were reaching for the bread. Alice was almost sick with hunger, and looked about the laden table eagerly. There was plenty of bread, cut in thick slices, with more uncut loaves in reserve; crocks of butter and two great cheeses; and at the butler's end a huge cold roast leg of pork and at the cook's end a vast game pie, partly cut. John and

Lucy seemed to have the job of slicing and dispensing these delicacies; bread and cheese was 'help yourself'.

'No use lookin' at the pie,' Katy told Alice, hacking a lump out of the nearest cheese. 'Us poor mortals won't get any. But we might come in for a bit o' cold pork if we're lucky.'

There was, besides, water or milk to drink, and jugs of beer were being carried round by the scullery maids.

'That's our 'lowance,' Peggy explained. 'Half a pint each for us girls and a pint for the men.'

'The last place I was at,' Katy said, 'we got beer money instead, eightpence a day. It's on'y old-fashioned houses like this still give the 'lowance.'

'Well, the beer's made here,' said Peggy, 'in the brewhouse. Stands to reason they'd give it. Sometimes in the autumn we get cider instead – they make that here too. I like cider better.'

'I'd sooner have the money,' Katy said grudgingly. 'I don't suppose I shall stop here much longer.'

Peggy winked at Alice and leaned across to whisper, 'She's been saying that since the day she arrived. The ones who say they're not stopping always stay the longest.'

The kitchen maid who'd taken the dish into the upper servants came back and slipped into her place, reaching simultaneously for bread and tearing a piece off to cram into her mouth. 'Lord, the smell o' that bacon were making me faint. Pass cheese, please.'

When the first edge of hunger had been taken off, Peggy asked, 'So what're they talking about in there, Molly? What's Mr Atterwith come to breakfast for?'

'More building work,' said Molly. A chorus of groans met this announcement. She nodded. 'Mrs H is beside herself. We've on'y just got over last lot.'

'What's that you say, Moll?' John called down from the foot of the table. 'If you've been eavesdropping on your betters, we might as well all hear it.'

The other conversations died away, and Molly told what she had heard.

'Well, it started with Mr Atterwith saying that Master

was for buying some more land. Mr Atterwith thought it were too expensive, but Master means to 'ave it.'

'Yes, that's Glebe Farm over to Hessay and Manor Farm over to Rufforth,' John said. 'Mr Goole mentioned it yesterday.'

'Master says they were Morland land once and ought to be again,' Molly said. 'Mr Atterwith sighed a good bit and shook his head and said he feared they weren't worth the purchase, and then Mrs Holicar up and says it's not the money's worth that's in question.'

'And what's that supposed to mean when it's at home?' Thomas asked robustly, spearing another slice of cold pork while John's attention was otherwhere.

'It means,' said John, without looking at him, 'that some of us have different standards to measure by. Go on, Molly.'

'I don't know that it's right to be listening to eavesdrop,' Mildred objected, looking down her nose at her inferiors in the middle seats.

John merely made an impatient gesture. 'Nobody's forcing you to listen, my dear. Shut your ears or leave the table if it minds you. Go *on*, Molly, and don't stop again, or I'll come up there and shake your head till your ears rattle.'

'He's a humorist, is John,' Katy whispered admiringly to Alice. 'Calls Mildred "Mildew" sometimes. Smart as a whip, he is, and cares for nobody, not even Mr Goole. Meals aren't like this when Mr Goole's in charge, I can tell you! We all eat in silence, and gossip about the gentry's a mortal sin.'

'I'll stick your head in the water jug, Katy Mappin, if you don't shut up,' John said, proving he had long ears as well as a quick mind. 'Well, Moll?'

'I forget where I was. Oh, yes, so Mrs Holicar says in her opinion it's the mistress, not the master, as wants the land, and she wouldn't be surprised if there was more changes to come. So Mr Atterwith says, "Yes, and after the present disappointment you won't have long to wait to find out what." And he says he's heard that the building scheme is to go forward to divide the dining-room – like she did the drawing-room, you know – and then to fill the moat on the north side and build the new kitchens.'

These last words raised such a clamour of groans, exclamation and comment that John was unable to quell it, and in the middle of the feverish outpouring of complaint about the mess, extra work, and sheer inconvenience and discomfort for servants the scheme would cause, the butler stalked in from the upper servants' parlour and said, 'What is the meaning of this uproar? Have you all gone mad?'

He did not speak loudly, but the noise was cut off as if with an axe. Every servant seemed to shrink in his place and eyes were hustled away from any likelihood of contact. Only John seemed unmoved, addressing himself to the rest of his breakfast as if nothing had happened.

'Prayers in five minutes,' Goole said. 'You'd better get this table cleared.' His roving gaze lit on Alice. 'Is this the new girl? Stand up!'

Alice, pinched by the girls on either side, managed to rise to her feet, feeling faint with fear. The awful eye of the butler seemed to flay her like an icy wind. 'Front hair inside the cap,' he snapped. 'And your face is dirty.' Mrs Holicar had appeared beside him and he said in her general direction, 'Is this the class of girl we have to put up with nowadays? I hope you can make something of her, Mrs Holicar, but I don't envy you the task.'

'Thank you, Mr Goole, but I can manage my own girls if I'm given a free hand,' said Mrs Holicar, annoyed at interference with her department.

Goole said no more, but stalked away down the kitchen, angular and black as the Grim Reaper; John, perhaps craving excitement, accosted him as he passed with, 'When does the building start, Mr Goole? Was a date mentioned?'

Goole paused only long enough to snarl at him, 'You'll go too far one day, mark my words,' before disappearing in the direction of his own room.

After all this excitement and emotion, Alice was glad

to follow the rest of the servants into the dim quiet of the chapel for prayers. Katy hustled her into place at the back; the nursery staff with the little boy came into the gallery above their heads; and then the gentry walked in and passed down to the front, the master and mistress, and two and a half of the three couples who were staying as guests (the other half not having managed to get out of bed in time).

The chaplain came out from his room, and the ceremony began. It was not long, but it gave Alice her first sight of the master, and a chance to examine him, if briefly. She was surprised: he seemed so very young, no older than the young footman who had accosted her that morning; certainly much younger than the mistress. He was a tall, healthy-looking man with an outdoor complexion, thick, wavy brown hair and bright blue eyes. Even to Alice's young and inexperienced eye, he looked as if he was in the wrong place. On horseback, or stumping about the woods with a gun, or leaning against a gate discussing the finer points of cattle with his stockman, that was how she saw him. Starched up in fine clothes, tightly collared, and reading a prayer to the large gathering, he looked so uncomfortable she felt sorry for him.

When the last amen had been said, the gentry left the front stalls to file out. As the master and mistress passed her, Alice could not resist looking up. The little movement must have caught the master's attention, for he turned his head and for an instant met Alice's eye. She felt an odd little spark of sympathy pass between them, and instinctively began to smile. His eyebrow rose slightly – and he was past and gone. The incident had taken no more than a second; it was nothing at all, really, but it stayed in Alice's mind.

The gentry went into the dining-room to take their breakfast; the servants dispersed about their work; and Katy grabbed Alice's arm and said, 'Come on, don't stand there daydreaming. It's bedrooms now, while the great folk are out of the way. Lord, if Molly's right about what she heard, there'll be the dickens to pay! We've on'y just got straight after the last lot, when the mistress had the old drawing-room pulled out and made into drawing-room and sitting-room! And before that it were the gentlemen's wing being built where the kennels used to be – Lord, that did make a mess! Ever since I've been at this place they've been tearing things up or tearing things down. If they're going to start again, I'll not stop long, I can tell you!'

George Morland, master of Morland Place, would have been surprised if he had known that he had aroused sympathy in his youngest and newest housemaid. Besides the fact that he did not know such a person existed – the pretty face had caught his eye for a second in the chapel, but not for long enough for him to determine whether or not it was a new one – he did not feel himself to be in any way pitiable.

He was master of all he surveyed. He had a wife of breeding and rank, who ran his house like a machine and enabled him to lead local society. He had a son to follow him – only one, it was true, and a rather puny lad, which worried him sometimes. He had horses, dogs, broad acres, endless credit at any shop in York, robust good health – and as good a cook, in his opinion, as had ever served under that ancient roof. Mrs Morland might fret that the cook was a female, which wasn't elegant, but Mrs Pender was a relief to George after Kemp, who had called himself the *chef de cuisine*, and whose regular outbursts of temperament kept the kitchen quarters in turmoil and sometimes interrupted dinner.

While he breakfasted – on bacon, eggs, kidneys, cutlets, several slices of home-killed ham, a peach from his own hothouse, and some toasted muffins buttered and topped with his favourite thing, a chunk from the whole honeycomb – he listened with only half an ear to the conversation of the guests. His mind was a litany of contentment. His wife, Alfreda, had been bitterly upset about the cancelling of the Southport wedding, at which she had intended to shine and to lay the foundations for a great deal of reciprocation. George, however, though pleased that they had been asked to the wedding – which proved the important ties between his end of the family and the titled end – was glad not to have to waste several weeks of the summer in London. The cancellation, he felt, gave him the best of both worlds, the credit without the trouble.

It was much more to his taste to stay here at Morland Place and have people come and visit. He liked showing off his house and his wife's elegant contrivances, enjoyed taking people round the estate, arranging shooting or hunting, according to the season, and receiving their admiration and gratitude for his condescension. Occasionally, he supposed, they would have to show willing and go and stay with other people at their houses, but if etiquette hadn't demanded it he would never have bothered. He liked his own house, his own horses, his own food and his own bed, and if he'd been offered the crown of England he wouldn't have taken it in exchange. Well, he thought, when this rousing sentiment occurred to him, Alfreda would probably have insisted he take it, but it wouldn't be his choice.

The trouble with Alfreda, he thought, looking down the table at the distant figure of his wife, was that she had never really got over the death of her brother, Lord Marwood. That frightful accident in London, tumbling downstairs and breaking his neck – she had been driven to the brink with grief when she had heard about it. There had been only the two of them (her pater having bankrupted and shot himself, and her mama having died of shame soon afterwards) and they'd been through hard times together. George had done what he could to comfort her, but he wasn't a great hand with women. Never had anything to do with 'em before he married Alfreda – and, come to think of it, not that much more since. Horses he understood, and dogs, and he got on very well with other fellows, as long as they weren't too clever. Women were a mystery. It beat him how they got through the days, with nothing to do and nothing to think about. In his view, that was why Alfreda had started up this plan again of knocking the house to bits.

Not that a smaller dining-parlour wouldn't be a good idea, especially in winter. The dining-room had been conceived and built on a grand scale, and the table, even with all the leaves out, would seat twenty, which was awkward when it was just the two of them, or a small party. With the end of the long room divided off into a neat, cosy dining-parlour, they'd still have a dining saloon large enough for grand dinners.

The other plan, to rebuild the kitchens and offices, was more problematical. Filling in the moat, now – he wasn't sure about that. He had an uneasy feeling that that was tampering with history. Sacrilege, almost. And the water would have to be diverted into an underground pipe, which would be a huge undertaking. Then knocking down whole walls and building virtually a new wing – the mess and inconvenience would be phenomenal. Not to say the expense. He had never had to worry about the cost of things, but there was Atterwith just last night saying those two farms he wanted to buy were too expensive. If Alfreda started up her bigger plan, Atterwith might say there wasn't the money for both.

On the other hand – and here he felt an upsurge in his brain that had him almost breathless with admiration of his own cunning – if he told his wife, magnanimously, that she might begin with her dining-parlour scheme, she would have to side with him against Atterwith in his farm-buying scheme. A *quid pro quo*. And those two farms he *had* to have. They would round off his estate. He felt so passionately about it, it was almost as if they were his already and someone was trying to take them from him. He was sure they must have been Morland land once, back in history. And they should be again, by his head! He would have a whole and perfect Morland estate to hand on to little James when the time came.

His face softened at the thought, and Mr Bosanquet, who was talking to him about the recent strikes in the coal and iron trades, wondered what Morland found to amuse in the worrying turn-down in trade. But George was thinking about James, and if there was one thing he loved even above his acres, it was his son. When the little fellow was brought down each evening, his face would light up and he would put out his arms and cry, 'Pa-pa! Want Pa-pa!' And George would scoop him up and whirl him round and the little chap would laugh and clutch at his hair, and then George would hug him tightly and ask him who he loved most in the world—

'—might spread to the agricultural workers too, don't you think, Morland?' Bosanquet's words interrupted his happy reverie.

'Oh, undoubtedly,' George replied at random.

'Indeed? You really anticipate trouble from that quarter?' Mr Chorton Eales put in anxiously.

'Oh, well, I dare say, on the whole, perhaps not,' George mumbled, glad that the spaces between them at table did not conduce to rigorous questioning. 'More coffee, Mrs Eales? Bosanquet, have you tried the ham? You must come out with me this morning and look round the home farm. My piggeries are the finest in the Riding – princely, everyone says. My father designed them, you know, and I remember he used to say if he lost all his money, he'd be happy to go and live in them himself.'

The gentlemen chuckled, but Mrs Morland felt pigsties were not an elegant subject at table, and interjected a cool comment about the weather, which stopped all conversation dead, as comments about the weather always do.

CHAPTER FIVE

George Morland's younger brother, Edward – always known as Teddy – was shown into the drawing-room of the rectory in Bishop Winthorpe. His sister Henrietta, Mrs Edgar Fortescue, rose to meet him with a glad smile.

'I'm so glad you're early – it gives us a chance to have a cosy chat before we have to go and dress. Would you like some tea?'

'No, thanks. But shouldn't you be bustling about seeing to things?'

'Not at all. Everything's arranged. It will only bother the servants to go checking on them.'

'Well, you're a cool one,' Teddy said, accepting his sister's offer of a seat. He took a sofa near the open french windows and stretched out his nicely-trousered legs. He had always been fond of clothes, and having an independent fortune and no-one but himself to spend it on, he could afford to patronise the best tailor in York, and patronise him often. 'I say, Hen, won't it look a bit rummy, though, having a dinner party without your husband?'

Henrietta sat opposite him, a slender girl with a narrow-chinned, pointed face, brown eyes and slightly tawny brown hair, which gave her something of the look of a pretty young vixen, Teddy thought. Her hair was dressed in a large plaited chignon behind, with a front of curls and some soft, wispy side bits, which made her look much too young to be married and mother of a child. But of course she had been married very early and she was still only – he worked it out – twenty-one.

Henrietta said patiently, 'But that's precisely why I've asked you to play host for me, so that it won't look rummy.'

'Well, you know what I mean. If the minute the rector's out of the country you go inviting hordes of people over . . .'

'Mr Fortescue's been away all summer; and it's only a small party, just a few good friends,' she said. 'It's for Regina, really. I can't give her a proper come-out, but she ought to have a little fun. She's been such a comfort to me these last two years.'

Teddy frowned a little. 'Now that *is* rummy, the way old Georgie cast her off.'

'Well, he didn't exactly cast her off,' Henrietta said in fairness. 'I asked for her to come and live with me.'

'And he's never asked for her back. And,' he added shrewdly, 'I'll lay odds he's never offered you a penny for her keep.'

'Oh, I don't mind that,' Henrietta said. 'You can't imagine what a comfort it is for a woman to have a female companion.'

'Yes, but dash it, what about a dowry? When Pa died he left both you girls to Georgie's care, and if that meant anything, it meant providing you with dowries. Things worked out all right for you, as it happened.'

'That's exactly why I want to throw Regina just a little in the path of Perry Parke,' said Henrietta.

'Oh, he's back from his travels, is he?'

'Yes, and since he hasn't seen her for a while she's bound to make an impression on him. She's so pretty, and he's such a good-natured man, I'm sure they'd be well suited.'

Teddy grinned. 'Aha! A plot! Well, he's certainly got enough fortune not to mind that she hasn't any.'

Sir Peregrine Parke, a merry young man of twenty-three, had inherited the estate and the baronetcy eighteen months ago on the death of his father, Sir Robert. Now, as the squire of Bishop Winthorpe, Perry owned all the land thereabouts not in the possession of the rector. As soon as his mourning had ended and the transfer of the estate had been completed, he had gone abroad to see something of the world.

When Perry had left Bishop Winthorpe, Regina had been sixteen and still 'not out'. Though it was obvious to Henrietta that Regina admired the young baronet, he had only ever noticed her as Henrietta's little sister. But while he was away Regina had turned seventeen, and though there could be no formal bringing-out in the circumstances, she had turned up her hair and let down her skirts and was now very much a woman – and a very pretty one.

'It would be wonderful to have her well settled,' Henrietta concluded.

'But you'd miss her,' Teddy objected. 'You've just this minute said how you need a companion.'

'As if I'd let that stand in the way!' Henrietta said. 'Besides, she'll only be at the other end of the village, at the Red House.'

Henrietta's life had been a strange one. Never in her carefree youth at Morland Place, riding about the estate and helping with the harvests and the lambings, could she have imagined herself in her present situation. Mr Fortescue was an aesthete and a noted scholar, a man more than twenty years her senior. What impulse had possessed him to abandon the celibacy of a lifetime and marry her she did not know; but for a strange, short while she had been the object of his passionate infatuation.

She had fallen in love with his love for her; but it had not lasted long. As soon as she had told him she was with child, he had seemed to recoil from her, as if she had become something loathsome. Throughout her pregnancy he had shunned her, kept her locked up, forbidden anyone else to come near her. And since the child, a girl, had been born, he had gone back to his old life, living quite apart from her in the large old house, treating her with grave civility when they met, but making sure they hardly ever did meet.

Then in June this year he had announced quite suddenly that he was going away for several months, to Heidelberg initially, and then to other German universities, to study some rare documents for a treatise he was writing. His curate, Catchpole, who also lived at the rectory, would perform his clerical duties while he was away. 'And you will be quite safe here with the servants,' Mr Fortescue had informed her. 'You may invite your brother to stay at some point, if it pleases you.'

He had left her, it seemed, quite without regret. His only qualm was at parting with his daughter; for against all expectations he loved Elizabeth. When she was brought down to see him every day, Henrietta thought she saw in the way he gazed at the baby the ghost of the passion he had once borne her. For herself, her only sadness in her husband's going away was the knowledge that she would not miss him. In the months of Elizabeth's life, she had reshaped her routines so that they now took little account of him.

His absence had made a difference to Regina, however. She was terrified of him, and when he was gone she seemed to revive like trodden grass springing upright. And then word had come via the servants that the Red House was being opened again for the return of the young squire. Regina had heard the news with shining eyes, and it was at that moment Henrietta had conceived the idea of a dinner party of welcome. She could not, of course, act without a host, but the rector's parting permission to invite Teddy had solved that problem.

The only difficulty had been Catchpole. He disliked Henrietta and disapproved of everything she did. When she told him her plan, he said loftily that Mr Fortescue would not approve, as if that was all there was to be said about it. But when Catchpole hadn't Mr Fortescue to appeal to, Henrietta was quite equal to defying him. He had no legal authority over her, and it was she who gave the servants their orders. He had no support in the house for his embargo, especially as most of them were eager for the party, which would bring a little excitement to their monotonous lives.

'I shall write to Mr Fortescue and ascertain his view of the matter,' was Catchpole's final threat; but Henrietta had an answer for that.

'You must do as you think fit; but Mr Fortescue said before he left that he particularly did not want to be troubled with anything while he was away, unless it was a matter of great urgency. You must decide for yourself how urgent he would think a dinner party.'

And Catchpole stalked away with a glare that told her he would not be writing. Probably he would complain bitterly about her when the rector returned; but she would have her party, she thought, even if she paid for it afterwards.

So now here she was on the very day, with all her plans in place, and dear genial Teddy sitting across the room from her. He was looking stout and well, she thought – stout in both senses of the word, for though he was only twenty-four, he had put on weight steadily since coming into his fortune, and now had the important girth of a much older man.

'So, tell me what you've been doing since I saw you last,' she invited.

'Oh, this and that,' he said airily. 'Nothing in particular, really.'

'How is the new railway station going along?'

'Slowly,' he said. 'Do you mind if I smoke?'

Henrietta waved a hand. 'How far have they got?'

'As far as can be expected,' Teddy said vaguely, lighting a thin cigar. 'To tell you the truth, I don't have much to do with it. I'm supposed to oversee it, but there's not much overseeing in the case, as far as I can tell. They get on pretty well without me, you know.'

'And how are your factories, and all your other business concerns?' Henrietta pursued.

Teddy looked at her sidelong. 'Now see here, are you catechising me? I may get my fortune from the factories and so on, but you don't really expect me to be down there every day fussing over them and getting in the way? The fellows know their business just as well as your servants know theirs.'

'Very well, I give you the point,' Henrietta smiled. 'But I do wonder what it is that you do all day long.'

'Oh, I'm always busy. I meet friends – go to stay with 'em sometimes – visit my tailor, go to the club. I don't know how it is,' he added, 'but once you've got up in the morning, what with this and that, there seems to be no time at all between breakfast and getting dressed for dinner.'

'In other words you're a thoroughly idle, worthless creature,' Henrietta concluded, and he agreed amiably. 'It's a pity you swapped your land for Georgie's factories. Looking after that would have given you something to do.'

'No, no, Georgie's the one for farming. I knew it wouldn't suit me, prodding pigs and fingering wheat and so on. Mud and smells and whatnot. I'm a town bird, really.' He sought for a change of subject. 'By the by, I went down to Trawden to see Manfred last week.'

'Did you? Oh, I'm so glad!'

'Well, I thought someone ought to. Georgie never will, and you can't, and he is our flesh and blood, after all.'

'Is he well? Does he like it there?'

Teddy frowned in recollection. Keighley Moor, on the edge of which the school was situated, struck him as a grim, bleak place, and he had always thought it unnecessarily far off for George to have sent their youngest brother. There had been, he was sure, an element of 'getting rid of the boy' about it, and he knew at whose door to place that! Georgie was a bit of an ass sometimes, but Alfreda, in Teddy's view, was a nasty piece of work.

Still, there was no sense in upsetting Henrietta. 'Oh, he likes it all right. I say, though, it's a rummy place, that school. Queerest set of boys you ever saw! Can't quite put my finger on it, but they all look as if they've been put together wrong.'

'But they aren't unkind to Manny, are they?'

'Lord, no! Kettleworth – the parson feller who runs the place – treats him like his own son. Made him a monitor now.'

'A monitor? They must think highly of him, then.'

'He only teaches the youngest boys, of course, but you should see him! So solemn and serious it'd make a cat laugh!'

'But how is he in himself? Is he well?'

Teddy thought for a moment. The school was housed in a large building like a barn, whose door opened straight onto the churchyard; the vicarage, slightly raised, sat on the adjacent boundary. It had been a wet but warm day when Teddy visited, and the puddles lying about on the graves and the paths, and the monotonous black drip from the dark overhanging trees, had made him wonder what it would be like in winter. He was not a man of much imagination, but the whole place struck him as clammy. And the queer set of boys – many of them the rejects of society, orphans, bastards and cripples – regularly gave him the jim-jams. But in all truth, Manfred had seemed settled and happy. He talked mostly about his studies, and seemed frightfully keen to recount some episode from the Trojan war he'd just been reading about, which was all Greek to Teddy – but then Manny always had been an odd little cove.

'Happy as a lark,' he said at last. 'Growing like a weed, too, all neck and elbows – you know how youngsters are.' Too thin and pale, Teddy thought, but then he was a scholarly fellow, not a sportsman, so it probably didn't matter. He sought for something else that would reassure Henrietta. 'The old dominie fellow has Manny up to dine at his house, and he sits at the family table with the Kettleworth girls. Four daughters, two older than Manny and two younger, and the way the old fellow looks at him, he'll be able to take his pick when the time comes!'

Henrietta smiled at that, but said, 'He never comes back even for a holiday, though.'

Teddy shrugged. 'Well, you know Georgie and Alfie.

But don't worry, Manny's perfectly happy. In fact, I don't suppose you could prise him away from the place now. Those Kettleworth girls are uncommon pretty. By the way, talking of Georgie and Alfie, did you hear about their terrible disappointment this summer?'

He told her about the cancellation of the Southport wedding. 'I feel sorry for the duchess,' he concluded. 'She and Papa were good friends, you know.'

'It is sad for her,' Henrietta agreed, 'but what about the daughter – Lady Venetia? What's to become of her?'

'She's been sent off in disgrace, from what I heard, into the country out of the way. The scandal will scotch her chances, I imagine.'

'Her chances of marriage, you mean?'

Teddy shrugged. 'Well, what else is there for a duke's daughter? She'll be known as a jilt now; but I suppose someone will take her eventually for her rank, as long as the duke comes down heavy enough.'

'Poor thing,' Henrietta said thoughtfully.

'Poor George and Alfreda, you ought to say. They're neck and ears into an orgy of building and buying land to make it up to themselves. You wouldn't know Morland Place any more.'

'I don't suppose I shall ever see it again,' Henrietta said sadly.

'I shouldn't think so, if Alfreda has her way.'

'But, Teddy, doesn't all this building cost a lot of money? I hope Georgie won't outrun his fortune.'

'Oh, he's safe enough, with the price wheat fetches these days. You can't go wrong if you have land. Farmers are all as rich as Croesus – always have been. That's why he wants to buy two more farms, so that he can extend his plough. And by the way,' he lowered his voice, though there was no-one near by to hear, 'I understand that they're hoping to expand in another way, too.'

'You mean Alfreda's increasing?'

'Not exactly, but Georgie hinted when I met him at the club the other day that he hopes it won't be too long before she is. He couldn't say it in so many words, of course, but he was nodding and winking so fast I couldn't help taking his meaning.'

'I wish them well. Children are a great blessing. Talking of which, would you like to come up and see mine?'

'Must I? I've just got comfortable.'

'Don't be such a pudding!' Henrietta laughed, jumping up and grabbing his hand. 'Come on, up, up! I'm determined now that you shall climb up to the nursery, just for the good of your soul. Don't you know that sloth is a sin?'

'Everything agreeable is a sin. It's no wonder clergymen always look so miserable,' Teddy said, but he grinned as he said it to show it was a joke. After all, she *was* married to Fortescue and he *was* a cleric, and for all Teddy knew, she loved him still. Women were like that, funny creatures.

It was a small party, and all old friends. As well as Perry Parke, Henrietta had invited his twin sisters, Amy and Patsy, who had spent six months in Switzerland in the care of a family friend while Perry was abroad. The other guests were the two sons of Mr Antrobus (a respectable gentleman with a large house on the edge of the village), who had been invited for the Parke girls; and Mary Compton and her brother Jerome. Mary Compton was a cousin of the Parkes' late mother, a handsome and independent woman who lived in a small house in the village. She shared it nominally with her brother, but he was a restless creature and as often from home as in it.

Jerome had been away the whole of this year, since just after Christmas, and this was the first time Henrietta had seen him since his return. At the first sight of him, when he entered the drawing-room with Mary on his arm, she felt the strangest jump inside her, like an electric shock, which she could not properly account for. He was a handsome man, well-made, with thick dark hair, and the formal black and white of evening wear suited him. But more than that, there was a vividness about him that made him seem twice as alive as anyone else in the room. As soon as he entered, he seemed to draw all the brightness and power into himself, so that he shone, to Henrietta, as though he were outlined in light. She knew she was staring, but she could not seem to help herself.

'Mr Compton, how nice to see you again,' she said, trying for a normal, social tone of voice as she held out her hand. He took it, but not in a handshake; he took both her hands, and his touch seemed to burn without destroying, as if she were salamander and he were flame.

'I hope it is *that* at least,' he said. His teeth seemed very white in his dark face as he smiled at her. 'But "nice" does not begin to describe the pleasure of seeing you.'

Henrietta was aware that Mary was watching her, and felt herself blushing. 'You have been away a long time,' she said.

'Did it seem a long time to you? I'm glad to know it! It was remiss of me not to call on you the moment I got back, of course, but I was like a child with a piece of cake, putting off eating the icing until the very last. Anticipation is a sweet and solitary sin, and peculiarly human. The lower animals know nothing of it.'

'Now you know Jerome is really here,' Miss Compton laughed. 'He's talking nonsense, as no other man does it.'

'It is a very pleasant nonsense,' Henrietta said. He was still holding her hands, and though she could think of no reason why he shouldn't, she felt at the same time that he ought to stop, and that she hoped he wouldn't.

It was a pleasant party, all young people, all friends, with plenty to say for themselves and plenty of good humour to carry things along. The Parke girls, Amy and Patsy, had grown into young ladies while they were abroad. They had subdued their rather fuzzy fair curls and turned them up, and their conversation was scattered with French words and references to a wider world than Bishop Winthorpe. But underneath the new polish they were the same unspoilt and merry creatures. With their rosy faces and round blue eyes they looked very like their brother, whom they adored and looked up to. Perry accepted their adoration as his right, but would have defended them to the death had anything threatened them.

Henrietta saw that he had been properly impressed with the change in Regina, and hoped that by seating them together at dinner she might promote matters. While they were still in the pre-dinner stage, he was already telling his traveller's tales more to Regina than to the rest of the company.

Mary came up to Henrietta to say quietly, 'Your sister is looking very well this evening. Is the gown your choice?' Henrietta admitted it. 'You have good taste.'

'Thank you.'

'Yes, and though the world at large might not say so, she will make him a pretty and pleasant wife.'

Henrietta shot her a startled look. 'Oh! But I didn't—'

'No need to perjure yourself!' Mary said. 'I honour your intentions. Your family is good enough, and Perry won't care if she has no dowry. Neither of them has an ounce of intellect but, then, most of the population manages to get along without any. I shall do all in my power to advance the cause, I promise you.'

'You don't blame me?' Henrietta asked.

'Isn't it what any sister would do?' Mary said solemnly. 'To help a sibling's love to prosper?'

When dinner was announced, Henrietta hardly needed to direct the pairs. Since Teddy was playing host, he had to offer his arm to Mary Compton, the senior of the female guests; and since the Antrobus brothers were as deep in conversation with the Parke girls as Perry was with Regina, it naturally left Jerome to Henrietta, which was as etiquette said it should be. She felt a deep sense of happiness as she laid her hand on his proffered arm; and why she should at that moment have seen in her mind's eye the momentary image of Mr Catchpole taking his solitary supper on a tray she couldn't determine.

She had taken a great deal of trouble over the dinner, and had designed the decorations of the table herself, and was pleased with the murmured exclamations at the sight of it, with its raised bowl of fruit in the centre, the small candles in glass funnels surrounded by flowers and the trails of ivy weaving all together.

'Elegance itself,' said Jerome. 'Who would have thought to encounter such sophistication in an English village?'

'Are you never serious, Mr Compton?' Henrietta complained.

He looked down at her, and she felt again that odd internal jolt. 'I am very serious. I've known Bishop Winthorpe most of my life, and I never thought I could be surprised in it again.'

During dinner the Parke twins talked about Switzerland, Perry about his travels, and Teddy amused Mary Compton with stories of his university days. Henrietta naturally asked Jerome where he had been all summer, and he told her of the various house parties he had been invited to, and how dull they generally were.

'I think you suffer from the same malady as my brother,' Henrietta said.

'And what is that?'

'A lack of anything to do. You ought to have a profession.'

'Heaven forbid,' he laughed. 'That would entail doing the same thing every day. I should go mad.'

'Well, then, you should have some land to take care of. Land is never the same two days running,' Henrietta said.

'You speak from experience?' he teased.

'Yes, for I was brought up on the land, and I saw it worked, and helped with it.'

'You must miss it very much,' he said, suddenly serious, 'your Morland Place.'

'It was never mine,' she said. 'But it was very beautiful and it was . . .' She hesitated, seeking the words.

'Yes?' he encouraged.

She looked to see if he was going to mock her, but his eyes were still and receptive, like warm water into which it would be so comforting to slip. 'It was important,' she said at last. 'The land is important. All this,' she waved her hand round the dinner table, 'everything else that people

87

do, it seems to me just a way of passing time. Even Mr Fortescue's work, though I know it is very clever and the greatest thinkers in the country admire it – well, it doesn't *matter* the way the land does. That endures.'

'You are so eloquent, almost you persuade me,' he said lightly. 'But what is one to do if one's father did not bequeath one an estate? Or, rather, if one's estate were in forms other than land?'

'You could buy one, perhaps,' she said, a little hesitantly, since she did not know how wealthy he really was.

'My dear ma'am, at today's prices? Land is dreadfully overpriced at the moment – but I daresay the bubble will burst soon, and things will even themselves out. However, I should not wish to be one of those caught in the explosion. I would sooner pick up the pieces afterwards. The jackal's part for me, every time.'

She saw that he was mocking himself, but there was something serious here she needed to know. 'My brother at Morland Place is in the process of buying some land. Two farms adjoining his estate.'

'I wish him joy of it,' Jerome said. 'Even marginal land around York is selling at forty years' purchase.'

'You think it too expensive?'

'Certainly. The price of wheat is high at the moment, but it may not last – will not last, if precedent is anything to go by. These things go in cycles, you know, and already there is a downturn in trade.'

'I don't understand what that means,' Henrietta said.

'Hardly anyone does,' he said, smiling. 'But it happens from time to time that money just seems to disappear. People have no spare wealth to spend on goods, so factories go onto short time and hands are put out of work. They have less money so they buy less bread and the price of wheat falls; which means that farmers have less income. And it's the income land generates that governs its selling price. Here endeth a short lesson in the national economy. I hope I made it clear to you?'

Henrietta did not answer, but said, with a worried

frown, 'He is spending a great deal on building too – enlarging the house and changing the rooms inside.'

'It sounds a little like *folie de grandeur*,' Jerome murmured.

Henrietta did not know what that was. She said, 'But Teddy says landowners are always rich, and that George cannot outrun his income.'

'Then probably Teddy is right,' Jerome said, seeing no reason not to comfort her – for what could she do about it, after all? 'I should like to see it – Morland Place.'

'Should you?'

'Of course. Your birthplace, the acres that nourished and shaped you? I should like to see anything that you loved as much as that. I'm only grateful it's an inanimate rival.'

She was troubled, understanding knocking at the door of her consciousness. There was something dangerous here, she felt dimly; enticing but dangerous.

And then he said, in a quite different voice, 'How have you been getting on with reschooling that horse of yours? Though if she were mine, I'd have knocked her on the head.'

'Oh, no, poor Ginger!' Henrietta reacted at once, as he had meant she should. 'It's not her fault that she was badly treated. I'm sure in time I can change her, but to say truth I haven't got very far yet. Bond, our head groom, said I must run her off for at least a year; and now, since he feels like you about her, he always finds an excuse not to help me get her up.'

'I thought you were going to ask Tobin up at the Red House to help.'

'Yes, but then Sir Robert died and I could hardly intrude, and then Perry went away—'

'And it was a case of "one thing after another",' Jerome finished for her. 'Well, now I'm back, I must see if I can't help you.'

'But you'll go away again. You never stay very long.'

He looked thoughtful. 'Yes, I shall have to go away again. I can't remain here for too long together. But,' he went on in a lighter tone, 'I may stay until the hunting starts, and we might achieve something in that time. Three months might work wonders.'

The ancient chaise which was passing an honourable retirement as a station cab must have been surprised to find itself carrying Lady Venetia Fleetwood, daughter of the Duke of Southport, when she might have been expected to be met at the station by a Wolvercote carriage. The driver, who left most of the navigation in any case to his horse, was certainly surprised to be jerked out of his daydream half-way between the park gates and the house by a peremptory demand to stop. It came not from a highwayman, but from a small but determined twelve-year-old girl in a plaid frock, straw bonnet and laced-up boots. Having stopped him, she gave him a winning smile, climbed up into the carriage, and rapped for him to continue.

'What are you doing here?' Venetia asked, almost as surprised as the driver.

The carriage jolted into motion. 'I came to meet you,' said Anne. 'I've been waiting ages. I wanted to talk to you without the others hearing.'

'What about?'

'About your day in London, of course. And *please* don't tell me you were going to see your doctor because I know that isn't true – though it was a jolly good excuse, because nobody could argue about it, could they?'

'Oh, Fairy!'

'Oh, Venetia!' Anne retorted. 'Nobody calls me that now. I'm too old for it.'

'Venerable,' Venetia agreed.

'Anyway, you know I won't give you away, so do, *do* tell me what you've been up to! I'm sure it's terribly exciting!'

'As a matter of fact,' Venetia said, 'it was true that I was going to see a doctor. I did my best not to tell any lies, but I had to make some excuse to get away.'

'I *knew* it was an adventure!' Anne cried triumphantly. 'Am I the only one who knows?'

'You don't know anything,' Venetia pointed out. 'But I had to tell Thomas because I haven't any money.'

One of the difficulties about her present banishment was that no arrangements had been made by her father to pay her allowance. On the whole she had not been unhappy down here at Wolvercote. The present Lord Aylesbury was an affable and approachable man, who had spent too much of his life *not* expecting to inherit the earldom to stand on ceremony now that he had. He had married a nice-tempered woman, and Wolvercote, which had stood sad and empty for so many years, now echoed again with the sound of voices, footsteps and laughter.

Since Venetia arrived there had been dinners, balls, picnics, drives, a treasure hunt and, most excitingly, a series of matches in a new game, organised by the earl's brother Maurice, who had seen it played in India while on his travels. It was called polo, and was nothing but hockey played on horseback. It sounded so dangerous that the countess had had grave doubts about letting the children join in. Protest overwhelmed her, and in fact the children proved best at it since on their ponies they were closer to the ground and therefore the ball. It was the adults who continually tumbled from the saddle, though sometimes it was only because they were helpless with laughter. As it was purely a piece of family fun, the girls were allowed to play too, and Venetia won the admiration of all her little cousins by abandoning ceremony and joining in astride a bare-back pony, then proving to have a quick eye and a firm wrist.

But for all the fun, she felt herself imprisoned. It was better to be here, away from her father's reproaches, but the fact remained that she could not leave, nor even go past the gates without explanation. And at night, in her bed, she went over and over things, by turns guilty and angry, lonely and frustrated.

'All right, I'll tell,' she said, glad of someone sympathetic to confide in, even if she was only a child. 'But you must swear not to tell anyone.'

'Earth, air, fire, water,' Anne said solemnly, going through a complicated ritual with both hands.

'Well, then, a few weeks ago I had a letter from Sir Frederick Friedman,' Venetia began.

'Who's he?'

'A great surgeon, an old friend of Mama's, and my sponsor when I was doing my medical training.'

It was only by the merest chance that Venetia had received the letter privately, for the mail was normally distributed at the breakfast table by the earl, and in the friendliest way everyone would demand to know what was in everyone else's letters. But on that particular morning Venetia had been out very early for a ride, and happened to be coming in at the Tudor door just as the footman who fetched the mail arrived back from the post office. Venetia had smiled at him, which had prompted him to volunteer that there was a letter for her in the bag. Many of the servants, particularly the younger ones, felt sorry for her ladyship. The details of the scandal were not known, but it was opined that it must have been a bad case for Lady Venetia to jilt her fiancé, since she was very level-headed and as affable and pleasant as they came.

'Oh, really? Just give it to me, then, Edward, there's a good fellow, and I'll read it upstairs.'

Edward couldn't resist being called a good fellow, and looked it out. He probably should not have done so, but after all, Lady Venetia was over twenty-one, and more in the way of being a guest than a young lady of the house. If the letter was in a man's handwriting and she wanted to receive it privately, who was he to say she shouldn't?

Up in her room she perused it eagerly. It had been sent to her at Southport House and redirected by one of the servants. Sir Frederick was writing to tell her that Dr Anstie had had further correspondence with Miss Jex-Blake in Edinburgh. It had been decided that there was little likelihood of legislation going through under the present government, and the best hope now was of a separate medical school for women. They were therefore gathering a council of like-minded people with a view to going ahead as quickly as possible so that the students could be in residence for the next session, which began in October.

'The meeting will be in August, on a date and at a location to be decided,' Sir Frederick concluded, 'and I do hope that you can be there. I do not know what your present or future plans may be, but whether you wish to go on studying or only to help others do so, I am sure the project will be of the greatest possible interest to you.'

'Of course,' Venetia told Anne, 'as soon as I read it I knew I had to go. But first of all I had to—'

'Nobble Edward,' Anne supplied promptly.

'Where did you learn such awful language?'

'From William, of course. He and Thomas are always talking about racing, and every time they lose a bet, which is every race, just about, they say the horse has been nobbled.'

'Well, don't say it when there are grown-ups present,' Venetia warned.

'Don't be silly. Of course I won't. Go on – you nobbled Edward?'

Having no money, she had had to rely on charm, but Edward agreed to bring her letters to her hand. Soon afterwards there was one from Mrs Anderson, telling her much the same thing, but adding some detail.

'You know I have never believed that separate medical education for women is the right way to go about things. It will only lead to their being marked as a different class of practitioner, subordinate and inferior to the ordinary doctor. But Miss J-B is headstrong and *will* proceed, and I know that the opponents of women in medicine will seize joyfully on any appearance of a split in the camp, so I shall have to bite my tongue and lend them my credit.'

A second letter from Sir Frederick told her that the meeting was to be on the 22nd of August at Dr Anstie's house in Wimpole Street. 'Mrs Garrett Anderson, I'm glad to say, has agreed to join the council, which will not only present a united front to the enemy, but will mean, one can confidently hope, that the future students will be admitted for clinical practice in *one* hospital, at least!'

He went on to urge Venetia again to attend if she was able, but concluded that since she had not replied to his last letter, she might be out of Town.

On the day before the meeting, Venetia had approached the countess to say that she wanted to go up to London the following day to consult a doctor.

'Oh, my dear,' said Lady Aylesbury at once, 'are you unwell? I thought you looked once or twice recently as though you had the headache.'

'No, no, I'm not unwell, Cousin Mary,' Venetia said, feeling guilty about arousing her sympathy for nothing. 'It's just that there is something I want to consult about.'

'Can't our good Dr Plomely help?' said Lady Aylesbury. 'He's as good a doctor as I've ever found, and *so* sympathetic. I never mind telling him anything – and the children adore him.'

'If you don't mind very much,' Venetia said, 'I'd sooner go to a doctor I know. It's . . . a little delicate.'

After that, the countess made no more objection, only told her to order the carriage at whatever time she liked to take her to the station, and to ask Benson, the butler, to look up the trains for her. Since she was engaged in deceiving her kind cousin, Venetia did not feel she could ask her for money for her fare, so she had been forced to go to Thomas – the Aylesburys' eldest son – who had a lavish allowance, and fortunately had not sustained any of his usual heavy losses since the last instalment was paid him.

'So was it a good meeting?' Anne asked, privately thinking it a very dull reason for all the subterfuge.

'Extremely. Everybody was there – Mrs Anderson, Dr Blackwell, Dr King Chambers, Mr Norton of St Mary's, my dear Mr Bentley, the Dean of St Agatha's – oh, everybody! You can't think how good it was to be with my own sort of people again, to be talking freely and about the most important matters in the world. I've missed London so! And my work most of all. At any rate, the meeting went well and there was a unanimous vote to found a medical school for women, with Dr Anstie as dean. Mrs Anderson and Dr Blackwell both accepted posts. Miss Jex-Blake is to look for suitable premises to lease, and promised me that if I can find the fee I shall certainly have a place when the school opens in October.'

Anne, who had been on the verge of yawning, sat up at that. 'Oh, Venetia, do you really mean you're going back to study medicine again? But won't everyone be furious with you?'

Venetia's animation leaked away. 'There *is* the little matter of money. There'd be living expenses to find as well as the fees, and I haven't even an allowance now. Papa would never agree to it, and there's no dear Aunt Fanny to help me this time. I don't see how it's to be done.'

Anne looked fierce. 'You *aren't* to give up! I think it's splendid that you want to do something, instead of just getting married and having babies like all the other stupid girls! When I grow up I want to *do* something too, and you can't let me down or I might lose my nerve, and then it would be your fault.'

Venetia began to smile. 'Oh, darling, don't be silly.'

'Just promise you won't give up.'

'I promise. But I don't see any way forward at the moment.'

'Something will turn up. I know it will.'

'Bless your optimism! And what field are you going to pioneer when you grow up?'

'I haven't decided yet, but it will be something important that women aren't allowed to do,' Anne said, with superb confidence.

'Then you'd better get us the vote. Everyone says it's important, but somehow I've never been able to work up an interest in it.'

'All right,' said Anne.

Cousin Mary asked so kindly about Venetia's health that she felt wretched with guilt for deceiving her, and as soon as she could she escaped to her room and sent away her maid so that she could think about the meeting and everything that had passed there. Particularly interesting had been a conversation between her, Mrs Anderson and Sir Frederick about surgery. Venetia had confessed it was the area of medicine that interested her most.

'It's a field in which you can actually *do* something, and see what a difference you make. So many diseases come down in the end to waiting and hoping. We know what they are, but we have no cures, and it's really more a matter of good nursing than anything else.'

'That's true in a lot of cases,' Sir Frederick acknowledged.

'I admit the logic,' said Mrs Anderson, 'but I must confess that I find operating a tremendous strain on the nerves. Fascinating, I grant you, but after every operation I feel spiritually exhausted.'

'You are in the unfortunate position of having no help in that field,' Sir Frederick said. 'You are the only surgeon at the New, aren't you?'

'I've had offers of help,' Mrs Anderson said, 'but all from men, of course, and I did decide at the very beginning that I should have none but female staff.' She turned to Venetia. 'If you manage to qualify, and you have the temperament for surgery, you'll be assured of a post. I'd take you on gladly to relieve me of the burden.'

That was something precious to think about, that there was a place ready and waiting for her, doing the thing she wanted most to do, if only she could qualify. If only! It was a big caveat. Would it be remotely possible to talk her father round? Once he was over his rage and disappointment with her, perhaps he would see that it was no use hoping she would marry in the ordinary way, and give in and allow her to do what she wanted. She tried to imagine the scene, and failed. Her father was as stubborn as she was, and had age and rank on his side. If she could persuade her mother to argue for her? But her mother was unwell, and it would be wrong to worry her. In any case, she'd be unlikely to agree. Though she sympathised with Venetia's desire to be active, she would not side with her child against her husband.

Venetia's thoughts went round and round. She saw no way out, no way forward. Finally her maid returned, rather anxious, to remind her that the dressing bell had gone and that it was a formal dinner this evening, and she yielded herself with a sigh to be furbished up, a process she called 'trussing', because of the tightness of the stays that were required under an evening gown.

They were all assembled in the drawing-room, and Venetia was trying to join in with the general chat and appear cheerful so as not to arouse the anxiety of Lady Aylesbury, when the interruption came. Benson came in, not to announce dinner, but with a piece of paper on a tray and deepest gloom in his eye.

'A telegraph, my lady.' He addressed the countess, but the awful eye swivelled round to Venetia, and she felt a cold foreboding grip her heart.

The duke had been taken ill while out shooting at Ravendene that morning and had been brought home. The doctor had been called, but before he could attend, the duke was dead.

CHAPTER SIX

Face down on her bed, a sodden handkerchief clenched in her hand, Venetia wept.

'I was always afraid for Mama,' she sobbed. 'She's been ill for so long, I've been trying not to think she might die. But I never thought Papa would go.' Lady Aylesbury soothed her head. 'I feel so awful! As if I brought it on him.'

'Hush! You're not to think that. It was nothing to do with you.'

'But I've caused him so much worry! And now!' Venetia had spent the whole of that very day doing what she knew he would not like, behaving in an underhand way, planning to defy him. And, like a punishment on her, he had been snatched away. 'I've been such a bad daughter! And I never even said I was sorry.'

The last time she had seen him he had been furious with her. The last words he had spoken to her had been angry ones. He had died not forgiving her. She was left stranded in his disfavour for ever.

'Venetia, dear,' Lady Aylesbury said gently, stroking her back, 'people don't die to punish other people. God has His reasons for everything, but He doesn't do things like that. He wanted your papa back, that's all.'

'But Papa wasn't even old!'

'It was his time to go. We mustn't question God's purposes. And you mustn't blame yourself. There's a temptation sometimes to think of ourselves as greater sinners than we are, and that would be the sin of vanity, my dear, wouldn't it?'

Venetia's sobs grew a little more moderate, and Lady Aylesbury bestowed a final pat on her shoulder, and said, 'I'll leave you to have your cry out. You needn't come downstairs again. I'll send a little supper up later on and you can pop into bed and have it there. Poor dear! I'm so very sorry.'

It was a sad and dismal journey across country to Ravendene. Lady Aylesbury, who was of an old-fashioned turn of mind and could not bear to think of a lady travelling without male protection, sent a footman with her, which meant Venetia spent the whole railway journey with him and her maid sitting opposite her, trying not to meet her eyes. The carriage was waiting for her at the station, and the sight of the coachman and groom in deep mourning livery, and the black lozenges on the horses' harness, brought it home to her what a cataclysm it was for a duke to die. He was not only her papa, but a prince of the realm, and master of a vast estate, and his removal left a chasm in many people's world.

At the west gate of Ravendene Mrs Horvath came running out to open for the carriage. She was in black, too, and her eyes were red and puffy with crying. When Horvath had died she had feared destitution, but the duke had said there was no reason she could not keep the gate just as well as her husband, and had let her stay on in the house and the position. So kind and considerate to underlings, Venetia thought. A good master, painstaking and generous – as long as you did not cross him.

Everyone they passed as they travelled through the park stopped and paid their respects, doffing their caps when they saw who it was. Venetia lifted a hand to them and gave a weary smile. Then they rounded the turn into the avenue and there stood Ravendene four-square at the end, with the lower windows all shuttered. Tears were making her throat ache. It was all so forlorn.

The Ravendene butler, a little bent man grown old in the service, met her in the hall.

'Welcome home, my lady.'

'Thank you, Arnold. This is a sad day.'

'It is indeed, my lady. His grace will be sorely missed – sorely missed.' The old man sniffed and applied the knuckle of one hand to his eye. Venetia thought suddenly that, quite apart from the affection that builds over a lifetime between butler and master, he must fear for his job now, for a new young duke would be likely to want a new young major-domo, and what would happen to Arnold then?

'Have you a bit saved?' she asked abruptly.

His mask slipped a little and he met her eyes nakedly for a moment. 'Thank you, my lady, just a bit. I shan't starve. But it's like the end of the world, all the same.'

She nodded, began to say something, then realised there was nothing appropriate *to* say. 'Where is everybody?'

'Her grace is in her room, my lady. She has been quite unwell. I believe Lady Augusta is sitting with her. Lady Olivia is waiting for you in the Octagon Room. Lord Marcus has not yet arrived from Town, my lady, and his lordship is with Mr Dabs in the library.'

Mr Dabs was the solicitor; and Arnold had not yet got used to the fact that Lord Turnhouse was now his grace. A dukedom, like the throne, is never empty. The duke is dead, long live the duke, she thought; but Harry would never be Arnold's master, and perhaps that was a very good reason why he should be replaced, even if neither of them had got as far as thinking it yet.

She gave him her wraps and walked up the wide, empty stairs to the Octagon. There was a fire burning under the chimney, and it made a glad sight: the day was chilly. Olivia was sitting patiently with her hands folded in her lap – not doing anything, not reading or writing or sewing, but just sitting in that way she had. It must be Court training, Venetia thought: *she* could never have sat unoccupied. Now Olivia turned her head, a look of gladness came over her, and she rose and almost ran to put her arms round Venetia.

'Oh, I'm so glad you've come! Everything's so terrible!'

'Dearest Livy! I've missed you.' Venetia hugged her hard.

'I've missed you too – you don't know how much!'

They walked with their arms round each other over to the fireplace and sat down. Olivia looked different, her beauty undiminished, but suddenly mature – a beautiful woman rather than a lovely girl. Her black gown, high in the neck, threw up the unearthly pallor of her face; her golden hair was dressed close, without curls.

'I suppose everything has fallen on your shoulders,' Venetia said.

Olivia didn't deny it. She said only, 'Thank God it didn't happen while I was in waiting. At least I could take the burden from Mama.'

'How badly is she?'

'She was ill before it happened. The old pains, you know, and a high fever. Since then she's been in a state of collapse. She loved Papa so,' Olivia said starkly. 'I don't know how she can go on without him.'

'Don't, darling! I can't bear it. Tell me how you've been.'

'I'm all right. I've been writing to all the relatives. It helps to have something to do. I had such a kind letter from the Queen. I'll show it to you later.' She stopped speaking and sat still again, hands in her lap, like a clockwork toy run down.

'I wish I'd been here to help you. But Papa—' Venetia swallowed and started again. 'I hate it that the last time I saw him he was angry with me. Now I'll never be forgiven.'

'Harry's very angry with you. He thinks – forgive me, dearest – that what you did brought it on. It was a stroke, the doctor said. Papa's been very low since we came down, and Harry's convinced it was the trouble and the scandal, and worrying about what was to become

101

of you that made it happen. I thought you ought to be prepared.'

'Prepared?'

'Because Harry's the master now. Over all of us. Even over Mama – not that she's well enough to—' She stopped again. 'I expect he'll get over it eventually. But I thought you ought to be warned.'

'He can't blame me more than I blame myself,' Venetia said.

Olivia looked up. 'Oh, I think he can,' she said.

There was no humour in Olivia, otherwise Venetia might have thought she was trying to lighten the atmosphere with a jest.

'Well, so you've come,' Augusta said. 'I think it's very bold of you, considering you practically drove Papa to his grave.'

'Gussie, you mustn't say such things,' Olivia said.

A spot of pink appeared in Augusta's cheeks. 'Well, Harry thinks so, anyway. You'll find out. And so do I. You've ruined *everything* for me, I hope you realise! I was having such fun before, and Mr Wentworth was on the brink of proposing to me, and now look! You did your best to spoil my coming out with pushing that horrid man down the stairs.'

'Gussie!' Olivia gasped, but her sister was unstoppable.

'And as if that wasn't bad enough, now you've ruined my chances of ever being happy again! My life is *ended*, thanks to you! No-one will ever marry me now. I shall be known for ever as *your* sister, and I'll go a spinster to my grave, not to mention the shame of it! No-one will even want to dance with me – not that there'll *be* any dances, with us stuck down here in mourning! You've made the whole family a laughing-stock, and we'll never hold up our heads again. And as for poor Beauty, languishing abroad, knowing everyone calls him your jilt and laughs at him behind his back.'

'Oh, Gussie, do stop,' Olivia pleaded wearily.

Augusta tossed her head, and Venetia said, 'You'll

get a husband all right, if that's what you want. People forget scandals as easily as favours, believe me. If some handsome man doesn't propose to you on the hunting field this winter, you'll be the belle of the Season next year. You're so pretty, Gus.'

'Good thing for me I *am*, with a sister like you,' Augusta retorted.

'I sent for you because it's right that the family should all be together at a time like this,' Harry said, from behind the desk in the library.

'*You* sent for me?' Venetia queried. If it weren't for the occasion, she might have laughed at Harry's newly magisterial mien. She reminded herself he was three years her junior. Sent for like a little girl in short frocks: she ought to put her hands behind her back and stick her stomach out!

Harry flushed a little. 'Mama is unwell – or perhaps you didn't know. I'm taking care of everything. And she's not to be upset,' he added, eyeing her as if she might defy him.

'How would I upset her? Do talk sense.'

'You upset everyone,' he said angrily. 'You always did. It was one thing after another with you, until Papa hadn't a moment's peace for worrying what you'd do next. And now see what you've done!'

It would have been funny if it weren't so sad, the inappropriately childish words, spoken with real passion, real anger and pain. A great weariness came over her. She could not – would not – justify herself all over again, and to her brother.

'Have you got nothing to say for yourself?' he demanded, thrown by her silence.

'Not to you,' she said. 'I owe you no duty. To Mama, perhaps, if she asks me.' She put her hand to her head. 'Don't rant at me, Hal. It's not the time or the place.'

He drew himself up. '*I* decide what's the time and place. And you'll listen to me in my own house, if you please. I'm the Duke of Southport now, and I'll thank you to remember it.'

'Quick to step into Papa's shoes, aren't you?' she said, provoked into retaliating. 'But are you big enough to fill them?'

She knew she shouldn't, and regretted it the moment she said it, but she was sore inside, and there seemed no respite for her, no comforting hand, no kind word.

Harry reddened angrily. 'I'm big enough to take care of my mother and my household, and what I don't know I'll find out. And I'm big enough to deal with you. I sent for you because I don't want any more scandal and there might be talk if you weren't here for the funeral. But after the funeral you'll leave this house, and that's my last word. You didn't see what he was like these last months! You broke his heart! It was that that killed him, and I hope you're satisfied now!'

Pain and grief scalded Venetia. She stared at her brother for a moment, seeing the childish, frightened tears in his eyes; understanding him, even though his accusation hurt her desperately. Without another word she turned and left him.

Marcus arrived in the evening, and provided a useful buffer state between the two camps, the righteously angry Harry and Augusta, and the anxious and grieving Venetia and Olivia. Marcus was a simple creature, made simpler by army life, and there were no difficulties for him here. Their father was dead: they must mourn him, bury him, and carry on with their lives, with due care and respect for their widowed mother. With him in the room, conversation grew conventional, only the expected words were said, and extreme emotions came to heel like good dogs. They dined, and went early their separate ways to bed where, contrary to expectations, Venetia slept at once and dreamlessly.

The arrival of other relatives the next day added to the buffer, and no more was said between brothers and sisters, though Augusta managed some theatrical lip-curling and some fine tosses of the head. More and more distant cousins arrived, and then favoured friends who lived far enough away to be offered a bed. The day passed in a procession of greetings, condolences and showings to rooms, the evening in a parade of reminiscences. The duchess remained too ill to appear, and Venetia had not yet seen her. Her nerves drawn tight by the atmosphere, she began to wonder a little hysterically whether her mother were being kept prisoner in her room; but Olivia shook her head and said calmly that she didn't want to see anyone, and that even she, Olivia, had only looked in and looked out again.

'She's taking laudanum and sleeping a lot, and the nurse is there. The least noise or upset plays on her nerves dreadfully. Better not to disturb her. She knows you're here, and I'll make sure you're told as soon as she wants to see you.'

The following day was the day of the burial. It was not the custom for widows to attend funerals, so there was no point in putting it off in the hope of an improvement in the duchess's health.

'Someone should stay at home in case she wants company,' Harry decreed. 'I think it had better be you, Venetia. We don't want people looking at you and talking when their minds should be on Papa.'

Venetia was glad enough to be spared the ordeal; and after breakfast her mother sent word that she would like to see her. She went upstairs, knocked, and was admitted by the nurse into the ante-room.

'She's awake,' said the nurse, in an undertone. 'Try not to upset her. And speak quietly – the least sound hurts her poor nerves.'

'Is she in pain?'

'It comes and goes – and the fever. She's a little better this morning. She was very badly yesterday, my lady, that's why she couldn't see anyone.'

Comforted a little by this, Venetia went through into the bedroom and approached the bed. Her mother looked white and frail, lying propped up amongst the pillows, her eyes blue-shadowed, her breathing faint and shallow. She smiled just a little as Venetia approached, but did not move or speak; it was plain from the limpness of her hands on the sheet that she could not.

'Mama,' said Venetia, 'I would have come to see you before, but they wouldn't let me. They said you were too ill to see me. Has a doctor examined you?'

Her mother closed and opened her eyes, in place of speech. Venetia laid a hand gently over her forehead. Despite the pallor, it was very hot.

'It's the old trouble, is it?' The eyes closed and opened again. 'Fever, pains in the joints? Pains in the head?'

She sat, taking her mother's hand so that she could check the pulse. It was faint but rapid.

'Not so bad today.'

The voice was so faint Venetia almost thought she had imagined it. She lifted the limp hand to her lips and kissed it. Her mother seemed to flinch.

'Don't touch – pains me.'

'Sorry, Mama.' She laid the hand down again.

Charlotte tried to smile. 'My good girl.'

The barriers broke. 'Oh, Mama, I'm so sorry!' Venetia whispered, her eyes filling with tears. The duchess shook her head, just once each way. 'Please say you forgive me! Please! It's too late to ask him, but you could—'

'Not your fault.' Charlotte's hand twitched with the desire to comfort her wayward child. She summoned all her strength. 'So like me – dearest.' A pause. 'Do what you have to. Be true – to yourself.'

Tears flowed. 'You do forgive me, then? Oh, Mama – I've been so afraid. So alone.'

Even at such a moment, Charlotte thought, deep in her debilitating weakness, when she had lost her husband and the one love of her life, still it was she who had to comfort others. No comfort for her, ever. And what hard row would this turbulent girl have to hoe? The weakness surged over her, and she drifted. Venetia sat beside her, grateful at last to have a sense of comfort, to be of use. The sun's shadow moved across the wall. Charlotte drifted and slept, and Venetia sat in silence, watching over her while they buried her father.

* * *

The reading of the Will took place when the guests had departed. It was something to give a focus to the day, which, now the funeral was over, seemed a loose and aching thing, without direction, making them nervous, like horses when the rein goes unexpectedly slack.

They all gathered in the library. There was a great deal of preamble, and old Dabs read slowly and not well, emphasising the wrong words, repeating ponderous legal terms he felt he had not pronounced just right. Outside it was raining – steady, thorough rain – and Harry glanced at the window from time to time, remembering that the agent had said they needed dry weather for the harvest. How bad was it? How much did it matter? Did he really need to understand all these things? The agent had praised his father, saying that he had known as much about estate management as he, the agent, did. But wasn't that what you employed people for? Where was the sense in both of you fagging over the same work?

At the end of the preambles, the solicitor came to the small bequests and pensions – pages of them, to old servants and old friends. Then the widow's portion, with her entitlement to reside at the dower house while she lived. *How sick was Mama? How long would she live?* And then he came to the children. Another preamble. Most of the Southport wealth was tied up in the land; it could not be realised without harming the estate. And estates had to be held together from generation to generation: that was the strength of England. Augusta looked sharply at Harry – was there to be nothing for them, then?

Nothing for Marcus. He was provided for – he had his career. A few keepsakes only, some personal things to remember his father by, a silver dressing-set, a painting of the battle of Waterloo by Wollen that he had always liked. Marcus showed no reaction. It was the way of things. He was the younger son, even if only by minutes – the spare, not the heir. He had lost the first and most important race of his life, but he was not bitter or angry. He was happy in his small world, and had never expected more.

And then it came to the girls. 'To my daughters Olivia and Augusta I give the sum of thirty thousand pounds each, to be held in trust for them by their brother Henry, my heir, to be used for their benefit, either to furnish a dowry or a pension, at his entire discretion. And I commend my daughters to his care, and enjoin them to obey and respect him as they would me.'

Venetia kept very still, staring ahead, not wanting to meet anyone's eye. Papa had changed his will, then. He had cut her out. She was not even mentioned – she did not exist. The pain in her heart was very bad.

'Thirty thousand?' Augusta was protesting. 'You must have read it wrong, Mr Dabs. Thirty thousand? Why, Anda Cornwallis has fifteen thousand, and she's nobody! Read the numbers again – you have it wrong.'

Dabs bowed towards her. 'To release such a sum as sixty thousand in cash from an estate such as this means selling something, Lady Augusta. His late grace had set sixty thousand aside in the Funds, but he preferred his money to work for him, and to reinvest it in the estate. His late grace expected to live many years more, and I dare say he would have made further provision at a later date, had his unexpected unfortunate demise not prevented him.'

Dabs's eye slid sideways for a moment to Venetia, and made perceptive by grief and pain she understood that the sixty thousand would have been divided by three – indeed, was so divided before the Will was changed. So her delinquency had benefited her sisters; but what would become of her?

Late in the day, when she had been sitting with her mother again, Harry sent a message summoning her to the library. He was less grand today, looked older, as though the reality of his responsibilities had caught up with him.

'How is my mother?' he asked first.

'No better, no worse. She is very weak and exhausted, sleeps most of the time. She hasn't spoken to me, if that's what you're wondering – not more than a word or two, anyway. She hasn't the strength.'

'I was just asking,' Harry said. He fidgeted with things on the desk. 'I've come to a decision,' he said at last.

'Indeed,' she said, not without irony.

'Papa commended his daughters to my care. He didn't mention you by name, but still you are his daughter – and my sister, after all, however badly you may have behaved. It would be a pretty poor show for me to let you starve. So I've decided to pay you an allowance. You can use it to live wherever you like, as long as it's not under my roof, and as long as you don't bring disgrace on the family name. And if you ever marry, provided it's a decent fellow – someone I can approve of – I'll let you have something by way of a dowry.'

'Or, at least, you'll let the decent fellow have it,' Venetia added.

Harry made a restless movement of annoyance. 'There you go again, spouting that tosh about women's rights when I'm trying to do the decent thing by you. Not a word of thanks – just the sort of stuff that drove Papa to his grave! Haven't you any proper feelings? He's hardly been underground a day. Can't you behave like a female, just for once?'

Venetia drew an impatient breath. What brother wouldn't provide for his sister, even if he had very much less than a ducal fortune to spend? Harry was talking more and more like an alderman. By the end of the week, she thought, he'll have reached the age of sixty and his beard will be white. But she didn't want to quarrel with him, especially as he was being far kinder than she had expected.

'An allowance to live independently is exactly what I want,' she said, 'and I do thank you. You might have made me live on as a pensioner under your roof.'

'Don't forget,' he said coldly, 'I said I'd pay you an allowance as long as you didn't disgrace us. That means you must find someone respectable to live with. I won't have you living alone.'

'Very well.' She hesitated. 'You know that I still want to study to become a doctor?'

He made an impatient gesture. 'I know it's of no use

109

to try to persuade you to reason. Do as you please – but you will not use the family name.'

It was phrased as a command, but it sounded like a plea. 'I shall call myself Miss Fleet, as I did before,' Venetia said. 'My title would be as much of an embarrassment to me as to you. And what about Mama?'

'*What* about her? I'll take care of her, don't you fret.'

'But can I see her from time to time?'

'You can visit her, provided you arrange it with me first.'

'And the girls?'

'That's up to them. I don't think Augusta will want to see you. As to Olivia, she has her career at Court. You might think of that. Consider whether keeping up a contact with you is likely to enhance your sisters' credit in the world.'

Venetia left the next day, to return to Wolvercote for the time being, until her arrangements were completed. She left with a sense of loss and of ending – but of beginning too. Though she was dependent on Harry's goodwill for her independent means, it did mean that she could resume her medical studies, she could take up the place at the new college that Miss Jex-Blake had offered her. Perhaps now at last her ambition was within her reach.

And it occurred to her that Miss Jex-Blake – though possibly not what Harry would have thought of as a suitable example on which to model herself – would know how to go about finding a place to live and arranging an independent life. Venetia was twenty-four, intelligent and capable, but she had never lived outside her family's boundaries before, and she felt in that respect very feeble and ignorant – an innocent abroad.

With the young squire of Bishop Winthorpe back in residence, village life had become lively. There were quite a few genteel families in the area, and many more a short carriage ride away. Perry began his reign by inviting them all to a grand ball. After that the floodgates had fairly opened, and all summer long invitations flew in all directions for dinners, picnics, dances, rides, suppers, and every other variety of social interaction.

In the middle of it all, a letter had come from Mr Fortescue to say that his researches were going well and that he was extending his tour in order to go to Italy. He had secured an invitation from the Pope to consult some documents in the Vatican Library, and such was their importance he was willing to overcome his dislike of all things papistical for the sake of a sight of them. Henrietta had felt guilty that her reaction to this letter was one of delight that the happy times were not to end yet. Mr Fortescue expected to be back not much before Christmas, and it was like an unexpected holiday to a school-child, to have him stay away so long.

The reschooling of Ginger, using the paddock up at the Red House, had occupied her all summer. At first the Parkes and the Comptons had seemed as interested in her progress as Henrietta herself. They stood behind the paddock rails and watched as Henrietta and Tobin, the friendly old Red House groom, worked her, some-times with a hand from Jerome. Regina went along to watch, too, and Perry could usually be found stationed at her side so that he could explain to her what was going on.

But progress was slow, and the audience often decided, after a few minutes of the endless lungeing, which Tobin thought necessary to good equine manners, that it would be more fun to go for a ride than stay and watch. As summer turned to autumn, more often than not the helping was left to Jerome.

One late November day Henrietta walked up to the Red House, where Ginger was now stabled permanently. It was early, but the sun was up and it was warm; the air seemed thick and bright, almost tangible, with the soft, smoky smell of late autumn. The last leaves hung limp and yellow against a hazy sky; the bare hedges were full of bickering birds, beginning to think of winter shelter and staking territory. The swifts were all gone, and the day seemed empty without their screaming, curving flight. In the verges the long grasses, ribby stalks and brown seed-heads were spread thick with the webs of autumn spiders. There was a finishing feeling to everything, a pleasant melancholy: winter was coming, but here was one warm day more to enjoy, to pretend that summer was still not over.

Ginger whickered from her stall as she saw Henrietta approach: it was wonderful, Henrietta thought, that she now anticipated a caress and an apple rather than a blow or curse. She petted and talked to her, murmuring the nonsense horses like to hear, and after a moment the mare did something she had never done before, thrust her muzzle up under Henrietta's arm, the ultimate gesture of trust.

A quiet voice from a little way off said, 'She has come a long way – you both have, together.'

Ginger jerked her head free, her ears going flat, and then forward. Henrietta turned. Jerome had arrived so quietly neither of them had heard him until he spoke.

'I saw you go past the house,' he said. 'I knew where you would be.'

'What were you doing up so early?' she asked, resuming her stroking of Ginger's neck. The mare watched Jerome over her shoulder, wary but not afraid.

'Why shouldn't I be up? You must think me a mere idle fribble like—'

'Like Perry, or my brother?' she completed for him. 'Well, not quite like them, perhaps.'

'Thank you for that small tribute. And what were you meaning to do with the mare all alone? Or were you waiting for Tobin?'

'He's at breakfast. All the grooms are,' she said, giving herself away.

'You weren't,' said Jerome sternly, 'thinking of riding her all alone?'

'I think she's ready,' Henrietta said defiantly. 'And it's better without too many people to fuss her.'

'My dear idiot, what were you thinking about? Granted

112

you don't want an audience, but how were you proposing even to get up on her without help?'

Henrietta blushed a little at his term of address, but she said, 'I was going to ride her bareback – across. Well, I've done it often before. As a girl I always rode like that.'

'Did you indeed! How remarkably improper, Mrs Fortescue!'

'And I thought I'd get up from the paddock rail. I've done that before, too.'

'Not with this horse, however.'

'She won't mind being ridden so much if there's no saddle. It won't be what she's expecting.'

'And if the surprise sends her mad and you are killed, what then?' He came a step nearer and the mare's ears moved quickly back and forth. 'If you don't care for yourself, think of the rest of us. How could we live without you?'

A stillness came over Henrietta, and from within it she spoke, almost as if she were outside herself and looking down from a great height. 'You can help me if you like. But you must be very quiet and gentle. Almost as if we are all asleep and in a dream. She will dream she walks with us to the paddock, that I float onto her back like a dream, and nothing is real at all, just mist on the grass or leaves drifting down the stream. Can you do that? Be part of a dream?'

He could only nod. Talking softly, she undid the pillar reins and led the mare out. Hoofs clopped hollowly on the cobbles. As she passed, Jerome fell in quietly beside her. They walked out into the lambent morning, and the mare wrinkled her nostrils to catch the soft smells of damp earth and dying leaves. Into the paddock – Jerome opened the gate for them – and Henrietta walked her round a circuit or two, bringing her back to him, giving him the reins and some slices of apple to reward her with. While he held the mare, Henrietta stroked her neck and shoulders, then her flanks, then leaned across her to stroke her other side, putting weight on her back. Ginger chewed her bit calmly, pursuing fragments of apple.

113

When she thought the moment right, Henrietta bent her left leg at the knee, and Jerome took it and put her up. She moved so lightly he had hardly anything to do. She was astride the warm golden back, her hands never ceasing the rhythm of her stroking. For a moment the mare didn't seem to notice what had happened. Then she put her ears back enquiringly.

'Let her turn her head,' Henrietta said, as Jerome instinctively tightened his grasp of the reins. 'Don't hold her. This is all a dream, remember?'

The mare turned and looked back at Henrietta, stretched her muzzle to touch her rider's leg. And then, as Jerome held his breath, she turned her head forward again, nodded it up and down thoughtfully a couple of times – and cocked one hind foot into the position of rest.

Jerome could have laughed, crowed, turned a cartwheel in amusement and relief; but of course he did nothing but smile a little. In a moment Henrietta slithered down and said, 'Enough for one time. Tomorrow we'll start walking. Shall we go back in?'

They returned the mare to her stall. Henrietta clipped on the pillar reins, and turned to Jerome, looking up at him with almost the same air of enquiry as the mare.

'You know,' he said in the dream, 'that I love you?'

She said nothing, and he took her face tenderly in his hands and kissed her. It was a long, close, quiet moment. Henrietta felt no surprise, only a great, sad yearning, and a feeling of belonging, of *home*, as though this was the place she had been travelling to all her life. She put her hands over his to keep him there a moment longer; and when they broke from each other, it was a terrible parting. They read the sadness mirrored in each other's eyes.

'There is nothing to be done,' she said. 'I am a married woman.'

'I shouldn't have let this happen,' he said. But she knew now, with retrospect, that he had been pushing and pushing for it to happen ever since they had first met. How could she have been so innocent, so ignorant as not to have noticed? But at first, of course, she had been in

114

love with her husband; and since then her senses had slept, protecting her. 'I knew I was in danger,' he said, 'and I did not draw back. Now I've put you in danger too.'

'But this is a dream, remember?' she said. 'It doesn't matter.'

There was a sound out in the yard. The grooms had finished their breakfast. They drew a pace apart, back to the safe distance.

'I shall have to go away,' he said.

She did not deny the necessity. 'But not yet,' she said. 'Not for a week or two.'

He regarded her steadily for a moment. 'I can't be here when he gets back.'

'I'll tell you when.'

'No,' he said. 'That would make it a conspiracy. I can't do that to you.' And he turned and walked away from her just as a gaitered boy came into the stalls at the far end, wiping his lips with the back of his hand.

The dreamlike quality lasted only until she had walked home. As soon as she stepped through the door of the rectory and saw the maid carrying breakfast dishes into the dining-parlour, it was gone. Reality was hard to breathe: she felt like a fish dragged out into the searing painful air. And here was Regina, coming down the stairs with her young morning smile, a girl in love for the first time and with every hope of return, licensed to talk about her beloved, to think of him as she chose. Not to anyone could Henrietta speak of Jerome; it was wrong even to think of him. She was a married woman, and he was out of reach for ever.

She almost gasped as the pain of it struck her. She loved him. She saw his face so clearly she could hardly believe he was not standing there before her. She wanted to run up to her room and lock the door, bury her face in her bedclothes so that she could keep hold of the precious single moment, which was all she could ever have. She understood now what he had given up in that moment of revelation. Now he could not be with her any more. If he

115

had kept his secret, he could at least have seen her; but it would have been like seeing someone through a window when what you wanted – so much, more than life itself – was to be in the room with them. He'd had to wake her: had to have her *know*. And now it was over. She knew quite certainly that he would leave at once, rather than have her taint herself with conspiracy: for if she saw him again now, she was as good as an adulteress.

Well, what was she anyway? She thought bitterly that he might have saved himself the noble gesture, for she would love him whether she saw him or not, and that was just as bad, just as much a betrayal of her marriage vows. Regina was talking to her, expecting a response, slipping an arm through hers – how she flinched at someone else's touch – leading her towards the breakfast table. Every word, every contact with someone who was not him dragged her further and further from that one moment which was her life's purpose. And yet she observed with amazement how she smiled and answered her sister as lightly and naturally as if she weren't being torn apart inside. This was how it would be, she thought, and the prospect of a lifetime of such dissembling sickened her.

Yet by the time Mary Compton walked up at midday to tell her – with a look of covert curiosity – that her brother had quitted Bishop Winthorpe that morning to go to stay with a friend for the hunting, she had already settled into it, adjusting to it as one adjusts to intractable pain.

A week later Mr Fortescue arrived home, without prior warning, looking very old and worn. The journey back had been hard, he told her, with a difficult crossing, and he had had a cold since Lyons. 'Draughty railway carriages, indifferent food, impertinent porters – all have exacerbated the condition. I am glad to be home, my dear,' he said, and in the relief of the moment, he looked at her kindly, and spoke with warmth.

'I am glad to have you home,' she said calmly. 'If I'd had warning of your arrival, I could have had the fires made up in your rooms ready for you.'

'No matter,' he said. 'I will sit with you in the drawing-room while it is done, and you may tell me what you have been doing all this while. And,' with a look of eagerness, 'you may have Elizabeth brought down to see me. I have missed her more than I expected. Yes,' he added, looking around him as he took a seat by the drawing-room fire, 'home seems very agreeable after so long away. Foreign travel is not an unalloyed pleasure. I believe I shall not wish to go away again.'

CHAPTER SEVEN

One March day in 1875, Henrietta was standing at the window watching the spring rain fall in torrents. It dripped from the budding trees, bounced off the paths, gurgled in the gutters; the daffodils, which ought to have been bright flags of cheerfulness, were flattened with it, their petals stuck dismally to the earth and turning brown.

Henrietta folded her arms round herself, not so much for warmth as for comfort. She hadn't been outside for days. She didn't mind riding in the rain, but the paths were now fathomless mud, and Bond made her life a misery if she wanted to take a horse out. He said he was worried about slips and sprains, cracked heels and mud fever, but she suspected rather that he disliked having to wash and dry two horses, to say nothing of his own boots and breeches.

The blankness of the sky seemed a counterpoint to her own feelings. She had two kinds of spirits: acute wretchedness, when she couldn't stop herself thinking of him, when she longed hopelessly for him and was torn with pangs of love and guilt; and numbness, when she managed not to think about the situation at all. The numbness was easier to cope with, but it never lasted long enough. Something would happen to remind her, and he would be before her in memory again, wanted so desperately, and out of reach.

He had been gone six months now. Where was he? Did he ever think of her? Was he miserable, or had he found comfort with someone else? She hardly knew which was the worse possibility. Mary never spoke of him, though sometimes Henrietta caught her looking at her in a particular way. She could have asked Mary for news, but would not allow herself. The degree of sin she was in by loving at all was the most she could bear; to indulge that love would be to lose what firm ground was left under her feet. Even Mary's friendship was perilous, for there was a look of him in her, and her way of speaking was like his. Solitary rides, accompanied only by Bond, was all that could blot out thought and give her respite. If only the rain would stop!

The door opened and a head popped round it. 'May I come in? The maid said it would be all right.'

Henrietta turned. 'Oh, Perry! Yes, of course, do. Are you wet through? Come to the fire.'

'No, no, I'm only a bit damp. Shed my greatcoat in the hall, and a monstrous great hat of the pater's I found in the gun room. I remember him wearing it fishing. Makes me look a figure, but the brim is so wide it could shelter half a Sunday-school class! I think,' he added hopefully, 'it might be easing off a bit.'

'It isn't,' she said, with certainty, 'but thank you for trying to cheer me up. I don't think it's ever going to stop. It's Noah's flood all over again.'

'It's making a mess of the wheat,' Perry said, suddenly serious. 'And the late lambs – never saw so many dead ones.'

'Yes, the one thing sheep can't stand is wet,' Henrietta said.

Perry raised his eyebrows. 'True – but how do you know?'

'I was brought up among sheep.' She remembered days spent with old Caleb the shepherd, sharing his dinner of bread and an onion, which he ate whole, crunching it like an apple. Suddenly she was there again, sitting on a rocky outcrop, in a sea of moorland grass gay with selfheal and wild thyme and toadflax, while the sheep grazed all about them, their bells making a sad, sweet music. For an instant she heard the murmur of bees and felt the sun hot on her head. Then she shook herself and was back in the present. It was all so long ago now.

'Was there something in particular you wanted, or did you just happen to be passing?'

'Oh, well, yes, now you mention it, there was something,' Perry said, looking a little conscious. 'Something rather particular, as it happens. It – ah – concerns your sister. Regina, in fact.'

'That is her name,' Henrietta said solemnly.

Perry looked at her sidelong and laughed. 'You're roasting me! The fact is – well, I suppose you've guessed, or noticed, that I'm very fond of her. In short—'

'Yes, do go the short way to work,' Henrietta encouraged. 'Spit it out, there's a good fellow.'

He squared up to the challenge. 'I'm in love with her and want to marry her. There now!'

'Spoken like a man! And I'm very glad,' Henrietta said. 'I've been hoping it would be a match – I know she's very much in love with you.'

'Is she?' Perry seemed pleased.

'Don't you know?'

'Oh – well – she did say she was, but it's nice to hear it from someone else. Confirmation, you know.'

'I'm amazed she's managed to keep your proposal a secret from me,' Henrietta said. 'She's usually such a gabble-puss. When did you ask her?'

He smirked. 'About half an hour ago. I happened to meet her at the post office and when she said she was going to the haberdasher's next I offered to escort her and hold the umbrella, and, well, while we walked along it – it happened.'

'I wondered why she was so keen to go and post my letters for me in all this rain,' Henrietta laughed. 'When was all this arranged?'

'No, really, it was quite by chance,' Perry protested; and then laughed too, and said, 'My sisters plotted it all, I'm afraid. They are two very bad girls, but with very good hearts. But the thing is,' he grew serious again, 'I need to know who I am to apply to for permission to marry her, Regina not being of age yet. I hoped you could tell me.'

'Ah, yes,' Henrietta said. 'Although she lives with me, her guardian is my brother George at Morland Place. His permission will be needed, although I can't imagine for a moment that he will object to such an excellent match. However . . .' She paused, thoughtfully. She imagined Perry riding over there, seeking an interview with George, being faced with indifference or even rudeness. George – probably at Alfreda's instigation – had never enquired once after Regina since she came to live with Henrietta, and she could imagine only too easily George saying something like 'She may do as she pleases – I have no interest in the matter.'

She didn't want to expose Perry to that; he was too nice a young man. She didn't want him to see in what low esteem his future wife was held. She didn't want a member of her family to expose himself in that way, to bring shame to the Morland name.

'It's a little delicate,' she said at last. 'No, nothing to do with your acceptability, I assure you! It's – oh, forgive me, I can't explain. But if you would be so kind as to wait a day or two, I think it would be best if I were to approach my brother first, and prepare the ground. Will you trust me?'

'Of course, I trust you absolutely,' Perry said, puzzled. 'But you don't think he'll refuse?'

'No, no! Never in the world! Just – let me go about it my own way.'

After some thought, she rejected the idea of a letter. Letters were all too easy to ignore, and there had never been any correspondence between Morland Place and the Rectory since her marriage. If she wrote and received no reply she would have to write again, and the matter would drag on, with cruel uncertainty to the young people. The best thing would be to send Teddy in person to interview their brother. But then Teddy was so lazy, he might not stir himself with enough urgency. And would he press for an answer if George was inclined to be difficult or indifferent?

No, on the whole she thought it would be better to go herself – and as soon as she decided it, she realised that she was partly influenced by a great desire to see her old home again. Yes, she would go herself – and without warning. If she wrote to ask if she could visit, they might say no, and she'd be back where she started.

Having come to the decision she wasted no time, and trotted along to the library where, in the absence of any information to the contrary, she expected her husband to be working.

At her tap on the door there was a long pause before he said, 'Come in.'

She went in. There was a big, good fire in the fireplace. The room was noticeably warmer than elsewhere in the house, and seemed cosily cheerful. The walls were lined with bookshelves, and the firelight moved over the ranks of leather spines, picking out the gilded letters with little sparking gleams; the old polished wood, leather chairs, crimson plush curtains all added depth to the warm glow.

The rector was at his desk, writing, and did not at once look up. She watched him for a moment, hands folded patiently before her, knowing better than to speak before she was spoken to. His bent head gleamed as if it had been polished too: the noble height of his forehead had grown yet higher these past years. His hair, which she noticed had gone almost white since last year, was rosy in the firelight. His gold-rimmed spectacles were perched near the end of his nose as he looked from a book to his notes and back again with the economical movement of the practised scholar. One of his thin, strong hands held down the book page, while the other held the pen, and the scratching of the nib over the paper was the only sound apart from the crackling of the fire and the measured heartbeat of the longcase clock.

She looked at him curiously, having one of those moments of standing outside a situation and seeing it with stranger's eyes. This man – this *old* man, with white hair and elderly hollow cheeks – what had he to do with her? Her husband seemed as remote as someone seen for a moment from a moving train, unnamed, unknown, unattached: it was hard to believe he was the father of her child. She watched his hands, and shivered a little, perceiving the strength of him. The hard fingers held down the pages while the hard mind pursued and tacked down facts, piercing them through and pinning them to his handwritten pages with the delicate ruthlessness of the entomologist. His years had not wearied him; he had not come to babbling of green fields. Everything about him was sharp-edged and purposeful. Beside him she felt loose, untidy, unregulated, something useless and unintended, like a stream that had burst its banks.

How could she ever have loved him? Not that he was not estimable, worthy of love, but how could she ever have *dared*? Her marriage had been like an enchanted sleep that had fallen on her in that frozen February garden when Fortescue had first said he loved her. And what, oh, *what* was it he had loved in her? Why couldn't she get it back? She was so lonely, she wanted to love him and to be loved. He was her husband, the only lover she had ever had – would ever have, now the bright eyes, the vivid face, the flame-like vitality that had woken her from her enchanted sleep were gone. Whatever warmth there was in the world for her could only come from her husband – this grey man, who had no more spark for her than cold ashes. Her life seemed to her just then so empty that she wanted to sink to the ground and weep with despair.

He looked up at last, over his glasses, at the quiet, composed woman, seeing nothing of the turmoil of her thoughts.

'Yes, my dear?' He knew it was something important – important to her, at least – because she never normally interrupted him. He was aware that he was lucky in his wife, having seen what other men put up with. She never troubled him with demands, emotional scenes, hysterics, meaningless conversation, imbecile questions. She never troubled him at all, in fact, merely lived her life in the other half of the house, on the whole quietly, thriftily, surprisingly tidily. She did not interfere with his work, and she appeared properly attired in the rectory pew at all times when it was expected of her. He was therefore prepared to listen patiently to what she had to say, and grant her request if possible.

'My sister has received a proposal of marriage from Sir Perry Parke,' she said, having had time to prepare the words – he liked them to be succinct.

The rector considered. 'That is more fortunate for her than she can have had cause to expect. Does she accept him?'

'Yes – they are in love.'

'You will be sorry to lose her companionship, but you will not wish to stand in her way.'

'By no means. It is what I hoped for her. But my brother at Morland Place will have to give his consent.'

'Ah!'

'And I would like to go myself to ask for it.'

He frowned. 'It is Parke's business to ask, not yours.'

'Still I would like to go myself to prepare the ground. My brother may be – ungracious; and I'm fond of Perry.'

The rector considered, looked carefully into her face, and then said, 'Very well, I have no objection. You may order the carriage. When will you go?'

'Tomorrow morning.' She thought he would ask more about her proposed trip, but he was not sufficiently interested.

'Very well,' he said, and returned to his book – not as if dismissing her, but as if his eyes had gone of their own volition and his head had been obliged to follow. He had probably never stopped thinking about what he had been reading, even while listening to her. She had the image of his brain rumbling on deep under their conversation all the while, like a great, underground machine – powerful, unstoppable. Perhaps, she thought, as she turned away, already forgotten by him, he was as much its victim as she was.

* * *

When George Morland came out of the steward's room, he noticed that the door to the chapel was open, and when he paused for a moment to wonder who would be in there at that time of day, he heard someone singing in a small, sweet voice.

Quietly he stepped up to the door and looked in, but saw no-one. The chapel was empty, but the singing came from the direction of the altar. A shiver ran down his back. The voice was so high and clear, like that of a child, but too old a child for it to be little James, and his mind naturally turned to ghosts. There were plenty of stories about hauntings in Morland Place, and not all Alfreda's modernisations could eliminate the folds of shadow and the things seen out of the corner of the eye.

But it was broad daylight, he told himself sternly – or daylight, at least – and he was a grown man and master of the house. He stepped over the threshold and walked boldly down the aisle.

'For why, the Lord our God is good;
His mercy is for ever sure;
His truth at all times firmly stood,
And shall from age to age endure.'

Well, he thought, no evil spirit would sing those words. Feeling braver, he joined in. *'To Father, Son and Holy Ghost—'*

The little singing voice broke off with a squeak, like a caught mouse, and at the same moment he came level with the front pew and saw a housemaid on her knees scrubbing the chapel floor. She looked up at him over her shoulder apprehensively. Her fair hair was escaping in wisps from under her cap, and her face was pink with effort; her eyes were tender blue, her forearms were bare and plump, and there was about her an air, if not an odour, of clean starch and soapsuds.

She scrambled to her feet and dropped a frightened curtsy, and he recognised her now as the pretty little one who always looked up at him as he walked out after morning prayers.

'No need to be afraid,' he said, as she gazed up at him wide-eyed. 'I'm sure singing a hymn in chapel can't be a sin.'

'I'm sorry if I disturbed you, sir,' she said, not wholly reassured. If you were an under-housemaid, there were so many things which turned out to be crimes after you'd done them. Especially, everything concerned with the Family – or Gentry in general – was fraught with hazard. The best you could hope for was never to encounter one of them in the flesh at all, and here she was alone and face to face with the very pinnacle of power.

'You didn't disturb me. You have a sweet voice,' George said. He was fascinated by her, now he had time to look at her properly. She was so little and young, and so pretty – he didn't think he'd ever seen a girl so pretty. But why was she afraid of him? 'It's a good hymn,' he added. 'One of my favourites.' And he smiled to reassure her.

She relaxed just a little. 'It's good for working to,' she said. 'Scrubbing or polishing.' And she demonstrated the movement for him, humming a single line. Then she stopped again, looking up to see if he would be angry.

'I've seen you in the chapel at prayers,' he said abruptly. 'You're—'

'Alice, sir,' she provided.

'Alice. That's a pretty name. And you're . . . ?'

She divined the nature of the question. 'Under-housemaid, sir.'

'Are you happy here, Alice?'

'Oh, yes, sir. It's a very good place.'

He was stumped for any more questions, but he didn't want the encounter to end. He carried on looking at her with a half-smile, and after a moment she took it to be an invitation to converse. But what could she talk to him about? The weather was always a safe subject.

'This rain is terrible, isn't it, sir?'

'Eh? Oh, yes.'

'I hear say there's no sowing the spring corn, the way things are.'

He wrinkled his brow. 'Are you interested in such things?'

'Everyone must be, mustn't they? The harvest affects everybody. It must be a worry to you, sir.'

'Yes,' he said. He remembered what Atterwith had been chattering about last time he'd been cornered by him. 'It's not just the corn. The stores are still in yard, and it costs money to feed them. And we've lost two good ewes this week, not to talk of dead lambs.'

The troubles were real, but what he felt most of all just then was the desire to tell her things. She was gazing into his face with intense and unshadowed interest, and he felt she would have been ready to hear anything he had to say. She would not dismiss him with a sharp wave of the hand, or speak impatiently to him as if he were of no account, or sigh in that way that made him feel clumsy and stupid. She was so young and pretty, rounded of limb and dewy of eye, as if life ran lightly and cheerfully in her veins. He felt a strong desire to go for a walk with her and show her his acres.

'I'm so sorry,' she was saying humbly. 'It must be a great worry for you.'

He nodded, bathed in her gentle sympathy. He racked his brain for something else to say. 'So – er – you are happy here, you say? Quite comfortable?'

'Oh, yes, sir. Well, except for the leaks.'

'Leeks?' he said, startled.

'The servants' bedrooms are up under the roof, and the roof leaks. With all this rain it's got very bad. We have a basin on our bed to catch the drips, and one of us has to get up and empty it half-way through the night.'

She said it not in a complaining way, but as if it were just an interesting story. Given her sympathy with his farming worries, he ought to commiserate with her, he felt; but while he was searching for the words, there was a sound of voices out in the great hall, which recalled him to reality.

'Excuse me,' he said, stopped himself bowing, added, with a wave of the hand, 'Er, do carry on,' and hurried away.

In the hall, Bates, the first footman, was talking to a lady in a neat brown costume and a hat trimmed with long pheasant feathers, explaining to her that the mistress was not at home. She turned her head as George appeared from the staircase hall, and at once a smile lit her features and she hurried towards him with her hands outstretched.

'George, there you are! Dear old Georgie!' His momentary recoil stopped her short and the smile faltered. 'Don't you know me?'

'Good God! Henrietta! I wouldn't have recognised you.'

'It's a long time since you saw me,' she said, trying not to sound reproachful. He appeared to be quite pleased to see her, and she did not want to annoy him. 'Four years, you know.'

'Yes, I suppose it must be,' he said. 'Well, you are looking prosperous.' He turned to Bates. 'This is Mrs Edgar Fortescue, my sister. Her husband is rector of Bishop Winthorpe.'

'Yes, sir,' said Bates stoically. 'The lady asked for Mrs Morland, sir, and I was explaining that Madam is *not* at home.'

'Quite right. Alfreda's in her room,' he said to Henrietta, walking with her towards the fireplace and waving Bates away with an impatient hand. 'She hardly leaves it at all now. We're – er – expecting a happy event.'

'So I understand,' Henrietta said. 'Teddy told me. My warmest congratulations. I hope she is very well?'

'Oh, tol-lol, you know,' George said, with a slight frown. 'The fact is,' he added, on a burst of confiding, 'that it doesn't go easily with her, this business. She was dashed ill with James, and she's that bit older now.' The last was spoken almost in a whisper. Alfreda had driven

128

the doctor from the house with icy rage when he had talked about her age, and George had had to get a new man in. That had been at the beginning of the pregnancy, and her temper was far worse now.

'I'm sorry to hear it. I hope everything will be all right after all. You have no particular fears?'

'Oh, no – the doctor says she must rest a lot, that's all, and not be upset. So, er, how is Fortescue? He's not with you today?'

'No. I came to talk family matters with you, Georgie. It was you I wanted, really, though naturally in politeness I asked for Alfreda. Are you at leisure? Can you spare me half an hour?'

She had not known what kind of reception to expect, but he was looking genuinely glad to see her, and this tentative question was met with a broad gesture and a warm affirmative. 'As long as you like. Glad to see you. What do you think of the old place? It must seem very different to you.'

It was not, in fact, as much changed as she had feared from Teddy's rather exaggerated accounts. The barbican and the face of the house were the same, and the great hall was unaltered; but there was a new wing where the kennels had stood, and building was going on on the other side of the yard.

'Are you knocking down the stables?' she asked.

'Most of them,' he said. 'Now we've got the new stable-yard, we don't need all those stalls up at the house and, frankly, Alfreda don't care for the smell. But we do need more kitchen accommodation.'

'Yes, I heard a rumour that you were going to build over the moat.'

'We did think of it, but it would have cost too much money, Atterwith said, so we came up with this idea instead. Kitchen quarters downstairs and more bedrooms upstairs, and we just keep three stalls to stand visitors' horses in, and a tack-room. But come and see what we've done with the drawing-room and dining-room. Vastly improved, I think you'll agree. And my gentlemen's wing is splendid – keeps the dogs and the tobacco smell out of the rest of the house, and I've a billiard-room and a gun-room and I can come and go as I please without disturbing anyone.'

It did not seem to occur to him, as it did to Henrietta, that it was odd for the master of the house to talk about not disturbing anyone. She let him show her the new accommodations, and approved wholeheartedly the provision of a small dining-parlour. She concealed her regret at the loss of the old drawing-room, for in her opinion the modern wallpapered apartment could not match the grandeur of the great panelled chamber with its moulded ceiling.

But George seemed to have no regrets. He listed the improvements and the cost of the new furnishings and carpets for her with pride. 'We do so much entertaining now, it was absolutely necessary to have more modern arrangements,' he concluded, 'and I think our guests all agree that we've done everything just as it should be. No-one ever refuses an invitation to Morland Place.'

At that moment he recalled that his sister and her husband had never been invited to Morland Place, that there had been no communication between them since Henrietta's wedding, and he fell awkwardly silent. He remembered the casual affection in which he had held his little sister, the ease there had been between them when they were living here together, before their respective marriages. He had never been a man of strong emotions, and had taken most things about his home and family for granted; but once his mother had died and his father had retreated into strangeness, Henrietta had been the warmest and most accessible thing at Morland Place. He remembered the rough-haired, hoydenish little thing she had been, and felt an odd pang, like hunger, for the simplicity of life then. He had hardly spared Henrietta two thoughts in the past four years, but now, this morning, suddenly faced with her, she seemed familiar and unexpectedly dear, and he was sorry fate had drawn them apart.

So when she told him about Regina's offer of marriage, he listened with more attention than he otherwise might have.

'*Sir* Peregrine?' he queried. 'What is he?'

'A baronet,' Henrietta answered.

He nodded approval. 'Good. A knight is nothing.'

'And he has a very good property. He's a substantial landowner in Bishop Winthorpe – in fact they call him the squire.'

'Excellent. It sounds like a good match for her,' George concluded. Then he wondered why Henrietta was telling him, and provided himself almost at the same moment with an answer, which made him frown anxiously. 'I say, he don't want a dowry with her, does he? Because, you know, anything of that sort . . .'

He was so transparent, Henrietta had been able to chart the course of his thoughts. 'No,' she said, a little sadly. 'He knows she hasn't a dowry. He's a very modern young man. He's quite willing to take her for herself alone, and there are no close relatives on his side to object.'

'Oh,' said George, and felt just a little ashamed. 'Papa left things in such a way, you know,' he floundered. 'The estate takes every penny, and more. There's never a groat to spare for anything else. I haven't even had a new coat this year.'

'It's all right, Georgie, I understand. All I want from you is your permission for the marriage.'

'My permission?'

'She is still under twenty-one, and you are her legal guardian.'

'Oh, of course! I was forgetting. Yes, I think I can give my permission,' he said judiciously, 'if you say the fellow is a decent sort. I trust your judgement.'

'Thank you.' She hesitated, and added, 'Will you come to the wedding? Will you give her away? It would mean a great deal to her. And it would put the seal of your approval on the match.' Better to put it to him that way than to say that his absence would cast discredit on the family.

'Oh, yes,' George said kindly. 'I think I can do that. Yes, I think I can say we will come. She is to be married from your house? Very good. Yes, I shall like the opportunity of seeing how you and Fortescue live. I'll be interested to see how you go on.'

'Thank you,' said Henrietta. She scanned his face a moment, then laid her hand on his arm and said, 'Are you well, Georgie? Is everything all right with you?'

'Yes, of course,' he said, seeming startled. 'Why not?'

'No reason. I'm interested in your welfare, that's all. I am your sister.'

'My favourite sister,' he said indulgently. 'That's what you always were.'

'And how is Manny? Have you any recent news of him?'

'Oh, he does very well at school. He's quite a pet of the schoolmaster – treats him like his own son. Couldn't be happier.'

She was about to pursue the topic further when there was a tap on the door and Alfreda's personal maid, Fanie, came in. She curtsied, quickly dissecting Henrietta with her eyes and storing away every detail of her appearance, and said to George, 'If you please, my lady wishes you to come at once.'

George blushed a little, for a reason Henrietta could not fathom. 'She's not unwell?'

'No, sir, she wishes to speak.' Having delivered her message she stood implacably in the doorway, to signify that her lady's wish must be obeyed.

George said to Henrietta, 'I had better go. The doctor said she ought not to be upset in any way, and if I were to keep her waiting . . .'

'Of course, I quite understand,' said Henrietta. 'I'll take my leave.'

'No, don't go! I want to show you round. You haven't seen the new stables yet and I know you were always nutty on horses.'

Henrietta smiled. 'I'd like to see them.'

He beamed. 'Excellent! And I'd like to talk to you –

we haven't had a comfortable chat in so long.' Or indeed ever, Henrietta thought, but she smiled her willingness to be his favourite sister now, which was better than never. 'Do make yourself comfortable. I shan't be many minutes.'

He disappeared with Fanie at his heels, and Henrietta settled herself to wait. His absence extended itself at first annoyingly and then embarrassingly. He must have forgotten her, she thought, which would be enough like him not to be surprising. She imagined him leaving Alfreda's room and trotting off down the nursery stairs, whistling, to let himself out of the postern without a thought that there was any such person as Henrietta in the world. She had just decided to ring the bell and leave a message for him when the door opened again and he was there, looking hangdog, his eyes anywhere but on her.

'I thought you'd forgotten me,' she said.

'Oh! No, not a bit, far from it,' he muttered. 'Alfreda – Mrs Morland – we had rather a talk. She's a little upset – that is, you know, ladies in her condition can be – well, I'm sure in other circumstances . . .'

'Spit it out, Georgie,' Henrietta said bracingly, surprising herself a little that she could talk to her older brother so freely. But what had she to fear, after all? The days when he could affect her life or even hurt her feelings were long gone.

George, too, looked a little startled. 'The thing is,' he said reluctantly, 'that she's not quite pleased with me for promising we'd come to Regina's wedding. Very cross, in fact. So I hope you'll forgive me for changing m' mind so soon, but she has to be humoured – could be dangerous if she gets in a tizzy – and, well, in short, she wants you to leave.'

'Leave?'

'Leave the house,' George said, his eyes begging for understanding. 'And never come back. She was quite – that is—' He coughed and shifted his eyes away. 'She says she doesn't want to hear your name or Reggie's mentioned again. So, in the circumstances, I'd better not show you round after all.'

He was smarting inside, not so much from the things Alfreda had said but the way she had said them, as if he were a delinquent servant. It was all very well to tell himself that she was not herself at the moment; he couldn't help feeling it shouldn't have been possible for her to address him with so little respect whatever her state of mind. Hen and Reggie were his sisters after all, damnit, and blood was thicker, as the saying went. But when he had shown resistance she had become almost hysterical, and cried that she hated Henrietta, and that she would bring bad luck if she were allowed to stay in the house a moment longer. He'd give something to know who told Alfreda that Henrietta was there in the first place – he suspected Fanie, who was a sly piece if ever there was one. But the damage was done now, and Alfreda was so close to her time that there was no taking risks.

'Why does she hate me so?' Henrietta asked, quite gently.

George stared at the ground and rubbed a marble square with the tip of his boot. 'Not herself, entirely,' he said. 'You know how these things go.'

Henrietta gathered her dignity and prepared to leave. 'You will send me your written consent to the marriage, however?' she said. 'It is a love-match, and a good one, and it will cost you nothing.'

George reddened. 'For my own wishes . . .'

Henrietta put out a hand. 'It's all right, George. I think I understand pretty well how things stand.'

He followed her, feeling wretched, to the great door. Bates appeared to open it for her; and at the last moment George called quietly after her, 'God bless you.'

She turned her head an instant and gave him a smile – warm, understanding, forgiving – which had him thinking for a surprised instant that old Hen had grown up quite pretty after all.

When Mr Catchpole had left the table and the dessert had

been put on, the rector roused himself from his thoughts to look at his wife, and after a moment said, 'You seem pensive, Mrs Fortescue.' Recollection came to him. 'Your visit to your brother had the desired outcome, I trust?'

'Not entirely,' she said. 'He has agreed to the match.'

'In worldly terms,' Fortescue said drily, 'it must be all he could ever have hoped for.'

'They are in love,' she said bluntly, 'and they are both good people. Why should anyone object?'

'Does anyone object?'

'You did not sound as if you liked it.'

He raised an eyebrow. 'The arrangement is of no consequence to me.'

She gave him a wry look. 'As the wedding will take place from your house, I should have thought you had every right to an opinion.'

'Your brother has given his consent, you say?' he prompted.

'Yes, but he will not come to the wedding or give her away.' In justice to George she wanted to say that the refusal came from Alfreda; but Alfreda was his wife, and how could you traduce a man's wife and not touch his honour? There was nothing she could say, just as there was nothing George could have said.

Fortescue looked at her across the table, as she sat with her head bent, crumbling a morsel of bread absently on her plate. He cared nothing about Regina, and the wedding would be nothing to him but nuisance, and a distraction from his work which he wished might never happen. But as he watched Henrietta thoughtfully, he saw a gleam of moisture under her lowered eyelashes, saw her draw in her lip under her teeth. She was his wife, and who acted against her attacked him.

'I'm sure your other brother will take the part – "give her away", as you put it. I would gladly undertake it myself, but as I shall be conducting the ceremony, I shall be otherwise engaged.'

Henrietta looked up, surprised and touched. She had assumed that he would leave it to Catchpole to conduct the service, as he did more and more these days. 'Thank you, sir,' she said softly. 'I know how you hate to be taken from your work.'

He smiled at her. 'You are my wife. It is little enough to do for you.'

She smiled back, but his words had lodged a barb in her. Given the wicked state of her mind, it would have been better not to have to be grateful to him; better to be ignored by him completely.

Two days later, Teddy rode over with news. 'I thought you would want to know,' he said. 'Poor old Alfreda!'

'Oh, Ted, no!'

'Afraid so. She miscarried yesterday. The child was dead, and she's pretty poorly. A girl, it was. Poor Georgie's beside himself.'

'Oh, Teddy, how awful! I'm so sorry!' Henrietta put her hands to her face. 'What brought it on – is it known?'

'Oh, nothing in particular, I gather. The sawbones said he wasn't too surprised – she'd not been well all through, and she was warned the last time not to try again.'

'But she'll be all right?'

Teddy shook his head. 'Touch and go at the moment. It's a wretched business.'

Henrietta thought of her visit and Alfreda's violent reaction. Could it have been that? Surely not? And even if it had been, how could she have known? It wasn't her fault, was it? Did George blame her?

'What will happen about Regina's wedding?' she asked aloud. 'George was to send his written consent, you know. I don't suppose he'll feel up to writing now.'

'Not until he knows how things are going to go with Alfreda.'

'No, of course not – I wouldn't expect it. I'll have to explain to Reggie that she must wait.'

Teddy put a hand over hers. 'I see it's knocked you off balance. It's a sad business. But give it a week or two and see how things go, and then if Georgie hasn't written, I'll go and remind him. Has any date been set?'

'No, not yet.'

'Well, then, there's no difficulty, is there?'

Henrietta raised her eyes. 'If Alfreda should – should get worse?'

Teddy shrugged. 'He'll have to attend to business sooner or later, no matter what happens. And even if it's a month or two, well, a summer wedding's better anyway, isn't it? Perhaps,' he turned his eyes to the window, 'there'll be a chance it will stop raining by then.'

CHAPTER EIGHT

A cool, damp June had given way to a wet July. London had always been disagreeable in summer, Venetia thought – still unconsciously a duke's daughter – but in a wet summer it was a thousand times worse. The rain seemed to wash the smoke out of the air and deposit it as a black slime on every surface; and the horse manure on the roads was turned into slippery mire, making every crossing a hazardous undertaking.

She was walking home. It had proved impossible to get onto an omnibus, and a man at the bus stop had jabbed her with his umbrella and almost knocked her hat off. He had said, 'Beg pardon, miss,' but he had said it in a way that suggested it would have been much better all round if Miss had kept her confounded hat out of everyone's way.

Home, she called it, but it was still hard to think of it that way – except that on a day like this any place she could call her own beckoned strongly. She was tired and her back ached and her feet hurt, and she rather suspected she did not smell quite as a gentlewoman should. Still, it had been an interesting case: a surgical intervention in a case of dysmenorrhoea. Mrs Anderson was to present a paper on the subject at the BMA conference in Edinburgh next month. Venetia wished her luck of it. The president of the conference was to be Professor Christison, the most virulent anti-feminist in Scotland and the former nemesis of Miss Jex-Blake. It had been rumoured that a motion against allowing women into the conference might be proposed, and Mrs Anderson might find herself embarrassingly ejected. Always trouble, Venetia thought wearily. Why can't they just let us be?

Home for the moment was number 90, Gower Street, conveniently placed for reading rooms and not too far either from Mrs Anderson's New Hospital in Marylebone Road or the London Medical School for Women in Henrietta Street. It was also tantalisingly close to many of the great hospitals, which were still out of bounds to the women students. Of all the hospitals in London, only the New had agreed to provide clinical teaching.

It had been calculated from the beginning that the female students would need access to a general hospital of at least a hundred beds; the New had twenty-six, and treated only women and children. Sometimes Venetia felt so discouraged that she wondered whether it was worth continuing – and, in fact, some of the students were saying that they would not return in the autumn. The school had opened the previous October with fourteen girls, all tremendously keen, and before long the numbers had gone up to twenty-three.

Miss Jex-Blake had been very keen for Venetia to join. 'It is most important that we *succeed*,' she said, in her emphatic way. 'It would be fatal to our cause to have anyone *fail* the course – that would simply give our enemies a weapon to use against us. And *you* already have so much experience, as well as a good basic education. I'm sure you could pass with the highest of honours.'

Venetia had not needed persuading; but she was not able to join the school on the opening day, for it had taken time to make her arrangements. At first Harry had seemed inclined to let Venetia wait until all the legal procedures had gone through before securing her allowance to her – which might have taken a year or more – but she wrote to him to point out how unfair it was to burden the Aylesburys with her presence and her keep.

In fact, the Aylesburys had shown no impatience to be rid of her. Wolvercote was a great rambling warren of a place, and Venetia had the impression that if they had run across nests of previously undiscovered relatives all over the house, they would have evinced neither surprise nor displeasure. No-one had suggested by so much as a raised eyebrow that Venetia should think about leaving, but the financial argument worked with Harry, and he had agreed to remit a certain sum every quarter to an account in her name at Hoare's, beginning seven months ago in December 1874.

In anticipation of the allowance, Miss Jex-Blake had put Venetia in touch with a Miss Hervey, who was to be one of the students and was planning to take lodgings in London with her widowed mother. They were respectable people – Hervey *père* had been a clergyman – and Mrs Hervey said she was quite willing to chaperone Venetia as well.

'It would be quite shocking for you to live alone,' she had said when they met in London to discuss the possibility. 'I should not allow Bel to do so for anything. But don't think,' she added with a pleasant smile, 'that I shall fuss and cluck over you. Bel is a sensible girl, and I'm sure you are too. You must be free to go about your business. But it's a censorious world, and people would think the worst if you hadn't an older person living with you.'

Venetia had liked her, and thought she would get on with Bel Hervey well enough once they got used to each other. Miss Hervey was a little reserved and brusque at first. She was ferociously determined to achieve her ambition, and not inclined to suffer fools lightly; but once she understood that Venetia was not just a bored woman amusing herself, she thawed appreciably.

Harry had expressed himself satisfied with the arrangement; it was only when Venetia explained it to Lady Aylesbury that any objection was raised.

'Venetia, dear, you can't seriously mean to go and live in lodgings! Oh, please, do reconsider! You can't think there is any desire on our part to be rid of you?'

'No, Cousin Mary, I didn't think that, but—'

'Then please stay. Make your home with us. We are more than happy to have you for as long as you like. I assure you, you will not like living in lodgings. It may sound exciting and novel, but you can have no idea of the discomfort and inconvenience.'

Venetia had suppressed a smile, for it seemed as though Lady Aylesbury had got the idea that living in lodgings was an end in itself, 'But, ma'am, I must live in London to continue my studies. I mean to be a doctor.'

Lady Aylesbury looked distressed. 'Oh, my dear, I hoped you had given that up! Stay here with us, do, and we'll find you a nice young man to marry. You can satisfy your philanthropic bent with committee work, as a lady should. What you contemplate is all very well for people who've been brought up to it, but you have not, my dear, and I'm convinced you would not be happy.'

It had taken a lot of gentle reaffirmation before Cousin Mary would stop begging her not to go. Anne, on the other hand, was all for it, and cried again and again, 'Oh, you are so lucky! I wish I could come too. I wish I were older. It's awful not being allowed to do anything. *Promise* I can come and live with you when I'm older.'

'You'll have very different views when you're seventeen or eighteen,' Venetia said.

'Eighteen? That's an age away!' Anne groaned. 'I can't bear it! And I *won't* change. How could you say so? *You* didn't.'

'No, that's true.' It occurred to her she was not being very fair to Anne, making the same assumptions as others had always made about her. 'Well, love, when you're eighteen, if your brother agrees, you can come and fight the good fight with me.'

'Oh, *thank* you!' Anne said emphatically. 'If only it weren't so long away.'

'It will soon pass. And you've lots of preparation to do in the mean time.'

'Have I? What's that?'

'You must attend to your education.' Anne looked startled. She thought of lessons as something devised by adults to annoy the young. 'You won't be of any use to me or the cause if you are as ignorant as other girls. You must be *more* educated than any man if you want him to take you seriously. Take every opportunity of learning, in every possible subject. Nothing will be wasted, I promise you.'

'Oh,' Anne had said thoughtfully. 'Very well.' It didn't sound much fun, and it wasn't quite what she had wanted to hear, but if Venetia said so, it must be so.

At last Venetia reached home. The pavement outside number 90 was crunchy underfoot, and she looked down with a tut of annoyance. The coal had been delivered today, and the coalman must have spilled some. If she carried it into the house on her boots there would be complaints. The house was one of a terrace, with three storeys and a semi-basement, drab grey-brown brick and white copings which were streaked with sooty rain. But she plodded up the steps with relief, longing just to sit down and be quiet.

It still seemed odd to be letting herself in with a latch key, rather than have a footman or doorman leap to anticipate her. The small vestibule smelt of soup, and was dim and dusty this overcast evening. As Venetia stood wiping her boots carefully on the mat, the landlady, Mrs Sidlow, popped out from the dining room to inspect her with a flinty eye.

'Why ever don't you get yourself an umbrella?' was all the greeting she proffered. She had been suspicious of Venetia from the beginning, divining in some mysterious way that 'Miss Fleet' was not of the same station in life as the Herveys. To her mind someone stepping outside their given sphere must be up to no good; and, in any case, the upper classes were well known to be devoid of all moral restraint.

'I don't like umbrellas,' Venetia said shortly.

'That's all very well, but you're wet through and you're going to drip all up my stairs – and who knows where else?'

'I couldn't get on an omnibus,' Venetia said. 'Excuse

me, I'm very tired.' And she turned away and started up the stairs to prevent any further conversation.

Mrs Sidlow didn't need an audience. Her voice floated up the stairs after her. 'Some people ought to have more consideration for others in this world. Betsy's got enough to do without cleaning the stair carpet all day and every day. And don't hang those wet things over the armchair or you'll mark the cloth.'

Mrs and Miss Hervey lived on the first floor, with a bedroom between them, and a sitting-room at the front which they all shared. Venetia's bedroom was on the second floor. The advantage of that was that it gave her privacy; the disadvantage was that the overworked maid, Betsy, sometimes could not be bothered to climb the extra flight to bring her water or coal, and Venetia would have to go down and fetch them for herself.

Now as she reached the landing she saw that the sitting-room door was open and a bright fire was in the grate. Mrs Hervey, seeing her at the same moment, said, 'There you are! Oh dear, how wet you are. I thought you might be, so I got the fire going. Not that it's cold, really, but these damp evenings feel so miserable without a fire, don't they? Bel's not long been in.' She gestured to another damp coat hanging over the clothes horse before the blaze. 'How did you get so wet?'

'I walked all the way,' Venetia said. She began to take off her coat and hat, aware that Mrs Hervey's fingers were twitching to help her. It would have been nice to give in and allow herself to be mothered. She remembered the comfort of having a maid to help you pull off your clothes when you came in exhausted from hunting or from dancing until four in the morning. But she had given all that up, and she would not be weak about it. She undid her own buttons now. 'Mrs Sidlow was her usual welcoming self. "Don't put your wet clothes over the chairs!"' she imitated.

'Never mind, come and sit down and dry yourself. Your boots look wet.'

'I ought to wash first,' Venetia said, but she sat, thinking wearily of tramping upstairs to find there was no water in her jug, then having to go all the way down to the basement, with the probability of bumping into Mrs Sidlow again.

Life was full of these petty annoyances, which, in her life of privilege, it had been someone's task always to smooth away. Cousin Mary had not been wrong when she said Venetia would not like boarding-house life. Even when she had lived in London with Aunt Fanny in the tiny house in Bury Street, it had still been their house, with servants, gingered up by Aunt Fanny's practised authority, to fetch and carry. Venetia had thought Bury Street the nadir of luxury, but she looked back on it now with longing. However, the allowance Harry was making to her was not generous, and with her tuition fees to find and books and equipment to buy, as well as living expenses, she could not pay enough to lift her and the Herveys to better lodgings.

There was a grittiness to life now – like the coal on the pavements – that made her realise how sensitive her skin really was. This sitting-room, for instance: it was a reasonable size, but the furniture was old and shabby and had not been chosen in the first place for aesthetic reasons. The curtains were a horrible shade of ochre, and when they were drawn across they did not quite meet – a small thing, but unreasonably irritating to Venetia. Now that her coat had joined Bel's before the fire, there was a smell like wet dogs in the air. It had seemed to her as normal as breathing to arrive home and hand her outer garments to a servant, never to see them again until they were dry, brushed, pressed and discovered hanging in the wardrobe as if they had never been anywhere else.

She had entered a world where things did not magically do themselves for you. It was a world of communal meals and having to ask for coal; of cheap letter-paper and ink that clogged; of washing your own stockings at night and hanging them over a chair by the fire to be dry by the morning. It was a world without horses and gardens and fresh air; of that curious kind of imprisonment which came with having nowhere but public places to go when you stepped out of your bedroom. It was a world of petty irritations and a general mild discomfort, which was no easier to bear for knowing that most people took it for granted and thought it the natural way of things.

Bel came in from the bedroom, her front hair a little damp, and said, 'Oh, Venetia, there you are! Have you seen the article in the *Queen* about the New Hospital? It's excellent! Didn't you show it to her, Mother?'

'Not yet, dear. Give the poor girl a chance to dry herself.'

But Bel waved that notion away, picked up the magazine from the table and came over to drop beside Venetia on the sofa and put the open pages before her.

'Look, isn't it first rate? The reporter has nothing but good things to say!'

Venetia read, her tiredness dropping away in the face of Bel's enthusiasm. 'You're right, not a critical note anywhere! "We were impressed with the orderliness which everywhere prevailed,"' she read aloud.

'Yes, and look, where it says about a patient waiting for an operation: "The thought could not but come before us, if we had something similar to undergo, how the suffering would be lightened by the fact that only women were present."'

'Just what the decent burgesses need to win them over! Mrs Anderson will be pleased.'

'Yes, it's good to know that one woman-thing, at least, is gaining approval,' said Bel. She put the magazine aside. 'Was the operation interesting?'

'Yes, very. You can have my notes to look at when I've done them. How was Anatomy?'

'Bones again. Interesting, but I don't know how I shall ever remember all the names. I wish I'd done Latin sooner. The names don't stick the way they would if they were in English. Will you test me later?'

145

'Yes, if you like. But don't worry, you'll have the whole recess to work on your Latin. It will soon become easier. By next session you'll have it down all right.'

'If there is a next session.' Miss Hervey sighed. 'Still no clinical work, and no prospect of being examined. Miss Cardoon says she's not coming back.'

'Miss Cardoon has good reason not to,' Venetia said, with grim humour.

'Perhaps; but sometimes I wonder if we're ever going to get anywhere.'

Venetia had been thinking much the same on her wet walk home. In March of that year Mr Cowper Temple, their champion in the Commons, had brought the Enabling Bill forward again, only to have it defeated by 196 votes to 153. Doggedly, he then brought a Bill to enable women with foreign medical degrees to be registered as practitioners, but that did not even get a second reading. And still all nineteen examining boards refused to examine any female applicant.

But meeting Bel's despondency, Venetia's own spirits perversely rose. 'Well, at least we have good friends in the Commons, with Mr Stansfield and Russell Gurney as well as Cowper Temple. And the Government *has* agreed at least to consider the matter of women's medical education, which they never did before.'

'Consider it, no more.'

'*Carefully* consider it during the recess, Lord Sandon said, with a view to deciding whether legislation should be brought next session.'

Miss Hervey made a face. 'Oh, yes! And what does that mean? He will ask the President of the General Medical Council for his opinion, and that will be the end of that, because we know what *he* will say.'

'Well, my dears,' said Mrs Hervey, 'you didn't think it would be easy to change the world, did you? You must either plod along or give up, there's no other choice.'

They looked at her, and then at each other. 'Oh, we shan't give up,' said Bel. 'But we reserve the right to have a little moan now and again.'

Venetia stood up. 'I'd better go and wash before dinner. I wonder if there's any water upstairs.'

But at that moment Betsy appeared at the open door, her face agape with curiosity, and said, 'There's visitors come, miss. Shall I let 'em in?'

'Visitors, at this time?' Mrs Hervey said in surprise. 'I don't know—'

But they had already appeared behind Betsy, and came in, wreathed with smiles, hands outstretched. 'It's us! Dear Venetia! How long it's been! Do forgive us' – to Mrs Hervey – 'but we simply had to come!'

'Emma! Tommy! Oh, you dear things!' Venetia ran to be embraced. 'Mrs Hervey, these are cousins of mine.' She performed the introductions quickly. 'But what are you doing here? You're looking very prosperous. What a smart hat, Em!'

Emma laughed and slipped her arm through Tommy's. 'We had to come and tell you. Guess what?'

'You're married?'

'How did you guess? We wanted to surprise you. I nearly laughed when you introduced me! I'm Mrs Thomas Weston now, you know,' she informed Mrs Hervey grandly, then spoiled the effect by giggling. 'Doesn't it sound funny? Well, not to you, I expect, ma'am, but to me it does.'

'But when did you do it?' Venetia asked.

'Just today,' Tommy said. 'We'd talked about a wedding for so long, but we couldn't decide where or when or who to invite, and it seemed whatever we did we'd be offending somebody. And then I thought, after all, we're not grand society people: why give the papers the chance to gossip about us? So I said to Emma, "Let's just slip away and do it, all on our own."'

'So we did. With two strangers from the street for witnesses – such fun!' Emma cried.

'And now we're off on our wedding tour,' Tommy said, 'but we had to come and see you first, because we knew you'd be glad for us.'

'Oh, I am, I am!' Venetia cried, hugging them again.

'I wish you every conceivable joy! You're so well suited I know you will be happy together.'

'You don't blame us for not having a wedding?'

'No, Emma dear, I think you did just right to please yourselves. But how did you find me?'

'Asked Mrs Anderson your direction,' Tommy said simply. He glanced round the room and tactfully didn't say anything. 'When we get back, you must come to us for dinner – and you too, ma'am, and Miss Hervey, if you will.'

'You're going to live in London?'

'Oh, of course! I've sold the old house, and we'll be taking something a little more cosy in Brook Street. I hope our home will become a centre for like-minded people, like dear old Langham Place.'

'Langham Place?' Miss Hervey's interest pricked up at that. 'You're interested in the cause, Mr Weston?'

'Tommy's an old campaigner,' Venetia said.

The clock on the chimney-piece struck, and Tommy started. 'Oh, Lord, we'll have to hurry or we'll miss our train. Come, wife! We must kiss goodbye and be gone.'

'I love it when he calls me wife,' Emma confided, lifting her rosy cheek to Venetia's lips. 'Goodbye, dear old 'Netia! We'll see you again soon!'

When the flurry of their leaving had died away, Venetia felt dreadfully flat. Their comfortable wealth, their happiness together, the freedom both things gave them, made her own situation seem more gritty by contrast, more of a prison. She thought a moment, searingly, of Lord Hazelmere, and wondered what he was doing at that very instant. She could have been doing it with him, wealthy, comfortable and beloved.

But not free, she reminded herself abruptly. The life of privilege had been a prison too – a softly lined, gilded cage, but a cage all the same. She had parted with it voluntarily, and it would be stupid to repine. She excused herself to the Herveys and dragged herself upstairs to wash before the dinner gong sounded. She had an aim in view, and she must always remember that. As to grittiness – that was a temporary ill. When she was a qualified doctor (it must be *when*, not *if*) she would have an income, which would do away with some of the discomfort, and what remained she would get used to.

It was only three days later that she met her brother, Lord Marcus, by chance in the street. His mind was evidently on other things, for he started to lift his hand to his hat to her before he realised why her face was familiar. Then he beamed, and greeted her with uncomplicated brotherly affection.

'Fancy meeting you here! Where are you off to?'

'Home.'

'And where's that? Queer thing,' he reflected, 'not knowing where my own sister lives.'

'Gower Street. Near the University.'

'Oh, really? I'll walk along with you, if you like. Thank God for a dry day, eh? I was beginning to think we'd never see one again.'

He was so easy to be with, it was as if there had never been any family trouble. Venetia took his offered arm with a feeling of comfort, and said, 'How are things in your world? Any prospect of a war to go to?'

Marcus took her literally. 'Can't say there is. Of course, there's this trouble in the Balkans – the Serbs are up to their usual tricks. Bosnia and Herzegovina are up in arms, and Serbia's egging them on in the hope of making it the excuse to seize territory. Can't blame them for wanting independence from Turkey, of course – who wouldn't want to be rid of overlords like that? – but, I don't know how it is, Serbia always seems to think it ought to own the whole of the Balkans, and that all the other folk living there ought to clear out and leave it to them.'

Venetia smiled at his analysis – much more succinct than the exposition in *The Times*. 'But we won't be drawn in, will we?'

'I don't know,' Marcus said doubtfully. 'Whenever there's trouble in the Balkans, Russia comes in to help the Serbs, and then we have to step in to protect Turkey

149

from Russia. But I dare say it might be sorted out with a few warships. We shall see.'

Venetia thought that though her brother was not over-endowed with brains he often had an instinctive grasp of foreign affairs. 'I'm sure you're right,' she said. 'To change the subject, did you know that Tommy Weston and Emma were married?'

'Yes, rum go, wasn't it?'

'Do you think so? They've been in love for ages.'

'No, I mean the way they did it. Didn't tell a soul. Still, I don't know but what they were right. Weddings can be prickly things. How did you hear about it?'

'They came to see me, on their way to the station.'

'Ah, yes, the wedding trip. South of France, I believe. I must call on them when they get back. Do the honours for the family. Harry won't be able to – he'll be in India.'

'In India?' Venetia said in surprise.

'Didn't you know? He's going with the Prince of Wales. Leaving on the twelfth of October. Four-month trip.'

'But Harry isn't part of the Prince's household, surely?'

'No, of course not. He's going along just as a friend. Paying his own way. He's got in frightfully thick with HRH and Carrington and that set since he came into the title. And although it's an official trip, the Prince wanted a few bosom chums along to make it fun. Aylesford and Sutherland are going too. The Queen kicked up quite a stink about Carrington going: don't approve of him, because of that business with the actress – thinks he leads the Prince astray. But then the Prince got mad and told Dizzy to tell Her Majesty that he'd choose his own friends, thank you very much. Well, not in so many words, of course,' he added, to Venetia's raised eyebrow, 'but that's what it came down to. I think HRH added Harry to the party for respectability. The Queen remembers that Papa was a particular friend of the Prince Consort, you see, so that makes Harry copper-bottomed as far as she's concerned.'

'Well, it should be a wonderful experience for him,'

Venetia said. To be one of only four companions taken along by the future monarch put Harry very high indeed.

'Oh, it will be! Wonders of the East, elephants, rajahs and all that sort of thing. Tiger shooting, I wouldn't wonder,' Marcus said vaguely. 'Gussie ain't above half pleased, though. Of course it's an all-male party, but she won't take that for an answer, even from Harry. That girl,' he added, with unusual vehemence, 'is getting out of hand. If Harry doesn't marry her off soon, she's going to be the worst flirt in London.'

'What will happen to her while he's away?'

'The Cornwallises are taking her. She wouldn't go down to the country for anything, even if Mama was well enough to take care of her, which she ain't.'

'How is she? Have you seen her?' Venetia asked quickly.

'Mama? Not recently. She's still down at Ravendene, at the Dower House. There's no cause for alarm, just that she's very weak – you know how the old trouble goes. She don't get out of bed much. Don't see anyone. Old Norton looks after her, and she totters out into the garden now and then and totters back again. But Harry says the quacks don't think she'll pop off, or anything. Why don't you go and see her?'

'I have to wait to be asked,' Venetia said bitterly.

'Nonsense!' Marcus said robustly. 'She'd be pleased to see you. Why don't you telegraph her? She'd be sure to say yes.'

'But Harry—'

'It's nothing to do with Harry. It's her house, to have anyone she wants.'

'But if I do anything he disapproves of, he may cancel my allowance.'

'Oh, he won't care about that, even if he ever hears of it. He's too bound up in his preparations for India. You never saw so many new clothes. He'll have so many trunks and cases, it'll be a wonder if the boat don't sink!'

Venetia laughed, and squeezed his arm affectionately.

'Dear Marcus, you do me so much good! And how's Olivia?'

'On top form. Du Cane's bitten the bullet at last, and they're talking about marrying next year when Harry gets back from India.'

'Oh, I'm glad for her! I'm sure they'll be happy.'

'No doubt about it. She'll be able to spend all her time at Court once they're married. She don't like living with Harry. Don't approve of his fast pals and noisy parties. Makes it awkward for her when she's not in waiting, having to arrange long visits to keep out of his way. Marrying Du Cane will solve a lot of problems.'

'And the Queen has approved?'

'Apparently so. What the Queen dislikes about marriage is people going away, and Livy marrying Du Cane is just the opposite – brings her closer.' They turned into Gower Street. 'Which house?'

'Number ninety. It's further up on the left.'

They walked in silence a few paces, and then Marcus said, 'Saw Hazelmere the other day.'

Venetia's heart jumped painfully. 'Oh, he's back in England, then?'

'Came back two months ago, but he went straight down to his estate and stayed there. Think he was only in Town to see his lawyer. Looked well.' He hesitated about adding the next sentence. 'Heard a rumour that he was interested in a girl. A Miss Parr from somewhere in the north – Cumberland or Westmorland or one of those. Heiress. Might be nothing in it, though.'

Venetia had nothing to say to that. Beauty courting someone else? It was not for her to mind one way or the other. It was foolish for her to feel a sharp little stab of jealousy, and hurt that she was forgotten so soon. But perhaps Marcus was wrong. He said it was only a rumour.

'This is it,' she said, stopping outside number 90.

Marcus said, 'I won't come in. Have to meet a fellow.' She thought he was loath to enter so shabby a place, but he said, 'Now I know where you are, I'll call again. No need for us to be at outs. Frankly,' he bent a little closer, 'I think Harry and Gussie got too hot under the collar.'

She kissed his cheek. 'Thank you. I'd welcome a visit.'

He studied her a moment. 'Chin up,' he said. 'And go and see Mama.'

'I will,' she said.

Mrs and Miss Hervey were going out of Town in August, to stay with a cousin who lived in Weymouth. They asked Venetia to come with them, but she was tender of burdening them, as from what she had gathered the cousin was not wealthy and the house was small.

There would be no classes to attend until October, but Mrs Anderson had asked if she would like to walk wards in September, to help her deputy, Mrs Atkins, while she and her husband took a holiday in Yorkshire. Venetia agreed gladly. There was only August left, then, to be dealt with. With some trepidation she wrote to her mother, and received a reply by return, though it was written in Norton's hand.

'Please do come. I am all alone here, and though I do not often leave my bed, you can sit with me sometimes and tell me about your life, and for the rest get some country air, which you must pine for. Come as soon as you get this letter. Take a cab from the station. If you haven't money for the journey, let me know and I will send some.'

The Dower House, on the far side of Ravendene Park, was small but charming: built in the reign of Queen Anne, it was symmetrical, square and trim with large, light rooms, sitting centrally in its small formal pleasure ground. Charlotte was the first resident there for a long time. It had been modernised for Oliver's mother on the death of his father, but Lady Turnhouse had managed never to live there. She liked to be at the centre of things, and preferred to make her home with Oliver even after his marriage, despite her dislike of Charlotte. But the Dower House had been so well built and thoughtfully modernised that very little had needed doing before Charlotte moved in.

When Venetia arrived she went straight to her mother's room, but did no more than salute her from the door. Norton, Charlotte's woman, said, 'She sees you, my lady. She's glad to know you're here, but better you go now. It's one of her bad days. I'll let you know as soon as she's up to talking to you.'

The household was very small – apart from Norton just a cook-housekeeper, two maids and a man – but Venetia was made very comfortable. After the lodgings in Gower Street, the rooms seemed huge and airy, and her eyes feasted on the beauty of the furnishings, and the clean, well-polished glow of everything. She dined alone that evening – the food seemed almost too exquisite after Mrs Sidlow's dried-out chops and boiled cabbage – and after dinner went for a solitary walk round the grounds. The beautiful silence of the countryside was all around her, and she did not feel lonely in it: a peace slid down like a cool draught of water into her soul, and the sweet cleanness of the air made her feel pleasantly tired. She went early to bed, and slept well, though she woke once or twice with a start because there was no traffic noise outside her window.

In the morning she was walking about the garden again after breakfast when Norton approached her.

'How is she today?' Venetia asked eagerly.

'Better,' said Norton. 'She wants to see you.'

'And how is she in general?'

'It's the weakness that's such a trial. Some days she can't lift a hand – it's all she can do to breathe in and out. Then it eases a bit, and she can get out of bed, sit in a chair, even walk a little on good days.'

'And the pains?'

'They come and go. Sometimes she'll be laid low for a week or more; then it will pass and we'll have no more of it for months. Well, you remember, my lady. It's the same pattern, only now the periods of prostration get worse.' She shook her head. 'I don't know how it will end. Nobody seems to know what it is, this Crimean fever.'

'You must be a great comfort to her. I don't know what she'd do without you.'

'Her grace was always very good to me,' Norton said gruffly, turning her eyes away as though a kind word would weaken her resistance. 'She'll be pleased to see you. You always were her favourite child, my lady. Go on up, now.'

Venetia found her mother propped on a bank of pillows. The room was very pretty, with green and gold bed hangings, a green carpet figured with faded pink flowers, and the same delicate, light-coloured, Louis XV bedroom furniture she remembered from Southport House. The curtains were drawn well back from the large window, from which a great cedar tree in the park could be seen.

'How are you this morning, Mama-duchess?' Venetia asked. Her mother extended a hand to her and she came to the bed to kiss the pale cheek.

'Better,' Charlotte said. 'Is it raining?'

'Not yet. I think it may pass over – the clouds are quite high.'

'Sit here where I can see you.' Venetia sat, and her mother surveyed her face carefully. 'You've lost a little bloom. You aren't working too hard?'

'I expect it's bad Town air, that's all. I'm not working hard enough for my liking. We still can't persuade any general hospital to give us clinical experience.'

'Tell me all about it,' Charlotte said. Her voice was faint, and short sentences were all she seemed to be able to manage, but she listened keenly as Venetia described her life and her medical studies.

'Some of the girls are discouraged and think of giving up,' Venetia concluded. 'And I must admit I wonder sometimes if it's all worth it. I seem to have caused such trouble – and for what?'

Charlotte gathered her strength to say something very important to her. 'I want you to know that I don't blame you for anything.' Venetia, who had been staring at nothing, raised perilously bright eyes to her mother's face. 'Papa's death was nothing to do with you. He was worn out. And never fully well since Balaclava. Harry and Gussie – foolish. They go too far.' She sighed. 'I never spent the time with them that I ought. Your grandmother spoiled Harry. And Gussie – brought up too much by servants.'

Venetia's eyes filled with tears of relief, and she struggled with them, not wanting to upset her mother. 'Harry's forbidden me the house – cut me off.'

'I never see him. Too busy with his new friends.'

'He's going to India with the Prince of Wales,' Venetia said. 'It's a great honour, I suppose.'

'That set's too old for him. I worry,' said Charlotte.

Venetia said, 'If he gets along with them so well, he must behave older than his years.'

'That's what worries me,' said Charlotte, and suddenly they both laughed. Charlotte took her daughter's hand. 'Dear love. I wish I had supported you more. But I couldn't go against Papa. And I was afraid you'd be unhappy.' She squeezed the hand. 'I feel differently now. Follow your ambition. It's right, what you're doing.'

A great weight seemed to have been lifted from Venetia's shoulders. She did not care what Harry thought of her, though it was sad to be at outs with one's family; and it was too late ever to recover Papa's opinion. But if Mama was on her side, everything would be all right.

'D'you know?' she said in a lifting voice. 'I think the sun's coming out. Perhaps you might be able to sit outside in the garden a little.'

CHAPTER NINE

The harvest of 1875 was very poor, after the wet summer. Usually the scarcity of corn raised the price, a natural mechanism which protected farmers; but that year there were increased imports from America, which kept the price down. It was a gloomy harvest festival in Bishop Winthorpe, and as Henrietta left the church she overheard several parishioners grumbling that the rector's subject for his sermon had not been well chosen. An exhortation to stoicism they would have understood, but a long panegyric on nature's bounty seemed to them deliberately provocative. Henrietta could have told them that it was far from likely Mr Fortescue had noticed the weather at all. He lived an entirely inward life, where the climatic conditions were governed by what he happened to be reading. He had probably been deep in the *Pastorals* for the past week.

But the grumblers stopped in courtesy when they came up to her, and even the gloomiest faces lightened at the sight of Miss Elizabeth Fortescue holding tightly on to her mother's hand. Having just had her third birthday, she had been deemed old enough to make her first appearance at morning service. The diminutive creature in the brown velvet frock and matching bonnet gazed up with large solemn eyes at the villagers who greeted her mother; and the worthy who stooped to say a word to 'rector's little lass' was rewarded with a shy half-smile.

But when Mr Fortescue appeared, Elizabeth's smile burst forth in all its radiance. 'There's Papa!' she cried

157

excitedly. There was something peculiarly delightful to the parishioners in the dour, ascetic Mr Fortescue being called 'Papa' by this moppet; and they lingered, enchanted, to see him abandon his normal reserve and lift the little child into his arms, where she leaned with utter confidence against his shoulder and rested her golden head happily against his grey one.

Henrietta watched, forgotten, from the background, and marvelled herself at the bond between her child and her husband. He who had never valued anything but the intellect was devoted to his daughter, even to the length of listening to her baby prattle, and helping her to read the foolish stories of *The Children's World*. Had Henrietta ever imagined that Mr Fortescue would have the patience or inclination to teach his daughter to read, she would have expected him to use the Bible or perhaps *The Iliad* as a primer. And she could never have imagined him greeting his parishioners after morning service with the child in his arms, or not correcting her when she called him 'Papa' in public.

When the last of the congregation had gone, Mr Fortescue returned Elizabeth to the charge of her mother. Elizabeth did not like the change and begged to be picked up again.

'I have things to do, child. Go with your mother,' the rector said, with the nearest thing to sternness he ever used with her.

'Will you come and see me?' Elizabeth asked.

'Yes, later. When you've had your dinner. Be a good girl and run along, now.'

Obedient to his command, she put her hand in Henrietta's and they walked off, but Elizabeth craned her head over her shoulder every few steps to see if Papa was still there.

'Did you like your first visit to church?' Henrietta asked, when she had Elizabeth's attention. She had been remarkably good all through, hardly a wriggle and never a whisper.

'Yes,' said Elizabeth decidedly.

'What did you like best, love?'

'Papa saying things,' she answered at once. 'And angels singing.'

Henrietta smiled. The angels were the choir, she supposed; and she remembered that when she had first fallen in love with Mr Fortescue, it had been his voice as he conducted a service that had enchanted her. So long ago, it seemed.

After all the rain, October began with a cold spell, which was a relief, and firmed the ground a little; and then it turned mild and damp, but not positively wet, for the start of the hunting season proper. Henrietta had decided that Ginger was steady enough at last to be taken out and shown hounds. She had brought her home from the Red House so that Oaks, the second groom, could make friends with her. It was he who would be riding with Henrietta this year, Bond having decided he was too old.

Oaks was a very different kind of man from Bond, and Ginger soon settled down with him. The meet Henrietta chose for Ginger's first outing was at the house of Mr Antrobus.

'I shall only keep her out an hour,' she said to Oaks. 'That's enough for a first time.'

It was a soft November morning. Henrietta hacked the mare along the lanes with Oaks leading Starlight beside her. Ginger seemed in a gay mood, putting down her feet well and playing with her bit. 'She knows it's a special day,' Henrietta said.

'They always knows, ma'am,' said Oaks. 'Hunting days is always special days. They smell it in the air.'

Henrietta felt a great lightness of heart herself. She loved to hunt. It was, she thought, the only time of real freedom a woman knew, and she thanked providence that not even the highest of sticklers had yet proscribed it as unsuitable for females. For the rest of her life, a woman must be defined by stillness and quiet, whatever she felt inside. Small, graceful movements, a low voice, a gentle lack of opinion were all she was allowed. But for a few

159

hours three times a week she could forget herself, her situation, her fears and frustrations: all were swept away in a joyful flood of movement. For those few hours Henrietta was aware of nothing but the exhilarating rush of air, the throb of her blood and the thrusting muscles of her horse as they scrambled over the country, up and down hills, across ploughs, through ditches and over hedges, until they were both blissfully used up and exhausted.

They turned off the public lane into a narrower one. It led only to Antrobus Hall, so it was not surprising that there was a sound of hoofs up ahead: other riders hacking to the meet. Ginger's ears shot forward and she pulled a little in her eagerness; Henrietta stroked her shoulder and hushed her. Another moment and a bend in the lane revealed five horsemen filling the road. The rear two were grooms: Henrietta recognised Tobin's back before he turned his head and touched his hat to her. In front of them was Perry Parke on his new heavyweight grey, chatting to Mary Compton on her elegant black Midnight. And as the road was only wide enough to ride two abreast, the fifth person was ahead of them, riding alone.

A great stillness seemed to fall over everything for Henrietta; the birds were lively in the hedges and the rooks were noisy in the nearby woods, but they seemed suddenly dumb, and the complex clatter of hoofs fell into silence. Everything seemed to move with weird slowness as if the air had become viscous. She recognised the big black horse leading the way, and she recognised its rider, even though she could only see his back. She would have known him anywhere, even if she had glimpsed just a hand or an ear or a fraction of a profile; she felt she would have known he was in the room with her even if it was pitch dark.

He was back! Mary hadn't said anything. Had he come unannounced, or had she deliberately kept it secret? Henrietta did not doubt that the wise and noticing Miss Compton had guessed how she felt, and was only grateful that she had never mentioned it. Now in Henrietta's

160

strange personal silence Mary turned her head and looked at her, a look that seemed full of significance. But Henrietta had no attention to spare for Mary: she could not take her eyes from the figure up ahead. She understood fully the meaning of the word *yearn*. Every bit of her strained towards him, aching with the desire to be nearer.

Ginger, perhaps sensing that her rider's attention was otherwise engaged, tossed her head to gain an inch of rein, then snaked a bite at Starlight, who, because of the narrowness of the lane, was closer than he should be. There was a scuffing clatter of hoofs as Starlight jerked away, and normal sound and movement were restored to Henrietta's world. She checked the mare, smiled an apology to Oaks, and found that Jerome had turned in the saddle and was looking at her. He favoured her with an odd, twisted smile, and raised his hat to her: an ironic salute, it seemed. *Why have you come back to torment me?* she thought. Oh, but she was glad, *glad* of the sight of him. He was like water to a thirst that had been tormenting her for so long she had almost grown unaware of it.

When they reached the lawn of Antrobus Hall, Mrs Antrobus came out to beg them to dismount and come inside.

'We have refreshments all ready, and a splendid fire – not that it's cold, wonderfully clement for the time of year – but a damp morning all the same.'

Mr Antrobus added his word. 'Plenty of time!' he said heartily. 'Hounds not for half an hour more. You are nicely early. The great pleasure of a lawn meet is having time with one's friends, don't you think?'

It seemed they were the first to arrive, but even as they dismounted other riders were coming in through the gates behind them, so there would soon be a crowd. Perry sprang from his horse and came to lift Henrietta down. 'I see you're riding your man-eater,' he said, with a smile. 'She looks quiet enough at the moment, but how will she be when she sees hounds?'

'We'll find out soon enough,' Henrietta said. 'How is

Regina?' Regina had never cared for horses, and did not hunt. 'I haven't seen her for a day or two.'

Perry gave his sister-in-law a conscious look, and pulled his lip under his teeth like a shy ten-year-old. 'Well, you know, she's been sticking to the house. It seems – that is, there's a suspicion – Dr Hill thinks she might be increasing.'

'Oh, Perry! I do hope it proves to be so.'

'Yes, I must say I do, too,' he said judiciously. 'I think it will be the very thing. But it's lucky she's not like you, or she'd be as blue as megrim, missing the whole hunting season.'

Perry and Regina had married in July, and Regina was now installed as mistress of the Red House. It still seemed rather absurd to Henrietta to think of her being the squire's wife. The twins were away at the moment, having a London Season in the care of a second cousin. Perry hoped they might find husbands in the larger pool of London, for they were twenty now and he was beginning to be worried about them. George, the elder of the Antrobus boys, had proposed to Amy during the summer, but she had refused him, which had been quite a shock to all concerned.

Miss Compton contrived to be beside Henrietta as she passed through the door into Antrobus Hall. 'My brother is returned, you see,' she said conversationally. Jerome was still outside with the horses. 'He arrived yesterday.'

'Does he stay long?' Henrietta asked, hoping it sounded like a disinterested question.

'He hasn't said. I wasn't expecting him,' Mary said. 'But it's his house, after all. He may come and go as he pleases.'

Henrietta looked at her for the first time and read a complex mixture of interest and pity in her eyes. She sought a neutral comment. 'I hope we shall have a good run for him,' she said.

Mary gave a wry smile. 'I expect it will be the best run of the season, now he's here. He has that sort of luck.'

A servant approached with glasses of sherry and another

with little sandwiches. Groups formed, conversation flowed, the likely outcome of the day was canvassed. More and more people joined the throng and the air twittered with fresh greetings, but still Jerome did not come to her. Henrietta kept her eyes firmly away from the door, yet she was able to turn her head at the precise moment he came through it. Mary was standing beside her, so it was natural for him to come straight to her. Yet there was nothing casually social in his burning look, which did not even take in their other companions. Mary had to engage Mr and Mrs Robertsbridge in light conversation to cover for him and whatever he might say.

He took Henrietta's gloved hand and lifted it to his lips. 'You look well. A little pale perhaps.'

'That's surprise, I expect,' she said. 'What are you doing here?'

'Where in the world should I be? This is my home.'

'You've managed to stay away from it for a long time.'

'Yes, it was an heroic effort. Now I'm here again, I ask myself if it was worth it.'

'Please, you mustn't—'

'Mustn't?'

'Talk like that,' Henrietta concluded. 'Not here.'

'Where, then?' he asked, hard and eagerly.

She shook her head. 'I didn't mean that.'

'Mean it now.' She said nothing. 'You must know this country very well indeed by now, Mrs Fortescue,' he said, in a different voice, as if she were a common acquaintance. 'I dare say you like to take your own line when hounds are running.'

'I know you do,' she said, very low. She was dismayed by how quickly they had come to this.

'I must be careful,' he said lightly, 'that I don't head my fox.' And then he released her hand and turned to join Mary and the Robertsbridges in general conversation.

Soon afterwards they were in motion again, going out to get mounted. Hounds appeared, and Ginger stood stock still, her ears so pointed they were almost crossed, quivering all over; then she let out a long, deep whicker of excitement that made her whole body shake. Oaks, hovering near, said, 'She sees 'em, ma'am. But she's still in hand. That's good.'

Ginger was still in hand, Henrietta thought, but am I?

Jerome edged Warrior up to them. 'You'll forgive me if I stay near, ma'am,' he said, so that Oaks could hear. 'I've had a hand in reschooling your mare, and I know a bit about her temperament.'

'She is much better since you last saw her,' Henrietta said, feeling as if she was speaking out of a dream. 'You've been away so long, I think you may not know how much she has changed.'

'But that may only be surface deep. Underneath she may be much what she always was,' Jerome said. 'Events will prove it, however.'

They drew two coverts blank before finding at the third, which gave them a short but exhilarating run across plough and stubble. At the end of it the fox took shelter in a small wood, and hounds lost the scent for a while. Ginger had behaved pretty well, but her excitement and the heavy going had put her in a sweat, and at the check Henrietta decided to change onto Starlight. 'She's had a good hour,' she said to the groom.

'Yes, ma'am. Quit while you're ahead, eh?' said Oaks, with a twinkle.

'Take her straight home,' Henrietta said. 'It's starting to rain and I don't want her to catch a chill.'

Almost as soon as she was remounted, hounds found the scent again and they were off. They were in different country now, pasture, hedges and woods, and the field began to spread out. Starlight took everything in his stride, and the great mind-emptying pleasure of the hard gallop took hold of her. She didn't precisely forget Jerome's presence – he was there in the corner of her mind like a flame – but she wouldn't allow herself to think about him directly, nor let it interfere with her day.

She was aware, without knowing how she was aware, that he was near to hand; Perry and Mary Compton were up with the first flight, just ahead of her.

They came to a big, heavy gate in a thick thorn hedge. Hounds went under and through it, seeming to dissolve and then spring back into shape on the other side in that way dogs have. The huntsman went over, and the whips, and then a queue formed behind the master to take it, for the hedge was too high and thick to jump. Henrietta knew this field: there was a place further down where the hedge was broken and had been mended with a rail, and she turned Starlight and galloped down to the gap. It was an awkward jump, for there was a ditch on the far side, but he was as sure-footed as a cat, and when they were over she could see hounds and the hunt servants some distance ahead, streaming away uphill round the side of a wood.

'This way! Follow me!' Jerome surged past her on Warrior, going away to the left, towards the thick of the wood. He must have jumped right behind her. One or two others had followed them to the gap but the first horse had refused, blocking the way.

'Where are you going?' Henrietta called breathlessly as Starlight followed the black.

'Short cut,' Jerome called.

She glanced back. The refuser was over now, and was cantering the other way, for though the pack was out of sight, the rest of the field could be seen straggling along the original line. She followed Jerome into the tree line. The hill was steeper on this slope, and Starlight slowed to a canter and then a trot; the trees began to close in; the path turned a bend and there was Warrior standing, flanks heaving, blocking the way.

Jerome cocked his head at a listening angle. 'No-one else followed us.'

'I don't think so.'

'We had better get off the path, just in case. From here you must walk. The branches are too low to ride.'

'What—' she began nervously; but he smiled.

'Do not ask what, or why, or indeed anything else beginning with a W. You struck your own line, as I suggested. You are here of your own volition.'

She felt her face burn. 'I didn't mean—'

'Did you not? Search your conscience, madam,' he said, with mock sternness. He came up to Starlight's side and held up his arms. 'Jump down.'

She untangled her skirts and jumped, her mind feeling curiously numb. He caught her, set her on her feet, and did not remove his arms. She was so close to him she could feel his heat, and her heart beat so fast she thought she might faint.

'No,' she managed to say through dry lips.

He smiled. 'You're quite right – someone might come.' He released her. 'Can you manage your skirt? Come, then.'

He led the way between the trees, and she followed him, Starlight walking behind her, bumping her with his muzzle. She didn't know why she followed him. She ought to leave him and go back to the others, but somehow she couldn't do it. *Weak, weak!* said one part of her brain. *You'll pay!* But she went all the same.

After a while he stopped. It was not a clearing, just a thinning of the trees. He hitched Warrior's reins over a branch and came to relieve her of Starlight, and she watched him as if she were in an enchantment, unable to move of her own volition. It was still in the wood, no sound but an occasional rustle and a drip of condensation from leaf to leaf. There were dead leaves underfoot, and moss; ferns and brambles all round; a little grey sky between the bare branches above; a smell of damp leaf-mould and blackberries.

He came towards her. 'Now, my love,' he said. She did not resist. She wanted him more than life, more than breath. She could not have held back from him then, if the penalty were death. He took her in his arms and looked at her a long moment, and then they were kissing.

'How you tremble,' he said at last. He enfolded her head tenderly against his shoulder and she closed her eyes, drawing in the perilous bliss of it through every sense, as though she might somehow stock up against famine to come.

'Why did you come back?' she asked, after a while.

'I had to see you.' He loosened his grip so that he could look at her. 'I thought that if I stayed away your power over me would fade, and then I could come back and be a common acquaintance. But the longer I was away, the more I wanted you. Life without you has no savour.'

'Oh, don't! You mustn't say so!'

'Mustn't tell the truth?' he said mockingly. 'Are you exhorting me to lie, madam? That is not the Christian way. And you a cleric's wife!'

She pulled back from him then. 'Yes, I am, though you seem to have forgotten it.'

He looked grim. 'You misjudge me. I might forget my own name before I forgot that ghastly fact.'

'Don't,' she said. Shame came to her, pushing down the joy of being with him. 'Look at us. What are we doing here?'

'Snatching a little respite from the awful dreariness of life.'

'It's wrong. We should not be doing this.'

'You came of your own accord.'

She bit her lip. 'I know. I'm so weak – but I must not. We must go back and join the others.'

He laughed. 'My dear love, now we have committed the sin, we might as well enjoy it. Stay a little longer and kiss me again. To have gone to these lengths for so little would be pitiful.'

'Don't joke,' she pleaded.

'I assure you, I'm not joking. I know the consequences as well as you do. Have the courage to be hung for a sheep, my darling, rather than this poor little undersized lamb.'

She still looked at him uncertainly, not understanding his humour, which was his defence against pain. In a different voice he added, 'Let me have something to remember.'

He kissed her again, and – weak, sinful! – she yielded. Tenderness lit to passion. She had never known anything

167

like this – this eager feeding of mouths. Mr Fortescue was the only man she had ever known, and she was beginning to realise that his ways were not the ways of all men. But she should not have thought of him at a moment like this. His image intruded, grey as ashes, into the fiery golden fervour of the moment, and cooled it. Jerome felt the change come over her and released her.

'We must go back,' she said. He did not argue, only stared at her, his expression unfathomable, and she said nervously, 'How long do you mean to stay this time?'

'I wasn't thinking of going away again,' he said. 'Bishop Winthorpe is my home.'

'You're staying for good?'

'Why not?'

'You know why not.' That inscrutable stare unnerved her. 'Jerome, we can't be like this.'

'Then we must be as common acquaintances, mustn't we?' he said. 'We can't avoid each other in a small community like ours. Indeed, if we tried to, it would give rise to gossip. You must treat me exactly as you would, say, Perry Parke. No coolness, Mrs Fortescue. No awkwardness. If I ask you to dance, you must accept, just as you would if I were nothing to you.'

She studied his expression. 'Why are you tormenting me?' she asked abruptly.

He gave a small smile. 'Oh, my dear, you have it quite wrong. It is you who are tormenting me. But come, if you want to go back we had better go now before the field gets too far away.'

The strain of having Jerome at home again was unendurable. As he had said, theirs was a small community, and she was meeting him every day, without ever getting used to finding him beside her. Repetition did not dull the effect. Her eyes sought him eagerly, in the street, in every room, in every group of people; her skin craved the touch of him, her lips and hands rehearsed their memories of him. He seemed to have developed an unnerving omnipresence. If she walked down the village street he would be coming towards her. If she went into a shop he would be there, lounging against the counter. If she visited a neighbour he would somehow be visiting too. When she hunted, he was of the field. At dinner parties she would be seated beside or opposite him. They were partnered at card parties. Hardest of all, at church he was always in the Parke pew, which was opposite the rectory's, and his profile tugged at the corner of her eye throughout the service. To the awful knowledge of her secret crime against her husband was added the sin of his coming between her and her devotions.

The rector did not mention Jerome's reappearance. He was just another villager, another parishioner, and though he had never been a regular churchgoer, the change in his habits did not seem to strike the rector as remarkable. Mr Fortescue had not always approved of Jerome, but that seemed all forgotten. Henrietta guessed that it was not so much Christian forgiveness but genuine lack of memory. The rector was more and more immersed in his work, less and less aware of what went on around him in the real world, and people outside the pages of his books all had the same shadowy lack of substance to him. Henrietta thought he probably no longer distinguished Jerome Compton from any other male creature in the parish.

But the worst occasions for her were those she attended with her husband, for then her sin was brought most vividly before her. Try as she might, she could not keep her eyes from Jerome, nor her mind from comparing her cold, grey, indifferent husband with the vibrant, passionate man she loved. Her animal self protested that it was unnatural and wrong for her to be the rector's wife instead of Jerome's, and her higher mind ran helplessly back and forth trying to catch and contain her feelings, like a poultry maid chasing two dozen loose chicks.

Jerome did not help. She quickly decided he was deliberately putting himself in her way, and when they were in company together he insisted on sitting with her and talking to her in what anyone else would have thought a perfectly natural way. Mary Compton was her closest friend, so why shouldn't Jerome be friendly too? Only Henrietta – and perhaps Mary – was aware of the perfectly devilish way he had with words, of how he could make an innocent sentence mean something quite different to Henrietta, of how he could look at her and smile at her when no-one but she could see it.

Christmas came with all its concomitant celebrations, and Henrietta's unease reached a peak, for the rector required all his household to take Communion twice a year, on Easter Day and Christmas Day. To refuse would be impossible, to explain why she wanted to refuse doubly so; so she was obliged to take the Sacrament with an unconfessed – and, at bottom, unrepented – sin upon her. It was a moment of utmost wretchedness. She half expected to be struck down by a lightning bolt as she opened her mouth for the wafer – and indeed that would have been a relief compared with the torment of guilt that followed.

Christmas seemed also to mark a change in Jerome's spirits. Throughout the weeks of his pursuit of Henrietta he had seemed to be enjoying himself, taking some kind of perverse satisfaction from her discomfiture. But after Christmas he seemed to grow sad and sullen. The looks he bent on her burned, and she found herself glancing round anxiously in case anyone else had noticed, for they were not the looks of a common acquaintance.

The climax came at the Twelfth Night ball at the Red House. Perry Parke liked to uphold the traditions of hospitality set by his father, and everyone in the neighbourhood was invited to this grand culmination of the Christmas festivities. Amy and Patsy were home from London, looking wonderfully elegant and sophisticated, and Perry invited eligible young men from as far away as York for their benefit.

Teddy was there, looking stouter than ever, and Henrietta realised with a start that Perry was regarding him as a possible husband for one of the twins. He was, after all, an eligible bachelor – handsome, independent and wealthy – and she was forced to wonder why the idea struck her as odd, and discover that it was because Teddy behaved like a man twice his age, and since coming into his fortune had never shown any interest in females. Food, fellowship, and a good cigar seemed to bound his horizons. He chatted pleasantly to married women, but seemed not to notice the unmarried ones at all. He was one of nature's bachelors, she concluded, and there were many such. Her own husband was one, her thoughts added bitterly, but he had been drawn out of his nature to marry her by a combination of chance and Alfreda's determination to get her off her hands.

The rector – who performed his unavoidable social duties with the same stoicism as his unavoidable clerical ones – had brought Henrietta to the ball, and at once handed her over to her hostess and disappeared into the smoking-room where he joined a group of older gentlemen in conversation about trades unions, social unrest, the price of wheat, the Government's recent purchase of a share in the Suez Canal, the ongoing trouble in the Balkans, and the appalling proposal to make elementary education compulsory, thus interfering for the first time in the relationship between parent and child and putting a father's authority at naught.

Regina told her sister at great length about her hopes, which had now been confirmed, and the matrons of the neighbourhood gathered round to swap confinements, servant problems and other topics suitable to married ladies. The dancing was going on in another room, but that was not supposed to interest the likes of Henrietta any more. There were some raised eyebrows, therefore, when at last Jerome Compton appeared at her elbow, asked her, rather impatiently, if she would care to dance, and hustled her away without waiting for an answer.

He seemed in a strange mood, and when they had taken the floor he danced without talking to her, looking almost morose. After a while she said, 'If you will make me a scandal by forcing me to dance, you might at least entertain me with polite conversation.'

171

'What?' He seemed dragged out of his own thoughts. 'Oh, hang polite conversation! I have been wearied to death chatting to a succession of witless young ladies so as to be seen to do the proper thing. I have asked every silly female in the room to dance so that no-one shall think it out of the usual when I ask you, but you don't seem a bit grateful.'

'You are in a mischievous mood,' Henrietta observed.

'No, I am in the devil of a mood,' he said. 'Let's be quiet a while, or I shall say things I don't mean.'

'As you please,' said Henrietta. 'What is there left to say? Only don't scowl at me, it looks too particular.'

His frown melted into a smile which, from the safety point of view, was no better. 'I wasn't frowning at you, dear heart. Perish the thought!'

They got through the figures more or less in silence. Henrietta felt tired to death and was glad just to be with him, however frail and perilous a comfort that was. Even in silence there was communication. At the end of the dance when they were lingering on the floor, waiting for sets to re-form, a waltz was announced, and Jerome looked at her with a glinting smile.

'The gods are with me! No, I didn't arrange this specially, but I would have if I could. Don't deny me the chance to put my arms round you for a poor little quarter-hour.'

The music started, and though she knew she ought to leave the floor, the resolve simply wasn't in her. Her body seemed to have a will of its own, separate from her mind, and stepped into his embrace. They swirled away, moving like a single animal.

'Henrietta,' he said, after a while, 'I can't go on like this. I thought I could, but it's too hard.' He squeezed her hand, and smiled. 'To be truthful, I thought I could wear you down by seeming to be at ease with the situation. Now it's a case of the biter bit. I am caught in my own toils. I can't go on being in company with you and not licensed to touch you or speak freely to you.'

She only half understood him. There was a part of her

172

that always tried not to listen when he spoke like this, in case she should lower her guard.

'So silent?' he said. 'Have you nothing to say to me, then?'

'I don't know what to say,' she said awkwardly. 'The situation is impossible.'

'Yes, it is,' he said. 'That is my whole point. We can't go on in this way. Therefore you must come away with me.'

'What?'

'Don't jerk away from me like that – someone might be watching.' He looked down into her face with a fervour that thrilled and frightened her. 'Is it such a hideous prospect? I love you, as I've never loved anyone before. Come away with me. I am independently wealthy – you shall not want. We will travel. You'd like that, wouldn't you? You're too wild a bird to be caged in this stifling village. Let the whole world be your home – our home. Let us be together – that above all. Together and free!'

Free? He should not have used that word. She saw in that instant that there was no freedom for her.

'I can't,' she said.

His eager look changed frighteningly quickly to a scowl. 'Don't say "can't" to me. You can! You will! What is the alternative? To moulder away to dust imprisoned by that old man?'

'I am his wife. I'm a married woman. What you ask is – impossible.'

'Only if you don't want it.'

'I do want – oh, so much!' The words broke from her and she was angry with herself. 'But I mustn't say so. I can't do what you ask – it would be wrong. And it's wrong of you to ask me. What use tormenting me?'

'What use indeed?' he said harshly. 'If you won't come with me, I will still go – you understand that? I can't stay here and not be able to have you. *That* is torment.'

'Do you think I don't know? Do you think I don't feel it too?' she asked, in a low voice.

'I don't know what you think or feel.' He glared at her a

moment, and then his expression softened. 'Please, love,' he asked gently. 'Don't sacrifice your happiness and mine for this stifling rectitude.'

'It's God's law,' she began.

'It's not,' he interrupted. 'It's man's law, that's all, designed to keep his chattels from being poached. There's no virtue in it. Not propriety, but property! It's a nonsense – an irrelevance. Come away with me, and we will be so happy.'

'But we wouldn't,' she said sadly. 'At first, perhaps, but only for a little; and then knowing we were doing wrong would poison and kill it.'

He looked at her keenly. 'Is that your last word?'

'Yes,' she said, though she had no idea how she found the strength.

'Then this is the end,' he said, his expression hard. 'I shall go away. And when you hear what you have driven me to, remember it was your wish. I must find some way to forget you.'

'I can never forget you,' she said, very quietly.

He relented suddenly. 'Oh, my love,' he said. He drew her tightly against him, and she did not resist, not caring who might be watching. The last dance together – she would have it, sin or not: a warm memory to keep out the cold of the rest of her life. The music circled, came back to the major key, entered a last brief elaboration, like someone turning in the doorway with a final thought, and came to its triumphant resolution. Their feet stopped; his arm loosened from her waist. She could not see him properly: he seemed wreathed in a bright mist. He raised her hand to his lips and kissed it as he bowed, then turned and left her without another word, walking across the floor, out of the ballroom – out of the house, she guessed – out of her life. She felt utterly bereft, and utterly exposed, standing in the middle of the ballroom, in an aching space and silence, washed by a river of tears.

And then Teddy was beside her. 'No partner, Hen? I suppose a brother would be no catch. Oh, but the orchestra is taking a rest. Shall we go in to supper together, instead?'

She looked up at him and smiled wanly, and found there was no space, no silence, no river. The earth had not cracked in two like a saucer, nor the heaven rained down fiery portents. No-one had noticed anything, and she was not crying – not outwardly.

'Yes, let's,' she said, and slipped her arm through her brother's. She felt hollow and defeated, and in that instant saw her life ahead of her as it must be, an arid, dusty circuit to be plodded endlessly like a horse in a mill: of domestic routine, varied only with visits to and by the same neighbours, with the same conversations, over and over, world without end. In that moment, she wished herself dead.

BOOK TWO

Going Astray

The widest land
Doom takes to part us, leaves thy heart in mine
With pulses that beat double. What I do
And what I dream include thee, as the wine
Must taste of its own grapes.

Elizabeth Barrett Browning: *Sonnets from the Portuguese*

CHAPTER TEN

In February 1876 London was treated to a State Opening of Parliament, something which had become rare to the point of extinction since the Prince Consort's death. Mr Disraeli had been far more successful than previous ministers in persuading the Queen to appear in public. Opening Parliament was the least favourite of her public duties, and that she did it with such good grace might be put down to Mr Disraeli's growing influence.

'On the other hand,' Tommy said to Venetia, 'it may have more to do with her showing support for the Royal Titles Bill.'

'You are a cynic,' Venetia said. The Royal Titles Bill, announced in the Queen's speech, was to bestow on Victoria the title of Empress of India.

Tommy had called to invite Venetia to dinner with him and Emma, and finding her unhappily confined to the house and poring over books, had persuaded her she needed exercise and whisked her out for a walk in the Park. It was a cold day, a little foggy, but bright, the low sun shining palely through the bare trees.

'Why does she want to be empress, anyway?' Venetia asked. 'It's never been an English title.'

'But it is generally accepted to be superior to "king" or "queen", and Her Majesty is miffed that her own daughter will be an empress one day and outrank her. Also, she feels being a mere queen puts her at a disadvantage when dealing with Russia.'

'I see. Well, I don't suppose it will do any harm,' Venetia said.

'Disraeli thinks India will like it. He says when you rule eastern peoples you have to work on their imagination as well as their reason.'

'I suppose he should know.'

'Gladstone is dead set against it. There'll be some fireworks when it comes to debate. There are many in the House who won't care for Disraeli imposing his orientalism – which is how they'll see it.'

'Talking of India,' Venetia said, 'the Prince of Wales should be home soon.'

'And your brother with him.'

'Babbling, no doubt, of tigers and mahouts and elephants and all the rest of it,' Venetia said. 'Shall you call on him?'

'We'll leave our cards,' Tommy said. 'Can't do less, in courtesy, but he may not welcome a call. He and I are not really in the same world any more. What will happen to Gussie now? Will she go back to live with him, or stay with the Cornwallises?'

Venetia gave him an amused look. 'My dear Tommy, *I* don't know. You can't suppose either of them confides in me.' He looked apologetic. 'You and Emma might invite Gussie to live in Brook Street. She'd be a companion for Emma. They were brought up together, after all.'

'I don't think she'd want to live with us now. Our lives are very dull even compared with the Cornwallises, and if there's a ducal house in competition . . .'

Venetia nodded. 'She's bound to choose frivolity over sense. Well, she'll be twenty-one in August – marvellous to say – so she'll be able to make up her own mind. If Harry wants her, she can act as his hostess until he gets married. It might keep her out of mischief to have a household to run.'

Tommy thought it might get her into more than it kept her out of, if what he had heard about the goings-on in the Prince of Wales's circle was true. He changed the subject.

'I must lend you a most interesting book Emma and I have been reading. It's called *Homes of the London Poor*, a series of essays by Miss Octavia Hill. Do you know her?'

'I haven't met her, but I've heard of her, of course. Miss Jex-Blake dotes on her. They were intimate friends at one time. They were even planning to live together, but it fell through – I think Miss Hill's mother raised an objection. But Miss Jex-Blake still thinks her the epitome of all virtue.'

'I didn't know that,' said Tommy. 'At all events, the essays are very interesting. The conditions of housing for the poor are dreadful. Her stories would make you weep – the filth and degradation. Of course, some of the tenants are drunkards and criminals and so on . . .' The *so on*, Venetia concluded with inward amusement, were prostitutes, which Tommy was too much of a gentleman to name even to one who must have known far more about them than he. 'But there are others who are decent enough folk, simply lacking the ability to organise their lives properly.'

'Yes, I can imagine,' Venetia said.

Tommy nodded. 'I expect *you* can. However, Miss Hill doesn't just deplore the situation, she actually does something about it. She has a scheme for buying up blocks of property – at least, she doesn't buy them herself, because she hasn't any money, but gets rich people to buy them – and then she manages them for the tenants' benefit.'

'In what way?'

'Well, to begin with she has them cleaned and repaired and improved, and removes the bad tenants, and chooses replacements from amongst decent folk. Then she arranges for a superintendent to keep them in order.'

'The houses or the tenants?' Venetia asked.

'Both. The superintendent collects the rent, supervises cleaning, manages repairs, and gives the tenants advice and help in things like finding work, saving out of their wages, teaching their children and so on. They even arrange outings and parties, and help them to grow flowers and make little gardens where there's room – anything that doesn't sap their independence. Miss Hill is very anxious the poor should do things for themselves and not rely on having things done for them, which I thoroughly approve of. It's enormously worthwhile work.'

'I'm sure it is,' Venetia said.

'Emma and I have talked about little else since we read the book,' Tommy said, looking, in his eagerness, much younger than his years, 'and we think perhaps we have found our work. Miss Hill is always looking for finance and helpers. We mean to talk to her about it; and if she thinks us suitable, we mean to buy a property for her to manage, and volunteer to be supervisors too.'

Venetia was surprised by the last. 'The work would be disagreeable, I imagine.'

'Probably,' Tommy said. 'But I feel I want to be properly engaged in something. We're always being asked for money, but this would be a chance actually to *do* something.'

'Giving money is doing something too,' Venetia said.

'Well, I hope I've helped a bit. But we've been dabbling in this and that for years, and though, of course, we'll still interest ourselves in women's rights and education and so on, the time comes when one feels one must specialise if one wants to make a real difference.'

'Yes, Tommy dear, I know.'

'Oh, of course you do! Well, you have your path set out before you, and I think now we've found ours.'

'I hope you have more luck of it than I have,' Venetia said, a little disconsolately.

The promise made by Lord Sandon on behalf of the Government to consider the matter of women's medical education over the recess had come to nothing. In January Mr Cowper Temple had written to Miss Jex-Blake in some exasperation to say that the Government had refused to tell him whether or not they would introduce a Bill in the next session; and given the weight of legislation already announced it seemed that 'wouldn't say' meant 'no'.

There was still refusal from all sides to admit any of the women students to hospital wards, and many of them had given up and left the medical school, believing the business to be hopeless. And Venetia had suffered a personal blow in the death of Sir Frederick Friedman, her own patron and mentor. If it weren't for the kindness of Mrs Anderson, who continued to involve Venetia in interesting cases and use her services in the New Hospital, Venetia would have been utterly frustrated. She had completed two and a half of the four years' training and had experience unique amongst the women students, but the goal of being a registered practitioner seemed as far off as ever.

She and Tommy had walked all the way to Apsley House while they were talking, and now crossed over Piccadilly into Green Park. There was a band playing, and it seemed natural to walk towards the cheerful sound. There was quite a crowd gathered round the bandstand, some seated on the park chairs arranged in rows, others merely standing around the periphery. Tommy and Venetia walked up to the outer edge of the crowd. The gentleman standing next to them moved over to make room, then turned his head to look at them. Venetia paled. It was Lord Hazelmere, and he also had a lady on his arm.

Tommy returned the compliment, pressing Venetia's hand against his ribs in reassurance as he said, 'How d'e do, Hazelmere. You're back from the country, then?'

'As you see,' said Hazelmere. He bowed to Venetia. 'Lady Venetia.'

She managed a slight curtsy. Her eyes were fixed on his face, hungry after all these months to see how he was. Handsome as ever, of course – but wasn't he a little pale? Had he been ill? There were lines of strain around his eyes, and no laughter in them as of old. He had said something else – she had no idea what, for her poor brain was gibbering with the surprise of seeing him again so unexpectedly, and there was nothing but roaring in her ears. The next thing she made sense of was Tommy saying, 'I think we'd better walk on. I'm afraid Lady Venetia's feeling the cold.' Lady Venetia was trembling like an aspen, but it had nothing to do with the cold.

They walked away, skirting the crowd, and soon found themselves at the Devonshire House gate onto Piccadilly.

'Are you all right?' Tommy asked, halting. 'I was afraid you were going to faint.'

'Faint? Nonsense!' Venetia said robustly. 'I never faint.'

'Well, you weren't very polite,' he said reproachfully. 'Didn't even acknowledge the lady when he introduced her.'

'Did he do so? I didn't hear.'

'She must have thought you were snubbing her. Hazelmere seemed quite put out.'

She looked rueful. 'To tell the truth, I was in a complete funk. I didn't hear a word he said. Poor Beauty! Was that his—' She made herself say it. 'His fiancée?'

Tommy raised his brows. 'I didn't know he was engaged. Who told you that?'

'Marcus said – oh, months ago – that there was a rumour Hazelmere was interested in a young lady from Westmorland. A Miss Parr, I think he said.'

'I didn't hear anything of that. But that wasn't Miss Parr he was with. It was Miss Graham, Lord Marstone's daughter. You've heard of her – the most celebrated débutante of last season?'

'Was she?' Venetia said, with stubborn indifference.

'She was in all the papers and magazines. She has quite a dowry, by all accounts, but she was famed for her wit and her looks – and I must say from the brief glimpse I had, the report didn't do her justice! You *must* have heard something about her. "Beauty" Graham, she was dubbed. Funny, isn't it, with him having been Beauty Winchmore all those years?'

'Astonishingly funny,' said Venetia.

'Like calls to like, I suppose.'

'Indeed.'

'I wonder if it's a case between them? They'd have handsome children, that's for sure.'

'Oh, shut up, Tommy!' Venetia exploded. 'Must you chatter on and on like a parrot?'

Tommy only raised an eyebrow, quite unperturbed. 'Why, 'Netia, are you still carrying a torch for him? I thought it was all over between you.'

'One more word, Tommy Weston, and I shall pinch you good and hard. And maybe kick your shins for good measure.'

'Sorry. Shall we look for a cab or do you want more walking?' He had had his revenge now for all the years of unrequited love, and like most revenge it had not answered. He felt rather a cad for baiting her, even though they were as good as cousins, and cousins were allowed a great deal of leeway. 'How quickly it gets cold when the sun starts to go down. Can you walk as far as Brook Street? We could have tea together – Emma will be home.'

The young Duke of Southport came home at the beginning of May, and in July Olivia was married to Charles Du Cane. Her situation since her father's death had been uncomfortable. She was only in waiting for three months of the year, and needed a home for the rest of the time, but Harry's attitude towards Venetia made her unwilling to stay under his roof, even though he was her trustee. His going to India had at least relieved her of that dilemma. Living with her mother at the Dower House was the obvious solution, but though the duchess's health had improved a little she still did not go out or see anyone, and it was a dull, isolated life even for a quiet young woman like Olivia.

So she had been dividing her time between her mother, the Aylesburys, and various distant relatives on her father's side; but she was unhappy away from Court, and more particularly away from Mr Du Cane. Marriage was the obvious solution, as then, since Du Cane was a permanent officer of the Household, Olivia would live at Court all year round.

Waiting for Harry was not necessary in the strict letter

of the law since Olivia was over twenty-one; but society at large would regard him as her guardian and think it odd if she married without his explicit approval, and she was very anxious not to give any cause for gossip. Harry also controlled her fortune, and since Charlie was not a wealthy man, it did matter to them that she should obtain her dowry.

She had come to call on Venetia at Gower Street towards the end of May to tell her the news, picking her way up the stairs behind the overworked maid with a valiant effort to conceal her surprise at her surroundings. Mrs Hervey had not been at home, and Miss Hervey had generously gone to her bedroom so as to give Venetia the privacy of the sitting-room.

Olivia paused in the doorway with a hesitant, is-this-right? air, taking in the smallness of the room and the shabbiness of the furniture, before her eyes lit on Venetia and she forgot everything but the pleasure of seeing her sister again.

'Dear 'Netia! Dear old Sissy!'

'Darling Livy! I thought you would have been at Balmoral?'

'Not this year. I'm not in waiting until the Court comes back to Windsor.' The girls embraced in the middle of the room. Olivia withdrew her arms and said in concern, 'But you've grown so thin! Dearest, are you getting enough to eat?'

Venetia laughed. 'Of course I am, silly!'

Olivia looked doubtful. 'But – this place – such a small room?'

'It is convenient for hospitals and such; and I'm too busy to mind the size of rooms. Don't worry, Livy, I'm not starving to death. My allowance is small but it's sufficient to my needs.'

'I don't see why it should be small,' Olivia said indignantly. 'Harry could afford to keep you in comfort.'

'I am comfortable,' Venetia insisted. It was not entirely true, but she did not want to upset her sister. 'You are looking very well,' she went on. Olivia, in a costume of lavender twilled silk, the draped bustle edged with close-pleated frill, looked out of place in this room. Her clothes were neat and not over-elaborate, but obviously expensive: she had that air of unadorned prosperity that distinguished those in Court circles. It made her look already a little matron, though her beauty was undiminished. 'You've a bloom in your cheeks and a sparkle in your eyes. Are you still in love?'

'That's what I came to talk to you about,' Olivia said. 'Mr Du Cane and I have decided a date for the wedding.'

'Oh, Livy, I'm so glad for you! Come and sit down and tell me all about it.'

Olivia sat, with only one doubtful look at the upholstery, on the sofa and told her all, with much loving detail about Mr Du Cane's many excellent qualities.

'So it's to be the twelfth of July,' she concluded.

'So soon? It doesn't give you much time to organise things.'

'Oh, but it isn't going to be a big affair like yours – as yours would have been,' she corrected herself awkwardly. 'Harry offered Southport House, though even if Papa had been alive I should have preferred to have been married from Ravendene. But as it is, neither would be appropriate either for me or for Mr Du Cane. So we are to marry at Windsor, in St George's Chapel. It was the Queen's suggestion – and a great honour.'

'Yes, I see that it must be,' Venetia said.

'Our friends are all Court people now, you see,' Olivia went on, 'so a big Society wedding would have been silly – and Mr Du Cane is not a wealthy man. It's to be a very small affair.'

'So small, I conclude,' Venetia said, reading her sister's expression, 'that I shall not be invited.'

Olivia looked distressed. 'It's all so very awkward! Harry has to give me away, or there would be talk, and he says he won't do it if you are there. And the Queen disapproves very much of ladies being doctors, and you do see, in my position, since I shall be at Court all the time, and there's Mr Du Cane's career to consider – well, I have to be careful. But it's not what I want. I wish with all my heart things could be different.'

A wedding, Venetia reflected, ought to be a time of unalloyed happiness; a bride should not be made to feel unhappy by warring elements in her family. It was unforgivable of Harry to spoil things for poor Livy, who had never harmed a soul, and Venetia would prove herself a better person than he. She smiled warmly and took her sister's hand.

'Dearest Livy, don't look so blue! I understand perfectly, and I promise you I'm not the least offended.'

Olivia's face began to clear. 'Really? Do you mean it?'

'Of course I mean it.'

'And you forgive me?'

'Sisterly love can encompass anything.'

'Gussie won't be there either,' Olivia said, and Venetia suppressed a smile at this offered comfort. 'It will be a *very* small wedding. I'm not even sure if Mama will come – she says her health isn't up to travelling.'

It sounded rather a poor show to Venetia, and she felt sorrier than ever for her sister. 'And will you go away afterwards?'

'Yes, to Scotland. Princess Louise is lending us a house on her husband's estate. It will only be for two weeks; but then the Court will be at Osborne, which is always almost a holiday in itself.'

'Well, I wish you very happy, darling, and I'm sure you will be. I don't know your Mr Du Cane, but Uncle Tom said he was a very nice man, and if he loves you, he must be.'

Olivia leaned her cheek to receive Venetia's kiss and said, in a much happier voice, 'Thank you, dearest. You've been so wonderful about all this. I shall send you a bit of the cake afterwards, in a little box, the way the Queen does.'

While Olivia's future was now assured, Venetia's grew more doubtful. Earlier in May had come cheering news from Mr Russell Gurney: the Government had said if he cared to reintroduce an Enabling Bill, they would allow it, provided Parliamentary time could be found. On the matter of time, things hung in the balance through June and July, and it looked as though it might fail again. But then in the third week of July Lord Shaftesbury decided quite unexpectedly to throw his weight behind it, and it went to its second and third reading in a matter of days, and was to receive Royal Assent early in August.

Yet all the Enabling Act would do was to tell the universities that they might admit women medical students if they wished, notwithstanding anything written in their Charters. But it was far from sure that any *would* wish – and indeed the noises coming from the English and Scottish universities were still very unwelcoming.

Meanwhile the London School of Medicine for Women had reached a crisis, for even if every examining board had opened its arms to women the following day, the girls at the school could not have presented themselves for examination, since they still had had no clinical practice. In June Mrs Anderson had suggested approaching the London Hospital in the Whitechapel Road to ask that certain wards should be set aside for women students. She had worked there years ago and knew that the vast hospital had eight hundred beds and that male students visited only a fraction of them. Setting aside whole wards, she hoped, would satisfy those who still thought that male and female students could not work together with propriety.

The House Committee expressed themselves willing, and for a few weeks hope was resurgent at the school; but then in July the medical and surgical staff at the London announced they would not entertain the notion for an instant, and that was that.

'I think the London School may close entirely,' Venetia said despondently to Tommy and Emma. 'Everyone is very gloomy, and there's no point in going on studying if it's all to be book work and lead to nothing.'

'What would you do then?' Emma asked.

'I don't know,' Venetia said. 'I can't bear to think of it.'

'Is it so very important to you, then, to be a doctor?'

Venetia gave a grim little smile. 'Dear Emmy, I thought I must have made that clear by now! It's all I want to do.'

The thought of going back to a life of idleness, a life with no intellectual challenge, no work of usefulness, struck her with such dismay that death almost seemed preferable. She knew how women passed their days, an endless round of giving orders to servants, changing their clothes, and visiting each other to say the same things that they had said yesterday and would say again tomorrow. Probably if she gave up being a medical student Harry would increase her allowance to a comfortable level, but would insist that she lived with someone respectable. Then either she would marry and become one of those vacuous women, or, unmarried, she would remain a companion to one of them with even less to do or to think about.

'I've gone too far along this road to go back now,' she said. 'But if the school doesn't reopen in October . . .' She sighed and stopped, sunk in gloom.

Tommy couldn't bear it. He would have been happiest for Venetia if she had married Lord Hazelmere and lived a normal life, but if that was really impossible now – and Hazelmere had been seen about Town all through this Season with the lovely Miss Graham on his arm – she should at least be allowed to be happy in her own way.

'Perhaps you should go abroad,' he said. 'Aren't there places abroad where women can study?'

'Yes, there's Switzerland. Zurich and Berne universities both admit women,' Venetia said. 'But foreign MDs are still not acknowledged here, so one would be no further on.'

Tommy thought a bit. 'Wouldn't it help if you went there for a few months and did some of the things you can't do in England – the clinical practice, for example? At least you would be moving along, and then if things did change here, you wouldn't have wasted the time.'

'I suppose there is something in that. But what's the use of talking? I can only just afford to live here, on what Harry allows me. How could I afford to go to Switzerland?'

Tommy said nothing more then, but the next day he went to see Southport. He found him preparing to go to Goodwood, where he would stay with the Duke of Richmond for the races, after which it would be Cowes week, and then a series of house parties culminating in one of his own at Ravendene in October for the shooting, to which the Prince of Wales had promised to come. 'And when HRH has shot my birds, we're to go to Sandringham in November and shoot his.'

'We?' Tommy queried.

'Oh, Gussie comes too, of course. She's regularly "in" with the crowd, and Carrington says the Prince finds her terribly amusing. She plays bridge better than me, and she's not at all a bad shot – and, of course, her looks are very much admired. Chetwynd and Cavendish are both mad for her. I'm planning a party for her twenty-first that I hope the Prince will come to. I've bought her the prettiest diamond necklace – shall I show you it?'

Tommy declined the treat. 'I expect I'll see it round her neck in due course,' he said kindly, 'and to better effect. But before you dash away on your whirl of pleasure, I have something serious I'd like to talk to you about.'

When he mentioned Venetia's name, Southport's brows drew down in a scowl, and when Tommy outlined his idea, they shot up in astonishment that Tommy should think he would consider it.

'Encourage her in her folly? Give her more money? I think you must have taken leave of your senses, Weston.'

'Think of the advantages,' Tommy said. 'You will have her out of the country. She will pursue this course to the bitter end anyway, so why not send her where you know you won't bump into her, at least for a few months?'

'There's some devil in you,' Southport said, narrowing his eyes. 'What is it to you, anyway?'

'I think she will make a fine doctor one day. And when she writes her memoirs as one of the pioneers of female

191

doctoring, she will mention me with kindness and I will have my place in history.'

'You are a humorist,' Southport said, looking at him oddly. 'Well, I suppose I don't much care, as long as she doesn't cause a scandal. But she can't go alone. Some respectable female will have to go with her.'

'I'm sure that can be arranged,' Tommy said.

It proved to be easier than expected, for when the idea was aired before the Herveys, Miss Hervey conceived a strong desire to go to Switzerland herself. 'It doesn't look as though there'll be anything doing for us here this autumn,' she said to Venetia. 'But won't it cost an awful lot?'

They made enquiries and worked it all out on paper, sitting at the table by the window of the little sitting-room with their cuffs rolled up. It was a wet and muggy August, and as the rain teemed dirtily outside, their hair stuck to their foreheads and the ink smeared on the paper where their hands had made it damp. Spreading Harry's new, more generous allowance between the two of them and adding what Miss Hervey usually had to live on, they would still be short.

'I have a little put by,' Mrs Hervey said. 'I anticipated that it might come to this, and set aside a little "foreign universities fund" just in case.'

'Dear Mother, you are a trump!' Miss Hervey said.

With the finances arranged, they had nothing to do but apply to the universities and arrange for letters of reference from Mrs Anderson, Mr Norton and Professor Masson. By the time warm wet August turned into cold wet September, it was all arranged, the tickets to Zurich bought, lodgings spoken for, and they had only to pack their trunks.

'It's the first time I've ever been abroad,' Miss Hervey said. 'I'm a little nervous – aren't you?'

'Yes, a little,' said Venetia. She had been abroad before, but never on her own, without an older person to supervise her. Now she was the older person, and it would be for her to take the decisions, to make sure they got on the right train and that their baggage stayed with them, to deal with foreign ticket collectors, porters, cab-drivers, signposts, notices and timetables. She hoped her German would be up to it. 'But excited, too,' she concluded.

'Oh, goodness, yes!' said Miss Hervey.

The first week of October arrived. Tommy and Emma came to see them off at the station, and the two young women departed their native shores with their hearts full of rather tremulous hope.

CHAPTER ELEVEN

George Morland was reading, without a huge amount of interest, a letter from his brother Manfred at Trawden School. The news that Manny had been made a pupil-teacher, at the tender age of fourteen and a half, left him unmoved, as did the revelation that the promotion had come about owing to the death of old Captain Morris, the visiting tutor who taught the boys on Mr Liddell's day off. George guessed there would be some appeal for money forthcoming – there always was these days. Everyone seemed to think that they had a right to dip their hand into his pocket. Hardly a day passed but some appeal for funds from one cause or another came in: orphans, retired cab horses, better houses for the poor, retired railwaymen's widows. Ask George Morland first, that seemed to be the motto, he thought self-pityingly. He turned the page. Ah, yes, here it was! Now he was a teacher, Manfred felt he ought to have a decent suit of clothes, so that the boys he taught would not laugh at him. He had grown so much taller in the last year that his trouser legs stopped short of his boots. Fortunately he had not grown any fatter, so he could still get into them, but Mrs Kettleworth said there was nothing to let down and the gap did make him look rather ridiculous.

'Rather ridiculous!' George exploded out loud. 'When the deuce does a fourteen-year-old boy *not* look ridiculous?' It was coming it a bit strong to be asking for new suits when George was already paying to keep Manny at the damned school in the first place. Now that he was a pupil-teacher, of course, the fees would be reduced, as Manny pointed out – and followed it up by hoping that George would see his way to using the money he saved to buy Manny the clothes he needed. Which, George thought, folding the letter and stuffing it in his pocket, was a pretty cool piece of cheek and made you wonder what old Kettleworth was teaching the boy. Not a suitable humility, at any rate!

He heard footsteps in the corridor outside, and one of the dogs lifted his head and whined softly, warning that someone was coming. George could move surprisingly swiftly when he wanted to, and in a twinkling he was out of his chair and, surrounded by a swirl of dogs, through into the gun-room, closing the door softly behind him.

Atterwith had been seeking an audience with him for two days, but he was not anxious to be interviewed. He had managed to avoid the man all day yesterday and all of this morning. He supposed he wanted to drone on about the terrible harvest again – as if it were somehow George's fault. He seemed to think it had been a bad idea to buy the two new farms and put them under the plough just as corn prices started falling. Well, corn prices had been high for twenty years, George thought indignantly, and no-one could have predicted the bad weather.

The dogs were looking at him curiously, wagging their tails, as he stood behind the door, listening. The footsteps went away again, and all was quiet. Good. He must have gone back to the steward's room. Looking out of the window George saw that the rain had actually stopped for a wonder, and slipped out through the other door into the yard. He strolled across it jauntily, and was not only shocked but aggrieved to walk into Atterwith as he passed under the barbican.

'Ah, Mr Morland!' Atterwith said, standing four-square in the middle of the path. The dogs surged round him, waving their tails. 'A word, if you please.'

'Oh, not now,' George said nervously. 'I'm just on my way out. Tomorrow, perhaps.'

'It had better be now,' Atterwith said implacably.

'But I'm going round the coverts to check the earths,' George said, surprising himself with his inventiveness. 'You know we've a party coming at the week-end, and I'm going to take the gentlemen cubbing. Must make sure everything's in order. You want our guests to have good sport, don't you?'

'You will find everything in order,' Atterwith said. 'And I must speak to you.'

George looked sulky. 'Well, if it's about the harvest again, you might as well save your breath. *I* can't control the rain, for heaven's sake!'

'It's not about the harvest. It's about a rumour I have heard that you are going to change things up at the stud.'

'Oh,' said George, not knowing whether this was better or worse.

'Is it true?'

'I don't know what you've heard,' George said, shifting his gaze away. 'Probably idle talk.'

'It was very specific for idle talk. I heard that you had decided to give up breeding and selling carriage horses and riding horses, and were going to give over the whole stud to racehorses. Do you tell me there's no truth in it?'

'There may be *some* truth in it,' George prevaricated. 'Look here, I must get on—'

'How much truth?'

George gave an exasperated sigh. 'Oh, dash it, why must you interrogate me like an inky schoolboy? I'm the master of Morland Place, though some people might be forgiven for thinking it was you!'

'It's my duty to look after the estate and to advise you on the best way to run it,' Atterwith said, unmoved by his petulance. 'So you will oblige me by answering my question. Is what I heard true?'

George stuck his chin out. 'Yes, it's true. I have decided to go all out for racehorses. Now, what of it?'

Atterwith looked grave. 'I must advise you against it. Carriage and riding horses are good commerce. There is a steady market for them and they bring in valuable income. Racehorses do not bring in money, they cost money. A racing stables is an expensive hobby, not a business.'

'And if it is a hobby – which I don't necessarily allow, because there are big winnings to be made—'

'Sir,' Atterwith interrupted, but patiently, 'for every horse that wins a race, you will have ten that don't win. And for every race it wins, it's likely to run three or four that it loses. And even when it does win, the prize money is rarely enough even to cover expenses.'

'Well, well,' said George. 'As I was saying, even if it is a hobby, what then? Am I not entitled to one? Am I not entitled to spend my own money any way I choose?'

'Of course, sir,' said Atterwith, 'if you can afford it. It is my painful duty to tell you that you can't.'

'Nonsense, man!' George looked genuinely surprised. 'What folly is this? I am George Morland of Morland Place. I am the leading man of York. If I can't afford it, who can?'

'The Prince of Wales, perhaps,' Atterwith said. 'He can appeal to Parliament for more funds when he runs out. But we've had two ruinous harvests, and we've purchased extra land at far too high a price, for which we had to take out expensive loans. We cannot afford to lose the income from the horses. Household expenses have risen year after year, and your style of entertaining is increasingly lavish.'

George had had enough. 'Now, look here, it's none of your damn business what I spend in my own house, or how I choose to entertain!'

'Indeed it isn't,' Atterwith agreed, 'but it is my business to warn you of impending insolvency. When you are declared bankrupt, it must not be said that I did nothing to try to keep you from it.'

George stared at him for a moment, speechless. His face grew redder, and the dogs, sensing the atmosphere, grew very quiet and crouched down. 'Bankrupt! How dare you? Insolent fellow, how dare you suggest that I – *I* am under the hatches?'

'Oh, not yet,' Atterwith said. 'Not quite yet. But if you go on spending more than the estate earns, that is the inevitable consequence. It is a matter of simple mathematics, Mr Morland, as you must see. And I most earnestly beg you to think again about your plan for the stud. Why throw away good income? You can have more racehorses, surely, without getting rid of the paying side?'

'Well, that's rather the point, you see,' George said. 'What was it you called it? "Good commerce"? It doesn't suit me to be thought of as a common horse-broker. It ain't gentlemanly, d'you see? Breeding racehorses – why, dukes and princes do that. It's a hobby, as you said. But selling carriage horses – it's like being in trade. It makes one little better than a grocer.'

Atterwith was silent in the face of this, trying to find the words to refute such folly. 'How is breeding and selling horses different from breeding and selling sheep or cattle? Or growing and selling corn, for that matter?' he said at last.

'Well, it is, that's all,' George said loftily. 'I shouldn't expect you to understand the difference, old fellow, but you must take my word for it.' Atterwith opened his mouth to protest further, and George interrupted firmly, but with averted eye, 'Besides, it is Mrs Morland's express wish, so that's all there is to it. Now step aside, and let me pass. I must be about my business.'

He went with such determination that Atterwith did not try to stop him. In any case, the clue was in the last revelation. *Mrs Morland's express wish*. What Mrs Morland wanted, she always had, and her advice on any subject was taken in preference to anyone else's, however great their expertise. If Mrs Morland said it was not gentlemanly to be a horse-broker – and Atterwith could just imagine her saying it – then George Morland would cease to be one. Probably, Atterwith thought bitterly, she had been reading something about the Prince of Wales's fondness for racing. It was on her initiative that all this lavish entertaining went on, Atterwith knew: George Morland could barely keep awake after dinner at the best of times. Naturally Atterwith expected his employers to entertain – it wouldn't have been right for them not to, given their position in society: but the large house parties, the shooting, the hunting, the racing – and George bet lavishly and unluckily at race meetings, not because he liked gambling but to keep up appearances – were draining coffers which the estate could not fully replenish.

As he watched his master's striding figure dwindle into the horizon, a great weariness came over Atterwith, and he thought perhaps he had been at Morland Place too long. Perhaps the time had come to move on, or even retire. Why should he struggle to keep things going when the master himself didn't care? But then, letting his eye wander round the fields, he realised that he loved Morland Place, almost as though it were his own. He couldn't abandon it. Though the task was thankless and perhaps even hopeless, he must keep on fighting for it.

George stumped along to an inward litany of anger at Atterwith's presumption, which usefully obliterated any anxiety that the man might be right. Alfreda had brought up the subject of the stables some days ago, and for much the reason Atterwith had imagined. The Prince of Wales had recently registered his own racing colours, and while there might be things about the princely lifestyle that Alfreda could not approve, there was no doubt that he was becoming a leader of society and an exponent of style in the highest sense. Equally, there struck her as something ungentlemanly in selling carriage horses for a living. Horse-coper, horse-trader – those terms had connotations of low life and dishonesty. She would like the words 'Morland Place Stud' to trigger in Society's mind an instant association with the elegant, fashionable and, above all, high-ranking world of racehorses, and nothing else.

And if George became noted for breeding racehorses, he, and therefore she, might soon be moving in that world, automatically on the guest list of dukes, marquesses and princes. The new Duke of Southport, she had read, had been a guest of the Duke of Richmond at Goodwood this year – and was Southport not their third cousin once removed? The previous duke's untimely death had thwarted Alfreda's legitimate desire to slip into his circle. But, then, the old duke had not been very sociable. The new duke was a much better prospect, going everywhere and knowing everyone. Let George build up a notable racing stables, and in a year or two they would be holding house parties for the York races to which perhaps even HRH would come.

George understood and approved of this ambition, and could only wonder he had not thought of it – purifying the stables – himself. He enjoyed the fact of their high style of entertainment, if not always the execution (fashionable clothes were dashed uncomfortable and guests kept him from his bed when his eyelids were drooping). He liked showing people round the estate and hearing their amazed and admiring comments, and he enjoyed telling the fellows in the club both beforehand and afterwards what eminent people he had had to stay and how impressed they had been by everything.

And besides all that, Alfreda must have what she wanted. She had been made very ill giving him his son and trying to give him another, and must be indulged. And she made his life a misery if she were thwarted. And besides again, there was little James to think about. His position in society must be secured, and it could not be too high for the future master of Morland Place.

At this point in his musings he reached the mares' paddock. He had been walking pretty much at random, and his feet had taken him there automatically. Now he saw that someone else was there, a female standing by the rails and petting the foals who had come up to inspect her. She turned when the dogs came racing up to her, and he realised with an odd jump of his heart that it was the maid, the pretty one who always looked at him and blushed so sweetly when he passed her in the house.

She was blushing now, and lowered her eyes and

seemed almost to be backing away from him, though the dogs were making it difficult, milling round her enthusiastically, licking her hands and trying to lick her face.

'Hullo,' George said, 'what are you doing here?'

'I beg your pardon, sir,' she said humbly, her arms full of hairy hound. 'I didn't mean any harm.'

'Good heavens, I'm not telling you off. Far from it. Don't worry about the dogs, they won't hurt you.'

'I know that,' she said, with more assurance. 'I like dogs.' And she rubbed behind the ears of the wolfhound who had his front paws on her shoulders, and sent him into drooling ecstasy.

'I see you do. And they like you.' Enough was enough, however. He called them off sharply, and they left her with reluctance and subsided onto the path. 'You're – er—' He racked his brain. 'Alice, isn't it?'

'Yes, sir,' she said, looking pleased that he had remembered.

'And what are you doing up here?' he asked, but tried to inject kindness into his voice. He didn't want her to think he disapproved, and run away.

'It's my afternoon off, sir. I came up to see the foals.'

'Don't you go home?'

'I do on my whole day. It's too far when it's just the afternoon.'

'And you like horses, do you?'

'Oh, yes! My father's a horseman, and I've always loved them. Especially the foals – they're so gentle and sweet, and their muzzles are so soft. I save a bit of bread from my dinner to bring them – I hope that's all right,' she added, in sudden anxiety.

'Of course it is,' he said. 'Don't be so nervous – you aren't afraid of me, are you, Alice?'

Her eyes crept shyly up to meet his, but only for an instant. 'No, sir,' she said, though it did not seem to be all the truth.

He looked down at her with a delightful sense of indulgence, of superiority and affection. There seemed to be admiration, even a little hero-worship in her hesitant glances, so different from Alfreda's steely gaze and frequent impatient offhandedness. With Alfreda she was the deity and he the acolyte; it was pleasant to try it the other way round for a change.

There were two mounting-stones by the gate. George sat on one and gestured to Alice. 'Come and sit and talk to me for a little. You aren't in a hurry to go anywhere, are you?'

'No, sir.'

'Good, then we can have a cosy chat.' She hesitated, and he added, 'What, then? You've said you aren't afraid of me.'

'No, sir. It's just that . . .'

'That what?'

'I'm only a housemaid, sir. And you're, well, the Master. If Mrs Holicar or Mr Goole were to find out, they'd think I was presuming, sir.'

George's sense of consequence was delightfully stroked. 'Don't worry about them. They are my servants too.' And seeing she had not followed his meaning, he added more simply, 'You shall not get into trouble, I promise you.'

'Thank you, sir,' she said, and sat.

She really was astonishingly pretty, George thought, especially with her cheeks so blushing – like pink velvet. 'How old are you, Alice?' he asked.

'Sixteen, sir.'

'I'm eleven years older than you – fancy that!'

'You don't look it, sir,' Alice said. She was thinking of how young he seemed in comparison with Mrs Morland who, if she didn't know better, Alice would have thought his mother.

The comment made George laugh. 'Well, it's true all the same. Perhaps I have youthful looks, I don't know.'

'I think you are very handsome, sir,' Alice said, in a low, shy voice.

George beamed at her. 'I used to be considered handsome in my bachelor days. I was said to be the most eligible bachelor in York at one time. But one doesn't

think of such things when one is an old married man.'
She said nothing, but her look was eloquent. George
seemed to swell with geniality. 'So you like horses. Do
you ride?'

'Oh, not like a lady. But I used to ride Dad's plough-
horses back from the fields when I was a girl.'

'I think you would look very good on a horse,' George
said.

'Oh, no, sir,' she protested, but with evident pleasure.
She sought for a question she might ask him. 'Are you
going to ride today, sir?'

'No, I was just on my way to look round the coverts. I
was going to check on the foxes' earths. Some gentlemen
are coming to stay at the week-end.'

'Yes, I heard Mr Goole say,' Alice nodded.

'I'll be taking them cubbing.'

Alice's face lit. 'Oh, I do love to see the fox cubs! When
I was little, Dad used to take me sometimes on summer
mornings to watch them play – like dear little kittens!'

'Hmm,' said George, wondering whether she knew
what 'cubbing' meant. And then an idea came to him.
'I know where there's a badgers' sett. Perhaps you'd like
to come with me one morning and watch for them?'

'Oh!' she said, and blushed deeply.

'On your day off, perhaps,' he said. 'I suppose you must
have to start work quite early in the mornings.' Her eyes
were down and she didn't answer. 'Wouldn't you like to
see the badgers?'

'Oh, yes, sir!'

'Then it's my company you don't relish.'

'Oh, no, sir! I mean, yes, sir! But—'

'We shouldn't tell anyone,' he said. 'They might take
it into their minds to dig the badgers out, or harm them
in some other way. It would be our little secret.'

She looked up – once, earnestly – and then down again.
'That would be very nice,' she whispered.

'I'm fond of animals myself,' George said, pleased with
himself. To spend time in the company of this sweet girl
with her worshipping eyes, didn't he deserve it? He was

the master, he gave employment to dozens, and did no end of good in the neighbourhood. Wasn't it practically his right? He would show Alice the badgers – and if he should indulge himself in a little squeeze or even a kiss or two, well, who was the worse for it? He was a man, after all, and men had their needs. What no-one knew wouldn't hurt them. And it was nobody else's business anyway.

Having settled this to his own satisfaction, he began to talk about his horses, and enthralled Alice on that subject until it began to rain again, and he packed her off hastily home.

As she came in through the servants' door, Alice came face to face with Lucy, the head housemaid, who said sharply, 'And where might you have been?'

'It's my afternoon off, please,' Alice said. 'I've been for a walk.'

'A walk? In this rain? You're soaking wet.'

'Only a bit damp. It wasn't raining when I set off.'

'I won't be answered,' Lucy said snappishly. She liked to model herself on Mrs Holicar, whose job she aspired to. 'Tea's finished. You'll get nothing now till supper.'

'Yes, I know,' said Alice humbly.

Lucy stared at her a moment, then said, 'Well, as you've nothing better to do with your time off than loiter about, you'd better go and make yourself useful. There's china to be rinsed and dried before the dining-room can be laid up. Go and get on with it.' And she flounced away.

Alice trailed reluctantly along the passage to the kitchen, and started as she saw that John, the second footman, was standing in the doorway watching her. 'Let yourself in for it, didn't you?' he said, not unkindly.

'I don't mind,' she said. 'I'd as lief do something as nothing.'

To her surprise, John didn't move to let her past. He contemplated her face in a way that made her blush. Since arriving here an innocent child two years ago, she had learned a great deal, both from whispered conversations with Katy – now moved on, as she had long threatened, to try her luck in the factories – and from experience. She had not been long at Morland Place before Thomas, the fourth footman, had tried his luck with her, and since then there had been approaches from and tussles with other male servants, both Morland Place employees and the servants of visitors. But John she had always thought a cut above the others, and if his way of speaking was sometimes quirky and often incomprehensible, she had always felt safe with him.

Blocking her way now, he said, 'As lief do something as nothing? You've a look about you, my girl, that I don't trust. What is it you've been doing this afternoon?'

'Nothing! What do you mean?'

'Why are you blushing if it's nothing?' he said. He took hold of her arm, making her start. 'You little fool, what do you think you're doing? I thought better of you, Alice Bone.' He shook her. 'Have you no sense? Have you learned nothing since you've been here?'

She looked up at him resentfully. 'Let me go. I've done nothing.'

'*I saw you,*' he said. 'I was coming back from the village. Lucky for you it wasn't anyone else! Oh, I won't split on you – but think, child! He's the master! He's gentry! I've seen you gazing at him like a sick sheep, and many's the time I've wanted to shake you for it.'

'I don't mean any harm,' she said, on the edge of tears. 'I've done nothing wrong.'

John's voice became more gentle. 'Look, dearie, I'm fond of you. You're a bright girl and you could do well for yourself. They were talking today about promoting you to upper housemaid, which would mean more money and less hard work. But that'd put you more in the way of the gentry than ever. You've got to know how to conduct yourself. And how to keep yourself out of trouble.'

'He was just talking to me, that's all. He didn't mean me any harm.'

John shook his head pityingly. 'You're such a green girl! There's only one thing men want from pretty girls – and that goes double for gentry men with servant girls. Now you heed me, Alice Bone, don't you ever go talking to the master again – no, nor any of his friends or relatives that might be staying here either. You act dumb and keep your eyes down and get away as quick as you can. And if anyone looks or says anything amiss to you, come and tell me.'

She was crying now. 'You said – men only – wanted one thing,' she said, between tears.

'Yes, well, I didn't mean me. I'm different. But don't you go trusting anyone else. They mean you harm, Alice, d'you hear me? Whatever they may say, they mean you harm.'

The servants'-hall tea – bread-and-butter and slabs of plum cake – was at a quarter to five, before the work of preparing the family's dinner began; and supper was had when dinner was away as far as the dessert. This was a meal of cold meat or pie, together with bread and cheese, cake, and sometimes rice pudding or treacle tart left over from dinner, or occasionally something more dainty left from family luncheon, like jelly or blancmange or a fruit tart.

After supper there was all the work of clearing dinner and washing up to be done, as well as preparing the bedrooms, making up the fires and attending to anything called for from the drawing-room. As she rose from the table, Alice was summoned to go to Mrs Holicar's room, and would have been quite glad to be spared some part of the labour, if she had not been in dread over the trouble she might be in.

But Mrs Holicar's expression was pleasant as she presented herself. 'Ah, yes, Alice. Wasn't it your afternoon off?'

'Yes, Mrs Holicar.'

'But I saw you in the kitchen after tea.'

'I went for a walk but it came on to rain so I came back.'

'Oh. Well, I'm glad to see you made yourself useful.

You're a good girl, and I've spoken to the mistress about you. She has agreed with me that you should be promoted to upper housemaid.'

'Yes, Mrs Holicar,' Alice whispered.

'I hope you are pleased. Your wages will go up to eighteen pounds. Your work will be different. You will only do the top of the cleaning – the dusting and polishing rather than the scrubbing – and there will be much more waiting on the family and guests: taking up morning tea, answering bells and so on.'

'Yes, Mrs Holicar.'

'I wouldn't have recommended you for this promotion if I had not been satisfied that you know how to conduct yourself with the gentry,' the housekeeper went on. 'The mistress likes pretty girls around her, and in the drawing-room, but she does not like pert maids, or those who do not know how to guard their tongues and keep their eyes to themselves. But you are a modest, sensible girl, so I think you will do well.'

'Yes, Mrs Holicar. Thank you, Mrs Holicar.'

'You can change your room tomorrow morning. Lucy will show you where; and she'll explain your new duties.' The housekeeper's voice became stern. 'You will be exposed to many temptations in your new position, Alice. I trust you will not let me down.'

There was nothing Alice could say except another, very humble, 'Yes, Mrs Holicar.'

Venetia loved her time in Zurich. Her German improved apace, for the family they were lodging with spoke no English, but were all great chatters. She never acquired the accent that Miss Hervey soon had, but she spoke more fluently and colloquially, and soon began thinking in German, which was a great advance.

The tall, narrow house on the Königinstrasse was cheerful and comfortable, with double windows and great colourful enamelled stoves to combat the snow outside – it was, apparently, a particularly cold winter. Apart from the numerous Grunberg family, there were several other lodgers, including two male students, and a professor of archaeology who had been lodging there since he was a student and seemed unable to find any reason good enough to move out.

Mealtimes were always noisy, with everyone – family and lodgers – crowding round the single long wooden table in the high-ceilinged, ground-floor dining-room. The house was mediaeval in its origins, though it had been continuously changed and improved over the ages, but the painted wooden frieze round the ceiling of the dining-room was original, with religious mottoes carved deeply in Gothic lettering and strange ancient High German. Together Venetia and Walter, one of the students, managed to decipher and translate one section as 'Unless the Lord watcheth the house, the watchman watcheth in vain', but they never did untangle the rest.

Conversation at mealtimes was always lively, often intellectual, sometimes frivolous. The Grunbergs and their lodgers liked simple jokes and jolliness, and one of the students had a turn for impersonation, while Professor Altheim could make up comic rhymes to order. Venetia enjoyed the ease and warmth of it all, and the sense of companionship – something that had not come much in her way before. Mealtimes were what she looked forward to most, although the food struck her as often very strange, with a great deal of vinegar about it, one way and another. There was also a prevalence of very dull cheese which, though it came in a variety of different shapes, with different names, always tasted exactly the same.

The work at the medical school and the hospital was fascinating, and she knew again that she was right in her choice, and that medicine really was what she wanted to do. Above all, it was wonderful to be treated as an equal: the school had been open to women since 1865, and after eleven years anyone with a prejudice against females had either got over it or left. It was a simple joy to be able to apply herself to learning without having to guard her behaviour or govern her language, without looking over her shoulder to see whom she might be offending; to be instructed and questioned as if the only thing that mattered was her intellect. She found that despite the handicap of her English background she was by no means at the bottom of the class; and in the practical work she shone, especially dissection and morbid anatomy, where her quick and steady hand and minute observation soon took her ahead of the others. Learning the German technical language was the hardest part: it was frustrating to know what she wanted to say and be grounded for lack of vocabulary.

Miss Hervey went home to England for Christmas, but Venetia stayed and celebrated Weinachten with the Grunbergs. The head of surgery, Professor Leinsdorf, had promised to give her extra tuition and let her attend his operations. He had taken a fancy to her and thought she showed promise, and she did not want to miss a single day of this experience which she couldn't get in England.

Her presence over the Holy Season endeared her to the family and made her something of a pet. She was already the object of hero-worship to the thirteen-year-old daughter, Katrina, who reminded her rather of Anne – not in looks, for she was a solid, sandy child with long plaits, but in her eagerness for life. And baby Wilhelm – or Villum as everyone called him because that was what he called himself – planted himself in her lap at every possible opportunity.

She learned the words of all the favourite Weinachten carols, though her singing was as hit-and-miss as always, and saw at first hand the German traditions that Prince Albert had tried to bring to England: the Christmas tree, the gilded gingerbreads, the stockings hung by the chimney, the stories about St Nicholas told to the round-eyed children. The Grunbergs clubbed together to buy her a wonderful present, a leather bag like a dispatch satchel, with a strap to hang over her shoulder, in which to carry her books to and from lessons. She was deeply touched by the thoughtfulness that had found something she really wanted and needed.

After Christmas the real winter weather set in, more snow than Venetia had seen in her life before. But snow in Switzerland was not like snow in England: it was regular, expected, and therefore was dealt with without fuss. It transformed everything into a glittering fairyland, and once Venetia had spent some of her precious funds on better boots, she enjoyed it. The streets were full of sleighs and the jingling of harness bells, and colours and sounds seemed brighter and somehow more real on the sharply frozen air.

She was walking home one day in February 1877, looking forward to supper and the heat of the potbellied stove in her room, her heavy bag dragging at her shoulder. She was alone, having stayed late in the library – Miss Hervey had gone home at the end of classes – and was stumping along through the crunching snow, her mind far away, when something hit her on the side of the head, painlessly, but enough to knock her off balance. Her arms flailed an instant, but the weight of the satchel tipped the balance and she sat down heavily.

She realised at once that it had been a snowball. There had been a fresh fall of snow, which had only recently stopped, and out of the corner of her mind she had noticed, though only subconsciously, that some youths were skylarking on the other side of the road. One of their missiles must have gone astray. Even as she was thinking this, one of them had run across the road to stand before her, sweeping off his hat, bowing, and saying something in German. For a moment she had lost the facility to understand a foreign tongue, and waved a hand at him, only a little crossly, saying, 'Yes, I'm sure you didn't mean to do it. Let me be, now.'

'Oh, so you are English!' The voice changed at once to the perfectly cut tones of the better quarters of London. 'Then I must apologise even more fervently. A Zurich native will be prepared for accidents like this, but a visitor, and especially an English visitor, can have no notion how frequently snowballs go astray.'

She looked up at him now, noticing first of all that his

expression held no hint of contrition, and that he was older than she would have supposed: her own age, or a little more – no mere youth or even undergraduate. The second thing she noted was that he was very handsome in a dark, slightly saturnine way, and that his hair was as densely curly as a ram's fleece.

'The speeches are all very well,' she said, 'but you might help me up.'

'I *beg* your pardon, ma'am. I was waiting only for permission to do so.' He offered his hands, and in a moment she was on her feet. The snow was so fresh and powdery that it brushed off without even leaving her coat damp. There really was no harm done, except to her dignity.

The other three members of the group had trailed across the road now and presented themselves shame-facedly with bows and stumbling apologies. Her language sense had re-established itself and she forgave them graciously in their own tongue, noting that they were much younger than the first-comer, probably only eighteen or so.

'You speak German very well, Fräulein,' said the first man. 'I do hope, by the way, that it is Fräulein? Your gloves conceal the truth from me, but I cannot imagine such a young lady, however beautiful, could be married already.'

'You will oblige me, sir,' she said coolly, 'by picking up my bag.'

As they had continued to speak in German, the younger men understood this and there was a concerted scrabble to oblige, in the throes of which several of the books were spilled out of the bag and had to be gathered up, dusted off and restored apologetically to their place. Venetia stood impassively while all this was going on, suppressing her laughter at the puppyish antics.

'But this is delightful,' the first man said, dropping into English. 'You are a student, I gather. So are my charges, the young lordlings here. And to judge from your reading-matter, you are a student of medicine. How fascinating that must be! I do hope, ma'am, that you will permit us to escort you home, carrying your heavy bag for you, naturally – it is the least we can do after abusing you so shamefully. And in the course of our journey, you could perhaps beguile me with an account of your studies.'

'Most certainly not,' she said firmly.

'But I promise you, ma'am,' he said, his eyes bright with mischief, 'that my young charges speak English so badly that they will not understand a word. It is only I who will be beguiled.'

'I prefer to walk alone, thank you,' she said.

He bowed and said, 'Then I beg you will allow me to call on you tomorrow – solely,' he added hastily, to the negative he saw forming on her lips, 'to make sure you have come to no harm.'

'On no account in the world,' she said.

'But this is too cruel!' he protested.

'And that is altogether too much nonsense, sir,' she said severely, bowed to the young men, and walked away. It had been an amusing incident, which she might have enjoyed mulling over later, had not Katrina met her at the door waving a letter that had come for her from England, which put it entirely out of her mind. It was from Emma, and was gratifyingly long, detailed and discursive. Venetia waited until after dinner when she could retire to her room and read it in privacy and comfort.

A large part of the letter was taken up with the news that Emma was going to have a baby. 'Tommy is so particularly pleased, because his father always regretted having no son of his own blood and talked sadly of being a "dead end in history", as he put it. In a funny way Tommy feels we are doing this for his father and mother, though I pointed out it had to be at least as much for mine, if he wanted to look at it that way. But he said no, that the first is to be a boy, and entirely a Weston, and after that I may have a daughter if I please and call her Fanny Hobsbawn! He is so funny about it, Venetia, but underneath he is truly moved, so much that it makes me want to cry.'

Emma talked about their part in Miss Hill's housing

scheme, the tenement block they were helping to improve, and various meetings they had been to. Then began a new paragraph.

I have kept this until the end, dearest Venetia, because it looks rather as though things are moving ahead at last on the medical front and I hope it will be a pleasant surprise for you. Tommy met Miss Jex-Blake at a meeting yesterday (I didn't go because I was feeling rather sick, which one does apparently in this condition – but of course I don't need to tell you that!) Miss Jex-Blake told Tommy that she has been in correspondence all winter with Mr Stanfield about something going forward at the Royal Free.

'Mr Stanfield' was in fact J. B. Stansfeld, the MP for Halifax, who was also the Hon. Treasurer of the London School of Medicine for Women, and one of their chief advocates in the House. Untangling Emma's syntax, Venetia read that Stansfeld had fallen in with a Mr and Mrs Hopgood while on holiday in Whitby, and it transpired that Mr Hopgood was the lay chairman of the governing body of the Royal Free, the large hospital in the Gray's Inn Road. The Royal Free had, like all the other hospitals, refused to admit women students; but as their friendship developed, Stansfeld had discovered that Hopgood was favourable to the women's cause, and 'not a bit afraid of the medical staff', as Emma put it. Hopgood had therefore undertaken to present an application from Mr Stansfeld on behalf of the London School to the Board of the Royal Free.

Negotiations have been going on for some time now, and according to what Tommy says Miss JB said Mr S told her, it is looking very hopeful and nothing but details are left to be worked out. So if it is as they say, you'll be able to come back and complete your course in England, and *won't* that be nice? Because apart from anything else, dearest V, I have to tell you that I don't feel at all courageous about going through this baby business without you to hold my hand and tell me what's what. I know that's selfish of me, but put it down to my condition if you please, and forgive me. The thing about having a baby is that once you start it, you are regularly in for it, and there's no getting out of it if you change your mind. Tommy says it's a good thing females don't seem to consider that beforehand, and I have to say I think he's right. If I could call it off now, I probably would – and if everyone else felt the same, then 'what would become of the human race?' as Tommy said.

On the twentieth of March another letter from Emma relayed the news that agreement had been reached with the Board of Governors of the Royal Free.

They will take in female students just as if they were men [Emma reported], and the only condition is that the hospital is guaranteed fees of at least £400 a year from the students, plus a further subsidy of £300 a year in case letting in women makes any of their regular subscribers so cross they refuse to subscribe any more. The guarantees have to last for five years, but Tommy says £700 is a small enough sum, and that if the School starts a fund for it, it will be covered in no time. He says Mrs Anderson has already offered £50 and her husband has offered to stand as a guarantor and that he will himself if anyone asks him – that is, Tommy will – which I know he is doing for your sake, to help hurry you home!

Venetia lost no time in showing the letter to Miss Hervey, and they hugged each other and laughed then indulged in a few tears by way of celebration.

'We can go home!' Miss Hervey cried. 'Oh, the bliss of dear old England! We've won!'

'Nothing can stop us now,' Venetia agreed. 'But it will take time to set things up, you know. I certainly mean to finish the year here, don't you? Leinsdorf has promised to let me observe all sorts of operations, and there aren't anything like the dissection facilities at home.'

'Oh, it's all right for you,' Miss Hervey said affectionately. 'You are everybody's pet. As for me, I can be mediocre anywhere just as well as here. And I want to see my mother and my brothers and sisters.'

'Ah, yes,' said Venetia. Home, for her, did not have quite the same connotations. The Grunbergs were as much family to her now as her own siblings.

CHAPTER TWELVE

The stirks stood in a corner of the barn penned off with rails. They looked poor and unthrifty, but more than that they were obviously sick. Their heads drooped, their breathing was laboured, and there was a discharge from their eyes and noses. Every now and then one of them gave a strained cough, which made its ribby flanks pant in and out like a bellows; and even as George stood looking at them, the thinner of the two went off its feet, folding down slowly at the front, then rather more rapidly behind as the hind legs gave way. It rested its head on the straw, stretching its neck forward like a swan in the effort to breathe.

'Pneumonia again?' George asked.

'I doubt if they'll last the night,' Atterwith said gloomily.

It felt cold and clammy in the barn, and the day outside was so dark that it was twilight inside. The rain rattled endlessly on the roof, and where a tile had slipped a steady rapid drip fell twenty feet into a puddle on the uneven brick floor. George was seized with sudden irritability. 'For God's sake, when will you get that damned roof mended?'

'When it stops raining, sir.'

'Be damned to the rain. Get one of the men up there straight away. I shouldn't have to tell you these things, Atterwith.'

Atterwith took the rebuke without comment; it was just George's way of letting off steam. This year, 1879, they had suffered an atrocious summer, chilly and with endless rain – the worst in a series of wet summers that seemed to have been going on for ever. The crops were flattened and ruined in the fields, and now cattle pneumonia had attacked herds weakened by the cold and the lack of sunshine. It was no comfort to read in the papers that the south of England was even worse hit, with, on top of everything else, an epidemic of deadly foot-and-mouth disease, apparently spread from a market where imported cattle had been sold.

'How many have we lost now?' George asked.

'These two will make ten. And four milkers.'

George stared a while longer at the suffering beasts, and then banged his hands impatiently on the rail. 'Well, damnit, I don't know why you're showing me. I can't do anything for them, can I?'

'No, sir. I just thought you ought to know,' Atterwith said.

George knew there was more to come, and sought for a lighter comment on which to take his departure, before he could be cornered with it. 'Oh, well, these things happen. We'll make it up on the sheep,' he said, turning away.

Atterwith stepped sideways to intercept him. 'There's something else I want to talk to you about.'

George had never seen Atterwith look so grim – and Atterwith lately had sported a variety of expressions, none of them cheery. He sighed and said, 'Well? Get on with it, man.'

'Your tenants at Glebe – the Jenkinsons – have asked me for a return of rent.'

'A return of rent?' George almost squeaked. 'They're supposed to pay me, not vice versa! Are they mad?'

'The harvest has been ruined,' Atterwith said. 'They haven't produced even fifteen bushels to the acre, and wheat is down to forty-five shillings a quarter at the market. They've nothing else to fall back on, and they have to live.'

'They must have money put away somewhere,' George

said. 'God knows they've paid me little enough the last two years.'

'There've been five bad harvests in a row. Any slack they had was taken up long ago. Their savings have all gone and they've sold anything they had of value.'

'Well, I can't be responsible for the weather. There are people who are just bad farmers.'

'It was on our orders that they put their pasturage under the plough,' Atterwith reminded him, but his tone of voice said, 'your orders'. 'It was on our orders that all our farms have been planting more corn year after year while the market collapsed.'

George shifted impatiently. He didn't like to be put in the wrong by an underling. 'If they can't pay me rent, they must get out,' he said. 'Damn their impudence! I don't run my estate for the benefit of thriftless wastrels. Get rid of 'em, Atterwith. There are plenty of good farmers looking for land.'

'I'm afraid there aren't.'

'What the devil d'you mean?'

'After five bad years, and with the price of wheat falling all the time, there are no suitable tenants left with the means to take on new farms. The Jenkinsons are good, steady people and they'll keep the land in good heart. Given a run of decent weather, they'll get back on their feet eventually. I would recommend a return, sir. It will be better for us in the long run. Other landlords are doing it.'

'They must be wrong in their heads!' George shook his head, baffled. 'I don't understand why the wheat price keeps going down. Shortage ought to push it up. It always has before.'

Atterwith kept his temper. He had explained it all several times, but George never seemed to take it in. 'Vast quantities of cheap American wheat are being imported. That pushes the price down.'

'I don't see why their wheat should be cheaper than ours,' George said peevishly.

'Because they are farming virgin land, which gives high

218

yields that we could never compete with, no matter how much we fertilised; and it's flat land that can be worked by machine, which saves them labour costs; and their weather is more predictable.'

'Oh, very well, I don't want a lecture,' George snapped. 'You're determined to be mumpish, I can see, so I shall just leave you to it. I have things to do.' He tried to sidestep the steward.

'What about the Jenkinsons?' Atterwith insisted.

George scowled. 'If they don't pay their rent by the end of the month, they must leave, and that's my last word on it. How the dickens do you think I'm going to live if I let my land out rent-free? A fine way to run things, that would be!'

'Sir,' Atterwith said in alarm, 'the last thing in the world we want is to have Glebe untenanted and back in hand. That would be a disaster.'

'It won't come to that. If you can't find another tenant, I shall do it myself. Now do get out of the way, there's a good chap,' George added, more genially, since he had put his foot down. 'I have to get back to the house and change before our guests arrive.'

'Another house party,' Atterwith said expressionlessly.

'Don't tell me you'd forgotten I have six gentlemen coming to shoot?'

'No, I hadn't forgotten,' said Atterwith. Six gentlemen and eight ladies, plus their servants and horses, to house and feed; further guests to dinner to meet the house guests; a ball on the Saturday night. He didn't suppose George had the least idea how much all that would cost.

'And then we're all going to Doncaster for the races,' George said happily. He was thinking that the Prince of Wales would be there, and that the Mundesleys, with whom they were staying, were well acquainted with the Saviles, with whom the Prince would be staying. The Mundesleys were bound to be asked to bring a party over on at least one day. Alfreda had had a new outfit made specially against that royal eventuality.

Atterwith was thinking that the money saved through

not having anyone at Morland Place for a week would be more than balanced by the money George would lose gambling, for in the presence of His Royal Highness he was bound to stake high, and he was always unlucky. He felt a weariness come over him; but it was his duty to warn his master and he wound himself up for one more effort.

'Sir, your pleasures are expensive, and if they are not matched by your rents and other incomes . . .'

George stared. 'Exactly my point! I'm glad you've got there at last. I'm not in the business of letting farms out for nothing, so tell those Jenkinsons to pay up or pack up!'

And, pleased with the felicitous turn of phrase, he slapped Atterwith on the shoulder and went whistling out into the rain, his mind on the pleasures of the evening to come, and on how good-tempered Alfreda always was when they had eminent guests.

Now that the building that replaced the stables had been finished – what Alfreda called the 'new wing' – there was handsome accommodation for guests and their servants, and the Morlands entertained frequently. This in turn meant that they were invited back, and the demands of social intercourse kept them busy most of the year round. That the Morlands were hosts more often than they were guests was less to do with hospitality than with the fact that George would always sooner sleep in his own bed and thought his own house, cook and horses superior to anyone else's. Alfreda knew herself to be far and away a better hostess than anyone of their acquaintance, so she did not object to the situation.

The new wing had servants' bedrooms in its attics and kitchen offices on the ground floor. There were more maids and men than ever in the servants' hall, which in turn meant less hard work for each of them (with the exception of the very lowest). Alice wasn't sure it made for a happier house. She noticed that when the guest rooms were full and everyone was kept busy, there were fewer quarrels and feuds 'below stairs'. Idle servants seemed to snap at each other like bored children.

For herself, she liked to be busy. There was a special atmosphere in the house when there were important guests, when the labels on the bell-board in the kitchen were inscribed in Lucy's careful handwriting with names like *Lord and Lady Micheldever* or *Sir Harold Monkton, Bart, and Lady Monkton*. The important guests brought their own personal attendants with them, who injected welcome new life into servants' hall conversations. They were always given the best of the new attic bedrooms, and were known by their master's name: Lord Micheldever's valet and Lady Micheldever's lady's maid were called collectively 'the Micheldevers'.

Younger or less important guests sometimes did not bring their own attendants, and then a Morland Place servant would be told to wait on them. Alice was often one of those given the duty, and that was fun too – a change of routine, a chance to see another lady's clothes and jewels; and sometimes the lady would unbend enough to chat while Alice helped her dress. And, of course, there would always be a 'tip' when the guest departed: sometimes money, sometimes a nice handkerchief or some other small thing from the lady's wardrobe.

Even when all the extras had gone, they still afforded topics of conversation in the servants' hall. Sometimes there was also whispered gossip, when gentlemen visitors had been spotted creeping along the corridors at night, or coming out in the morning from bedroom doors not their own. There was never, Alice was glad to note, any gossip of that sort about Mr and Mrs Morland. She shouldn't have cared to hear her master and mistress talked about in the way some of the gentry were.

For the shooting party Alice was instructed to wait on Miss Worsley, the eighteen-year-old daughter of Colonel and Mrs Worsley. The young lady was new enough to the whole business of country-house visiting to be excited by it and eager to quiz Alice and confess in her turn. Having dressed her for dinner the first night, Alice slipped out of the room and was heading for the back stairs when the door of George's room opened and he emerged. Alice froze to the spot as she had been trained to do. There was no reason for the master to see her at the other end of the corridor, when he should be heading for the main staircase; but almost as if he heard the pattering of her heart he lifted his head and looked straight at her. Still she expected him to go on; but after a glance around, he walked quickly and quietly down the corridor towards her.

Alice's heart was thumping. Her lips parted, but she had no idea what she might have been going to say, for he put his finger to his to silence her, caught her wrist with his other hand, and drew her after him into the linen room. There, in the little light coming from the door, which he had left open a crack, surrounded by the fragrant heaps of clean starched linen, he took her into his arms and kissed her.

His embraces had become much more practised in the three years since he had first invited her to watch for badgers with him. The first time he had kissed her it had been hesitant, clumsy and brief, and he had looked at her as though he expected her to scream or hit him. Now he kissed with firm intent, and after a moment he held her against him with one arm to free the other hand to roam inside her clothing.

Alice's part was simply to acquiesce, which she did with fear and trembling. So far they had not been caught, but the danger was always there, whether they kissed out of doors or in, and though she loved him and lived for these infrequent encounters, they never failed to terrify her. But she half thought that George (as she called him in her mind, with mental blushes for her forwardness) enjoyed the element of danger. As time passed he grew bolder, more devil-may-care about where and when he embraced her.

Sometimes when he was kissing her she heard John's voice in her head delivering his warning. If they were discovered, Alice would be dismissed instantly without a character. There would be no appeal and no help to be looked for from George – this she knew and accepted as a simple fact of life. All the risks were hers. He had nothing to lose. Yet there was no question in her mind of resisting: she was in love with him, more so with every month that passed. He was the prince in her personal fairy-tale, the dream that made her life worth living.

Hard work and spartan conditions were a servant's lot and accepted as naturally as breathing, but what they hated most was the monotony of much of their lives. Boredom plagued them and they relieved it by living vicariously through the gentryfolk they served; and where the gentryfolk's lives did not quite come up to scratch, they had to rely on their imaginations. Performing the same mindless tasks day after day provided plenty of mental leisure, and left them vulnerable to fantasy.

Alice was a bright girl, and perhaps more in need of mental food than many of the others. While dusting and polishing, trotting back and forth fetching and carrying – most of all, in bed at night – she made up stories about the master. He (either miraculously freed from Mrs Morland by means unspecified, or, better still, never having married her in the first place) accosted Alice on the way out of church, or met her at a ball and asked her to dance, or passed by her father's house and saw her in the garden. The early scenes varied, but always after gazing at her enraptured for a while, he told her she was the most beautiful girl he had ever seen and asked her to marry him.

Alice's daydreams got as far as the wedding ceremony and the driving away on the wedding tour, never any further. Romantic love was what she was after, and what happened when she was alone with George did not conflict with this. His attentions were confined to kissing her and fondling her body. The 'harm' that John had warned her about (and she had always known what he meant) had not come to her. She liked to think that it was because Mr Morland was a gentlemen and really loved her; in bed at night she told herself that he would have married her if he could.

Their limited encounters seemed to satisfy George, but sometimes, as now when his hand was inside her dress and fondling her breast, and she felt herself grow hot and weak, she wished he would ask her for more. She would have given it, and gladly, and laughed at the consequences. But he never did, and afterwards she would be grateful for his restraint, while wondering shakenly what it would be like. All for love, and the world well lost – who had said that? How she yearned for love!

'Oh, Alice, Alice,' George was murmuring. 'You're so lovely. So soft.' He kissed her again, lengthily, then suddenly stopped, pulling back his head and listening. 'Thought I heard a door opening,' he said. 'I'd better go.' He let her go, adjusted his clothing, patted her cheek, peeped out cautiously into the corridor, and was gone.

Alice, feeling languorous, hot, unsatisfied, afraid and guilty all at once, put herself to rights as well as she could in the dark, and made her own cautious exit.

Despite the late nights inevitable with entertaining, George had never lost his early-rising habits, and was always down to breakfast long before his guests. Often he was early enough to eat, go out to the stables or walk round a covert or two, and return to the house with enough appetite for a second breakfast when the visitors and ladies came down.

He felt enormously satisfied with life this morning. It had actually stopped raining, for a wonder, and though the sky was grey and unpromising it was enough to lift his spirits. He had a delightful day ahead of him, of driving his guests to the coverts, showing them some of the estate on the way, and then of displaying his prowess with a gun before them. The ladies would come out with a picnic luncheon, and would exclaim in wonder at how many birds he had taken. And when the shooting was over there was the prospect of a fine dinner and agreeable talk, everyone telling him how splendid Morland Place was and applauding Alfreda's hospitality, and more of the same to come on the next day, and the next.

And there had been that delightful and unexpected encounter with Alice last night: he thought of her sweet, soft body and the excitement of touching it in the dark cupboard only inches from discovery. Even remembering now in daylight gave him a pleasant tingling feeling. The element of secrecy and danger added to the thrill, and he assuaged his conscience with the dictum that men had natural urges, which had to be fulfilled. He did not have marital congress with Alfreda – except on very rare occasions of her choosing – and a man was a man, after all. In fact, he had never been very active in that sphere, though he didn't think in those terms: he had no way of knowing what the norm was, since he had never indulged in talk of that sort even when he was a growing lad. His infrequent encounters with Alice were enough to satisfy his sexual urges, which were otherwise used up by his energetic outdoor life. When he was not actually kissing Alice in a cupboard or behind a bush, he forgot her entirely, and hadn't the least idea that she daydreamed about marrying him.

But today, having quelled the first pangs of hunger with a plateful of cold ham and a quantity of bread and butter, he collected his dogs and went out with the pleasant thought of Alice's breasts to the forefront of his mind. Her image reigned until it was ousted completely by the sight of his brother riding up to Morland Place.

'Hullo,' he said, with unusual cordiality. 'What brings you here?'

Teddy swung down from the saddle into a sea of dogs, all smiling and waving their tails and threatening to stand up and put muddy paws on his chest. 'I've had a letter from Trawden,' he said, without preamble, fending off the canine affection.

'Who's that?' George asked vaguely. 'Dogs, dogs, come off! Heel, boys! Sit!'

'Trawden,' Teddy said. 'It's not a who, it's a where. Trawden, the school where your brother has been these eight years.'

'Of course I know Trawden,' George scowled, his happy moment spoiled. 'Well, what now?'

'It's from Mrs Kettleworth. She writes to say Manfred is ill. She says she wrote telling you the same thing two weeks ago and had no reply.'

'I don't see what I'm supposed to do,' George said crossly. 'I'm not a physician. What does she want of me?'

'She hoped you might go and visit him,' Teddy said, with ironic calm. 'He is your brother.'

'Oh, pish!' said George. 'He's a grown man now. What is he – seventeen? Why should I go prancing about the countryside at his beck and call? Do I summon you every time I get a cold in the head? Not that I ever do,' he corrected himself, with pride. 'Never know a day's illness from one year to the next. That's the result of a healthy life. Fresh air, exercise and good food – that's the way a man should live! I always say—'

Teddy interrupted him harshly. 'Shut up, Georgie! Manny's ill, I tell you, and it's no cold in the head. Mrs Kettleworth says his condition is grave. Here, read her letter.'

He held it out but George didn't take it. 'I've no wish to read her letter, thank you. Women always fuss about health.'

'She says,' Teddy said, fixing him with a stern eye, 'that it's only a matter of time, and she asks whether he might be brought home before the end. We ought to go and see him.'

'We? Why don't you go?'

'You're the head of the family.'

George looked uncomfortable. This was not what he wanted to hear on a day that had started out so well. He *had* a conscience, though he preferred to ignore it whenever possible, and he had hoped that Manfred was out of its reach for ever by now. Manny had done well at the school, graduating at sixteen from pupil-teacher to assistant master and taking over the classes of Mr Kettleworth, the principal, when that gentleman decided to retire from active teaching. George had news of him from time to time via Teddy, whether he wanted it or not. He gathered that Manfred was a favourite with the whole Kettleworth family, had been invited when he was sixteen to live at the house and given his own room, and that there was some thought that he would marry one of the Kettleworth girls and inherit the whole business when the old fellow died. George had been glad to think Manny was settled for life. Alfreda had been glad that they no longer had to pay for his keep.

So the letter saying Manny was ill, which he vaguely remembered, had intruded an unwelcome note, which was why he had put it aside and promptly forgotten it. Now here was Teddy, intruding it on his notice again. Relations were the very dickens, he thought. There ought to be a law that said they had to move as far away from the family home as possible the moment they were twenty-one and never come near it again.

But, as Teddy said, he was head of the family. He liked people to remember that, so he said at last, 'Oh, very well. You can leave it with me. I'll deal with it all right.'

Teddy stood firm. He knew from long experience about George's ability to forget things. 'I'll wait until you make up your mind what to do.'

'You can't expect me to come to a decision right this minute,' George said indignantly.

'I really think you have to, Georgie. The matter's urgent.'

'But I'll have to talk to Alfreda about it.'

'Then go and talk to her.'

Alfreda was awake. Since her miscarriage she didn't sleep well. She usually managed no more than four hours before the pains in her back woke her, and then she would sit up in bed through the small hours reading, making guest lists for future entertainments, planning menus, designing gowns. Sometimes she would drop off again at about six or seven in the morning, and as this was her best sleep, it was an iron rule that she must not be disturbed until she rang for Fanie to bring her tea.

Today she had not gone back to sleep, and was sitting in bed in a very frilly wrapper making detailed plans about the shooting luncheon – the exact disposition of each servant and the precise time at which every action would be initiated, as if it were a military campaign. The essence of hospitality, she believed, was perfect planning. She enjoyed entertaining, not because she liked people but because she liked the exercise of her intellect and the sense of achievement it gave her to see her plans made actual. It was her own particular act of creation. The pleasure she took in other people's hospitality came only from knowing herself important enough to be invited, and was therefore better in retrospect. She needed to rub shoulders with the highest in the land, but did not actually enjoy their company.

George was turning out to be quite satisfactory as a husband, despite her early doubts about him. He was good-looking and dressed well, she had mended his manners, and he was an attentive host. He was entirely biddable and relied on her for direction in everything. He never troubled her sexually, and was happy to spend any amount of money she suggested on improving the house and their way of life. There were occasions when she even felt quite fond of him, and would have been grateful to him for rescuing her from the hell of dependent poverty, had it not been obvious that he had gained far more from the transaction than her.

All the same she was not pleased when he came to her room at an hour of the morning when no-one but Fanie was allowed in. It wasn't even breakfast time yet. She would not have been disposed to favour any request he made, even had it not involved one of his siblings, whom she had ruthlessly excised from his life. She listened to his stumbling exposition, and noted with alarm that he seemed to be having an attack of conscience about the wretched creature.

'Nonsense,' she said robustly, when he paused. 'What

228

on earth should you go there for? What purpose would it serve? Are you a physician? Are you in holy orders?'

'I am his brother. I was always fond of him.'

'You've been content to forget that for the last eight years. Why remember it now?'

'But if he's dying?'

'Sentimental nonsense! Besides, I doubt for a moment that he is. The lower orders exaggerate these things out of ignorance.'

George persisted. 'Mrs Kettleworth says he wants to come home.'

'Home?' She was alarmed at this turn. 'This is not his home. And would you bring someone riddled with God-knows-what disease into this house where he might infect our little boy? Have you no sense? Besides, if he is going to die, far better he dies where he is. It would throw out all our plans to have to go into mourning at this particular time, to say nothing of the expense of a funeral. Let them bury him, since they're so fond of him.'

She saw now she had gone too far. A wounded look crossed his face, and his mouth set stubbornly.

'If you think I'd begrudge my little brother the cost of his funeral . . .'

'No,' she said placatingly, 'I'm sure you wouldn't. You are the most generous of creatures, Mr Morland. But think how it would upset our plans. We haven't a day between now and Christmas when we're not entertaining or being entertained, and it would all have to be cancelled if we went into mourning. And the danger to our little boy cannot be risked. Your brother is better off where he is, I'm sure you must see that.'

Her gentler tone of voice softened his resistance. 'I expect you're right. But I ought to go and see him, to say goodbye.'

'We have a house full of guests,' she protested. 'You can't desert them. And as soon as they are gone we are going down to Doncaster. The Mundesleys are expecting us. We can't possibly let them down, when the Prince of

Wales is expected.' She saw him waver. 'Let your brother go, if someone must – let Edward go.'

'Teddy says we ought both to,' George said weakly. 'He's waiting outside.'

'Good heavens, Mr Morland! With your guests about to emerge from their rooms at any moment, and a day's shooting to come? We can't have a situation like this embarrassing everyone. Go and get rid of him at once! Send him down to – wherever it is as your envoy. Send a suitable message – I'm sure no-one would expect more. They know how busy an important man like you must be. And if your youngest brother is really as ill as they say, in all probability he wouldn't be able to see you if you did go.'

This last argument swayed George. 'That's true. You're right, Teddy should go. He has nothing else to do. And I'll send a note down with him – a few comforting lines. I expect it's a fuss about nothing, anyway.'

'Just so. He'll be perfectly well again this time next week, and you'd have felt a fool for wasting your time if you went.'

The journey down to Oakworth was tedious, involving slow trains and slower coaches, and the further west Teddy travelled the more it rained and the wetter the rain seemed to be. It was almost a relief to reach the moors where at least a dreary vista of wet rocks and heather did not remind one of the ruined harvest. The grey buildings of Trawden School seemed to hunch their shoulders to the steady downpour; even the smoke from the chimney could not rise through it, but trickled over the lip and down over the roof like more water.

It was a dismal place, Teddy thought, with a shiver, as he got down from the ancient cab which had been his transport over the last leg of the journey to Trawden. The graveyard was sodden, hung about with dripping black yews and autumnal elms. Water had gathered into sheets in the lowest places: some of the gravestones rose out of unbroken water. The church and the house, being built on a slight rise, were above it, but around the schoolhouse duckboards had been put down along the path, and its door sill was only just above the flood level.

In the house it was more cheerful, with good fires in all the rooms, though such was the clammy chill of that summer that Teddy would not have called it warm inside, and there was a distinct odour of damp under the peaty smell of the smoke. Mrs Kettleworth, looking drawn and anxious, greeted him, and regretted her husband could not receive him as he was ill in bed with a cold he could not shake off. The four girls, not pretty but pleasant-faced and with intelligent eyes, came forward to welcome him, and the gravity of Manfred's condition was there to be read in their suffering faces. They had all regarded him as a brother for many years; the second daughter, Margaret, had hoped to marry him.

Teddy refused refreshment and was taken immediately upstairs to Manfred's room.

'He always had the attic bedroom,' Eliza, the eldest, explained anxiously, 'and though we would have moved him to a better one when he – grew ill, he wouldn't have it.'

'I'm sure he couldn't have been looked after better,' Teddy reassured her.

Eliza raised naked eyes. 'We all love him dearly,' she said.

The attic room was small with a sloping ceiling, but at least that meant that the small fireplace was adequate to warm it. The narrow iron bedstead took up most of the room. In it, under a spotless white counterpane, Manfred lay propped on three pillows. Beside him on a bedside table was a bowl covered in a clean towel and a small vase of flowers – purple asters and springs of heather.

Teddy wouldn't have known his brother. Manny had wasted away to nothing, and his hollow-cheeked face looked ten years older than he was. His hands rested on the fold of the sheet, all knuckles like an old man's, and his wrists looked too big for them. He had a woollen shawl around his shoulders over his nightshirt. His eyes were very bright, but what struck Teddy most was the sound of his breathing, shockingly noisy in that small room.

Eliza quietly placed a chair for Teddy at the bedside, and then the girls withdrew to give him space. Teddy sat, and tried to smile, tried to think of something to say.

'Well, old chap, how are you?'

Manfred didn't answer. It was such an effort to breathe, he couldn't waste words. His eyes went past Teddy to see if they were alone, and then he said, 'Shut the door.'

Teddy obeyed, and, returning to his seat, said, 'Is that better? A draught, was there? Georgie sent all sorts of messages by me, hoping you're better soon and all that sort of thing, and to say that if there's anything you want—'

Manfred moved a hand to hush him. 'I want to go home,' he said. His breathing roared between short sentences. 'I haven't long. Don't want to die here. Not fair on the girls.'

'They all seem very fond of you,' Teddy said.

'They are angels,' he said emphatically. 'I love them like sisters. Their mother too. So kind to me. And Mr Kettleworth – owe him more than I can say.'

'Then – aren't you better off here?' Teddy said awkwardly. 'It seems a shame to leave them – not that you're going to die. Of course not, old chap. You'll be well again by and by, and then you'll . . .'

Manny shook his head wearily, once each way, closing his eyes a moment against tears. 'Don't,' he said. 'I've faced the truth. I haven't long now. But it's not fair on them – to die here. Burden on them.'

'I'm sure they don't see it that way,' Teddy said gently.

'*I* see it. Take me home, Ted.'

Teddy felt his way carefully, looking for words that wouldn't hurt. 'You can come home with me, and welcome, old chap, if that's what you want. I'll be glad to have you.'

Manny's fever-bright eyes searched his face. 'Not Morland Place?'

'They've – got a houseful of guests at the moment. It's a bit difficult. In a few days, or a week or so, when the guests have all gone . . .'

Manny nodded, closing his eyes. 'I understand.' He swallowed a few times, and then said, 'Call the girls in. I'll tell them.'

The Kettleworths did not protest at Manfred's decision, and set quietly about preparing for his departure, but wherever Teddy turned there was a girl wiping her eyes or discreetly blowing her nose. They packed up his few things, and then Mrs Kettleworth and Eliza together helped him get up, and dressed him. Teddy offered his services, thinking Manfred's modesty might be offended by having two unrelated females dress him, but he was waved away. He had no nursing skills, and the women had taken care of him for weeks now. He was too weak, and they were too fond, to worry about modesty.

When he was dressed – looking like a scarecrow, poor sticks propping out human clothes – they began to help him down the stairs. Step by step, supported by Eliza, the other hand gripping the rail, he felt his way downstairs, stopping every few feet to rest and drag his breath. At the first landing Margaret ran forward with a chair for him to sit for a while to recover; at the second he leaned against the wall, and Teddy had to turn away to hide his own tears at the sight of his brother's weakness. When he reached the ground floor the girls gathered round and escorted him to the sitting room, helping him into the armchair by the fire to gather his strength again.

'Mr Kettleworth's coming downstairs to say goodbye,' Mrs Kettleworth told Manfred. 'He'll be down soon. The carriage won't be here for a bit, so don't worry.'

Teddy followed her out of the room, and in the passage asked, 'Have you sent for a carriage?'

She met his eyes only for a moment before reaching for her handkerchief. She shook her head, and he took her meaning. A cold weight seemed to settle in his chest.

233

Mr Kettleworth appeared, in dressing-gown and slippers, a woollen cap and a shawl round his shoulders. He was obviously unwell, full of cold and looking a little feverish himself, but he made nothing of it, and by an act of will came to sit by Manfred and talk cheerfully to him, thanking him for his good work, discussing the progress of some of the pupils, talking about future plans. Manfred didn't speak, but he seemed to listen, his eyes fixed on his mentor, only sometimes moving to seek some other face in the room. The light faded outside and dusk came on, and the firelight grew brighter by contrast. The girls and their mother stood near, huddled together as if for comfort, while their father talked on to the accompaniment of the rattling, dragging breaths.

At last the old man's voice cracked and stopped. Manfred looked from face to face in desperation. 'I don't want to die,' he said. 'I'm afraid.'

Margaret began to sob quietly, and Eliza put her arm round her to muffle the sound on her shoulder.

Kettleworth laid a hand on the boy's bony knee. 'There's no need to be afraid. You are among your friends. Everyone who loves you is here,' he said.

Teddy thought that sounded a little odd. He should rather have said, 'Everyone here loves you.' He rehearsed the two sentences over and over in his mind until at last he couldn't remember which had been said, or what the difference was.

After a while, Manfred said, 'Is the carriage here yet?' Mrs Kettleworth said no, not yet, and he nodded, acknowledging her answer. They were the last words he spoke. He died shortly afterwards, between one breath and the next, sitting upright in the fireside chair, the light of the flames moving like water over his face.

They found room for him in the highest corner of the Trawden churchyard, and Teddy paid for a handsome headstone, though he asked the Kettleworths to choose the wording. 'You've been more of a family to him than his own family,' he said. He was glad he had not taken Manny back to York. This had been his real home.

Mr Kettleworth took the funeral service, despite his ill-health. The boys from the school filled the church, along with the villagers and farmers from nearby smallholdings, all of whom seemed to have known Manfred and liked him well. The four girls led the singing, and the trebles of the younger boys gave it an unearthly sound, despite the coughing and sniffing that spoke of a multitude of colds. It struck Teddy that this was not the healthiest place to be in a wet summer, but out of gratitude and consideration to the family, he stayed on another day after the funeral at their request.

The Doncaster races were not a great success, owing to the condition of the track after all the rain, but the social events surrounding the meeting gained by contrast. The Morlands went to everything important, and were particularly delighted to be introduced to the Prince of Wales as 'distant cousins of your friend Southport, sir'. He chatted for some time to Alfreda about the Duke and Lady Augusta, and remembered some distant relatives of the Turlinghams (Alfreda's family) he had met on another occasion, leaving her with the opinion that he was a charming and intelligent man and that those people who disparaged him were speaking out of ignorance and probably jealousy that they did not know him.

George and Alfreda arrived home at Morland Place after a delightful week to be met by Atterwith in a state of deepest gloom. The ewes in the lower pasture were sick, and the vet he had called in had said it was liver rot. They were probably going to lose the whole flock.

CHAPTER THIRTEEN

Venetia had stayed on in Zurich through the summer of 1877 to enjoy the fine Swiss air, and to gain more invaluable clinical practice, going back to England only at the last minute, in September, when Emma had begun sending nervous telegrams, reminding her of her promise to support her through childbirth.

It was a sad farewell of the Grunbergs. Katrina was in floods of tears, begging her to write often; Frau Grunberg, wiping her eyes on her apron, pressed food on her for the journey in ridiculous quantities. The various menfolk shuffled their feet and sniffed manly-wise, and even baby Villum, who had been happily plastering her cheek with kisses, suddenly sensed the atmosphere and began to wail. The professor gave her a pocket edition of Schiller, against the horror of being delayed somewhere *en route* with nothing to read, and the two students carried her bags to the station and accompanied her with a triumphal march on the jaw's harp. When her train finally pulled out, they ran alongside clowning and making faces and crying, 'Goodbye! *Gute Reise*! *Komm' gut nach Hause*!' until the platform and their breath ran out.

Emma and Tommy met her at the station in London and took her home with them to stay until the baby was born. There was much talk to catch up on, though at first Venetia had difficulty in thinking in English and kept using the German words for things. The baby – a girl they named Fanny after her grandmother – came soon afterwards with no difficulties, and Emma recovered so quickly that Venetia had no doubts about leaving her when the new session began at the London School on the first of October.

The session opened with real hope for the thirty-four students, for much had changed in the time Venetia had been in Zurich. Firstly, the Royal Free was now open to the women students for their hospital practice, making it possible for them to complete their study. Secondly, it was now at last possible for them to be examined, for the Irish colleges had taken advantage of the passing of the Enabling Act and opened the medical degree to women. Miss Jex-Blake and her friends Mrs Thorne and Miss Pechey, who had completed their studies abroad, had sat the examinations in Dublin and passed with honours. By the time Venetia returned to England the three were already entered on the medical register.

And there was more good news during the winter of 1877/78: the University of London accepted a new Charter, admitting women not only to the medical but to all degrees. The state of mind of the gentlemen by whose power this came to pass was summed up by Sir James Paget, who said that while he thought women were sadly mistaken in wanting to enter the medical profession, he could see no sufficient grounds on which they could justly be excluded. It would have been nice, Venetia thought, to have been warmly welcomed, but she and her colleagues were grateful enough simply to be allowed in.

So Venetia did not have to go to Dublin: it was the University of London examination that she took in June 1878; and by the time Emma's son Thomas was born in December 1878, she was a registered practitioner. It was a moment of great, but quiet triumph for Venetia. She had succeeded against all the odds in doing what she wanted; she had achieved her goal and proved that she was as able as any man. But for praise she had to look to her fellow pioneers. Mrs Anderson and Miss Jex-Blake sent warm congratulations, but her family was silent on the subject, except for a letter from Norton saying that her mother was very proud of her but too ill to write just then. Even Tommy and Emma seemed a little muted in their pleasure on her behalf: they praised her effort and endurance, but hoped only in very wistful tones that it would make her happy.

Now, Venetia thought, real life would begin: at the age of twenty-eight she was to pass at last out of studenthood and into her chosen adult world. Miss Hervey, who also passed with high marks, was going back to Portsmouth, her home town, to set up practice there, and they parted with fond embraces and promises to write. Venetia had no doubt that London was the place for her: not only was there a larger pool of potential patients, and the largest number of hospitals, but it was where all the major new work was being done, and where thought on all subjects was the most advanced. To go anywhere else would be like separating herself from the main stream of life.

The drawback was that setting up would be more expensive in London, especially as she meant to choose a smart enough area to be able to charge two guineas. She needed capital for a deposit on a lease, and to undertake the alterations that would be necessary to make the house suitable for her purposes; to refurbish it smartly and to furnish it – for she possessed nothing of her own – and for the wages of a minimum of servants. She would also need enough money to see her through until her practice had grown enough to support her, which could be as long as a year – she hoped not more.

Despite his silence on the subject of her success, she approached Harry first. It galled her a little to do so, but she salved her pride by making it clear that it was a loan she wanted, not a gift, which she promised to repay with whatever interest he thought fair. In the back of her mind she had thought this would provoke him to generosity, if only to salve his male pride, and that he would write back saying there was no question of its being a loan. But Harry had refused point blank to lend her anything; indeed, he even stopped paying her the allowance that had kept her through her student years.

I hoped still that you would come to your senses and lead a quiet and respectable life of atonement [he wrote]. But it seems you are lost to all decency, determined to make a figure of yourself – and in London itself, where you can be of the greatest embarrassment and handicap to your family. I cannot prevent you at your age from doing what you like, but I can at least refuse to help you shame yourself. If you follow this course you must consider yourself no longer my sister, and having made your bed, must lie in it as best you can.

Given their qualified rejoicing over her success, she did not like to ask Tommy and Emma: they might have felt compelled against their will not to refuse her, and she did not want to embarrass them. So she turned to her mother, though she didn't like to bother her when her health was so poor. When Venetia went to see her, it seemed to her that her mother was shrinking – not just physically, but, like a snail, back into a smaller and smaller world. She was proud of her daughter's achievement, and believed in the good she could do, but her pleasure was somehow that of a person looking in from beyond a window, marvelling at the bright images within, but irrevocably separated from them.

Charlotte did not, however, hesitate to advance Venetia a suitable sum out of her jointure. So in the autumn of 1878 Venetia hung her brass plate outside a small, neat house in Welbeck Street, and contemplated it with a frisson of excitement: *Dr Venetia Fleet, MD*. She had done it! And if she wept a tear or two that night for what had been lost along the way, she met the new day with a pleased anticipation.

Welbeck Street was nicely placed for the homes of the middle and upper-middle classes who would be her paying clients, and the house had a semi-basement in which to set up her dispensary for the poor. Paying patients were to be received by a smart maid, Patty, and shown into a small sitting-room at the front, where they would wait until summoned through a communicating door to Venetia's consulting-room at the back. Afterwards they would leave the room by a different door onto the landing, whence Patty would show them out. A second maid, Lotty, a cook, and a daily charwoman for the heavy work completed the minuscule household.

As a sop to convention Venetia did not live alone. She shared her house with a Miss Ulverston, a middle-aged lady who worked as a secretary to the *Englishwoman's Journal*, and who was plain and steady and respectable enough to give the lady doctor countenance. They shared a drawing-room and dining-room on the first floor, but in reality she and Miss Ulverston did not see much of each other, for she was enormously busy with her patients, while Miss Ulverston spent all her time at meetings and rallies and at the houses of like-minded friends.

Venetia had expected the first year to be hard going, but fellow doctors who had taught her at the School were generous in making referrals, and within three months there was a steady demand for her services. In six months she had begun paying back her debt to her mother, and to her great pride it was cleared within the year. At the end of eighteen months she knew herself to be successfully established.

Her paying patients were female, but they often consulted her on behalf of their male children and servants as well. One or two gentlemen had sought her medical opinion on matters that did not require undressing, but on the whole 'lady doctors' were still an amusing curiosity to the male sex, like performing dogs: they agreed it was clever but could not see the point of it.

Venetia would have liked to treat more men; equally she would have liked more surgical practice, but the only hospital she operated in was the New, where Mrs Anderson often called her in to assist. Inevitably much of Venetia's work was obstetrical – her least favourite area. The demand for women doctors in matters of childbirth could not be overestimated: she was asked to attend confinements at considerable distances – as far away as Norfolk on one occasion.

She was completely absorbed into a world almost as far removed from that of her birth as could be. The world of fashion, of the *ton*, the Season, and the great house continued all around her, occupying the same city, almost the same streets, and yet it never touched her or impinged upon her unless she lifted her head from her work deliberately to look for it. Harry and Augusta spent a large part of their year in London, but she never saw them, though she occasionally read about them in the newspaper, when she had time to open it. Marcus's world was further removed and more different, so though he did not avoid her she never bumped into him; Olivia, at Court, was the most distant of all, though she wrote sometimes, and always spoke wistfully of longing to see her 'dear old Sissy'. Of all the friends of her youth, it was only the Westons whom she still saw, partly because they had descended from the ducal heights to the middle-class world of the Cause and good works; but mostly because, out of kindness and loyalty, Tommy consulted her on behalf of Emma and the children. For his own needs, he continued to go to his old physician.

When the third Weston child, Ada, was born in March 1880, Venetia brought her into the world single-handed, by then an experienced midwife. Ada's arrival had made the Westons' move to a bigger house necessary, but they liked Brook Street and simply moved further up the road, nearer to Grosvenor Square. They chose a house with a large suite of nurseries on the top floor, for the children's sake, but there was another reason for their wanting grander rooms below: Tommy had at last fulfilled his father's ambitions for him and gone into politics.

Lord Beaconsfield – the former Mr Disraeli (Queen Victoria had ennobled him in 1876 when his failing health made the rough-and-tumble of the Commons too much for him) – had dissolved Parliament at the beginning of March 1880 over Irish Home Rule. Beaconsfield had known that the Conservatives were unpopular because of the economic crisis; but they had won two recent by-elections and he thought they were safe. Both he and the Queen, according to Olivia, were taken by surprise when the Liberals were returned with a large majority. There was much talk that the election had been won by unfair means: Mr Gladstone had defied precedent by 'stumping about the country' in person, giving political speeches in major cities and whipping up a ferment among voters. It was simply not done for statesmen to campaign like that, and Lord Beaconsfield had refused to follow suit; but Tommy said appealing to the voters directly in that manner was, after all, the logical response to the widening of the franchise, which Beaconsfield himself had brought about.

Mr Gladstone had asked Tommy to stand some time previously, having heard about his various reforming interests from the MP Henry Fawcett (who was married to Mrs Anderson's younger sister Millicent). The disadvantage of his marriage to Emma was outweighed by the fact that Gladstone had been acquainted with his father: Tom Weston had sat as a Tory, but in those pre-1832 days when he had first entered the House, there was nothing much to divide Whigs from Tories except family tradition. Tommy said, 'Pa always believed politics should never get in the way of government,' and accepted Mr Gladstone's invitation, expecting to have to wait for a by-election; but the general election had provided the earlier opportunity. Tommy's philanthropic reputation went before him and he was returned with a comfortable majority by the newly enfranchised artisan class.

With Gladstone's Liberal Government carrying a majority of 137, the hopes of reformists in all fields were running high, and the Weston house was transformed on the instant from a family home to a centre of agitation, with meetings and dinners and comings and goings. Two whole rooms were set aside for Tommy's political business, two secretaries dealt with his correspondence, and it seemed before you could sit down anywhere in the house you had to remove a box of pamphlets from the seat of the chair.

Tommy obviously loved it all, having found his *métier*; but since Ada's birth – right in the middle of the campaign – Emma had seemed discontent, and two months later was still fancying herself delicate. Venetia suspected a connection. Tommy had been an adoring husband, but now Emma was struggling to hold her own against a flood of other claims on his attention.

One early summer day in 1880 Venetia was called to the Westons' house to examine a crop of colds in the nursery.

'All these stairs!' Emma complained, as she and Venetia mounted to the top floor. 'Every time I go past the old house I look at it and sigh. It was so snug and nice.'

'Isn't this nice?' Venetia asked. 'It seems very grand to me.'

'Draughty,' Emma sniffed. 'The fireplaces eat up coal by the hundredweight and don't give the smallest drop of heat in return. And it's impossible to keep clean with maids as lazy as they are nowadays.' She caught Venetia's amused look and said, 'A big house is not all pleasure, you know.'

'No, how would I know anything about big houses?' Venetia laughed.

'It's different when it's your parents' place and you don't have to run it,' Emma said. 'I do miss our dear little house. It was so comfortable and we had such nice parties in it.'

Some other cause of discontent was working on Emma, Venetia thought – it wasn't really the fireplaces or the maids. It would emerge sooner or later. She suspected she had been called not on account of nursery sneezes but to be confided in.

'Tell me what's wrong with the children,' Venetia said, as they climbed the last flight to the nursery.

'Feverish colds, every one of them, even the baby,' Emma said. 'Fanny started it, of course – she always does.

I wonder if I ought to let her play with other children. She always seems to bring something back.'

'You can't isolate the children from everything,' Venetia said. 'It isn't reasonable. And catching minor ailments like colds probably strengthens them in the long run.'

'All very well for you to say,' Emma said. 'You don't understand a mother's feelings. The fear of losing the little ones hangs over you like a ghastly spectre.'

Venetia managed not to laugh, but she could not conceal a smile. 'Emma! Ghastly spectre indeed – where did you get such language?'

Emma frowned crossly. 'The nursemaid has a cold too, and a sore throat to go with it, and I don't know anyone in the world who wouldn't call diphtheria a ghastly spectre. But if you don't want to attend my children you needn't.'

Venetia patted Emma's arm comfortingly. 'Don't get upset, Emmy dear. I don't take any sickness lightly. I just don't want you to worry before there's any need.'

In the pleasant, light, airy nursery (she had had some say in the disposition of things) Venetia examined the children and then the sniffing, coughing, croaking nurse. She took her time about it, knowing that a quick diagnosis would not satisfy Emma's fears, but she could see at once that it was not diphtheria and that none of the four was seriously unwell.

'Nothing but a cold,' she pronounced at last. 'Keep them warm, keep the windows open, and get them out in the fresh air as much as possible. You too, Betty. Outdoor exercise is the best thing for a cold.' She prescribed warm salt gargles for the maid's throat and eucalyptus oil at night to help everyone's breathing. Despite their colds the children were stout and bonny, and little Fanny already promised to be a beauty like her grandmother.

'Come downstairs and have some tea,' Emma said, when she was satisfied that her brood was not going to be snatched away. In the back parlour she used as her private sitting-room, she presided over the tea kettle and chatted lightly of neutral topics. Venetia responded without emphasis. There was evidently something on Emma's mind and it was a matter of waiting until she brought herself to the point.

At last Emma stopped in mid-sentence, got up, and went to open the door quietly and look out into the passage. Then she came back to her seat and said, 'I wanted to be sure there was no-one nearby. Can I talk to you about something – something rather delicate?'

'Of course,' Venetia said.

Emma hesitated. 'You're not married,' she began, 'so perhaps you don't know . . .'

'I am a doctor,' Venetia helped her along kindly, 'so I probably do.'

Emma began again with a little rush. 'I do love Tommy. He is the nicest person, and the best husband in the world. I don't want you to think that there's anything wrong, or that I'm not – not . . .' She stopped again.

'Is it about your intimate relations?' Venetia asked. Emma nodded. 'You can speak quite frankly to me,' Venetia urged. 'Nothing you can say will surprise or shock me, you know. A husband may wish to do things—'

Emma coloured richly. 'Oh, it isn't anything like that!' she gasped. 'No, it's – well, I've had three children in three years. I love them dearly, but, oh, I would be glad not to have any more for a while.'

'Ah,' said Venetia. 'Well, of course, that's really up to Tommy, isn't it?'

The blush did not subside. 'Yes, I know what you mean, but – but Tommy loves me so, and – and I can't—'

'Refuse him? No, I quite understand. As a loving wife you couldn't.'

'Oh, please, isn't there anything?' Emma said. 'I've heard that there are things a person can do. There was that book, wasn't there, a few years ago, the one all the fuss was about? I didn't read it, of course, but I wondered if you knew anything about it – in a professional way, I mean.'

The book to which Emma referred was *The Fruits*

of Philosophy; it had been the subject of a notorious prosecution under the Obscene Publications Act of 1857. The book had been around for forty years in various guises, but the publishers Charles Bradlaugh and Annie Besant had reissued it, and deliberately provoked the trial in 1877 to bring its subject matter, contraception, into public debate.

While Venetia was thinking how to answer, Emma took fright and said in a low, miserable voice, 'You think I'm wicked for asking you. I'm sorry. Please forget it.'

'No, no, I don't think you're wicked at all,' Venetia said hastily. 'In fact, you're not by any means the first lady who has asked me for advice, so you needn't feel ashamed. Whatever people say in public, there are many – and from very respectable families – who practise it in secret. I personally don't think there is anything wrong with it. Husbands do enjoy having marital relations, that's simply a fact, and intimacy ought not to become a thing of dread for the wife just because she's afraid of the outcome.'

'You don't think it would be irreligious?' Emma asked anxiously.

Venetia smiled faintly. 'Darling, I'm not in holy orders! It's no use asking me for spiritual advice.'

'But the Church's view – one's marriage vows, even—'

'I don't know that the Church has the last word on everything any more. You and Tommy and I, we are all trying in our own ways to change the status of women, aren't we? And if women are to be more than mere breeding machines, they need to escape from constant childbirth. It seems to me that if you accept that women are individuals in their own right, then you pretty well have to accept contraception, whatever the Church might say.'

Emma was made uneasy by hearing the word spoken aloud. 'It sounds awfully selfish put like that.'

'Is it selfish? I don't know,' Venetia said. 'I wonder if it might not be a duty for educated people to show the way. I've seen so many pitiful wrecks of women among the lower orders, their health ruined and their lives endangered by constant childbirth. Is that really God's will? And it's no use telling them abstinence is the answer, because that's almost never in their power. It's the men who decide on when and how often to have relations.'

'So, if you're not against it, can you help me?' Emma asked, not terribly interested in this abstraction.

'I'd like to help you, Emma, but you do know, don't you, that a doctor can be struck off the medical register for giving contraceptive advice?'

'No, I didn't know that. Oh, Ven, I'm sorry!'

'It's all right. I will advise you, but I must ask you to be very discreet about it, and not let anyone know that I've obliged you.'

'You can be sure of that,' Emma said fervently. 'I should simply *die* if anyone knew I'd even asked.'

So Venetia went through carefully the different methods of checking conception – the *coitus interruptus*, the 'safe period', the *baudruche*, the sponge, and the syringe – and Emma listened bravely, not lowering her eyes though her cheeks burned throughout.

At the end Emma asked, 'And which do you think best? Which do you recommend?'

'You must decide that with Tommy. They all have their advantages and disadvantages, but it would be no use to fix on one before talking to him.'

Emma put her hands to her hot cheeks, her eyes wide. 'Talk to Tommy? Oh, no, I couldn't!'

'But – do you mean he doesn't know you're consulting me?'

'Of course not! He'd be terribly shocked and angry.'

'*Would* he? Are you sure?'

'I know he would! He loves me to have children. He's always talking about them being a blessing. He'd never agree to me doing anything like that.'

'But, Emma, you can't do it without him.'

'Why not?'

'Apart from any other consideration, he'd know you were using something.'

'What about this sponge you mentioned?'

Venetia shook her head. 'I think he'd notice. Syringing is the only thing you might possibly manage somehow without his knowledge, and that's the least sure of the methods. I couldn't advise it, love, really. In the end he's bound to find out, and if you've done it without his agreement he'll be even more hurt. It could destroy your marriage – not to mention my career.'

'I wouldn't tell him it was you told me.'

'I think he might guess, don't you?' Venetia said, gently ironic. 'Why don't you talk to him? I'm sure you'll find him more sympathetic than you fear. He's a modern-thinking man, and a great advocate for the Cause. It must be something that's come in his way before, and if he loves you he'll be receptive to the idea.'

But Emma continued to shake her head. Talk to a man about something like that? 'I couldn't possibly. You don't understand. How could you?'

At home, Venetia pondered that last comment. Since she had set up in practice she had found that, on the whole, her unmarried status was no handicap. The women who consulted her were happy to trust in her qualification. Occasionally their husbands demurred, but among the educated middle class the wives generally had their way in such matters. Among the lower orders, of course, they were only too glad to have anyone attend them, no matter what age, sex or marital status.

She knew all about the reproductive process, from erection to afterbirth. She had delivered countless babies, had treated sexual diseases, seen the consequences of illegal abortion, operated on prolapsed wombs and fistulas, dissected the organs of generation in anatomy class, advised on dysmenorrhoea and impotence, fought vainly against puerperal fever.

But she was not married. That was just a fact. She was not married and probably never would be now. Who was there for a woman doctor to marry, after all? Mrs Anderson was so lucky: her husband was content for her

248

to be herself, treating her career as equally important with his own, but such a man was a rarity. Even in the pro-Cause circles that Tommy and Emma inhabited, the men who would accept a wife on those terms were either married already, or too old, or both. Younger men might espouse the idea on behalf of other people, but when their turn came they chose traditional wives who would take the subordinate position. And who could blame them? If it were possible, wouldn't she prefer a spouse who would carry out all the dull, domestic part of marriage and leave her free to follow her career?

Well, probably marriage was not all it was said to be after all. There was Emma, for instance, married to Tommy whom she loved and who was as kind and open-minded a soul as could be imagined, yet she didn't feel she could talk to him about something as essential to her welfare as birth control. Whether she was right or wrong, it proved that being married to someone didn't mean you were able to understand them. And what was the point of it all, if physical intimacy did not breed mental and spiritual intimacy?

She had finished dinner and was catching up on her reading when she heard the bell ring downstairs. Listening for clues, she wondered if she was about to be summoned out to a birth, and hoped that if she was, it would prove a straightforward one. But after a moment there were two sets of footsteps up the stairs, and the maid opened the door and announced, 'Mr Weston, madam.'

Venetia got to her feet. 'Tommy, how nice to see you. I hope this is a social visit? The children were all right when I saw them this morning – nothing but an ordinary cold-in-the-head apiece.'

Tommy did not speak until the door had closed behind him; then he said, 'No, it is not a social visit.'

Venetia's smile faltered before his dark expression. 'Won't you sit down?'

'No, thank you,' he said curtly.

She waited, but he didn't go on. 'Tommy, what's the

matter?' she asked. She had never seen him like this: easy, affable, ordinary Tommy was holding himself up stiffly, his brow drawn with stern disapproval, his eyes avoiding hers.

'I think you know very well what the matter is,' he said. 'What have you been telling my wife?'

'*Your wife?*' She almost smiled at the way he said it. 'Why not "Emma"? You sound like an alderman.'

'Do you think this is a joking matter? Your humour has never been more misplaced! I came home to be greeted by my wife in an agitated state of mind, and as soon as we were alone she began babbling about the most shocking, shameful things – I would never have imagined she knew such words! And to hear them coming from her mouth – to think she would employ them in the presence of a gentleman!'

'You are her husband, for heaven's sake!' Venetia said impatiently. 'To whom else should she talk about contraception?'

His face reddened suddenly as if she had hit him. 'Yes, I thought it must have been you who put that word in her mouth! She wouldn't say, but I guessed it was you, even though I could hardly believe it.'

'Oh, Tommy, do stop canting! There's nothing wrong with the word "contraception".'

'And I suppose you think there's nothing wrong with the fact, either?' He began walking up and down the room, turning jerkily at the end of each beat, his hands twitching with anger. 'It's a filthy, disgusting, degrading practice, fit only for prostitutes. That you could use the word so calmly shows how you've been coarsened by the kind of life you lead!'

Venetia raised her eyebrows in astonishment. 'You always supported my desire to be a doctor.'

'That was a grievous mistake on my part. I didn't fully understand how it would debase you – you, a duke's daughter, to be advocating the harlot's habit, disseminating such filth in respectable drawing-rooms!'

Venetia was deeply hurt, but more than that she was

puzzled. 'You've always been so liberal, so forward-thinking! I don't understand.'

He wheeled on her. 'Perhaps you don't! Being unmarried yourself, perhaps you don't understand the nature of the bond between man and wife. And, given your state of ignorance, perhaps you should refrain from advising others on a subject you know nothing about.'

'I *do* know—' she began.

'Then you shouldn't! Good God, even your basic Christian upbringing ought to tell you that the sexual act was ordained by God for the purposes of procreation. To interfere with that order is a sin.'

'Tommy, you don't believe that?' Venetia cried. 'Surely the emancipation of women from the chains of—'

'Matrimony is not a prison!' he interrupted. 'Perhaps if you'd married as you ought you'd know that! Perhaps you'd know better than to talk to another man's wife about things so intimate they should never be mentioned outside the marriage bed!'

Tears were stinging Venetia's eyes. Tommy saw them and rejoiced, loving her and hating her almost equally at that moment. She had attacked him where he was most vulnerable with regard to her. His manhood was outraged. He had loved her and she had rejected him; that had been hard to bear. But now the woman he had loved so much had intruded into the most intimate area of his life, had discussed with his wife what he did in his own bed. He was seared with embarrassment and shame. That any unmarried woman of good family should know, let alone discuss, such things was bad enough, but that it should be Venetia, of all people!

He had been happy with Emma, and now Venetia had taken away his refuge, spoilt his peace, humiliated him. Innocent, shy, good Emma; bold, worldly, tarnished Venetia. He would never know what they had said to each other. He would never know what she knew about him. In the dark, secret warmth of the act of love he would know no safety now, seeing her eyes watching him, her smile mocking him. As she still haunted his dreams – fevered, sometimes, those images of her, naked, desirable, for ever out of reach – so she would haunt his waking thoughts and come between him and the wife he had chosen but never loved as he had loved his goddess.

'I'm sorry,' Venetia said. She knew all the arguments, of course. Contraception, 'the harlot's habit', was universally condemned – at least in public. For a husband, the practice was tantamount to masturbation; in employing it he induced in his wife the condition of mind of a prostitute. Even the *Lancet* had stated categorically that the only legitimate check to population was to marry late, all other checks bringing physical and mental disease in their wake. The woman who consented to the use of contraception was tacitly admitting that she had sex for pleasure: no decent female therefore would allow it even to be mentioned in her presence.

Privately, of course, there were many respectable women who practised it. But Tommy was evidently more old-fashioned in this regard than she would have expected; and she had a suspicion that his resistance was more to do with it being *her* who advised Emma than the advice itself. So she said, 'I'm sorry.'

But Tommy's hurt was too deep to assuage. He did not yield. 'I hope you are,' he said, 'but I have little confidence. You've changed, Venetia, and I have to say I don't like the new person. And as it seems I can't trust you to behave decently in my house, I shall have to forbid it to you. You will oblige me by not calling on or writing to my wife again.'

For a moment Venetia was on the brink of arguing with him – pleading, perhaps, for Emma's sake as much as her own. But pride had always been what sustained her in adversity, and it reared up now. She straightened and looked at him with all the hauteur a duke's daughter could summon.

'As you please,' she said. 'I will ring for the maid to show you out.'

'Don't trouble. I'll see myself out,' he said, and left her.

CHAPTER FOURTEEN

In February 1880 the SS *Strathleven* landed forty tons of frozen beef and mutton from Sydney and Melbourne in England. A whole lamb was sent to the Queen, a sheep to the Prince of Wales, and both pronounced themselves impressed with the quality of the meat. It was the marvel of the moment. The press was full of the wonder of it, that meat should have been sent half-way round the world, and from a place where it was high summer, without spoiling. Here was an end, said the pundits, to the inconvenience and expense (not to say cruelty – a consideration with Her Majesty) of shipping live animals around the world for slaughter! Here was a source of cheap and plentiful meat to feed the increasing multitude of town dwellers!

George Morland had read about it in the newspapers at the time without particularly heeding it. He was not a thinking man, and was unable to project in his mind what it might mean for him. Now, a year on, as the price of bullocks fell another three-ha'pence a pound in the market, he began to wonder if there weren't some kind of conspiracy going on. Despite five disastrous harvests, wheat was down to thirty-eight shillings, an unprecedented low. The country was being flooded with cheap imported grain from the American prairies: new efficient steam engines raced cargo ships back and forth across the Atlantic, coal out and wheat home, as if hell-bent on destroying George Morland's fortune.

The liver rot of 1879 had wiped out his entire flock of sheep, including his precious merinos, with not only repercussions on his purse but with the result that the spinners and weavers of Morland Fancy were suffering enforced idleness. Some had other work they could turn to, or at least a patch of land where they grew vegetables and kept a pig, and a wife who could take in washing; but others begged George to give them work (as if he had it lying about for the asking!) or, failing that, to give them relief. Grown men, George fulminated to his nodding wife, expecting him to earn their livings for them! He already paid his dues and more. If his wool-workers had to go on the parish, well, he had paid his rates, hadn't he? In irritation at their demands, he had pretty well decided that the Morland Fancy business was not worth reviving. There was a small, steady market for it, but it would be years before he could build up a flock again, and in that time the customers would have learned to go elsewhere. As to buying in the wool for the interim period, as Atterwith suggested, it seemed to him an illogical notion. They only made the cloth in the first place because they had the wool. If they didn't have wool, they might as well forget the whole damn' thing and turn the estate to something else.

But then that convict-infested wilderness, Australia, had started sending frozen carcasses to undercut his beef! No wheat, no sheep, no beef – what was next?

'If only you hadn't got rid of the working horses, sir,' Atterwith said, on more than one occasion.

'Good job I did,' George snapped. 'There's no demand for plough-horses now. Three-horse land is useless with the price of wheat so low – you couldn't give it away. Nobody's buying plough-horses.'

'But there's always a demand for carriage horses,' Atterwith argued.

'There'll be a demand for my racehorses after Ascot, you'll see!' George interrupted. 'Dryad's going to win the Gold Cup, no doubt about it! My stud will be famous throughout the country. They'll be begging me for horses!'

A spell of Atterwith's gloom always cheered him up. He

could not be unaware of the depression that was creeping over agriculture, for there was plenty about it every week in the farming papers, and articles in the national newspapers too from time to time. In the census that year, 1881, it was shown that there were ninety thousand fewer men working on the land than ten years before, and unemployment was rife in agricultural areas. Farm hands were migrating to the towns to look for other work; arable farms were being abandoned to scrub grass; speculators were buying up corn land, evicting the inhabitants and turning it over to uninhabited sheep runs.

There had been a call in Parliament for tariffs to protect farmers from the cheap imports – Belgium, France and Germany had all imposed them – but the Prime Minister had refused. Things were different on the Continent, as Atterwith tried to explain to his master: over there they had military conscription, so they needed to support farm labourers, who were the natural conscripts. In England more than half the population now lived in towns, and the towns were prospering. England was the workshop of the world, and cheap imported corn and meat fed the workshop labourers, the enfranchised artisans. The agricultural labourer, having no vote, had no political weight, even in distress.

While neither understanding nor articulating this reasoning, George acted on it quite naturally, turning surplus men off and reducing wages to his remaining workers. It was what everyone else was doing, and he argued that he could not jeopardise his fellow landowners by paying more than them. The tenant he had got in for Glebe Farm (a ruffianly fellow, and no husbandman, but the best he could find) had his labourers working for their food alone – and still he was paying no rent. The situation was only marginally better than at Manor, which they'd had to take back in hand when the tenant had upped sticks and gone. And all his other tenant farms had asked for remissions – his rents were horribly reduced.

But if ever George really started to worry, Atterwith's prophecies of doom made him cheerful out of sheer contrariness. And however difficult things might be in the field and barnyards, indoors, at home, everything was delightful: Alfreda arranged entertainments with the almost frantic dedication of a condemned soul. During the hunting season they were never without people to stay. George hunted his own pack five times a week, and Alfreda followed, almost as often, in her smart, fast pony-phaeton, which George had had made for her since she didn't ride any more. And as the hunters were being let down the Season was starting – last year, despite Atterwith's protests (damn his impudence!), George and Alfreda had taken a small house in London for three months. This year they were staying at home, but York was a lively place, and there were plenty of good families in the county. When the Season ended, the time for country-house visiting began; then it was the shooting; and then hunting started again.

George's first inkling that there might be something amiss (apart from old Atterwith's philippics, which he put down to a bad digestion – the fellow was as thin as a rake, which was not a natural way to be, to his mind) came one morning at breakfast. He was reading the paper about the new ship from Cunard's, made entirely of steel and with a triple expansion engine, that could do over seventeen knots. She was to ply the transatlantic passenger run. Conditions of unbelievable luxury and privacy for the passengers! Electric lights in all the cabins! All the wonders of New York only a fortnight's travel away! He was thinking he wouldn't half mind taking a trip himself one day when he was disturbed by a cry of exasperation from his wife.

'The impertinence!'

'My dear?' he asked, looking up.

Alfreda had been opening her letters, and had in her hand a stiff sheet with the unmistakable look of a bill about it. 'It's from Madame Étoile,' she said. 'How dare she? Why, I *made* that woman! She was nothing before I took her up – a provincial seamstress. It was my patronage that made her fashionable. When I think

256

how much I must have spent with her over the last ten years!'

'Let me see,' George said.

Alfreda handed the letter over. 'I would be grateful,' it said, 'if you could see your way to settling some of the outstanding accounts by the last of the month, as I should find it difficult to fulfil your latest esteemed order without at least some lightening of the burden.'

George looked up. 'Damned impertinent female,' he commented, though without heat. One expected shop-keepers to be impertinent, if they were not kept down. It was their breeding – or lack of it, rather. 'Threatening you – *you* – with a shut-down over some paltry amount. What's the total, my dear?'

Alfreda handed over the bill. It proved to comprise two sheets, and as he glanced over them, his eyebrows went up. Who would have thought it would cost so much to cover a woman's small body?

'Well, I suppose it is quite a lot for her to be owed,' he said cautiously. 'And some of these bills have been running almost two years. Why not send her something, just a token amount, to keep her quiet? Settle the two oldest, say?' The suggestion was not going down well with Alfreda: her expression was grim. He hastened to placate her. 'I know it is damned impertinence and you ought not to be worried by this class of person, but I suppose the wretched female must eat, and we don't want talk in the town. Why not be gracious, my dear? It would make her feel bad for bothering you,' he added cunningly. 'Coals of fire and that sort of thing.'

'Have you quite finished?' Alfreda said icily when he paused. He nodded humbly. 'In the first place,' Alfreda said, 'I shall pay my bills when *I* want to pay them, not when some thick-fingered provincial has the impertinence to demand settlement. And in the second place, I have no money in my account to settle it *with*. I settled Peckitt's bill for my shoes this month, and then Obadiah's had to be paid for the repairs to my phaeton.'

'You shouldn't have been bothered with that,' George

said in surprise. 'You should have told Obadiah's to send the bill to Atterwith.'

She gave him a level look. 'They wouldn't release the phaeton without payment. They said the last bill they sent to Atterwith – for the shaft on your gig – hadn't been paid. They were quite polite about it, but quite determined,' she added bitterly. Above all things in the world, she hated to feel powerless, and she had been powerless to move the coachmakers by anger, hauteur or threats. The humiliation had been extreme.

It did her some good to see George angry on her behalf. 'By God, I shall have something to say about this! Atterwith shall beg your pardon for putting you on the spot like that – aye, and Obadiah's shall as well! The impudence of refusing you your own carriage! But you should have come to me. You of all people shouldn't have to worry about money. Nothing could be easier than to give you some more.' He thought a moment. 'I haven't anything by me this morning, but I shall go into York straight after breakfast and see the bank. I'll transfer a month's allowance to your account, and take out some cash too, to make you comfortable.'

'Thank you, Mr Morland,' she said, a little stiffly. She seemed about to add something, and then changed her mind.

It was one of those May days when it was good to be alive. The sky was a deep, satisfying blue, and the brisk little breeze that bowled the occasional cloud across it was warm as the south. The earth was damp, and gave up a sweet breath of greenness and growing. George's road horse, Arthur, usually the most phlegmatic of characters, seemed to feel it too, and broke into a trot of his own accord as they turned off the drawbridge onto the track, and put in a little frisk and half buck as the pack of dogs rushed after them and streamed past on either side, to fan out ahead, nose-down to the grass for a delicious trace of rabbit.

He always sent the dogs back when he reached the

main road, but they had left him before that, slipping away under hedges to make their own way home. He rode into York touching his hat to acquaintances, turning his head appreciatively after a nice-looking horse, and smiling affably when anyone turned their heads after *him*. At thirty-two – all but a fortnight – he was in the prime of life, a big, stout, red-faced, healthy man, expensively dressed, and with those touches of care about his hat, boots, neck cloth and the cut and curl of his hair that showed an experienced valet's hand. If it hadn't been for Alfreda's prejudice in favour of clean-shaven faces, he would have grown his beard, like the Prince of Wales: he fancied it would suit him even better than HRH. Here in York, he was the local equivalent of the Prince. No-one counted for more than the master of Morland Place; no-one had more influence; no-one was better known or more popular. His brother might live in York itself, but he was a nothing by comparison, no more than an idle man of moderate means, a mere pursuer of pleasure. George was the one who counted; and having finished his business at the bank, he was going straight over to tell Obadiah's a thing or two, and then perhaps finish up by chastening Madame Étoile. No use letting the shopkeeping class get above itself; and it occurred to him with an inward snigger that, in fact, brother Teddy was a shopkeeper, when it came right down to it. He might make up a joke along those lines, he thought, to have ready for the next time he happened to bump into him.

An hour later George was standing on the Lendal outside Dykes's bank feeling – and looking – like a poll-axed bull. His interview with Mr Dykes senior had not gone as he had expected. His plans for venting righteous anger on the merchants of York were set aside. He had himself just undergone an experience that fell short of carpeting only by the depth of Mr Dykes's professional courtesy.

He was glad to see Mr Morland, said Mr Dykes, because he had been on the point of seeking an interview with him. An urgent interview. There was the matter, it seemed, of a cheque – a substantial cheque – presented by

259

Arbuckle and Bryan, the builders and civil engineers, to meet which there were insufficient funds in Mr Morland's account. Mr Dykes confessed himself unwilling in the greatest degree to return the cheque unpaid, and would be greatly obliged if Mr Morland would deposit funds to cover the cheque, or indicate when, in the very near future, he would be able to do so.

To George's astonished and piqued exclamation, Mr Dykes, steepling his fingers and pursing his lips, regretted that Mr Morland's overdraft had reached a level where Mr Dykes felt it would be imprudent on his part, and unhelpful to Mr Morland himself, to extend it further. It was a great privilege to have the handling of Mr Morland's esteemed account, but Mr Dykes had a responsibility to the shareholders, and also, if he might presume, felt a fatherly interest in Mr Morland's welfare, having handled Mr Morland's respected late father's account before him. If there was any advice that Mr Dykes might have the honour of proffering to Mr Morland—

To George's angry explosion, the now eternally damned Mr Dykes looked grave and begged to mention that it was impossible to close and remove to another bank an account which was overdrawn to the extent that Mr Morland's was. Mr Dykes deeply regretted that he would feel unable to honour any further cheques or issue any further cash until Mr Morland or his agent had addressed the situation to Mr Dykes's satisfaction.

Bruised in his vanity and astonished at the turn of events, George wandered along the street, bumping into passers-by he was too stunned to notice, vaguely accepting apologies from people whose toes he had trampled. Where had all the money gone? What had Atterwith been about? Of course things had been bad for the last few years, what with the terrible harvests, the cattle pneumonia, the sheep liver-rot, and various expensive ailments and accidents among the horses; but he was George Morland of Morland Place! It was not possible for him not to have money. Simply not possible! Why hadn't Atterwith said anything? But, to be fair, he remembered now, unwillingly, that Atterwith had been warning him, or trying to, only he had never taken it seriously. Atterwith was a gloomy old man and a professional doom-sayer, in George's eyes, so he always discounted everything he said. Perhaps he had discounted too heavily? But, damnit, he thought with a fresh surge of anger, it was Atterwith's business to see that George *did* listen to him! It was his *job* to make sure George understood the state of things. Atterwith was culpable – almost criminally culpable. If George wouldn't listen to him, Atterwith ought to have followed him about and kept repeating it until he did!

The last person he had bumped into seemed to have taken hold of his arms, and coming back from his churning thoughts, George found himself looking into the broad, smiling face of his brother, under a jauntily tilted top hat and above a sack coat, check trousers and spats.

'Hullo-ullo-ullo!' Teddy exclaimed. 'You're barging along today, old fellow! Miles away, by the look of you.' As George didn't answer, Teddy noticed the unnatural pallor of those usually ruddy cheeks and said with concern, 'I say, ain't you well, Georgie? You look as if you've had a bit of a shock.'

'Eh? Oh – yes! I mean, no! I'm all right,' George muttered incoherently.

'Look here, I was just going up to the club for a splash of something. Why not come with me? You look as though you could do with a spot. My treat! I've had a bit of good news today.'

'You have?' George said, falling in beside his brother, which was less trouble than resisting him.

'I have! My agent in Manchester tells me that we've landed an excellent contract to provide bed-linen to Cunard for all their passenger ships. Won it against stiff competition too – but the new machinery I installed last year is the best there is and we've been able to knock quite a bit off the nearest rival and still leave ourselves a decent profit. The outlay will pay off in less than a year with this new contract. Wonderful thing, business! But,' he recollected himself, 'I was forgetting, you don't have any opinion of factories and such. Mustn't bore you with my nonsense.'

The factories in question had been George's, and he had swapped them with Teddy for land – the outlying farm at Moon's Rush, as it happened, on whose damp pastures the sheep liver-rot had first shown itself. He groaned, catching his toe against an uneven paving-slab at the same moment and stumbling.

'Hold up, old chap!' Teddy said, grabbing his arm again. 'I say, Georgie, you don't look so very spry. Are you sure you're all right? Look, here we are at the club! Come on in and let me get you a large brandy. That'll set you up.'

The meeting was between George, Alfreda, and Atterwith only, and took place in the drawing-room. Three of George's dogs, sensing that he was in trouble, followed him in, and Alfreda opened her lips to demand their ejection and then, seeing her husband's face, folded them again. George sat very upright in a wing chair, and the dogs sat before him with their chins on his knees, doing everything they could by way of speaking eyes and dripping tongues to comfort him.

'I did try to tell you, many times,' Atterwith said wearily. 'If you spend ten times what the estate brings in, the only possible end is bankruptcy.'

'There's no need to exaggerate,' Alfreda snapped. 'And I do not wish to hear that word spoken in my house.'

Atterwith drew breath to retort, and let it out again. There was no point in losing his temper. He was tired of the struggle and the situation and of being ignored, and they hadn't even asked him to sit down now, though they were expecting him to get them out of trouble by some magic that didn't cost them any of their luxuries. But he had been steward here for so long he almost regarded Morland Place as his own, and he couldn't let it down. He had to be patient with them.

'Recrimination will get us nowhere,' he said. 'Now that I have your attention at last, what we must do is to draw up a plan of retrenchment and try to put the finances in order.'

'Retrenchment?' Alfreda said in alarm. 'I don't know what you mean by that. There is no unnecessary expenditure in this house. There is nothing that can be given up without compromising the gentlemanly standards expected of Morland Place.'

'If the tradespeople are not paid at least some of what's owing them, Obadiah's will not be the only firm that refuses to supply you. And where will your gentlemanly standards be then?'

'Don't be impertinent!' Alfreda said, mottling.

But George lifted his head from gazing into his pointer's eyes and said, 'What have you in mind, Atterwith? Let him speak, my dear. We ought to hear him out.'

Atterwith gathered his mental notes. 'Morland Place is well-founded: you can supply many of your own basic needs from the home farm, so there is no need to starve. What you must do is to stop buying unnecessary goods from outside that require payment in cash. That means no more clothes – make do with what you have. No more wine – you make your own cider and beer. No luxuries. The staff wages will have to be cut down – I suggest you get rid of half the servants at least.'

'It is impossible to run this house and entertain properly with fewer servants,' Alfreda said angrily. 'It would be an insult to one's guests.'

'Then perhaps you will have to give up entertaining,' Atterwith said implacably. 'I suggest also that you give up the hunt. It costs a small fortune to keep the pack, the hunt servants and the horses. You cannot afford it.'

'Give up hunting?' George fell back in his seat, aghast. To give up hunting would be tantamount to giving up life.

'By no means,' Atterwith said calmly. 'You can hunt with someone else's pack. Let them stand the expense.'

'But there've been hounds at Morland Place since – well, since there *was* a Morland Place!'

Atterwith nodded. He had read the family histories.

263

'But fox-hunting is a more elaborate and expensive sport than what was practised years ago; and it used to be a family activity, not sport provided for any person of fashion who cares to come along. You can't afford it, I assure you.' George looked mulish. 'At least consider charging a subscription.'

'*Charge* for hunting? Charge my guests for hospitality?' Alfreda cried.

'It's being done already in the shires. The Quorn, I believe, has a voluntary subscription, and the—'

George interrupted, 'Well, well. Pass on for the moment. What other "economies" have you in mind?' He gave the word an arch intonation, and glanced at Alfreda to show he was on her side.

'The racing stables.'

George sighed. 'But that's my principal source of income, now that farming doesn't pay. I can't seem to get it into your head!'

'It might perhaps pay if you ran it on more rational lines, concentrating on the promising horses and getting rid of the losers. *And* if you didn't go to all the fashionable meetings and bet on every race.'

'It seems,' Alfreda said frigidly, 'that you wish to deprive us of every innocent pleasure.'

'Besides, you don't understand,' George informed him generously. 'Going to the meetings is part of the business. Yes, and the betting, too. I don't particularly enjoy it, but one must be seen as the right sort of fellow if one's to sell one's horses. A fellow won't buy a fellow's nags otherwise. People have to know one's name – it has to get about.'

Atterwith let it go. 'But retrenchment is only half the story. Even if you lower your rate of expenditure, and even if your income improves, that will not clear the debts as they now stand. A capital sum will be needed to pay off sufficient of the outstanding accounts to restore credit. And to raise capital, something will have to be sold.'

George and Alfreda exchanged a look. 'I don't know what you think there is to sell,' George said doubtfully.

'The hunt and the racing stables, to begin with,' Atterwith said.

George moved restlessly. 'I don't know about that. What else?'

Atterwith shrugged. 'You know better than I do what personal effects you may have that are of value.'

'I suppose you mean my jewels?' Alfreda said sharply.

'You may put that out of your mind,' George intervened. 'Mrs Morland's jewellery is not to be touched. And as to the plate and pictures and so on, well, they're heirlooms. What sort of a father would I be if I sold off little James's patrimony?'

'Then that leaves only the land. Sell some of the outlying farms.'

George shrugged. 'It's the same objection. My son is to inherit one day, and I mean to keep his inheritance together. The only land I might agree to sell would be Glebe Farm and Manor Farm, as being the most lately acquired, but you know yourself as things stand I wouldn't get what I paid for them, if I could find a buyer at all.'

Atterwith spread his hands. 'You have rejected every suggestion I have to offer. What, then, do you propose to do?'

There was a silence in the room, at the end of which Alfreda said, 'If we cannot sell, we must borrow.'

George's face lightened. 'By Jove, yes, you're right!'

'Sir, madam, we are in difficulties precisely because we cannot borrow any further. What is an overdraft but borrowing? Or unpaid bills for that matter?'

'Ah, but what about a mortgage?' George said. 'Mortgage Morland Place. That should fetch in a tidy sum, enough to pay off all the damned creditors at one go. No sense in muddling around with a pound here and a pound there. Get them all off our backs once for all!'

'Now, *that* is good sense,' Alfreda said approvingly. 'You do not look as though you thought so, Atterwith – but I dare say you cannot like any idea that is not your own.'

'I only wondered,' Atterwith said, passing over the slur, 'how you proposed to pay off the mortgage?'

'Oh, Lord, you don't need to bother about that. The joy of a mortgage is that it runs more or less for ever. And things are bound to pick up sooner or later. We can worry about that when the time comes. As I see it, it is the perfect answer. I don't like a mortgage myself, of course,' he acknowledged generously, 'but it's a last resort, and better that than to sell any of little James's heritage. I couldn't live with myself if I robbed my own son of what he had the right to expect.'

George felt he had come out of it rather lightly, all things considered; and he had been particularly pleased with the way Alfreda had supported him all through the interview with Atterwith. The fact of the matter, as she had said afterwards, was that he – Atterwith – was getting too old. Running Morland Place was a huge and important task, and the old fellow was past it. Certainly he should not have let things get so bad before doing anything about it; and most of his suggestions for retrenchment were ludicrous. As to selling anything, George had his own reason, other than those stated, for not wanting to do that. If he sold any part of Morland Place, Teddy would certainly hear about it, and George didn't want to give his brother any opportunity to gloat. Over the brandies in the club Teddy had not again mentioned his prosperity or the factories George had parted with so lightly, but if he knew George was struggling, he would realise how he had got the better of the deal. Rather than that, George would have burned Morland Place to the ground.

Discussing the matter further the next day, Alfreda conceded generously that perhaps there were one or two economies that might be made without material discomfort. She could manage without any more new clothes, at least for the time being: she already had a new outfit for Ascot, and Fanie could alter one or two things that would do for occasions when no-one of the highest rank would be present. George was deeply touched by this, knowing how violently his wife hated 'made-over' clothes. Alfreda accepted his worship calmly, knowing that she could neither pay Madame Étoile, which would be giving in to blackmail, nor go elsewhere for her clothes, which would be admitting defeat.

The other economy Alfreda proposed was to do without one or two of the servants. They had, perhaps, multiplied to a greater extent than necessary, she said; and idle servants were more likely to be difficult and quarrelsome. George agreed that they were eating them out of house and home, and that the wages bill was enormous. He proposed getting rid of some of the footmen: male servants were more expensive than female, not only because their wages were higher but because they were subject to a tax. A householder had to pay fifteen shillings per head per annum for every male servant he employed.

But Alfreda vetoed that idea, very firmly and for the same reason. Because male servants were so expensive, the middle classes had themselves served almost exclusively by females. What marked out the wealthy, the fashionable and the upper classes was the number of menservants in the house. It would be intolerably *petit bourgeois* not to have those ranks of liveried men lining up at the door to welcome them home when they had been away; to have their guests admitted and announced not by footmen but by the abomination of 'parlour-maids'.

She did not express it that way to George, however; she merely said in the flat tone he never contradicted, 'We cannot manage with fewer footmen, Mr Morland. It would be very inconvenient.'

'Whatever you say, my dear,' he agreed meekly. The household was her concern. As long as his grooms, kennelmen and gamekeepers were not touched, he had no opinion on the matter one way or the other.

'I think, however, some of the housemaids might go,' Alfreda said. 'We don't need so many in the establishment: we can always hire more on a casual basis when we are entertaining a large party.'

'Dismiss housemaids?' George glanced at his wife with

the panicky thought that she had somehow discovered about Alice, and that this was her way of getting rid of her. But Alfreda's face was serene, and he reflected that if she really had found out it would not be like her to hide her wrath, or to act indirectly. Still, if the reduction of staff were done on a random basis, the lot might still fall to Alice. He cleared his throat and asked casually, 'Have you any particular ones in mind?'

'The more junior ones, of course,' she answered impatiently. She seemed to find it a foolish question. 'It would not be sensible to dismiss a maid we've spent years training. And we could lose a kitchen-maid, too, and one of the sewing-maids and one of the laundresses. No-one would notice that.'

So Alice was safe. That was good. On the other hand – the thought came to him quite suddenly – if she did leave, other possibilities came into being. Away from the house, he could see her whenever he liked; he could even (and it seemed naturally to deserve capital letters) Make Her His Mistress! His face grew hot at the picture it conjured in his mind. He had never taken full advantage of Alice's willingness, mainly through lack of opportunity, and the fear that Alfreda would find out. The physical pleasures he had allowed himself were well enough; but he was a grown man, after all, and he no longer had congress with Alfreda, and surely a man in his position was entitled, if the girl were willing, to more? Alice was in love with him, and his for the asking, and now that she was twenty-one there could be no irate father in the case, should anything come of it.

If Alice were not one of the dismissed he might persuade her to leave, and then he could set her up in a little place of her own somewhere. There was a house of his in York that was without a tenant at the moment: a tiny terraced cottage in Goodramgate in which a widow had lived, making biscuits and toffee and cakes and selling them from the front room. She had died two months ago, and the cottage had not been re-let, because it was in poor condition and the widow had left it very dirty, and

George was unable to afford the renovations needed and unwilling to lower the rent. Alice could live there, clean it up herself – she was a trained housemaid, wasn't she? – and when he was not visiting her she could supplement her keep by taking in sewing or washing or something of the sort. That way it would cost him very little more than it cost him now in her wages.

It seemed like an excellent idea until the difficulties began to occur to him. How would he explain the situation to Atterwith? It would be damnably embarrassing to expose himself to his steward's disapproval while demanding his discretion, especially as he was under no illusion that Atterwith liked him. And what if Alfreda looked through the books, which she did from time to time, and wondered why there was no rent coming in from the cottage, or why her former housemaid was living there?

Suppose someone in York saw him going in there and mentioned it to Alfreda? The thought of her asking him and his trying to work off a reasonable story made him sweat: he was not a good liar, and Alfreda's cold eye and rapier mind unnerved him at the best of times.

And then, when he came to think about it, how often would he be able to visit Alice there anyway? He was always so busy about the estate, and didn't often go into the city; making a separate trip, going all that way just for a – well, it seemed to him like a lot of effort for not much return. The very thought of it made him feel tired. And then, what if he got bored with her? It would be difficult to turn her out of the cottage for that reason, and there he'd be with an unprofitable piece of property and the danger of meeting a reproachful woman every time he went in to York to call at the bank or consult his tailor.

No, on the whole (and he felt an indefinable relief as he came to the decision) he was better off as he was, with Alice safely on hand for a little fondling and kissing when he had a mind. The rest he could do without.

He realised with a start that Alfreda was looking at him

curiously, wondering at his long silence, and he roused himself hastily to answer.

'I'm sure you're right, my dear. Some of the girls could go. I'm always seeing housemaids standing about doing nothing. We can do without some of them very well.'

CHAPTER FIFTEEN

Venetia thought that Tommy's anger would dissolve once he had had time to think about it quietly, but it seemed her crime was too great to be forgiven. There was no letter, no call, no card left. She was cut surgically out of his and Emma's life. She heard about them occasionally through common acquaintances; learned that poor Emma had had another child in May 1881 – a boy, Alfred – so evidently there had been no contraception for her. Sometimes in the course of her day she would even find herself in Brook Street, and would glance up at the windows as she passed their house. But though they lived in the same part of the city, she never met them. Once only she saw Tommy, when her cab and his were halted side by side by the traffic at the corner of Edgware Road. She stared at his profile under his tall hat, not knowing whether she wanted him to look up and see her, or hoped he wouldn't. But he was reading a newspaper with great attention, and after a moment his cab jerked him forward and out of her line of vision.

The Westons were still doing good work in the housing scheme, according to Miss Ulverston – who knew a Miss Jekyll who was a friend of Miss Octavia Hill. The work was more necessary than ever, since the agricultural slump was sending more and more unemployed labourers into the towns and cities, desperate for work, and putting a greater strain than ever on the lower grade of housing.

Venetia came across the consequences of bad housing all the time in her work. Three-storey houses in which ten families lived, each occupying a single room – perhaps a father, mother and up to six children in a space fifteen feet by twelve – anything from sixty to a hundred souls sharing a single privy and water tap: such places bred disease, deformity, drunkenness, incest and vice. They came to her dispensary in a sad procession: the women with broken jaws, gonorrhoea, prolapsed wombs; children with tuberculosis, rickets, skin diseases, scurvy; old men with ulcers that would not heal and bronchitis that made their chests roar like broken-winded horses. Saddest of all, though, were the child victims of the overcrowding, girls of thirteen pregnant by their brothers or fathers, dull-eyed ten-year-olds of both sexes with venereal diseases, babies born to women who drank or took cocaine or heroin, already exhibiting the symptoms of their mothers' addiction.

With Emma busy with her family and Tommy with his political career, the Westons were less personally involved, these days. They no longer directly managed a building, though they owned three. Miss Hill was becoming quite a national figure, and as the housing question was moving upwards towards being a question for the Government, Tommy, along with Sir Charles Dilke, was one of her leading advocates at Westminster. Miss Ulverston brought back snippets of information from Langham Place for, given the limited number of people involved, all Good Works overlapped at some point in their existence; but what interested her was the Vote. All the 'franchisists' were building their hopes on the next Reform Bill, promised by Mr Gladstone's government, which was to give the vote to the countryman. This time, they believed, a women's suffrage amendment would be added and carried: a majority of the Liberal Party seemed willing to support the cause, and various Party meetings had passed suffrage resolutions. The only difficulty, according to Miss Ulverston, was deciding the question of whether the amendment should refer to all women, or whether married women should be excluded.

Venetia knew something about this from Mrs Anderson,

whose sister, Millicent Fawcett, was a leading name in the suffrage movement.

'It is such a *difficult* point,' Miss Ulverston said, in her breathily emphatic way, her brow furrowed. 'There is such *hostility* to the idea of married women having the vote, because men see it as a *second* vote for the *husbands*. We might more easily get *unmarried* women and *widows* through, since they are such a small group – but, then, would that not be to compromise our whole *argument*? Or would it be better to secure what we can and hope that more follows – a *foothold*, you see, or the thin end of the *wedge*?'

Venetia listened without comment when Miss Ulverston raised these questions, but inwardly she had little hope that the amendment would go through in any form. Whatever the state of play in the Commons, there was still the hurdle of the Lords. Lady Anne Farraline, back from a year abroad and in London in May 1881 for her come-out, came to visit Venetia one day, and told her that 'Cousin Aylesbury says the Lords will never pass a women's amendment, and William agrees with him. The Lords are amazingly against it.' William – her brother, Lord Batchworth – had also told her that Lord Salisbury (who had taken over leadership of the Conservatives on the death of Lord Beaconsfield that April) had said that whatever Mr Gladstone said in public, in private he was determined women should *not* have the vote, and if a Commons majority in favour looked at all likely, he would invoke party loyalty to reverse it.

'Which only serves to make me more determined than ever that women *shall* have the vote one day,' Anne said. 'Do you remember, Venetia, how you said once that I would have to work for the vote because you were too busy conquering medicine?'

Venetia looked with affection at the lovely girl sitting opposite her: Anne at eighteen had inherited all the Farraline good looks, and was one of the great beauties of the Season, the most desirable débutante of the year. To her ash-blonde hair and violet eyes, elegant figure and lovely features, she added a fortune that her father and grandfather had worked hard to restore, and a name that had now recovered from the disadvantage laid on it fifty years before by her grandmother's divorce. Anne would be presented at Court; and Anne would surely very soon be making an advantageous match.

'I remember,' Venetia said. 'But I wasn't serious, you know. And it won't be long before you'll be married and then you won't have time for dull things like the Cause.'

Anne opened her eyes wide. 'I'm shocked to hear you speak like that! You, of all people! Everyone said you couldn't be a doctor, but you proved them wrong; and I'm going to prove them wrong about the vote. I'm *going* to. And as to marriage, do you think I would marry anyone who didn't agree with me? You showed me the way, dearest Venetia. You are my model in everything.'

'Oh, Fairy, don't say that!' Venetia said despairingly.

But Lady Anne only laughed. 'Nothing fairylike about me now! William says I'm a regular Boadicea!' She gathered up her little dog, preparatory to leaving, and then added, 'Oh, by the way, I saw Marcus last week at the Tonbridges. I said I would be coming to see you and he sent his love.'

'That's nice. Mine to him, if you please, if you should see him again.'

'He's such a nice man,' Anne said, 'but strangely *old*. He's only ten years older than me, but very like a dear old uncle; whereas you only seem the same age as me – or just a year or two more,' she added, with transparent honesty.

'I expect a soldier's life is terribly hard,' Venetia said, smiling at the flattery.

Anne hesitated, and then went on seriously, 'Had you heard that Augusta was getting married?'

'No,' said Venetia.

'Yes, Marcus told William. He doesn't approve at all. It's one of the Prince of Wales's dreadful racing friends, Colonel Vibart. Well, he calls himself colonel, but Marcus says he's never been in any regiment that *he* can discover. And he's loads older than Augusta – he really *is* forty, if not more.'

'I suppose that doesn't matter if she loves him,' Venetia commented, at a loss for something to say. She had read something in the newspaper last year about 'Johnny' Vibart: he was part of the Prince's racing, gambling, hard-drinking, actress-chasing 'fast' set, to which her brother Henry belonged. Gussie was Harry's hostess, and as much part of the set as any of them.

'Well, the queer thing is that it seems she does,' Anne said. 'She's quite nutty on him. Marcus saw her at Marlborough House with him. She was smoking cigarettes and drinking champagne and laughing just like a man, he said. He was terribly upset, poor Marcus, but if that's what she likes to do . . .' Anne shrugged. 'They're quite the heart and soul, she and Vibart. Everyone calls them "Gussie Girl" and "Johnny Boy". But Marcus says Vibart's in financial trouble, and if Cousin Southport refuses her dowry they'll have nothing to live on and Vibart might end up in prison. I hope that's not why he's marrying her,' she ended soberly. She met Venetia's eyes. 'This marriage business is fraught with pitfalls, isn't it? You're very wise to avoid it. I think I shall too.'

Anne's visit gave Venetia a great deal to think about, and much of it disturbing. She hoped her beautiful cousin would not follow her example, for though Venetia regretted nothing about her chosen course, achieving her goal had come with a price. Her days – and often her nights – were immensely busy; her work was absorbing and exhausting and for the most part left her with little time to think. But when she did find herself at leisure, she was usually alone. Miss Ulverston was rarely at home, and Venetia hardly knew what it was to eat in company. She was invited out to meals sometimes, but she early learned the value of Mrs Anderson's iron rule: 'Never make a friend of a patient.' On the few occasions she weakened and accepted an invitation, she found she was expected to sing for her supper. There were still not so very many lady-doctors, and for a hostess to produce one at dinner was a matter of pride. Venetia quickly grew tired of being quizzed and baited. Even those who did not disapprove of her calling tended to regard her as something of a *lusus naturae*.

Mrs Anderson had the benefit of a large family to provide her with company. Venetia's only social contact tended to be with fellow doctors, who talked 'shop', or others like Miss Ulverston, who talked about nothing but the Cause, which she found wearisome. She remembered with wistful fondness the days of her youth (a lifetime ago!) when she had been surrounded by handsome young men all talking witty nonsense for her amusement.

What she missed, she thought, was probably not to be had – the intimacy of equality with a member of the opposite sex. Who knew even if Mrs Anderson, who had married for love, had it? Given her busy life of practice, hospital, committees and lectures, she probably hadn't time for it; and Venetia could see that, if her own work went on multiplying at the present rate, she would soon be in the same boat. Perhaps that would solve the problem.

She had read in one of the society papers some time ago that Miss Graham had married the Marquess of Westhaven, so there had been nothing serious between her and Beauty after all. She had tried not to feel glad – poor Hazelmere, rather, if he had cared for her! She had not read anywhere that he had married anyone else; but he lived permanently in the country now, according to the threads she picked up through gossip. Not that it would matter if he did come to London, of course. And he might well have married some local girl and not sent a notice to the papers. He was not a man one could imagine living alone for ever. He would not cope well. Not like her. Though, of course, coping was not the same as enjoying. She was, it had to be admitted, damnably lonely.

Occupied with these thoughts as she walked up Welbeck Street one day, she did not notice someone on the other side start at the sight of her, raise his hand to his hat, and begin to cross the road. Traffic held him up, and only as Venetia was about to climb her own front steps did he gain the pavement and call out, 'Hey! I say, hullo! Hold up there!'

She turned. The man removed his hat as he reached her, and stood before her, smiling as if he expected her to know him. After a moment, the curly dark hair struck a chord in her mind.

'You are the man who hit me with a snowball in Zurich!' she exclaimed.

'Alas for what might have been!' he said, his eyes bright with laughter. 'You ought really to have been able to say, "The amusing man who befriended me in Zurich and took me to all the most fascinating places". But though I searched high and low for you, I never could find you. No-one in my circle seemed to know anything about the lady medical students, and the old wigsters at the university wouldn't reveal a single thing, no matter how I probed them. Close as oysters!'

'You tried to find me?' she said in surprise.

'Oh, how I tried! It took up all my waking moments for weeks.'

'But – why?'

He smiled a slow, intimate smile that made the back of her neck tingle. 'My dear ma'am, what an *interesting* question! Can you really not know? Ah, there's a blush! You understand me now.'

She tried to be haughty. 'I really don't know what you mean. You must excuse me – I am very busy.'

'Oh, but it's almost five years since we last met. You can't brush me off so cruelly,' he said. 'Now don't frost! To think of stumbling across you like this, when I wasn't even looking any more. How perverse fate is! One can't defy it.' His eye went past her to the plate beside the door. 'Is this your house? Dear ma'am, is it possible that you are the Dr Venetia Fleet here celebrated? Your studies bore fruit, then? My heartiest congratulations!'

He said it as if he meant it, and her sore heart was comforted by his warmth.

'You don't think it wrong for a woman to be a doctor?' she asked cautiously.

'Why should I? I am all for women doing whatever they like. *I* always do. And I do admire people who have an ambition and carry it through. Isn't that generally considered laudable? Surely the crustiest old specimen must grant you that?'

'You'd be surprised what crusty old specimens can deny when they put their minds to it,' Venetia said, smiling despite herself.

'Well, I should hate it if someone said I might not do this or that because I'm a man, so all power to you, Dr Fleet!'

'You have the advantage of me,' she pointed out.

'I beg your pardon.' He bowed. 'Jennings is my name. Ivo Jennings. At your entire service, Dr Fleet.' He straightened up. 'How delicious it is to call you that! Have you got used to it yet, or does it still give you a thrill?'

'I'm too busy often to have time to be thrilled.'

'Now *that*'s a sad confession!'

She suppressed a smile. 'But really, Mr Jennings, I can't stand talking to you in the street—'

'Of course not,' he said promptly. 'You had better invite me in so that we can continue to chat over tea. I adore chatting, don't you?' He saw that she hesitated and went on, 'A little late for tea, is that it? But your busy life must often make you late for meals, and I haven't had any yet – not a drop nor a crumb.'

'I'm not sure I ought—' she began.

'You are a doctor, and I wish to consult,' he said, his face suddenly serious. 'I have been suffering for some time from a dreadful pain here.' He put his hand to his chest. 'Do you prescribe for gentlemen, or does your husband insist you attend only ladies?'

She was stung to answer, 'I attend anyone who is genuinely in need of my services, and I have no husband.'

'Excellent,' he said, almost skipping up the steps. 'Come along then – and do hurry up, Doctor! It wouldn't do your reputation much good if I were to drop dead on your doorstep under your very nose, now, would it?'

She followed him perforce, and opened the door, ringing the bell at the same time. Inside the vestibule she said, 'How long have you had this pain?'

'In my heart? Almost five years,' he said solemnly. 'Since the first moment I laid eyes on you. Ah, now, don't poker up! I had to make you take me in somehow, poor helpless waif that I am! Give me tea and I shall be good. I am tremendously respectable, I promise you.' He lowered his voice. 'Look, your maid's coming. If you make her throw me out I shall resist, and that will make far more row and scandal than being nice to me.'

'You are impossible!' Venetia hissed. But she hesitated. What could be the harm in having tea with him? She was not a green girl any more; and hadn't she flouted far worse conventions by being here at all? 'Oh, Lotty,' she began, not sure what she was going to say.

He made up her mind for her. 'I've heard so much about you, Lotty,' he said airily to the maid. 'I'm an old friend of your mistress, from her student days, you know.'

Lotty eyed him with interest, beguiled by his good looks. 'Are you a doctor too, sir?' she asked.

Venetia intervened, lest he say something indiscreet. 'Is Miss Ulverston at home?'

'No, Doctor, she's not come in,' Lotty answered.

'Very well. Mr Jennings and I will have tea in the drawing-room, and when Miss Ulverston arrives you can ask her to join us.'

'Yes, Doctor.'

Climbing behind her to the drawing-room, Jennings said into her ear, 'Nicely done! Miss Ulverston is the duenna, I take it? Some ferocious old dragon who keeps undesirables at bay. Is she really expected home, or did you say that to impress the innocent Lotty?'

'What is it to you if she is or isn't?' Venetia asked, holding down laughter.

'I like to know how much time I have,' he said, with

dignity. 'My performance is best when allowed to develop at its own pace. However, if time is short I can leave out the overture and first movement and go straight to the *scherzo*, though it would be a pity for you to miss them.'

In the drawing-room she turned to face him. 'Mr Jennings, do you mean to talk nonsense the whole time?' Even as she said it, she remembered how much she had enjoyed nonsense as a girl, and a sharp needle of excitement tingled in the pit of her stomach. Close to, he was very handsome, and he was smiling at her in a way that suggested he knew everything she thought before she thought it.

'It occurred to me,' he said, 'that the life of a lady doctor must be one of great struggle and seriousness, and that if anything was lacking, it would be laughter.'

'You're right,' she said, yielding suddenly and completely. 'Talk nonsense to me, then. I shall welcome it.'

'And Miss Ulverston? Will I be turned to stone when my eyes first strike her face?'

'She is very nice, but she rarely comes home before six thirty.'

'Over an hour away! Excellent! I can manage quite a lot of nonsense in that time.'

Over the teacups, buttered toast and Swiss tarts, Mr Jennings exercised himself to entertain, and laughter improved Venetia's appetite so that she made a better tea than she usually did. Through the nonsense, she managed to glean quite a bit about him. He had been sent to Europe by his father to study music: 'A last effort to make something of me – something other than an idle man-about-town, that is. Of course, I had to obey because the old fellow held the purse-strings.'

'You could have earned your own living, perhaps.'

'Please! Never suggest such a thing again. It pains me that you can even frame the words. Besides, my father was frightfully rich, and I was the only son. It would have been sheer wanton waste to give up a fortune of that size, besides breaking the old fellow's heart. He was uncommon fond of me, when he wasn't beating me for my sins.'

'You say "was"?'

'Yes, he's dead now. Died in the winter of 'seventy-seven. That's what brought me home.'

'I'm sorry,' said Venetia, seeing the sadness under his flippancy. 'Is your mother still alive?'

'No, she died a long time ago. I'm a complete waif, and in desperate need of your sympathy.' His eyes gleamed.

'Ah! Well, you had it up until then. And who were those young men you were with in Zurich, whom you were teaching to disrespect women?'

'Nothing of the sort. I was teaching them accuracy of eye – essential to the man who means to pursue women as they ought to be pursued.'

'And how is that?'

'Single-mindedly.'

She ignored that. 'But what were you doing with the young men? You do not strike me as the bear-leading type.'

'Don't I? But that's what I was, all the same. Two of them were the sons of a friend of my father, whom my father obliged me to chaperon for a few months on their Grand Tour. Not as a job, you understand,' he added, 'but to teach me responsibility and steadiness; and to do the baron, their father, a favour, because Papa owed him one, and the fellow the baron had engaged had broken his leg. I suspect the boys broke it themselves to get away from him – he sounded both vulgar and dull, a lethal combination. And the other boys accumulated round me, for no better reason than because I was there. Like river flotsam catching against a tree root. Before I knew where I was, I was practically an usher.' He gave a delicate shudder.

'Didn't you like your work?'

'Oh, the boys were very good boys and admired me to an embarrassing degree, but it put an unhappy restraint on me – far worse than studying music. There was no going anywhere or doing anything with those innocent eyes fixed on me, like so many winsome puppies.'

Venetia laughed, though she feared she should not. 'I suspect you were not a very proper person to take charge of them.'

'Well, so I told Papa – and the baron – and anyone else who would listen,' he said, raising his eyebrows. 'It was a piece of folly from beginning to end. Much better to have left me in Heidelberg, and the boys in ignorance.'

'*Are* you musical?'

'Yes, very. But too lazy to make anything of it. I ought to have been a composer, but though my head is full of music, I can never be bothered with the fag of writing it down. All those lines to draw, page after page of orchestration – ugh! You can't think how wearisome.'

'If you are so very rich, you could hire someone to write it down for you, I imagine?'

'But I'd have to spend hours and hours mewed up with them, so it would have to be someone I liked enough. Where would I find such a person? You, perhaps – are you musical?'

'Not at all. I was taught as a child to play the piano, but I do it mechanically, not with any spirit or talent.'

'If you can play at all, you must have the ear for it. I expect you were just badly taught. So many people are put off music by an awkward tutor.'

'So if you are not writing music or chaperoning boys, what do you spend your time on in London?'

'Why, nothing at all. I told you I inherited my fortune when my father quit his lease, so I am an independent gentleman now. There's nothing takes up more hours of the day than being an independent gentleman, I can assure you.'

'Now *that* I can't understand,' Venetia said. 'I could never bear doing nothing all day long.'

He smiled at her in a very particular way that made her scalp tingle. 'There again, you see, you've been badly taught. From what I observe you have the native talent, plenty of it – all you need is a good tutor. Doing nothing is a complete delight, as long as one does it the right way, and in the right company.'

She couldn't look away from his eyes, which she discovered were the most wonderful green-gold colour – it would be insulting to call them hazel – like young beech leaves with the sun shining through them. They were brighter than any eyes had a right to be. 'Where,' she heard herself ask, 'would I find a tutor for such a subject?'

'I was rather hoping you would ask that,' he said. 'I think the best thing for such a promising student would be for me to undertake it myself. We should begin, I fancy, with music. It's a crime that you should not love it. You will come with me, if you please, to a concert tomorrow night. Hans Richter conducting Wagner at the Albert Hall. There, you can't say no to that!'

She licked her lips, which were unaccountably dry. 'You – you are making up a party?'

'No,' he said, smiling that particular smile again. 'It will be just you and me. I can't afford any distractions if I am to teach you properly.'

Properly? she thought. But it was most improper for a single woman to go to a concert alone with a man – indeed, to any public place.

'Perhaps,' she said faintly, 'if you were to ask Miss Ulverston—'

He shocked her by roaring with laughter. 'Not for anything in this world or the next! What do you take me for, Dr Fleet? I am proposing to spend an evening teaching you to swoon with rapture, not making teacup chit-chat with a duenna and a schoolroom miss! Come, now, you have already flouted every convention I suspect you were brought up with, just in becoming a doctor. What is one more – and such a minor one? We are two independent adults – may we not choose where and how we spend an evening?'

'I think you are hypnotising me,' she said, 'but yes, you are right. I choose for myself now.'

'And what do you choose for tomorrow?' he asked. 'Miss Ulverston or me? You can't have both.'

'I choose you,' she said.

He fell back in his chair with exaggerated relief. 'Thank God for that! I thought for a moment my skills were waning.'

It was the most perfect October day: a clear sky the colour of flax-flower, with just a few faint, misty veins of cloud high up; the sunshine warm, and the chestnuts just coming into their full gold-brown glory. It had been a clear night and there was a heavy dew on the grass that only just fell short of frost, but the sun was drying it up rapidly. The air was fresh with a smell of autumn about it, that blackberry tang of dead leaves and woodsmoke, which is half exciting, half melancholy.

George shed his dogs in the gentlemen's wing, paused to inspect his hair in the glass beside the door, and went in to breakfast. In the small dining-parlour the fire was blazing up, warning him that Alfreda was going to join him. It was too warm for him, but she felt the cold, and always sent ahead to have the fires roused when she went from one room to another. Breakfast was already laid out on the sideboard, and George, who had been out walking about with his dogs since before sunrise, helped himself lavishly to bacon, sausages, eggs and kidneys and hastened to secure five minutes with the paper before his beloved should arrive.

He had almost finished his first plateful when she appeared. He rose, wiping a trace of mustard from his moustache in case she required kissing, but she waved him back down and glided to the sideboard to serve herself with buttered eggs.

'Perfect day, my dear,' he commented. 'You and the ladies will enjoy your luncheon *al fresco*. The wind's all from the south today.'

'I will do my duty whichever quarter the wind is in,' she replied unanswerably. But indeed, she was rather looking forward to the shoot today. Sometimes joining the gentlemen out in the fields for luncheon was a trial, even with a canvas canopy, which she insisted on nowadays if it positively rained. She was as stoical as the next person, but once the damp got into her bones she would be stiff for days. Today, though, there was that soft, buttery warmth to the sunshine that made going out of doors a positive pleasure.

George got up to replenish his plate with pork pie, cold ham and pickles. 'We should show good sport today,' he said. 'And then – roast pheasant with juniper sauce! Partridge with gilded apples! Game pie! Oh, my!' His eyes gleamed at the thought. 'What a wonderful thing it is that a man can enjoy himself and fill his larder at the same time!'

'I wish you would not talk about filling your larder as though we were indigent!' Alfreda rebuked him.

George, who had not meant it that way, looked hurt. 'I only meant—'

'Well, don't! And pray don't speak in that manner before our guests. That is the way ridiculous rumours begin.'

'Our guests will have every Morland Place hospitality, as they always do,' George said. 'No-one has ever gone away believing he was stinted in anything. You wrong me, Mrs Morland. I merely expressed a pleasure in the seasonal nature of good eating.'

Alfreda did not answer. She ate very little herself these days, and what she did eat usually gave her indigestion. It was another unfair burden laid on her shoulders by a cruel and arbitrary God. Through her young womanhood, in what ought to have been the most carefree days of her life, she had suffered under the sting and humiliation of terrible poverty, passed from relative to relative, dependent for her every crust on charity – though until her father's reverses she had been Miss Turlingham of Turl Magna, only daughter of a proud line. At the point of her greatest desperation she had married George, demeaning herself to become the wife of a Yorkshire farmer, though the Morland family – and more importantly the Morland money – was old. With immense effort and perseverance she had trained and moulded George into a consort who, if not *quite* worthy of her, at least did not shame her in company. She had supervised the spending of his wealth so as to make him ever more respectable, and accepted in the highest circles.

She had given unstintingly of herself, had worked and laboured to raise Morland Place, had sacrificed her health to provide it with an heir. And then, just at the point when she ought to have been able to relax at last and enjoy the fruits of her efforts, it all seemed to be coming unravelled. Unpaid bills. Turning off servants. Hideous talk of retrenchment. Worry about the future, when the future ought to have been a glorious increment on the comfortable present. Being obliged to pay cash for things. Having tradesmen look askance at her. It wasn't to be borne! She had not deserved this, she who had given all her life. She was nearing forty, she couldn't, she simply *couldn't*, be poor again! The idea filled her with despair and panic. She hadn't the energy or the strength any more to struggle. And what of her little boy, whose inheritance she had fought so hard to preserve? Before he had even been born or thought of, she had ruthlessly rid Morland Place of all those who might take from him what should be his.

Where had the money gone? She didn't understand what had happened. How could they so suddenly be in danger? How could a great estate like this fail? She couldn't cope with the idea, or with the terrifying spectre of want. Her only recourse was to look away, to continue grimly to live as they had lived and do what they had always done, and hope that the threat would go away.

George had gone on talking, and she gathered his thread without really listening. He was talking about today's shooting party and the affairs of their guests, seeming quite unalarmed by any prospect of financial failure. It was to be a small party only, and of local people, who would arrive at eleven and spend the day: the Chubbs, the Coweys, two sons of Lord Grey, Lord and Lady Lambert and their son and two daughters. The gentlemen would go out shooting, the ladies would stay home and chat, and all would meet out of doors for luncheon. The gentlemen would shoot again in the afternoon, there would be dinner (sixteen at table – a small affair), and carriages would be called afterwards.

And the reason for the modesty of the arrangement now came into the dining-parlour, accompanied by a nurse-maid. 'Good morning, Mama, good morning, Papa,' said James, and only a slight tremor in his voice betrayed the excitement under his formal greeting.

'Good morning, James. You may kiss me,' Alfreda said.

He walked up to her rather stiffly, on his best behaviour, and she made pretence to inspect him a moment. How handsome he was! And how like her brother – her beloved, wicked, deeply missed late brother Kit, the last of the Turlinghams! Unable to help herself, she reached out a hand to touch his face, pushed an imaginary strand of hair from his brow. Bearing him had cost her dear, and she had suffered terrors that she might lose him, for he had been a frail and sickly baby; but now he had grown strong and straight, a handsome little boy, golden-haired and blue-eyed like her, well-formed and healthy. She inclined her cheek for his kiss. His breath, sweet and innocent as hay, brushed her skin. Overwhelmed by love she kissed him back; and when she had straightened, she smiled, and said, 'Happy birthday, darling.'

James's smile broke forth in response – crooked with the gaps and growths of ten, but brilliant and beguiling. He thought his mother as beautiful as an angel, and her stern remoteness did nothing to cool his adoration. Her smiles were the more precious for being so rare. His love for his big, jolly, outdoors, dog and horse-surrounded father was a simple and straightforward thing; loving his mother was more like religious worship.

'Yes, happy birthday, my boy,' George said now, breaking the spell. He held out his hand and James went to him and shook it. He raised his eyes to his father's in eager appeal. After all, a birthday had a certain significance, and a boy could hope. George beamed. 'Yes, you're right, I have something for you! Over there, under the side-table, there's a box. Bring it here, my boy.'

He watched the lad with pride as he ran eagerly across the room. He had had his fears, too, when James was born so pale and small, and they were only enhanced when the two attempts to give him a brother had failed. Now, given Alfreda's state, there could never be another child, and the Morland inheritance hung by this slender thread.

But James had confounded fears, and grown lusty – a perfectly normal, well-knit little boy, a good rider already, and promising to have a good way with dogs. Next year he would be going away to school – George had agreed with Alfreda that it was right and necessary, though it was his mind that agreed and not his heart – but all this winter, by way of compensation, James would be his. He would show him what it meant to be a gentleman, and more importantly a landed gentleman. James had had a tutor, and had been given the lessons a gentleman's son ought to have. He would have sufficient grounding to get by at school without being too often thrashed; and later, at Eton, he would learn how to behave in men's company, and make important friends. But the thing that really mattered, that deep love of the land which marked out the landed gentleman from the Town fribble, was in his blood, and would be brought out and cultivated at his father's side.

The box – long and narrow, of polished wood – was heavy, and James carried it over with an effort and deposited it at his father's feet, looking up at him with suppressed excitement. 'Open it,' George said. He exchanged a smiling glance down the table with Alfreda as James squatted down, undid the catches, and threw up the lid. In awed silence the boy gazed at the gun, gleaming barrel and glowingly polished stock, which nestled deep in the velvet lining, chestnut against purple.

'Oh, Father!' James breathed at last.

'Yes, it's for you,' George said. 'Take it out, try it for size. Yes, it's all right. It's not loaded.'

'That's right, James, you must always remember,' Alfreda said, 'never bring a loaded gun into the house.'

James took it out, held it, stroked it, feeling the lovely balance, admiring the rich patina of the polished stock, like the shine on a well-groomed horse. 'It's a beauty,' he murmured. 'Oh, Father, it's a breech-loader too!'

'The very latest thing,' George confirmed. 'With a choke bore. There'll be no excuses now! Anything you don't hit, it will be your own fault. You can't blame this little beauty.'

James lifted it to his shoulder, turned and levelled it at the sideboard, the door handle, the fireplace. 'Thank you,' he said, with simple profundity. He turned to his mother. 'Thank you, Mama.'

'The shoot today has been arranged in your honour,' she replied. 'You will go out with your father and his guests and shoot with them, just like a man. I hope you will behave yourself.'

The boy was so overcome he could only bow his head, pulling his upper lip down over his lower in exquisite delight and embarrassment.

'Do everything your father tells you,' Alfreda went on.

'And you can take Jupiter,' George added.

James lit like a candle. 'Oh, Papa, can I?' He had been given a pointer pup last Christmas, and had been working hard in every spare hour to train him.

'Yes, I think so. He's quite sensible now. It's time he was shown the guns; and if he seems to be getting too excited you can keep him on the leash.'

James caressed his gun's sleek barrel. 'I bet we get lots of birds,' he said happily. 'Mama, I saw Goole laying out the magazines in the library once, and there was a picture of some gentlemen with guns, and they had heaps and *heaps* of birds all round them, like great featherbeds!'

Alfreda had no chance to answer, for George interrupted sternly, 'Ah, that was a *battue*. That's not the way we do things here.'

'Isn't it?'

'No, my son. In a *battue*, the birds are beaten out of the

cover by servants and driven up to the guns. The shooters do nothing but stand still and fire. There no sport in that. It's a massacre, nothing more. At Morland Place we walk up the game with dogs in the old manner. That's the way a gentleman shoots.'

'I believe,' said Alfreda in her most distant voice, 'that *battue* shooting is becoming popular with some of our leading families. If James should ever be invited to Sandringham . . .'

George rarely contradicted his wife, but this was one occasion when he felt compelled to. 'My dear, if any of us is invited to Sandringham, we will, I hope, know what is proper in a guest and behave accordingly. But at Morland Place,' he said firmly, 'we walk up the game.'

The visitors were expected at eleven, and at a quarter to George went out to the courtyard to check that everything was in hand, the grooms prepared to deal with the horses and the servants who were to accompany them ready to go. While he was there Atterwith came out from under the barbican and said, 'Might I have a word with you, sir?'

George straightened from stroking a spaniel's ears and read his steward's face. 'Oh, not *now*, man!'

Atterwith was not deflected. 'I'm at my wit's end. After all I've said to you, and all you agreed, I now find . . .' He flourished a piece of paper, and George hastily grabbed his elbow and turned him aside so that the other servants should not hear.

'Now, mark me, I won't be harangued,' he said crossly. 'I have guests arriving at any minute.'

Atterwith shrugged himself free, but spoke in a lower voice. 'I have just been apprised, sir, of your latest venture. A letter from Laxton's Bank—'

'Oh, that's old stuff!' George said hastily.

'So I discover.' Atterwith's anger was clear in his voice. 'After you agreed in April to retrench in order to set your finances at rights, you went out in June and borrowed more money. A large sum, which you didn't tell me about, and on which you have somehow omitted to pay the interest. I should like to know,' he added with bitter irony, 'what you expect me to do about it!'

'Now, look here,' George said, trying to be reasonable. 'I had to raise a little sum. I'm having to pay cash for some things, and so is Mrs Morland – and I blame you for that entirely, Atterwith. Oh, yes! One way and another, your ideas about retrenchment have leaked out and people are getting the notion that we may not pay our bills. It's damned embarrassing! I met Laxton at the club and he offered in a friendly way to advance me something—'

'At a ridiculous rate of interest!'

'Well, you see what you've done, driving me into the arms of usurers! I must say I thought it a bit off of Laxton to take advantage of a fellow, but there, I had to settle some playing debts, and Mrs Morland had to have something to wear, so what was I to do?'

'You could have told me,' Atterwith said.

'I knew how you'd make a fuss – and I was right, wasn't I?'

'But how did you expect to pay the interest?' Atterwith asked, in wild frustration. 'You were only adding to your debts!'

'Ah, well, there, you see, I'm not as heedless as you seem to think me,' George said, with wounded pride. 'I was simply unlucky. I knew Flora had a litter coming, and her pups are worth their weight in gold. Selling them would have paid the interest for the first quarter – and I wasn't even going to keep one for myself, though it broke my heart to see them all go. But I had the money all right. Only then I had a stroke of bad luck at the August meeting, and debts of honour have to be paid first, you know. And the gunsmith would only take cash for James's birthday present. So I found myself unable to pay Laxton anything.'

Atterwith could not speak. He shook his head slowly from side to side like a goaded bull. At last he said, 'You do see, don't you, sir, how you have simply made matters worse? You have not decreased your former debt by a whit; and now you have another capital sum to repay, and as long as you don't repay it, more interest to add to your outgoings. You must retrench! This cannot go on or you will become bankrupt.'

George wanted to say, 'Oh, nonsense!' but something in his steward's lined face and pouched eyes gave him pause. 'I won't give up the hunt,' he said defensively.

'Then at least cut back to three days a week. And raise a subscription.'

'It ain't gentlemanly to ask for subscriptions,' George objected.

'Is it gentlemanly to be bankrupted and have everything sold out from under you?' George didn't answer that. 'Hunt three days only. Raise a subscription. Reduce the pack. Sell half your hunters. If you do that, I may be able to keep you afloat. If you refuse,' he went on, preventing George from answering, 'I shall be forced to give you my notice.'

All the harvests were in, and the stubble stood crisp and yellow over the plough; the thick, well-kept hedges were still in leaf, and full of autumn berries and teeming insect life. It was the time of year when birds were eating hard to fatten themselves against the winter. Pheasants and partridges were plump and delicious, and even rabbits were worth potting if they happened to break nearby. Not hares, though: no-one had ever killed a hare on Morland Place land. The tenant farmers complained bitterly that they damaged the crops, but it was an inflexible rule dating back hundreds of years.

The gentlemen walked out with their dogs – spaniels to work the hedges and pointers to work the stubble – and the servants to carry their guns and the bags. James insisted on carrying his birthday present himself, and the gentlemen smiled indulgently, remembering their own first gun and how hard it was to part with it. 'I believe I even took mine to bed for a week,' Lord

Lambert murmured. James walked beside his father, holding himself very upright, as though he were so full of happiness and pride he was afraid he might break. His pointer Jupiter frisked about him and tried to get the other dogs to play until, aware that they were letting the side down, James issued a stern rebuke, which was only spoiled by his voice acquiring an unexpected squeak at the end.

'Nice youngster,' Mr Cowey said, to cover the boy's embarrassment. He called Jupiter to him, seized his head and examined his teeth and eyes. Jupiter, incorrigibly good-natured, swung his tail as he submitted.

'Comes from good stock,' George said. 'You remember my bitch Biddy? She was his grand-dam.'

'By Jove, yes! I had a pup of hers once. You stung me pretty hard for him, too, Morland, as I remember!' said Mr Chubb.

'Good blood costs good money,' said George complacently; and then the mention of money reminded him of the unpleasant interview with Atterwith. Damn the man! Cut back the hunt? It was blackmail, plain and simple! But he had laboured to put it out of his head so as not to spoil the day, and he would not let it return to haunt him now. 'Still,' he added, 'it's all in the working, you know. All in the working.' He smiled down at his son. 'You've the knack of it, my boy. You'll be a good man with dogs. Firm, but kind.'

To raise an unpleasant subject like that when he was expecting guests at any minute! And on James's birthday, too! No matter how he tried to forget it, it had taken some of the shine off the day. Damn Atterwith to perdition! He'd a good mind to let the man give his notice. Morland Place could do without him. He took too much on himself.

But the shooting was good, and gradually George relaxed and began to enjoy himself. He tutored James in loading and aiming his new gun, criticised his shots, praised his better ones. Jupiter, while keen and not at all gun-shy, was still rather too excited by the sudden increase in company and activity, and after the first half-hour George ordered him leashed so as not to put up the birds too soon.

The morning broadened and soon half George's attention was on listening out for the arrival of the luncheon wagon and the carriages of the ladies. They had worked their way out past the Ten Thorns and Knapton to the pasture towards Harewood Whin, when they finally saw the procession of vehicles coming up the track which led from the Wetherby Road towards Huntsham Farm.

'Ah, there's luncheon, gentlemen,' George said. 'Just time to flush this last hedge, I think, before they get here.' He put his spaniel, Flossie, in, and the gentlemen loaded and cocked their guns.

'Nothing but rabbits in it, I wager you,' Mr Cowey said. 'Looks like typical rabbit country to me.'

'Ah've seen partridge in there this last week, sir,' volunteered one of the Huntsham men, who had come down to watch.

'Well, it takes a good eye to get a rabbit,' Lord Lambert said slyly, 'especially when it bolts out of a hedge. Perhaps you're too old, Cowey. It's a young man's sport, really.'

'Shooting game is sport,' Cowey said, with dignity. 'Don't denigrate the term, my friend.'

'Definitely too old,' Lambert said, winking at the elder Mr Grey. 'What say, Robert?'

'I can see Mama!' James exclaimed eagerly: he had been watching the carriages. He raised one arm and waved vigorously, as children down the ages have waved at carriages, and trains, and boats. George looked too, and wondered suddenly if Atterwith had spoken to her this morning. Damn the man! Trying to spoil their day.

A blackbird, disturbed by the approaching dog at the hedge-foot, shot out on the farther side with its loud chip-chip-chip of an alarm call. At the same instant a rabbit bolted out of the near side.

'There he goes!' cried the younger Mr Grey, swinging up his gun.

'Mine, I think!' Lambert called, laughingly.

Jupiter, whose leash had grown slack in James's hand as the boy's attention was on the carriages, snapped into action. He was bored with merely watching, and a rabbit practically under his nose was too much for a young dog to ignore. He shot after the rabbit; the guns were already up and swinging round, following the bobbing grey shape. 'No!' cried James, as the leather whipped out of his hand, and flung himself after his dog.

George felt some sound rip out from his throat, heard someone else shout something, and at the same instant – or perhaps it was even before, as it seemed to him afterwards – several guns spoke. The rabbit jinked and the dog jinked with it, and James threw himself, arms outstretched, full length on the ground, as if trying to catch the dog in the way one catches a pig in an alley.

But the boy didn't get up. In the moment of silence that followed the guns' percussion, George heard birdsong – robin and chaffinch, the sweet shrilling of a wren, and far off a distant blurred chorus of rooks in the misty elms: the day going on just as if nothing had happened. But a red flower was unfurling itself in James's pale silk hair. There was a splurge of voices behind him, protests of disbelief and shock; Flossie, pressing against him, whined anxiously; and then somehow his legs were carrying him to that crumpled figure in the rough autumn grass.

'James,' he said. 'James.' His voice sounded dreadful, not like his at all. He knelt, touched the boy's shoulder, lifted him a little, and he was horribly limp, limp as no living thing is. George had been handling dead birds all day: he knew that feeling. But this was James: it couldn't be! He didn't want to look at the damaged head, the spoiled hair. He looked instead at the distant trees of Harewood Whin; at Jupiter trotting back, leash trailing, tail swinging uncertainly. He looked up, and saw the shocked faces of the men, staring at him. Don't, he wanted to say, but he couldn't speak now.

A faint cry drew his attention the other way. The carriages had stopped, and someone was coming across the pasture towards them, and it was that which finally pierced George's brain and made him understand fully, because it was Alfreda, and she was *running*. And still the birds were singing: only minutes had passed since he was a father.

CHAPTER SIXTEEN

In December 1881 *The Times* reported that 'the most distinguished audience ever seen in a theatre' had attended the opening night of Goldsmith's play *She Stoops to Conquer*. The particular attraction of that particular performance was that the leading role was being played by Lillie Langtry, the most beautiful woman of the age and the acknowledged mistress of the Prince of Wales.

London had just about managed to get used to the idea of the Prince having a mistress and not trying to conceal the fact – a grudging acceptance only possible because the Princess of Wales obviously knew about her, and gallantly and graciously invited her to parties at Marlborough House. If the Princess tolerated the situation, Society more or less had to follow suit, but it didn't have to like it. Mrs Langtry was the most talked-about woman in London. Her looks – that pale skin, the hour-glass figure – were admired even by her detractors; her vivacity praised with faint damns; her charm acknowledged with shakings of heads; her ambition mentioned with condemnation. She had not only lured the Prince into her bed and kept him there for four years, and charmed the Princess into tacitly accepting the situation but she had recently even beguiled the Prime Minister, the crusty and misogynistic Mr Gladstone. He was now said to be monstrously smitten, was seen at parties deep in conversation with her, and had even sent her presents of books.

All that, London had grown tolerably used to; but for her to act in a play was beyond the bounds! No decent female would dream of becoming an actress, or receive one into her house; for a woman to act on a public stage was to step into deepest degradation. Many still believed that women should not take part even in private theatricals, despite their growing popularity; there were great houses where the mere suggestion of charades would be met with a sharply indrawn breath. Yet here was Mrs Langtry acting in a play in a London theatre as if it were the most normal thing in the world, and the Prince of Wales ensuring that all his influential friends attended the performance!

Venetia was there that night, for Ivo Jennings vowed he wouldn't miss it for worlds and managed to acquire two tickets, though fairly humble ones at the back of the dress circle. Venetia was doubtful at first about attending, but her curiosity overcame her scruples – and Jennings assured her, with a sidelong grin, that no-one would be looking at *her* that night! She enjoyed the play, and thought that Lillie Langtry looked very beautiful on the stage and acted very well, as far as she could tell from her limited experience; but perhaps even more interesting to her was to catch the first glimpse in years of her relations.

There was Lady Augusta Vibart in one of the expensive boxes, her celebrated red hair elaborately dressed with flowers and feathers, diamonds at her throat, her white arms resting on the red velvet as she laughed down at admirers in the pit. She seemed to be laughing a great deal (her vivacity was often mentioned in the popular papers), but 'Johnny' Vibart was not much in evidence, and the seat next to her experienced quite a traffic in the raffish and handsome gentlemen of the Prince's circle. If one man occupied her attention for longer than another, it was Sir George Chetwynd. Ivo told Venetia who he was: a wealthy baronet, very prominent in the racing set, but best known for his philandering ways. There was also a good deal of movement between boxes, and much of the time Venetia's views were of the back of Gussie's head as she leaned over to talk to the Prince in his box next door, or engaged in conversation with Carrington or Knollys or McDuff as they lounged gracefully on the back of her chair.

Venetia saw Harry, looking handsome in evening dress, but rather pale – though that may have been the gas light – at the back of one box after another, talking to the Prince and various friends, leaning over to say something to Gussie, standing by the curtains smoking a cigar with Vibart and, in the interval, walking in the promenade with a dark-haired young woman on his arm. But he did not sit and watch the play, hardly stayed in one place more than a few minutes at a time, and was as often out of sight as in it, coming and going on the edge of things like a restless ghost.

When they were returning to their seats after the second interval, Venetia saw Harry with the dark-haired woman at a distance, standing together in the loge drinking champagne. The duke was smiling indulgently, one hand behind his back under his tails in a gesture she recognised, poignantly, as her father's. The woman was evidently being very vivacious, with much display of teeth and tossing of her glossy dark head; and as she tilted her head back to laugh, she revealed a fabulous necklace of rubies and diamonds round her white throat.

Venetia felt a little faint, and pinched Ivo's arm to ask who she was.

'I don't know,' he said, 'but she's got a fortune round her neck. Why do you ask?'

Venetia didn't answer, only shook her head slightly. She had recognised the fortune in question. Jennings looked at her and she forced herself to smile and speak lightly about an unconnected subject. She had never told him her real name or anything about her family or background, so she could not voice her real concern.

Whether by the Prince's influence or not, Mrs Langtry's career as an actress was successfully launched, and she appeared in another play in April 1882, which was equally well received.

It was in April that Venetia received a visit from her

brother Marcus, and the subject of Mrs Langtry's theatrical career came up in conversation.

'Don't know if she's any good at it,' he said. 'I suppose if you say so she is. But the fact is her star's on the wane and she's got debts to pay. HRH is tired of her, though he's too much of a gentleman to let it be seen publicly, but he won't pay them for her, and the wolves are gathering round her. There are disgusting stories circulating . . .' He paused a moment, his eyes stationary as he considered them. 'Well, they ain't for your ears,' he concluded. 'But whether they're true or not, the fact that they're being circulated means she's out of favour. She'd better make what she can out of acting, before her reputation makes her untouchable.'

'Dear me,' Venetia said, 'and that's the sort of company Gussie and Harry are keeping! I saw them at the theatre when she made her début. Gussie seemed very sprightly, though she didn't seem to talk to her husband much.'

Marcus gave a just perceptible sigh. 'The word is that the Prince is interested in her, so he's stepping back. He's got an actress of his own, as it happens, so he doesn't mind.'

'Gussie seemed to be talking to another man quite a lot – Sir George Chetwynd?'

'Oh, yes. He's after her too, and she's playing him off to bring the Prince to the point. I know it was foolish to think I could make any difference, but I felt forced to remonstrate with her about Chetwynd. He's not the sort of man a fellow wants his sister associated with – not at all the thing! She thinks she's got him on a leash, but I warned her he's more dangerous than she realises. Whatever her airs, I don't believe she's up to snuff, and even being Harry's sister and the Prince's new pet, she's not untouchable. But Vibart and Chetwynd are old pals, and Gussie believes "Johnny" will see Chetwynd toes the line. Fact is, they both want her to take Langtry's place, so that they can use her influence with the Prince for their own benefit.'

'Oh, Marcus,' Venetia exclaimed. 'What would Papa

300

think if he saw how she'd turned out? I suppose it's no use expecting Harry to intervene?'

'None,' said Marcus shortly.

A week before, their mother had summoned Marcus down to Ravendene in order to ask him to speak to Harry and persuade him to leave off his wild life, at least for long enough to marry and beget an heir.

'Otherwise,' Charlotte had said anxiously, 'the title will die out. I know *you* don't intend to get married.'

'Couldn't afford it, even if I wanted to,' Marcus had said. 'And I don't want to. I like my life as it is.'

'I sometimes think,' his mother had added rather pathetically, 'that it might not only be the title – the *line* might die out. Olivia doesn't seem to be going to produce, and my poor Venetia will probably never marry now, so unless Gussie and Vibart have a baby, the stream will run into the sand. Who would have thought I could have five children all grow to adulthood and still not have a single grandchild?'

So Marcus had undertaken to go and see his brother, though it was out of pity for his mother rather than because he thought he might have any effect. Charlotte didn't know, and Marcus didn't tell her, that if Augusta had a child it was unlikely to be Vibart's – there was enough salacious gossip around for him to be aware that Vibart had other interests entirely and was perfectly happy for his marriage to be a nominal one. The most likely outcome at the moment seemed to be that if Augusta produced an offspring it would be half royal – and then, of course, it would have to be smuggled away and would never be acknowledged.

So he went to Southport House and was admitted, and after a considerable wait was escorted up to his brother's private suite. In Harry's sitting-room he accepted the glass of sherry offered by his manservant, lit one of his own cigars, and after a moment the door to the bedchamber opened and Harry came out, wearing a dressing gown of gold-coloured silk figured with scarlet,

301

Turkish slippers on his feet, and his hair still tousled from sleep.

'This is a filthy hour to disturb a fellow,' Harry grumbled. 'I suppose *you* were up at dawn on some parade or other.'

'Not quite,' Marcus said.

'God, you look damnably spruce and sprightly! It's not good manners to come before a fellow gleaming with health – not at this hour of the morning.' Harry flung himself down on a sofa and extended a stringy hand. 'Give me one of those cigarettes – box on the table there. Can't function without a ciggie.'

Marcus obliged, helped his brother light it, and said, 'You looked in damned bad shape.'

Harry raised his drooping eyelids at his brother. 'If I was one of your horses, you'd shoot me, eh?' he said cynically.

'What the deuce have you been doing to yourself?' Marcus asked.

'Oh, I think you know the answer to that,' Harry said. Marcus didn't deny it. Harry was pale, underweight, and his hands shook. His cheeks were hollow, his eyes red-rimmed and watery. His nose was red too, and he sniffed and wiped it constantly. Marcus was a simple fellow, and a soldier, but it didn't mean he didn't know what the more louche and raffish part of Society got up to.

'You're a damned fool,' Marcus said abruptly. 'That stuff is no good for you, and you know it. Why don't you give it up?'

'If you'd ever tried it, you wouldn't ask such a damn fool question.' Harry drew deeply on his Turkish cigarette and blew the scented smoke upwards. 'What d'you want, anyway? If you've just come to harangue me you might as well give it up now.'

'Mama asked me to come and see you,' Marcus said. 'She wants to know when you're going to get married and produce an heir.' Harry began to laugh weakly. 'I'm glad you think it's funny. You know perfectly well that I can't afford to marry – and I'm damned sure I don't want to

302

inherit the title if you kill yourself with your idiotic way of life.'

'*When* I kill myself, you would rather say – I can see it in your eyes. Well, I haven't got on to opium yet, but I dare say that may be down the line. What can one do, when life is so deuced flat? And I know too many women – and too much about them – to want to marry any of them, thank you.'

'You've been seen with Harriet Dacres,' Marcus said. 'Perhaps if you didn't waste your manhood on actresses, you'd have the inclination to marry decently.'

Harry only laughed louder. 'Dear boy, if you could hear yourself! Wasting my manhood, indeed! Little Harriet gives me pleasure, and charges very little. It would cost me a very large settlement to marry some frozen-faced daughter of an earl, and I don't suppose she would give me any pleasure at all. Quite the contrary. Besides' – he blew his nose again – 'this stuff doesn't conduce to very much activity of that sort, even with Harrikins. Increases the desire but seriously impedes the performance, if you know what I mean.'

'All the more reason—'

'Oh, she's very understanding,' Harry assured him. 'Knows there are times when I want to be with her just for the pleasure of contemplating her smooth cheek. Your pleasure, of course, comes from the contemplation of the smooth cheeks of your horses.' He grinned suddenly at his brother. 'Or is it the smooth cheeks of your young soldiers, these days?'

Marcus coloured angrily. 'How dare you?'

'I've never been sure,' Harry went on, unconcerned. 'You've always been such a close hand, there's no fathoming you.'

'I can see I'm wasting my time here,' Marcus said, gathering his dignity. He rose to leave, but before he reached the door, Harry called him in a different voice.

'Don't go! Please, I'm sorry. I feel so devilish rotten in the mornings it makes me bad-tempered.' Marcus turned and looked at him warily. 'I didn't mean it. I'm sorry.'

Marcus paused. He had loved his twin in childhood, and they had been inseparable. It hurt him terribly to see him suffering now. Though they had grown apart and lived entirely separate lives, Harry was a part of him still. 'I can't bear to see you like this,' he said, more gently. 'Can't you take yourself in hand?'

'It's too late now,' Harry said. 'There's nothing to be done. I'm damned, Marcus. Lost and damned.'

'Don't talk rot,' Marcus said. 'You're not thirty yet.'

'I'm a great deal older than thirty, in everything that counts. I've eaten the apple from the forbidden tree, and there's no going back now. You can't *un*know what you know.'

'You're just being silly,' Marcus said gruffly. 'Talking in that damned theatrical way because you mix too much with actresses. All you need to do is to pull yourself together.'

Harry stared at him a long moment, and Marcus knew he hadn't reached him at all. And yet there was a great sadness in Harry's eyes as he stood up and said, in a light, bantering tone, 'Now I've been lectured enough. The novelty wears off, you know. I think I shall go back to bed and seek the solace of a little blow. See yourself out, will you?'

Marcus thought of all this as he answered, 'None,' to Venetia's question.

'I saw him with a pretty dark-haired girl at the theatre. I suppose she wasn't anyone we should be glad about?'

'She's an actress,' Marcus said shortly.

'Ah! I thought she might be. But, Marcus, she was wearing the family rubies! I recognised them.'

'I believe they were only lent for the evening. I've never heard that he showers her with gifts. I suppose we should be grateful she isn't more rapacious,' Marcus said, as though it were not much satisfaction.

'Perhaps. But it was a shock to see her in something I've seen round Mama's neck so often.'

Marcus was silent a moment, and then said, 'Still, we can be glad that Olivia's happy.'

'Yes, I had a letter from her at Christmas,' said Venetia. 'Very little about her, of course: it was all about the Queen and the Royal Family – pages about how Prince Leopold is going to get married. She says his fiancée, Princess Helen, is really nice and sensible and, for a wonder, the Queen approves of her – because usually she hates anyone who marries her children. You've seen her, Marcus: is she really happy?'

Marcus frowned in thought. 'Well, she worries a good deal about his health, of course, and it's not to be expected that she'll like losing her private secretary . . .'

A slow smile spread over Venetia's face. 'Not the *Queen*, silly, I mean Olivia!'

'Oh! Well, yes, I think she is. Du Cane is a very decent chap and devoted to her, and she seems to love him just as much.'

'Good! And it's as well, really, that she's away from all this, at Court, where she'll be protected. It would hurt her terribly to see how Harry and Gussie carry on.'

'And what about you?' Marcus asked.

She looked at him cautiously. Had he heard? Surely not? '*What* about me?'

'Are you happy? Do you still like being a doctor? Was it worth it?'

She smiled. 'Yes, I like being a doctor. And yes, it was worth it. Whatever else happens in my life, or doesn't happen, that is a constant. It's unendingly fascinating and worth while.'

'Hmm,' said Marcus. 'Well, I suppose the two of us are being useful at least, you a doctor and me a soldier. Balancing the books a bit. I've probably not said this before, but I believe you were right to stick to your guns. I did think being a doctor was a bit indecent for a girl, but you've made a go of it, and I'm proud of you.'

'Thank you,' Venetia said, touched. 'I'm proud of you, too.'

He coloured a little, and cleared his throat with a

soldier's embarrassment at such emotional display. 'And I'm glad to know you're settled in your life,' he went on. 'Thing is, I may be going abroad soon. This Egyptian business starts to look serious. We might have to send troops, and then, well, I'd be glad to be able to leave you with a clear conscience.'

Venetia laid a hand on his arm and leaned over to kiss his cheek. 'Bless you, Marcus. It's nice to know someone cares about me.'

Venetia had held out against Ivo almost the whole of that first summer after she met him in Welbeck Street. She had gone with him to concerts, to the opera, twice to a play; to an open-air band concert in the Park (bringing back memories of the time she had seen Beauty there), to a regatta on the Serpentine, to a military review at Wimbledon (which had made him laugh very much – he had a reprehensible attitude towards old-fashioned entertainments). Once they had driven out to Hampstead Heath for a picnic and once they had gone riding in Richmond Park, on hired hacks (oh, for the horses of her privileged upbringing!).

Finally, on Bank Holiday, he had taken her for a trip on a steam launch to Hampton Court, all among the cheerful lower classes out on the spree with their wives and children, sandwiches and cold tea, bottled beer and lemonade. She suspected he had meant it as a joke, but the joke had been on him, for she had enjoyed every minute. It was relaxing to be among people who would not know or judge her. She had made him go round the rooms like any shilling tourist, and had insisted they try the maze, where they got lost along with everyone else. Finding themselves at last in the centre, they were taken under the wing of a stout couple with four children who, while waiting for rescue, had stoically unpacked an ample picnic from a large basket and insisted on Venetia and Ivo sharing it.

It was after that outing, back at the pier at Westminster as he was helping her into a cab, that he hesitated a moment and said, 'Will you come to my house? I should like to play to you; and you, as I have remarked, have no instrument.' She looked at him doubtfully, and he said, 'We have been lost in the Hampton Court maze together – reputation can face no sterner challenge! Come, what do you fear? My servants will bring us supper while I play and you listen. I'd take you to a restaurant but I know that would be too high a hurdle for you at present.'

She felt herself blush, and was angry with herself for reacting to the mere mention of a restaurant, as if she were seventeen. His expression was perfectly grave, but there was a mocking smile in his eyes, and she felt it would be too ridiculous to scruple over something so ordinary. So she said yes, and though he only nodded and said, 'Good,' in an ordinary voice, and gave the address to the cabbie, she felt her heart beating fast as he climbed in beside her.

He had a house in Eaton Place, in what was these days called Belgravia. It surprised her a little – and worried her. Whereas St James's at this time of year was deserted, with all the great people down in the country, Belgravia people lived in London all year round.

'You don't go out of Town?' she had asked Ivo some weeks earlier, and he had said, 'No, I like London when everyone else is away. I like the illusion that it's all mine.'

Belgravia also was not the sort of place one expected a bachelor to live, and the house he took her to was not a bachelor's house. Now, as she climbed out of the cab and trod warily up the steps to the door, she supposed that this must be Mr Jennings's family home, which meant he must be very much richer than she had suspected. The sight of the elderly manservant who opened the door confirmed it. A servant who has been trained in a great house has something about him that the experienced eye can detect; and by the same token, she was rather afraid Gethers might recognise her for what she was. His face, however, was a perfectly well-governed blank as he bowed and stepped back for her.

'Gethers, Dr Fleet and I will have supper in the white drawing-room as soon as it is ready.'

'Very good, sir.'

He went away, and Ivo led her up the stairs, saying, 'Excellent man, that. One of the best things my father left me.'

'This was your father's house?' Venetia asked.

'His Town house. He had a place in Berkshire, too. I never go down there. I'm not a country man. I ought to sell it, really.' He saw her raised eyebrow and said, 'Oh, I've no sentimental attachment to it. It's not the ancestral seat: Father bought it about twenty years ago. He fancied becoming a squire, but that's not my idea of pleasure.'

'Your father lived in greater style than I had imagined,' Venetia said, trying not to sound surprised, but he divined her, and grinned.

'Oh, the old man was as rich as Croesus, and consequently I am, too. How unworldly of you not to guess!'

It came to her suddenly then. 'You're Jennings' Bank!' He bowed assent. 'Not unworldly – stupid! But surely – you said you were an idle man-about-Town?'

'My dear madam, I don't *go* to the bank, except to draw money. I dare say my father would have *liked* me to like the world of finance more, but he wisely realised nothing would have been more fatal to his fortune than to force me to follow his footsteps. I'd have bankrupted him in a fortnight. So he sighed and left me alone, and I remained comfortable and he remained rich.' He looked at her quizzically as he showed her into a room on the first floor. 'Does it make a difference? Are you less uneasy at being here alone with me, now that you know I am a very large and respectable private bank?'

She couldn't think of an answer to that, and said only, 'Don't be silly.' And then, glad to be distracted, 'What a lovely room!'

It was a panelled drawing-room with a pretty bay window onto the street. The panelling was painted white, and the furniture was French Empire, the settles and chairs upholstered in gold and white brocade; the carpet was a thick Chinese, white patterned with rose and green. There were some pretty pieces of porcelain and white biscuit here and there, a few gilt-framed glasses, and the pictures were Arcadian pastoral scenes, which at a quick glance looked like Watteaus and Bouchers.

'It was my mother's favourite room – her taste, I imagine,' Ivo said, looking round indifferently. 'A little too sugar-rose for me, but it is pretty, I grant you. And that was her instrument – the best thing *she* left me.'

It was a very large grand, and its gleaming dark brown wood looked too heavy and masculine in the light, dainty surroundings. It stood in the bay. At the other end of the room were double doors, folded back, beyond which was a second room, unlit, in darkness.

'Now, sit,' he said briskly, 'and I will play you something before supper – and a great deal more after it. Sit there, where I can see your face.'

He sat himself at the piano, opened it, and began playing, a stormy, energetic piece full of pedal and flourish. It was quite short. At the end of it he said, 'Chopin. Or is that too emotional for you? Perhaps you prefer . . .' And he went straight into another piece, more lyrical and symmetrical.

She recognised it. 'Schubert,' she said, when he finished.

'Quite so. Too sentimental, perhaps? Between the two we find Schumann – the unsung genius – no, perhaps I will save Schumann for later. I might need him. For now, to last us until supper, we will have Beethoven. For a Bank Holiday, I think the *Bagatelles* would be suitable, don't you?'

He played. Venetia had been thoroughly taught, though she had no natural talent, and she knew enough to know he was good. She could distinguish between an amateur and a professional performance, and his was professional; but whether he was better than any other professional she couldn't judge. It sounded miraculous to her, and she was carried away on a flood of pure sound. While he played there was movement in the next room as Gethers (and only him, as far as she could tell) entered from the far end, lit the candles, and began quietly laying a small

309

table for supper. She was aware of this, saw it out of the corner of her eye, though it did not disturb her. She watched Ivo's face and his hands and listened to the marvellously intricate and yet transparent music, and felt her body relaxing and her mind expanding.

He stopped at last and said, 'Supper's ready. Shall we?'

She had forgotten Gethers by then, and when she looked round, saw that everything was ready for them in the other room, and that the servant had gone. She walked before Ivo to the table and he seated her; his place was laid cater-cornered to her, and he said, 'It is easier this way for me to serve you. Gethers has gone to bed. We are quite private now.'

'Is he your only servant?' she asked, and he gave her that mocking smile.

'An indiscreet question, madam, if ever I heard one! Suffice it to say we shall not be disturbed. I thought you would prefer that – and I prefer to know that your listening will not be interrupted.'

Now she was thoroughly confused. She did not know what he intended towards her or what her reaction should be. He had invited her to hear him play, and the sight of the manservant had reassured her. But he had not had to order the supper, which argued a predisposition; and the candles in the white drawing-room had been lit ready for them. And had not Gethers's performance been as practised as his master's? Had Ivo brought women here before, or had he instructed the butler this morning what to expect? Whichever it was, she felt she was being manipulated.

And yet now he was talking about music again, and was helping her to supper and pouring her wine with no more archness than if she were his sister, or these the tea-rooms at Bath. What could she do but go along with him? His smooth confidence was very comfortable, like a sofa into whose embrace one could relax. She had come here of her own free will after all; and he *was* a marvellous musician; and she was hungry.

310

While they ate, they chatted; they had been friends for long enough now for the conversation to flow. When she said that she had had enough, he poured two more glasses of wine, carried them back to the other room, sat her again with her glass to hand, and said, 'Now you shall have Schumann – quite my favourite composer. The wine will complement him perfectly.'

He played. She found she had to concentrate, really to listen, for it was neither simple nor symmetrical; but it was the more satisfying for that, she thought – like Ivo's face. The regular features of a Greek god might attract to begin with but one would soon tire of them. The very irregularities of Ivo's face one could go on looking at and looking at, always finding a new plane, and new angle of light, a new conjunction to intrigue and delight.

He came to the end of the piece; without looking at her, he drained his glass and sat a moment flexing his fingers, one hand against the other. Then he stood and came across the room to her. Her heart began to beat rapidly, with that familiar hard, tight feeling in her chest. He held out his hands and she stood up and gave him hers, facing him at arm's length.

'Do you like Schumann?' he asked.

'Very much.' It was not enough, so she said, 'Better than Schubert.'

'Good! You have taste. Tomorrow, you shall have some Brahms.' He paused, looking her over consideringly. 'I think you may be ready for it now. What do you think?'

Did he mean Brahms? His shining, mocking eyes invited her to trap herself; her breath was tugging as if she had been running. She struggled to find a neutral answer. 'I don't know,' she said. 'How can I tell if I am?'

He drew her by her hands so that she was as close to him as she could be without their bodies touching. '*Don't* you know?' he said. 'Why, Venetia Fleet, you're vibrating like an A-string.' He let go her hands and put his arms round her, drawing her the last fraction to him, so that her body was against his all its length. 'Do you want me? I think you do. But you must tell me so. Say it, then, say you

311

want me.' He kissed her, very lightly, on the lips. 'Oh, Venetia,' he said, almost reproachfully, as if half jokingly rebuking a child, 'how you do betray yourself! The truth now! Tell me.'

'I can't,' she whispered.

'I think you can.' He extended his tongue, elegantly, and with the tip traced the shape of her upper lip. The shock of the sudden intimacy was so great she thought she would faint. She could feel the exotic hardness of his male body; his warmth, like the radiation from a stove; the splay of his hard hands against her back. Every fibre of her, every drop of blood, every nerve ending wanted him, wanted him so much that the hard knot of passion in her stomach made her feel almost sick.

He took pity on her, and his smile was kind now. 'In French then,' he said gently. 'That will do.'

'*Je te veux*,' she said, and there was such release in it, she said again, fiercely. '*Je te veux!*'

'Then thou shalt have me,' he said, and kissed her fully.

She yielded then. Her hands went up around his neck, her head tilted back like a hungry bird wanting to be fed, and the quality of her response made him catch fire. They were kissing, then, like lovers, with the abandon of long-restrained desire let loose suddenly and at last. When he paused to draw breath, he seemed a little dazed, and for a moment put his hand up to cup her face, stroke her cheek, gazing into her eyes from only an inch or two away.

'*Tu m'énivres!*' he whispered, and she felt her stomach clench with desire – something so deep and primitive it half frightened, half elated her. But she knew this feeling would have its way, and it seemed as if she had come deliberately to this point, that she had selected and rejected and turned and moved in all she did according to some unseen and elegantly elaborate pattern which had always to deliver her to this moment.

So when he released her, took her hand, and led her to the door, she went with him without struggle, embracing her fate with a look of fierce joy, like a Byzantine martyr.

★   ★   ★

'Well,' said Ivo Jennings, leaning up on his elbow. 'Well.'

Venetia, lying in the spread pool of her hair in his unfamiliar bed, gazed up at him with a bruised look. She had known all about the physical act in theory, and had long known that it would be something that mattered to her; but nothing could have prepared for the emotional turmoil it caused in the breast even of a woman of science.

He drew a wayward strand gently aside from her lips and kissed them, and then stroked the trace of moisture from beneath her eye. 'Tears, or sweat? I hope not tears.' He drew a shaky breath. 'You didn't say, my love, that you were a virgin.'

'Did I need to?' she asked, and for the life of him, he didn't know what she meant by that.

'We are on rather perilous ground here. My God, I feel as if I'd stepped into a familiar room and gone through the floor into a volcano. You have taken my breath away, Dr Fleet.'

She heard his voice change through that sentence, from the shaken sound of the beginning to the familiar teasing note of the end. He was drawing back behind his safe barriers, she thought. She must do the same. She was too exposed to him as she was: the wrong words might hurt her.

'Well,' she said, as lightly as she could, 'you were my first lover. What then?'

'What then, she says! It was a momentous occasion, and ought to be recognised as such. If I had known, I would have ordered champagne.' He laid his fingers against her cheek. 'No regrets?' he asked tenderly.

She turned her lips to kiss his hand. 'No,' she said. 'Why should there be? It was – wonderful.' She needed to ask something, but wasn't sure how to. 'Was it – I mean, I know it wasn't your first time . . .'

'My first time with you. And first times are always special.' She wanted more than that. Her eyes were unwavering. He said seriously, 'You have amazed, and dazzled, and astonished me. I have never known anything like it, or anyone like you.' And then the teasing look came back. 'If I had known how wonderful it would be, do you think I'd have waited all summer while you made up your mind?'

It was then that Venetia realised that if she was to survive this experience at all, she was going to have to learn to laugh at moments like this. So she smiled and said, 'There, and all this time I thought I was waiting for you to make up yours!'

By the time of Marcus's visit in April 1882, the affair had settled, as all human interaction will tend to, into something of a routine, though they did not meet often enough for the excitement or pleasure to fade – certainly not for Venetia. The demands of her career were such that they could not often have time together, and she was deeply grateful that he never suggested that she should give it up, or even complained about the long hours she worked. The fact of the matter was that as a new and female practitioner, she did not dare turn away a paying customer; and her work with the patients in the dispensary gave her the experience essential to give them confidence in her. She tried to keep one evening a week free, on which she and Ivo would go to a concert or some other public entertainment, and if that were impossible she would try to see him on a Saturday or Sunday afternoon; but even if they did meet, it was not always possible to make love, which meant that their desire always outstripped opportunity. They could only do it at his house: she did not dare take him to her own bed, for fear of the servants talking; she hardly dared have him enter her house when she was alone, even in daylight, in case gossip started. And when visiting his house, it must always be late at night, for she never forgot there were plenty of people in the neighbourhood who might recognise her.

So when they did finally find themselves in bed together, they caught fire from each other, and each time was a miracle to Venetia. To abandon oneself utterly, after a lifetime of self-discipline and struggle, was the deepest pleasure she could imagine; the feeling of being completely accepted by him, which came with their nakedness, was perfect satisfaction. He was experienced – she had never expected otherwise – and he led her gently through a world of sensual pleasure that was new and wonderful to her; yet she always felt his equal, giving as much as she received.

When she was away from him, she worked with the more dedication and single-mindedness because she was happy: it was like a pleasant fire glowing in the background of her mind, a satisfying warmth she was aware of, but did not have to think about. What he did with himself when he was not with her she never found time or inclination to wonder. How a man of fortune passed his days and endured his idleness she had never been able to imagine – nothing was new about that. Privately she wondered that he did not want to involve himself in the business of the bank, or run for Parliament, or seek some other public office; but as he never criticised her career, she felt it only right that she should never voice those questions.

CHAPTER SEVENTEEN

George scratched on Alfreda's door, and after a long delay was admitted by Bittle. The elderly maid didn't say anything, only stepped aside to let him pass, her red-rimmed eyes reproachful, her down-curving lips set tightly as a trap. He thought it would have depressed him terribly to have that sour old woman around him, looking like an undertaker with a grudge, but Alfreda seemed to take comfort from her. She had dismissed all the other nursery staff and ordered the nursery rooms locked up, but Bittle, who had been her nurse in childhood, had come creeping and sidling to Alfreda's rooms and somehow managed to stay there.

Everyone else received short shrift – even the chaplain, Roding, who had naturally thought comforting the bereaved mother should be his particular province. George acknowledged that one didn't necessarily want to hear the religious line peddled when one was racked with grief: he himself had had to bite his tongue when Roding had come evangelising, with the little fellow not even underground. But George had simply nodded away and shut his mind to it. Alfreda, though, had gone for the chaplain's throat like a maddened wolf. And even now, three months later, she would not set foot in the chapel.

Only yesterday Roding had begged her again to seek the comfort of religion, and the balm the Almighty alone could lay on a grieving heart.

'It was your Almighty who took my child away,' she replied. 'I hardly think He can have any comfort for me.'

'We must not question His ways. He tempers justice with mercy, He who made the world and all that is in it—'

'*I* made my son, out of my own flesh. I gave my health and strength to do it. And He took him from me. What justice is there in that, let alone mercy?'

Roding sucked in his breath at the blasphemy, but he persevered, though in terror of Alfreda's bitter eyes and flaying-knife tongue. 'He knows the secrets of all hearts,' he bleated nervously. 'He can understand all, forgive all—'

'Well, *I* don't forgive *Him*,' Alfreda said, 'so you can take your pious platitudes away and leave me alone!'

So it was cautiously that George entered the bed-chamber, in which Alfreda spent more and more of her time. She hardly ever came down to a meal now, and when she left her room it was usually only to walk about the gardens alone for a while, her arms wrapped round her and her eyes fixed unseeingly on some inner horizon. There had been no more entertaining, of course – a mixed blessing – but she had refused to see any of the former friends who called with their condolences, or even to look at any of the letters and notes that arrived. George had had to do everything.

He found his wife now on her daybed, drawn up near the fire, a rug over her legs and a shawl round her shoulders. It seemed warm to him in the room, but still she sat hunched, holding the shawl round her as though she were cold. Her face looked pinched, and so pale it was almost blue, and as she turned a sour and glittering look on him, it struck him that she looked like an old woman – a mad old woman at that. She and Bittle were a pair now. Pity tugged at his heart . . . and a little resentment.

'What do you want?' she asked, as he stood before her.

'I came to see if there's anything *you* want,' he said.

'Well, there isn't,' she said, and turned her head away to stare at the flames.

'I thought you might think of coming out today. It's

317

a beautiful day, really mild,' George said. The tragedy had at least stopped Atterwith talking about getting rid of the hunt, or even cutting down. George hunted five days a week as before, though there were no 'lawn meets': the field, in deference to their bereavement, joined them along the way. 'It's a shame to waste weather like this – it can't last at this time of year. And the scent will be breast high,' he went on coaxingly.

'How can you think about scent at a time like this?' she interrupted.

'I just thought it would do you good to get out in the fresh air. A little healthy exercise. Take your mind off it for an hour or two.'

'You think *hunting* will make me forget?'

'Well, not forget. Of course not. But I've found it helps not to think about it all the time,' George ventured gently.

'*You* may find that easy enough. I can't shut him out of my mind so easily.'

'I didn't say it was easy—'

'Oh, leave me alone, can't you? Go and hunt and enjoy yourself! Do whatever you want to do! My child is dead!'

Her eyes filled with tears, and the sight of them made George's lip tremble. He said, 'He was my child too.'

'What does a father know of love or pain?' she retorted.

He was hurt. 'I *did* love him. Good God, do you think I don't suffer just as much as you?'

She looked at him, and he almost flinched before the black despair in those exhausted eyes. 'He was my *only* child,' she said.

George knew what she meant; but he couldn't let her claim to be the only sufferer. 'Alfreda, I loved him. When I saw his little body lying there—' He swallowed. 'Must we be like this?' He made a huge effort, unfamiliar with this talk of feelings. 'I'm lonely without you. Can't we comfort each other?'

'I can't comfort you,' she said, in a low voice. She turned her head away again, and he saw her sigh as though she were weary to death. 'I have nothing for you, George. I'm sorry for your pain, but I want to be left alone. Go away now. I can't bear you near me.'

It hurt so much more because she said it quite gently, as though dredging up from the depths some last dregs of kindness for a stranger; and because she called him by his given name, something she had hardly ever done in all their years together. It hurt him, and it frightened him. He felt she had gone away from him, started off on some journey without him which would take her beyond his reach for ever, leaving him alone and cold in a dark place, like an abandoned child. What would he do if she left him? How would he order his life? Ever since he had reached adulthood, she had been there, directing him, and everything he had done had been done for her. He turned from her averted face, stumbled from the room.

His throat was hurting and tears were seeping from his eyes. A few paces led him to the upper hall, and he leaned against the balustrade and looked down blankly, seeing far below him the black and white marble squares of the great hall's floor. His son was dead, and he would never get over it – he didn't see how anyone could – but he had thought they would go on somehow, get back to some semblance of normality. Now he saw that she had given up, that she was not going to come out of the black cave where she had retreated after that terrible day. He felt the house around him like a living entity, something so familiar it was like his own carcass. He had grown up here. His son had been growing up here. One day, in the proper course of things, he would have been laid in the crypt and his son would have become master. That was how things had always happened, how it was supposed to have happened for him. But it was his boy who had been lowered into the dark place to lie among the bones of his ancestors, and without James life seemed pointless. What was Morland Place for, if there was no heir? There was no purpose in his going on. A tear fell from his down-tilted face, and he saw it fall, glinting, to hit the hard, shining floor far below. Perhaps there was a way out for him, too

– a way to end this misery. He leaned further over, and the chequered squares seemed to swell and subside like the sea, beckoning him . . .

There was a warning cough from somewhere near at hand, and he jerked upright, and saw the second footman, John, standing there at his elbow.

'I beg your pardon, sir,' he said. George looked at him in a bewildered way. 'I was just passing on my way downstairs and wondered if there was anything you required?'

'No – no, nothing,' George managed to say.

John smiled kindly. 'A fine hunting day, sir. You'll have a good run.'

'Yes, I expect so,' George said, and, shaken back into himself, turned and went away.

In the kitchen there was a general lingering after dinner. These days, with no company, the master out hunting until dark, and the mistress never leaving her room, there was not so very much to do in the afternoons. John was describing the incident that morning. He was speaking principally to Alice, but everyone in the kitchen was listening; if not overtly, then as they pottered about various tasks.

'I wonder if I hadn't come along whether he might have jumped,' John concluded. 'He looked fit for it. I've never seen him in such a black.'

Alice began to answer, but her response was pre-empted explosively by the mistress's French maid, Fanie, who paused on her way past the table to say, 'Pah! And if 'e 'ad jomp, what then?' She curled her lip. 'A brokken leg, my friend, zat is all! You make yourself grand wiz your stories, but 'e is not ze man *pour se tuer*, zat one.'

John merely shrugged, not prepared to argue with her, but Aggie, the elderly kitchen-maid who had replaced Peggy and Molly, sucked her teeth, shook her head and settled to the enjoyment of a good piece of bad news. 'Ah don't knaw so much. There's no knowing what folks'll do when their hearts is broke, an' all hope is gone,' she said, with gloomy relish. 'He's a desperit man, is the master. Aye, an' Ah'll tell you what else, an' all: there were an owl on't roof last night.' She looked round at the company, nodding, and lowered her voice sepulchrally. 'Aye, Ah'm not jestin' 'n' jokin' – Ah saw it plain as day! There it sat on't roof tree a full hour after moonrise, and you knaw what that means.'

'Hit means you are a stupid old woman,' Fanie answered obligingly. But Aggie had most of the other servants with her, and carried on unperturbed.

'It means sorrow comin' to the 'ouse, that's what it means. Dark an' deadly sorrow coming to this 'ouse, and nowt anyone can do to turn it away.'

'I should think there's sorrow enough come already,' John said impatiently. 'A portent's supposed to come before the act, not after.'

'You do not know what sorrow means,' Fanie said. 'I tell you what sorrow is, my friends: it is zis waste of all my talents! All zese years I work 'ard to become skilled at dressing my lady, to be ze best lady's maid zere is, and 'ow am I rewarded? She never leaves 'er room! I give 'er ze best years of my life, and all for what? Does she appreciate? No! She refuse me and shut 'erself up wiz zat Bittool!' She scowled round the table. 'She is *hideuse*, zat Bittool! I 'ate 'er! I 'ate all hugly people! I shall not stay 'ere to be surrounded by hugly hold women and un*grrrate*ful ladies!'

Alice, at least, was impressed. She had rubbed shoulders with Fanie enough to know that when her Rs rolled like that, she was genuinely upset. 'I'm sure Madam appreciates you really,' she said. 'You wouldn't leave her now, when she's so unhappy?'

'*Bien sûr* I shall leave,' Fanie said, tossing her head. 'I am not being ze best ladies' maid in ze world so zat I can wait on an hinvalid in 'er bedchamber! I shall go to Madame Chubb.'

'Mrs Chubb's got a maid,' Mildred pointed out.

'Ha!' said Fanie triumphantly. 'I see 'er in York last week, and she say 'er daughter is to get married in March and will need a ladies' maid of 'er own. She will be Mrs 'Avergill and verrray rich. Madame Chubb say if I will go to 'er she will pay whatever I hask.'

'But Miss Chubb's not a very pretty young lady,' said the cook, coming to sit down to rest her feet after her morning's labours.

'I make 'er pretty,' said Fanie.

'And she's not what you'd call a leader of Society,' Mrs Pender went on.

'I *make* 'er leading! Zat is my genius!' Fanie snapped. She cast a glittering look round them all and stalked out, and though the rest of the company muttered, Alice felt a sadness, for she thought she had seen beneath the anger the fear of a woman past her prime, faced with the prospect of losing her livelihood, faced with lonely and perhaps destitute old age. Fanie's arts concealed the truth from many, if not most, but Alice had sometimes had the duty of taking up her morning tea, and she knew that she must be well over forty.

Alice leaned close to John and said in a low voice, 'Will she really go? Doesn't she think the mistress will entertain again when she's out of mourning?'

John didn't answer at once. He stared after the French-woman with troubled eyes, then turned his chair a little so that they should not be overheard. 'This is not for repeating, but I tell *you* because you're different. Things are in a bad way. The master's over head and ears in debt and the mistress has lost the will to live. Fanie's afraid she may just give up and die – and if the master goes broke, she will. Fanie's right to get out while she can.'

Alice had paled a little. 'But – but if the mistress dies, what will happen to him?' She did not need to specify to John who she meant. 'He dotes on her.'

John only shrugged. 'We should all get out while we can. The ones who jump while the ship's still afloat will have a better chance of a new billet.'

'*You* wouldn't go?' Alice said, shocked.

He gave a grim sort of smile. 'You've a queer notion of where my loyalties lie. D'you think any of *them* will give a tuppenny dam what happens to the likes of us if things go wrong? They'll be too busy worrying about their own hides. We'll get turned off without warning to fend for ourselves. Now you keep this to yourself, Miss Alice, d'ye hear me? Don't go blabbing to the other servants. I've warned you because you've got more up here than the others,' he tapped his forehead, 'and you could make something of yourself. Don't you go throwing yourself away on a lost cause, that's all.'

'But I *couldn't*—' she began, aghast, and he laid a warning hand briefly over hers.

'Don't look like that. People are watching.' He eyed her a moment. '*He* doesn't care a jot for you, and never will. Don't be a fool, Alice Bone. Don't throw your life away.' And with that he got up and left.

Passing the butler's room and hearing Mrs Holicar's voice from within, John lingered outside the door and listened.

'. . . a house without a mistress,' Goole was saying in reply, in his ordinary voice, which was far less plummy and exalted than his butler's accent. 'As good as, anyway. It's not what I'm used to.'

'I know.' Mrs Holicar sighed. 'I may have to leave myself if things don't get any better. I remember the times before the mistress came, Mr Goole, and I don't want to go back to them, believe you me. Mess and muddle and nothing done as it should be. It'd break my heart.'

'I don't see how it *can* get better,' Goole said. 'Where's the money to come from? Mr Atterwith's as tight as an oyster, but it don't take a mind-reader to know he's worried. Master ought to pull in his horns, but will he? And then there's that marble memorial *she*'s ordered – a Gothic folly, Mr Atterwith calls it.'

'Based on the Albert Memorial in Hyde Park, so I understand,' Mrs Holicar said, with faint reproof.

'Based on my foot! It'll cost a fortune, that's all. Folly's right, if you ask me! And it's the only thing she shows any interest in.'

'Poor soul,' Mrs Holicar said, though to John it sounded perfunctory.

'It's *him* I feel sorry for,' Goole said. 'He could have more children, if it wasn't for her. That's what comes of marrying a woman so much older than him. It was a bad business! His father ought to've stopped it.'

'His father had passed away by then,' Mrs Holicar said. 'You wouldn't know – it was before your time.'

'Well, however it was, he ought to put her aside now, and take a younger wife.'

'Mr Goole!' Mrs Holicar cried, and John backed away a little, in case she should come storming out in indignation. 'There's never been a divorce in this family and there never will be! The very idea!'

'That's all very well, but there's the estate to think of. He needs an heir, and that's all there is to it.'

'Whom God hath joined together—'

'Well,' Goole said, 'it might not come to that. If she goes on the way she is, she'll release him another way.'

John heard someone coming, and slipped away.

During Venetia's period as a medical student at St Agatha's, nothing had been spared her. She had come in contact daily with the suffering of the lowest of society, and learned about the diseases and injuries that afflicted them. The horrible sights she had witnessed had bred in her a determination not to abandon the poor when she was qualified and able to do something to help them. Hence she had set up the dispensary in the basement of her house, and the word soon travelled through the mean streets that Dr Fleet would not turn you away.

This generosity had its negative side, for it was not to be expected that the paying customers would relish picking their way through all that poverty and suffering in order to get to the doctor's door; and without the paying customer, there would be no more help for the poor. So she had been forced to set up a second dispensary in a court off nearby Marylebone Lane. The respectable working classes, who could afford to pay a few pence for their cures, and would not offend the eyes of the paying clients, attended the Welbeck Street dispensary; the pauper class, in all their multitudinous misery, went to the Marylebone Free Dispensary for the Poor.

Given how frequently the pauper class and the criminal class overlapped, it was inevitable that Venetia should come into contact with the Marylebone and Paddington Division police. There was a certain amount of suspicion on either side to begin with, but though a policeman's basic nature might be deeply conservative, his daily experiences demanded that he be adaptable, and she did not find nearly so much hostility to the idea of a lady doctor as in society at large. Besides, working side by side bred a community of interest, and it was not long before she found the local police were not only staunch allies but were calling on her for help in various incidents. Inspector Morgan of the CID became a particular friend, and one day in the late spring of 1882 he called on her at her house, sending up his card and asking if she would see him on a confidential matter.

She had him shown up, and Miss Ulverston, who happened to be at home that evening, politely absented herself. The inspector – a heavy-built man with bushy hair, unexpectedly handsome brown eyes, and the almost inevitable side-whiskers – looked round him with a swift, keen eye that took in everything, and then accepted the proffered seat, sitting very upright on the edge of it with his hat on his knees.

'Very nice of you to receive me, Doctor. I've often gone past your house, of course, wondered what it was like inside. Very comfortable, if I might be so bold as to pass comment.'

Venetia smiled. 'Did you think I would live in *dis*comfort?'

He cocked an eye at her. 'Well, now, there you have me! Because it did occur to me to wonder whether a lady who succeeds so well in a man's world might not have something of a man's nature to make it happen. And I know my own house would be a very sad place if Mrs Morgan did not see to the creature side of it.'

'Well, now you see for yourself,' Venetia said, not sure whether to be offended or amused.

'I see that a man is only obliged to be a man, but a woman has to be both to get along. It's a useful lesson.'

Venetia bowed her head, laughing. 'Glad to be of use to you, Inspector! Was there anything else?'

He smiled too, but only briefly. 'It was something quite else I came about. I wonder if you have heard of the House of Lords Select Committee on the Protection of Young Girls?'

'Yes, of course,' she said. It had been sitting through the winter, gathering evidence on prostitution and procurement and other matters relating to the sexual exploitation of girls. The age of consent had been raised in 1875 to thirteen, and there was debate as to whether it should be raised further, and whether any other legislation was needed in that area.

'Well, ma'am, I have been giving evidence relating to my experiences over the years concerning brothels and accommodation houses and other such matters. The gentlemen of the committee seemed to take to me – were so kind as to say I put things very clearly for them – and they asked me if I knew of a doctor who could give evidence on some related topics.'

'What topics?'

He made a deprecating face. 'Well, Doctor, disagreeable ones, so I won't deceive you. They want to know about the effects of prostitution, in particular on young girls, with respect to injury, disease, childbirth and so on.'

'I've seen plenty of that at the free dispensary,' Venetia said. 'More than anyone should see in a lifetime.'

'Well, that's what I thought,' he said. 'So I told them—'

'You told them my name?'

'Without permission? Lord, no! Bless you, ma'am, what d'you take me for? I only said that I knew of a doctor I'd worked with, experienced in such matters, and that being as she was a lady doctor, she might very well know things a male doctor would not – a female's view, d'ye see? The Committee was very keen to have you sent for, but I said in view of the disagreeable nature of what would have to be spoken of, I would have to put it to you. So I am here to ask if you would consider letting yourself be called. It's in a good cause, as you know.' His expression changed. 'I'd do anything I could to get some of these poor little scraps off the streets. I've a little girl myself, just nine years old, and when I remember – well, it's hard to get your dinner down of an evening sometimes, when you think of what you've seen.'

Venetia said, 'When you put it like that, I have no right to refuse to give evidence, have I?'

He shook his head. 'You shouldn't feel that way, ma'am. Like I said, it would mean talking about very disagreeable things, and in front of gentlemen. That's not something I could lightly ask any lady to do. And if you felt it would be too unpleasant to you, why, there are other doctors, men, who can do the job instead, so it's not as if you'd be letting anyone down.'

'But you are right, I do have unique experience,' Venetia said slowly. 'I became a doctor because I wanted to be able to make a difference. I would be letting myself down if I did not take this opportunity.'

'Well, ma'am, take your time to think about it,' said Morgan, standing up to leave. 'No need to jump in hasty-like.'

Venetia stood too. 'I have made up my mind. You may give the Committee my name, Mr Morgan. I will answer their questions. And you needn't look so anxious,' she added, smiling. 'I'm accustomed to discussing what you call "disagreeable things". I can do it without blushing, in a scientific cause.'

Venetia was duly called, and armouring herself in her plainest suit and least frivolous hat, with veil, she presented herself and was conducted by an usher to the committee room where Lord Salisbury was sitting. She was not worried that he might recognise her: though he had known her father, of course, and had been at Eton and the House with her uncle Cavendish, he had not set

eyes on her since she was fifteen years old, and had no
reason to associate her with the Southport name.

The marquess stood courteously as she came in, a
dignified, bearded man in his fifties, with a shiningly
bald front and the Cecil dark eyes, and said, 'Good
morning, Dr Fleet. Is that the way you preferred to be
addressed, by the by? Very good. May I say at once how
grateful we are that you feel able to help us in this matter.
It cannot be very agreeable for you, and I am sure we all
applaud your courage and the sense of duty which must
have brought you here.'

Venetia inclined her head, hardly hearing what he was
saying, for if her first glance had been for the marquess,
her second had quickly scanned the other three people
in the room, and the shock of what she saw seemed to
be making her ears sing. Lord Salisbury begged now to
present his colleagues to her: one was the secretary, Mr
Elder; the other two were his fellow peers, Lord Verney –
a stout and pop-eyed gentleman quite unknown to her
– and Lord Hazelmere.

All had, of course, stood up. Hazelmere had put his
hands down on the table edge as if he needed it to support
him, and he seemed to have gone rather white. Venetia
wondered for a rippling moment what he would say.
Would he expose her – denounce her – refuse to have
anything to do with her? *This woman and I were once
engaged to be married: I cannot remain in the room with her!*
But when his name was mentioned he merely bowed his
head without speaking or meeting her eyes, and, grateful
for his silence, Venetia returned the compliment and
sat down.

She wondered, however, how she would be able to
answer on delicate subjects, knowing how he felt about
her profession, how he would hate the fact that she knew
what she knew, would despise her the more for unsexing
herself. Perhaps she ought herself to declare the impedi-
ment? But there was work to do here, important work;
and Salisbury had begun speaking again, was engaged in
a preamble about the purpose of the commission and the

areas of its enquiry which, she guessed from its length, was meant to put her at her ease. By the time he reached a pause into which she could have voiced an objection, it was too late, really, to object.

And when the marquess got down to the questions, she quickly became too absorbed in the matter in hand to do more than register Hazelmere out of the corner of her eye as an embarrassment. To the scratching of the secretary's pen, she answered what was put to her, speaking concisely and frankly, schooling any emotion out of her voice and manner, feeling it was what they would have expected of a man doctor, and was therefore what they should have of her.

To their credit, neither Salisbury nor Verney displayed any discomfiture. They listened with sober care to what she said, asking for elaboration or clarification as they required it, but exhibiting no more shock or disgust than if she had been an engineer describing damage to buildings. Her own tension evaporated in the face of their matter-of-fact handling of the subject. She described the evils she had seen, the pathetic cases she had treated: a nine-year-old girl to whom she had been called to deliver a baby; twelve- and thirteen-year-olds with the marks of venereal disease plain upon them; the physical damage caused to a small child by adult sexual intercourse.

Hazelmere spoke for the first time. 'You speak very calmly about it all,' he said. He looked shaken. 'Don't you find such things shocking – appalling?'

She turned her face towards him, but did not quite look at him. 'My feelings are nothing to the point. I am here to testify to facts.'

'Quite so, Dr Fleet,' said Salisbury soothingly.

But she was not soothed. How dare he criticise her? 'There is an introduction house in South Molton Street,' she said. 'That is what they call these places. They specialise in selling maidenhoods.' Hazelmere averted his face a little, and she went on, shaking just a little, 'Sometimes, of course, the girls are not *virgo intacta* – there are ways of faking the condition – but they must appear to be, so

329

all are young and fresh-looking. The highest prices can be charged for genuine innocents, country girls lured by the offer of more money than they can earn in service. The procurers say you must get them at twelve or less, to have any chance that they are intact.'

'I don't—' Hazelmere began, but Venetia overrode him.

'The customers believe,' she said, only just in control of her voice, 'that the act of deflowering a virgin is a cure for veneral disease.'

There was a silence then; even the scratch of the pen stopped. Venetia was swallowing hard to stop herself from crying. Hazelmere was looking down at his hands, turning his signet ring round and round, his lip under his teeth.

At last Lord Salisbury spoke, gently. 'Thank you, Dr Fleet. We are all aware, I am sure, of how distressing your work must often be. If I may turn now to the question of the age of these girls. It is, I imagine, impossible to verify the exact age of a child prostitute? But as a medical practitioner you would have some means of knowing the approximate age through physical examination?'

Venetia gathered herself together and answered, and the interview continued. Hazelmere also seemed to recover his equilibrium, and later asked a question of his own.

'Inspector Morgan of the CID – who I believe is an acquaintance? – has stated to this committee that he has never known of a case of a girl being held in a brothel against her will. Is that your experience?'

'I cannot claim as much experience of brothels as Mr Morgan,' Venetia said gravely, recovering her sense of humour a little. To have Hazelmere ask her that question as if she spent her life popping in and out of them was too absurd. 'I can only say that I have never heard of a case of coercion of that sort.'

Lord Verney was about to ask another question when Hazelmere said, 'Of that sort? Is there another sort, then?'

Now she met his eyes. 'There is what I might term economic coercion. When a girl is left pregnant and her seducer abandons her, she is regarded as a fallen woman, whatever the circumstances of her fall. Society makes no distinction between ignorance, determined vice, and sheer bad luck. So an otherwise decent girl with a baby finds she cannot get respectable work or lodgings, and the only recourse open to her is to turn to prostitution to support herself.'

'The *only* recourse?' Hazelmere asked, with a hint of disbelief.

'As long as she has the baby,' Venetia said. 'Less particular girls might smother the baby, or drown it, or simply abandon it. Without the child in tow, she might become respectable again. Ironic, isn't it?'

When the committee had finished with her, Lord Salisbury thanked her with grave courtesy and asked if she would be willing to attend again if more questions arose. She assented, and left the room. The usher was waiting to show her out. They had not got very far down the corridor when the door opened again and Hazelmere came out and called her. 'Dr Fleet! Wait, please.'

Venetia stopped and turned. She was not entirely surprised. She had thought he would not miss the opportunity to tell her how much he disapproved of her.

'A moment of your time, if you please,' he said.

She watched him approach, seeing his face dark and working with some emotion; and suddenly she had had enough. She said coldly, 'I will answer questions in the committee room, and nowhere else.'

'It isn't a question. There's something I want to say to you.'

'No doubt there is, Lord Hazelmere, but do *I* want to listen to it? I beg your pardon, but I have a very great many things to do, and I cannot spare you any more time. Good day to you.'

She turned very determinedly and walked away, feeling that being snubbed so firmly in that place must prevent him from any further attempt to follow her. And so it proved. When she turned at the end of the corridor to follow her guide down the stairs, he was still standing at the far end, looking, she was annoyed with herself for thinking, rather small and forlorn.

The event had rather an unexpected consequence. A few days after her deposition to the committee, Venetia received a letter from Tommy Weston.

Dear Cousin Venetia,

I have heard about your giving evidence to the House of Lords' Committee, and wish to say that I admire your courage and think you did just right. The coldness between us since our late disagreement two years ago gives me much pain, and I know that Emma misses your friendship in the greatest possible degree. I cannot think that you acted rightly in giving the advice you gave to Emma without my permission, but I am willing to believe that you acted from pure motives and that it is a case of a genuine, if irreconcilable, difference of opinion. If you can find it in yourself to put the past behind and close the said unhappy chapter, I would be more than willing to do the same, in the interest of restoring intercourse between our two households. If we can agree to disagree on this head, I assure you the subject will never again be referred to by,

Your humble obedient servant,
T. Weston.

Venetia hardly knew whether to laugh or cry. It fell so far short of an apology that it was plain he did not regard himself in the wrong at all, and was suffering severe mental contortions in the effort to restore their friendship without having to remove the cause of their enmity. Absurd to suppose they could forget their disagreement, when the very reason for his writing to her now was bound to remind them! It would be a strained friendship that had to tiptoe round the sleeping wolf of an unresolved and 'irreconcilable difference of opinion'. And yet she did miss them both; and was it not equally absurd for them to live within streets of each other and be engaged in similar good works and yet never speak or visit?

Well, if he could bury his pride – which as it was male, and connected with sex, must be hurting a great deal more than hers – she could be just as generous. She wrote back, and the next day Tommy called in person, sending up his card first in a chastened manner, as if unsure even now whether she would admit him. The meeting was a little awkward, inevitably. They exchanged rather stilted greetings, discussed a few public events of the day, and only then came to personal things, when Venetia asked how Emma was. Tommy answered, as men do, not of his wife, but of his children. They now had four, and Emma was expecting again.

It was on the tip of Venetia's tongue to say, 'Ah, then the contraceptive advice was not taken?' but she managed to control her madness at the last moment and say instead, meekly, 'You must be very happy. I hope she is well?'

'Oh, yes, in rosy health. I hope you will come and dine with us? We shall be alone tomorrow. Emma hopes very much to see you.'

'It happens that I am free – yes, thank you, I will come.' He beamed and thanked her, with an appearance of relief, which made her wonder whether Emma had been making his life difficult for very long over the quarrel. He was taking his leave – perhaps wisely cutting this first meeting short – when she thought to ask him, 'You heard of my deposition to the Committee from Mr Gladstone, I suppose?'

He paused and looked at her thoughtfully. 'Well, no, as a matter of fact I had it from Hazelmere. We still belong to the same club, you know. I met him there and he mentioned it.'

'I see,' Venetia said neutrally. She could guess in what terms he had described it.

'He was surprised to see you,' Tommy said.

'So I imagine. I was even more surprised to see him.

I thought he never came to Town these days. I thought he'd retired permanently to his estate.'

'He did at one time,' Tommy said, and seemed about to add something else, then changed his mind.

BOOK THREE

Coming Home

What if we still ride on, we two
With life for ever old yet new,
Changed not in kind but in degree,
The instant made eternity –
And heaven just prove that I and she
Ride, ride together, for ever ride?

Robert Browning: *The Last Ride Together*

CHAPTER EIGHTEEN

Ever since 1875, when the canny Mr Disraeli bought the bankrupt Khedive Ismail's shares, the Suez Canal had effectively been under joint French and British control. But the canal could not be isolated from what was happening in the territory through which it ran, and Egypt was not a happy nor a peaceful place. Native Egyptians hated their Turkish overlords, and in the Egyptian army the officers, who were mostly Egyptian, hated the government ministers and functionaries – mostly Turkish – who surrounded the khedive and controlled their lives.

Early in 1882 one of the officers, Colonel Arabi Pasha, executed a kind of *coup d'état*, and while leaving the khedive in place, dismissed the prime minister, made himself war minister, and demanded a new constitution. The French and British hesitated. Neither country wanted Turkey to intervene, upsetting their own delicate balance of power; neither, remembering the Crimea, thought it could mount an effective joint action with the other. Besides, France was so afraid of the rise of German power that she declared she must avoid all risks outside Europe so as to be able to meet those within it. Gladstone, unwilling to commit British troops without French support, tentatively suggested employing a Turkish army as their common instrument, but the French refused to consider it.

Meanwhile, the assurance to the khedive that his maintenance on the throne was regarded as essential to the welfare of Egypt inflamed the Egyptian nationalists. They believed France intended forcibly to transfer Egypt to her own empire, as she had recently done with Tunis. In June 1882 nationalist riots broke out, with many Europeans, including the British Consul, killed. The British and French fleets arrived at Alexandria, and Arabi Pasha's soldiers began fortifying it with earthworks and batteries. In July the French fleet received orders from Paris to avoid confrontation, and sailed away. The British fleet, left alone, successfully reduced the fortifications with a ten-hour bombardment.

'It's obvious that from now on we shall have to act alone,' Marcus told Venetia, when he called on her on the 20th of July. 'The French have let us down, and we can't rely on them. Gladstone and his cabinet know that, thank God! I've just been told that we are ordered to Egypt under Sir Garnet Wolseley.'

'Oh, Marcus, you're going to war?' Venetia said, not knowing whether to be pleased for him, or anxious.

'Oh, don't worry, those Gyppy fellows won't be a match for us. We should clear it up in a few weeks. And then, if they've any sense, the Government will take control, get rid of the khedive and Arabi alike. Turks in government are always corrupt and cruel, and the Egyptians will never settle down under them; and we can't afford the Canal to fall into rebel hands. The only sensible course is for us to take over and make Egypt our protectorate.'

'I doubt if the French would like that,' Venetia said, 'or the other European powers, for that matter.'

'Oh, they'll see it's in everyone's best interest. If it were up to me,' he added firmly, 'all these strategic places would be under British control, like Gibraltar. Take Constantinople, for instance, or the Panama Canal—'

'I thought that had been abandoned?' Venetia said, puzzled.

'Oh, quite. But if it were ever finished, it would be too important to leave it under foreign control. Who but the British can be trusted to treat everyone fairly?'

Venetia had no answer to that. 'What's Wolseley like?' she asked.

'He's a good soldier,' Marcus said, as if that were all that needed to be said. 'I think we shall have a good scrap of it. I can't tell you how much I'm looking forward to it. We've a sort of family interest in the Canal, in a way, haven't we?'

'You mean because Mama's cousin Benedict Morland worked on it?' Venetia said. 'And died out there, too,' she remembered. 'You will take care, won't you?'

'Of course.' Marcus shrugged that aside and changed the subject. 'By the by, I'm glad to know you're friends with the Westons again. Saw Tommy Weston in Whitehall this morning and he mentioned you. Did you know he might be up for a Cabinet post?'

'No, how's that?'

'Well, Johnny Bright resigned over the bombardment of Alexandria – he's a Quaker, d'ye see? – and Gladstone's thinking of giving Weston the Duchy of Lancaster. Quite a step up for him.'

'Uncle Tom would have been so pleased!' Venetia said. 'And Papa too – he always thought Tommy was able.'

'Anyway, I said I was off to Egypt and he said he'd keep an eye on you for me, which rather relieves my mind.'

'Don't be silly, I don't need looking after,' she said.

Marcus ignored that. 'No good expecting Harry to do it,' he said. 'Got in with a thoroughly bad lot. Gussie too. I did hear,' he added, as though reluctant to believe it, 'that she's thinking of going on the stage, like the Langtry woman.'

'Oh, Marcus, surely not! Not Gussie?'

'They seem to think it's nothing but a lark,' he confirmed gloomily. 'I tackled Harry but he simply said it was Johnny Vibart's business now; and Vibart thinks it's something to be proud of, for his wife to be able to act and sing in public.' He sighed. 'I don't know how HRH got mixed up with a rum set like Vibart and Chetwynd and that Baird feller. They're not at all the thing.'

'The racecourse attracts many strange people. All are equal in the face of the great god Chance,' Venetia said.

'I don't know about that,' Marcus said, 'but the Prince

ain't a bad sort at heart. Mad keen to go out to Egypt himself, so I hear, especially with his younger brother commanding the Guards contingent. Connaught's a brigadier, you know. But the Queen would never let HRH go, even if he had any military experience. Seems a shame.' To him, the desire to be a soldier redeemed most of a man's failings. 'So,' he reverted, 'I shall have to leave you to Weston's care. It's a pity,' he added, 'that you didn't marry Hazelmere when you could. Of course, it's too late now.'

Venetia felt herself pale inwardly. 'What do you mean? What's happened to him?'

'Oh, he's all to pieces. His estate's in a bad way – he had all his money in the land, so this agricultural depression's hit him hard. Putting it up for sale, I understand.'

'Is that what he's doing in London? I asked Tommy but he wouldn't say.'

'Not his business to say,' Marcus said, 'but you're my sister. Hazelmere's selling up, going to live in London from now on. Looking for a government post – something that will pay him just enough to live on. I dare say Gladstone will put something in his way – used to know his pa. And Weston will speak up for him.'

'Lord Hazelmere was on a House of Lords' committee earlier this year,' Venetia said.

'Probably by way of a try-out. No fees involved in that. Poor feller won't be able to marry now – can't afford it.'

'I thought he had it in mind to marry an heiress,' Venetia said casually, remembering Miss Parr and Miss Graham. 'What became of that plan?'

'Pride,' Marcus said elliptically. 'No, it's the bachelor life for him now he's penniless – and he's an only son, last of the line. As I say, it's a pity you didn't marry him while you could.'

Venetia suppressed a smile. 'But, Marcus, if I had, he'd still have been ruined, and now I'd be penniless too,' she pointed out.

He pondered a minute. 'Hadn't thought of that.'

★   ★   ★

From Marcus's failure to mention it, Venetia gathered that her affair with Ivo Jennings had so far gone unde-tected. It was a source of great strength in her life: she loved him more madly as the months passed, and had she not been so busy she felt she might have suffered all the youthful miseries of being in love, the longings and doubts and the agony of not being able to be with the beloved object every moment. They could not often be alone together, so when they were, these were times of intense passion. For the rest, he remained a warm glow in the back of her mind, something delicious to think of in the few moments she had before falling asleep at night. She looked forward intensely to the next tryst, but had no time to fret that it might be a week off.

But as London emptied for the summer months and her paid work slackened off, she began to wonder what the future would hold for them. In the beginning of the affair, she was too overwhelmed with the experience of being in love, and of making love, to go any further in her mind; but now she began to ask herself when the next step would be taken. From love to marriage is a natural progression for a woman; but for all her worldly experience, Venetia knew little about the working of men's minds. When she was with him, Ivo was amusing and affectionate; when she was alone with him, fiercely passionate; but though he expressed disappointment when circumstances kept them apart, he never seemed to extrapolate from that a need for their circumstances to be changed.

One day in August he called at her house, something he did not often do. Miss Ulverston was at home, and he chatted politely to her. She was in raptures that the Married Women's Property Act, passed in Scotland the year before, had now been extended to the rest of Britain, and was eager to explain how that resolved the problem of whether the women's franchise amendment should apply to all women or exclude married women. 'Now they can own their own property in their own right, their having the vote won't be regarded as a second vote for the husband. Or,' she added realistically, 'it *ought* not to be, but some people will not see reason even when it's explained to them.' But at last she recollected her tact and took herself off.

'Thank you for being so patient,' Venetia said, when they were alone. 'Amelia has worked so hard for it, she deserves her moment of triumph.'

Ivo shrugged. 'Oh, I don't mind. She amuses me. But I wonder if these women realise that the more "rights" they snatch for themselves, the less attractive they make themselves seem. They kill any desire in men to be chivalrous or generous; the desire even to be kind will go next. They may come to regret all this "equality" in the end,' he said, with a hard smile. 'There's an old Eastern proverb that says, "Be careful what you wish for: you may get it."'

'I don't understand,' Venetia said. His tone made her feel uneasy. 'What do you mean?'

'Oh, I don't mean you,' he said lightly. 'You have other qualities that lift you into a different sphere altogether, my lovely odalisque. On the subject of which, I must say you are looking rather pale and worn. Are you quite well?'

She abandoned the puzzle and said, 'I'm just tired. The heat breeds diseases amongst the poor so my dispensaries fill up as my consulting-room empties.'

'Quite so. I must say, darling Dr Fleet, that even my love of London is wearing just a trifle thin at present. It's so damned airless! And I don't see enough of you. I've long suspected that London gets in the way, and now you've confirmed it. So I come to you with a proposition.'

'What proposition?'

'I must warn you it's really more of a demand – refuse me at your peril! I want you to come away with me.'

Her heart fluttered. 'Come away with you?'

'For a few days, so that we can be together properly, without having to watch the hands of the clock all the time. There is a charming hotel I know by the river, as secluded and quiet and pleasant a place as exists anywhere on this benighted planet. We can be together the whole

time, eat a great deal, drink even more, talk to our hearts'
content – and sleep together all night! What do you say?
Doesn't it sound appealing? Isn't it the very description
of the joys of heaven, somehow transported to earth?'

'It does sound wonderful,' Venetia said, 'but—'

He put out a hand and stopped her lips with his finger.
'No, I can't accept any sentence beginning with "but"!
There isn't a "but" in the case. We'll go incognito,
travel down on the train on Friday morning and stay
until Monday evening. I promise you the hotel staff
are discretion itself – they wouldn't have any business
otherwise. You shall close your dispensaries and put off
any remaining patients who are wanton enough to remain
in London at this unfashionable season, and take the rest
you amply deserve and even more amply and obviously
need.' He smiled beguilingly. 'And if you need any more
reasons, I have to tell you that the chef at the hotel is a
master of his art. His *poulardes à la crême Toulouse* would
make a strong man weep.'

She laughed. 'Oh, now you have persuaded me! How
could I resist such culinary temptation? Where is this
nirvana, pray?'

'Maidenhead,' said Jennings.

Venetia had been awake for a long time, staring at the
movement of the light outside against the curtains, listening to the birdsong. Her thoughts were far away when
Ivo addressed her.

'What time is it?'

'Early,' she said. She felt him push himself up on
one elbow; she was turned away from him, half on
her side, her folded arm under her head. His bare arm
reached across her to the bedside table for his watch,
and she looked at it, the skin and muscle and shape of
a male forearm she knew so well. How could that be?
To know someone's face was one thing, but to know so
intimately every part of another person's body was still
strange to her.

'Ten past six,' he said. His arm came down on the other

side, bridging her, so she turned on her back to look up at him. He was smiling. 'Couldn't you sleep?'

'It seems such a waste,' she said. 'It's our last day today.'

'Mm, you're right,' he said, bending his head to kiss her lingeringly. 'Have you enjoyed yourself?'

'It's been wonderful.'

'We haven't seen much of Maidenhead,' he said. 'Somehow there always seemed better things to do.' He propped himself with his face in one hand and with the other toyed with a strand of her hair. 'What would you like to do today?'

Venetia looked past him at the room, which had become so familiar to her. The hotel was not, as she had feared, the very famous one, the Mecca of the *demi-monde*, with the lawns that went down to the river, where the *poules de luxe* could be seen strolling with their keepers. Once or twice in the past she had been to Maidenhead on an innocent family outing, and from the safety of a boat drifting by had had the muslin ladies pointed out to her. When Ivo had said, 'Maidenhead,' she had been afraid she was to be numbered among them.

But she ought to have trusted him. They had come to a small, out-of-the-way hotel which, because it had no river-frontage, was not popular with the wilder set. It had a very discreet and expensive air, and the staff had not suggested by so much as a raised eyebrow that they thought 'Mr and Mrs Jennings' were anything but a properly married couple.

It had been a bad moment for her, all the same, when they stood at the desk and Ivo announced them and asked for their room. She was sure she had blushed. It was ridiculous and infuriating, when she had gone past the point of no return so long ago. She was a grown woman, and what they were doing was not against the law. Yet she had had to turn her face away, and under cover of fidgeting with her veil, had cast an anguished look around to see if there was anyone who might know her. It was one thing to flout the conventions in the privacy of his house and the darkness of night, quite another to be standing with him in the foyer of a public hotel where anyone might see.

Their room was well appointed, even luxurious, but in a solid, respectable style, which reassured her somewhat; and when they had gone down to dinner that first night, she had found the dining-room similarly subdued, and with the tables set well apart from each other and screened by palms and ferns in pots, so that each had its privacy. Yet as they passed to their table, she couldn't help seeing that at each other table was a man and woman so deeply involved with each other they did not glance up. It was plain to her that they were enjoying 'assignations', and if she thought that about them, she knew they must think it about her.

But it had been heavenly to be with Ivo for four whole days, to be able to make love whenever they wanted, and, above all, to sleep together. It was odd, but that act of falling asleep in his arms and waking still beside him, though it encompassed several hours of unconsciousness, seemed more precious to her than anything else they did together. And in this room she felt safe. No-one could see her, recognise her, or judge her, as long as they were here inside. It was fortunate, perhaps, that he was as happy as her to spend almost all day in bed: they did not seem to be able to get enough of each other, and any moment when they were not touching seemed a wasted one.

And now it was their last day. This evening they would have to catch the train back to London and normality: the idyll would be over. How should they spend their last day? They ought perhaps to try to make it memorable.

'What do you want to do?' she temporised.

'I asked first,' he said. He twisted her hair round his finger. 'We could hire a vehicle of some sort and go for a drive. Or we could take a boat on the river. Or walk about the town and see the sights. There's a church of some sort, I believe, and a bridge that echoes strangely if you stand underneath it and shout.' He slid the finger out of her hair and ran it slowly down her throat and across her breast, making her shiver. 'I suppose since we are in Maidenhead we ought to sample its peculiar delights. What say we have them make us up a basket and take a boat on the river? It shouldn't be so crowded today.'

'Mm, that sounds nice.'

'And then we can find a secluded spot to tie up and eat. A pastoral scene – I picture a rustic gate, a willow tree and perhaps a picturesque cow or two to witness our riot.' He was stroking her body in a way that made it hard for her to concentrate. 'There's only one thing I insist on, and it may be hard for you to grant me.'

'Hm? No – I'm sure – whatever you want.'

'I insist,' he said sternly, 'that it must be I who take the oars. Independent female you may be, but I cannot allow you to do the rowing.'

She laughed. 'No, how can you be so foolish! Oh, Ivo—!' His caresses overcame her, and she reached up and pulled him down to her.

It was a fine day, and though it was a Monday, it was August. The river seemed very crowded to her as Ivo helped her into the boat at the landing stage near the bridge. He held it steady while she settled herself and the boatman handed down the picnic basket, then they were shoved off. Ivo handled the oars with skill, but at first he was manoeuvring his way through a throng of boats, and Venetia felt awkward and exposed, sitting there, helpless to escape or hide herself. The other boats came very close, and the people in them seemed hardly genteel – almost vulgar. Even the females made no effort to avoid looking at her; some positively stared. Most of them were laughing too freely, and many were dressed too loudly. Not to put too fine a point on it, some were what she recognised by now as expensive tarts.

Ivo didn't seem to mind the throng. He dipped and pulled, looking over one shoulder then the other, concentrating on the river. Despite his skill, a less expertly handled boat bumped into them, its prow hitting them amidships. The two young women in the stern shrieked

346

with abandon, clutching each other with simulated fear. Their companion, a red-faced, middle-aged man with large grey moustaches, was jolted almost off his seat in the bow, grabbed at his dislodged hat, dropped an oar, and then, twisting round to see what had happened, huffed a confused apology.

'I beg your pardon, sir. Dear me! By Jove! Crowded today, ain't it? Didn't see you, sir. I'm so sorry!'

'Not at all, sir,' Ivo called genially. 'Rowing's hard enough, and I see your attention must have been otherwise engaged. Indeed, how could it have been otherwise, with so much beauty before you?' He lifted his hat with mock gallantry at the women. 'Ladies, don't distract him, now! I warrant he has his hands full as it is.'

They shrieked again, this time with knowing mirth. 'Hands full? Ooh, I get you! You naughty boy!'

Venetia looked at the wide open mouths, gaping like black holes in the artificially white faces. She turned her face away, embarrassed, and said, 'Please, Ivo! Get us away from them.'

One of the women was amused, and cried, 'Ooh, parding me, m'lady! 'Ev I ho-fended you?'

The other seemed inclined to be piqued. 'Give yourself fancy airs, don't you? Ain't no difference between us, love – Rosy O'Grady an' the colonel's lady!' And they both laughed.

The man tried to hush them. 'Please, Maisie dear! I beg your pardon, sir. Truth is,' he smiled a little lopsidedly, 'we've all lunched rather well.'

'Ain't *that* the truth!' Maisie's friend giggled.

'Not at all, sir,' Ivo said, grinning. 'What's the river for, after all? Let me shove you off. Left oar, sir – *left* oar! That's right. Pull both now.'

The boat swung and wobbled and began drifting away as the man tried valiantly to co-ordinate his movements and avoid hitting himself on the chin with the inboard part of his oars. The women grinned amiably at Ivo as they receded. 'You won't get much change out o' that one, love!' Maisie called pleasantly. 'Too old and sour.

347

Why'nt you come over here and join us? We'll see you have a good time.'

Ivo only laughed, and seeing a gap open up, dug his oar in and shot away, leaving them behind as they turned helplessly on the current and tangled with two more boats.

When they were clear, he looked at Venetia with the old, mocking smile as she sat staring unhappily down at her hands. 'What is it? Do they bother you? They shouldn't – they're only a couple of gay girls having a good time. Why should you mind what they say?'

'I don't think you should have encouraged them,' she said in a low voice.

'My dear idiot, females like that don't need encouragement!' he laughed. 'I know what's annoyed you: your nose was put out of joint by their polish and elegance!'

She didn't like his teasing, but it would have made her more ridiculous to object to it, so she kept silence, her cheeks hot. She was wishing heartily they had not come out in a boat, wishing even that they had never come to Maidenhead. He should not have exposed her to this sort of thing. And yet, suppose the gay girls were right? Were they all the same after all? But no, that was a foolish thing to think. She and Ivo were in love. It was not a business transaction – which made it all the more important to ensure that appearances did not suggest it. He shouldn't have brought her here.

Yet as they pulled further up the river and it grew quieter, the magic of the place began to work on her. They glided almost silently between green banks, gazed at by nothing more threatening than a stately swan or two, a few busy moorhens dabbling in and out of the rushes, half a dozen red cows standing in the shallows with the ripples of passage lapping their fetlocks. Gradually Venetia regained her composure. The only sound was the creak of the rowlocks and the chuckle of water against the boat's stem; the smooth motion, the strange, flat smell of the river, the little fresh breeze on her forehead, the swallows dipping and skimming were all so soothing.

She trailed her fingers in the cold, green-brown water, and watched the sunlight dance on the broken surface, watched the handsome play of muscles in Ivo's forearms as he feathered and pulled so competently. It was lovely to watch a man do something he did well. It was almost like the feeling she got when she watched him play the piano: the word that came to her was *puissance*. His ability to do things, his *puissance*, excited and attracted her. He felt her eyes on him and smiled at her, and she wanted him again. This endlessly renewable passion between them seemed a marvel to her.

He found a tying-up place, a narrow inlet parallel with the river, between overgrown banks shaded with willow. It was only just one boat wide and hardly more than a boat's length, so they would be unlikely to be disturbed. Without conversation they disembarked, spread a rug over the grass, passed up the basket and cushions, and settled themselves in the moving, dappled shadow of the trees.

'Well,' he said at last, engaged in opening a bottle of wine, 'have you recovered your temper?'

She was hurt. 'I never lost it. How could you think so?'

'You didn't like the tarts laughing at you. In your world, such creatures are always the helpless supplicants, aren't they? Humble, silent and grateful.'

'You don't know much about them if you think that,' she said, with dignity. 'They might be grateful but they aren't often humble, and they're *never* silent. Nothing those women could say would shock me, I assure you. I'm quite accustomed to rough talk, from all sections of society.'

'Then what upset you?' He gave his teasing grin. 'I know! You thought it was my fault we collided, and you were shocked at having to revise your estimate of my skills. But you can rest assured, I am the master of everything I undertake. Too much liquid refreshment in the other boat, that was the long and short of it. There now, have I dispelled your unease?'

There was no resisting him. She laughed, and he

poured the wine, and they ate and drank and talked of everything and nothing, as friends do. When they had finished, she lay down and put her head in his lap, and the dreaming afternoon poured down like honey through the gold-green leaves, the molten sun refracting into dazzle on the moving water beyond their haven. Later he lay down beside her, and they kissed and caressed, wrapped in a cocoon of summer afternoon bliss.

Later still she propped her head on her hand so that she could look at his face, traced with her eye the line of his forehead, his surprisingly delicate eyebrows, the curve of his closed eyelids and the feather of his eyelashes against his cheek; his nose, straight except for one bump, which was beguiling in its imperfection; his mouth – looking at his mouth made her shiver with desire. She wanted him so much, always. What was this wildness in her? Did all women in love feel it? Did it last throughout married life?

He felt the shiver. Without opening his eyes he murmured, 'What is it? Are you cold?'

'No, of course not.' She hesitated, and then, thinking a better moment was not likely to come, she said, 'I was wondering what was going to happen to us.' He didn't reply. Was he asleep? She didn't believe so. Why should she be shy about mentioning the subject? But she was, brought up to believe it was for a man to ask, and unable to break the habit of mind. She swallowed and said tentatively, 'I mean, where do we go from here, you and I? What—'

She got no further. He gave a sort of grunt, and murmured, as if almost asleep, 'Oh, not now, lover. Don't spoil a perfect day with questions.' And he reached up a strong arm and pulled her down against him, and kissed her very long and thoroughly, then tucked her head against his chest and rested his chin on top of her hair. All without opening his eyes. Venetia, half relieved and half frustrated, yielded and said no more.

It was beginning to turn cool when they went back down the river: in August the shortening of the days accelerates, and there is sometimes an autumn chill in the oncoming dusk. The sun was going down, crimson and gold behind the trees. Shadows crept out from their hiding places under bridges and banks and slipped across the river, painting an indigo crescent on the back of every rosy and gilded wavelet. The smell of the water now seemed somehow melancholy.

Boating parties all seemed to have had enough of the water at the same moment, and there was a queue to get back to the landing stage. As they got nearer, they found themselves in closer and closer proximity to the other boats. Ivo was quite relaxed, resting on his oars, looking over his shoulder and pulling up when the opportunity came; Venetia tried to curb her impatience, sat with her attention rigidly inboard, so as not to catch the eye of anyone nearby. She did not want another brush with the muslin company.

But the boat that was being funnelled alongside them contained a very different kind of party, as she could tell from the clothes and demeanour without ever directly looking at them. It was a larger boat than theirs and contained an elderly gentleman and lady, two young women with parasols, two young men, and a girl of about ten in white muslin and ringlets. It was moving just a little ahead of them, and as the older gentleman passed so as to be able to see Venetia's face, he started with recognition and began automatically to lift his hand to his hat.

Venetia caught the movement and looked at him. It was Mr Walcott, an exporter and the husband of one of her patients. In a panic, her eyes widened, and she gave a tiny, warning shake of her head, which stopped his hand, but plainly puzzled him. Mrs Walcott turned to see what her husband was looking at, just as, with a glance of embarrassment towards Ivo, understanding came to him and he frowned and turned his face away. Venetia turned her head away too, but not before she had seen the recognition in Mrs Walcott's eyes.

351

Now that it was too late, she saw how much better it would have been to acknowledge them. To be sure, she was out on the river alone with a man to whom she was not married; but after all, Ivo was not married either, and he was perfectly respectable, and she was not a child. If she had greeted the Walcotts naturally and introduced Ivo as if nothing was wrong, they probably would have assumed they were engaged to be married. Now she had given the game away completely.

The two boats were locked together for what seemed an eternity. Venetia had turned right away and was leaning over the opposite side of the boat as if staring at something in the water, but she could feel what seemed like a thousand eyes boring into her back. No-one said anything, but they must all have seen and recognised her. Oh, what a fool she was! She was furious with herself. The guilty man flees, she thought – how apt that was! But there was nothing to be done about it now. Surely, surely the Walcotts would not say anything? They would be discreet – they *must* be discreet.

The agonising moment was over at last. The other boat pulled ahead of them, reached the landing stage, and with her head still firmly averted Venetia saw, without looking, the party disembark, gather themselves together and walk off. Did they look towards her a moment before they left? She thought they did – but perhaps they were just looking at the river. Ivo's turn came, the boat was tied up, he helped her out, and said, 'Your hand's as cold as ice. Are you all right?'

'It's getting chilly,' she said. 'And don't you think the river looks almost threatening when the sun starts to go down?'

'You have struck a *triste*,' Ivo said wisely. 'Natural reaction to the approaching end of a day of pleasure. You see it in children all the time.'

'No, what do you know of children?' she said, trying to meet his light mood. They were walking away from the pier now. He stopped and turned her to face him, taking both her hands.

'What's the matter?' he asked, for once with unteasing concern.

'As you say, it's just a *triste*,' she said. 'Do you think we could go straight back and have supper in London instead of dining here? I've had a lovely time, but it would be rather like a prolonged goodbye, and they're always painful.'

'Of course. Just as you please,' Ivo said obligingly. 'We can go to my house, and have some music. I'll find something very hot and dry to play, so that it doesn't remind you of water. Do you think you might be up to playing a duet with me? Oh, yes, I know you think you are hopeless, but you can play well enough to keep up with me, and I'll forgive you the interpretation for the pleasure of being able to hear both parts for once.'

She guessed that he was chatting to distract her from her thoughts, and was grateful, even while it puzzled and faintly annoyed her that he displayed no curiosity as to what those thoughts were.

The assembling, shipping and supplying of an army of 16,400, over a distance similar to the crossing of the Atlantic, was accomplished with tremendous dispatch and efficiency, in complete contrast to the Crimean campaign of sorry memory. On the 13th of September General Wolseley defeated Arabi's rebel army at Tel-el-Kebir with fewer than 450 British casualties. There had never been a neater business, everyone said, and even Marcus agreed, writing to Venetia from Cairo, that a great deal of the credit had to go to Cardwell and his reforms.

I thought at the time that he was a complete outsider and that his tinkering would be the ruin of the Army, but I admit now that I was wrong. I wish I were able to tell Papa so – it must have vexed him to have me against him. The transport and provisioning go like clockwork, and, far from making the men soft, it seems to do them good to have proper meals and

353

decent tents at night. The climate here is so tire-some, any little comfort is welcome, I must say.

He told about his own part in the 'magnificent cavalry dash' which had taken Cairo and routed the last of the enemy forces, and then went on,

I hear that Sir Garnet is very pleased with Prince Arthur, and has written to Her Majesty to praise his cool courage under the hottest fire Sir G had ever seen. He takes good care of his men and is active in his duties – which, in translation, means he is a good soldier and a good egg! I know Olivia will be pleased to hear it. You will be pleased to know I haven't a scratch on me and will be bringing you a present of a very fine carpet from the tent of one of the rebel cavalry officers. We expect to be going home quite soon, having done all that needs to be done here.

Tommy Weston, visiting Venetia, disagreed with this last sentiment. 'With the khedive and Arabi both scup-pered, the situation out there is anything but stable. The moment is ripe for us to annexe Egypt once for all – for the sake of the Canal, we can't allow any other power the opportunity to do so.'

'But surely the rest of Europe wouldn't stand for that,' Venetia said.

'I don't know so much,' said Tommy. 'I believe it's what they expect, and they'd be quite glad to let us get on with it. It's in everyone's interest to have things quiet out there, and if we want to undertake the dirty work, well and good. And, quite frankly, we're trusted where other powers aren't.'

Venetia smiled. 'That's more or less what Marcus said.'

'Don't sound so surprised. Marcus isn't an idiot. He has his own way of putting things, but he's quite shrewd.'

'So, if even Marcus can see the sense of annexation, why don't we?'

Tommy made a face. 'The Cabinet is funking it. Bright's resignation made them nervous about the moral aspect, and, frankly, Gladstone is an old man and he'd sooner wash his hands of the whole problem. What we need is someone with fire in his belly to grasp the nettle.'

'You?'

He laughed. 'I'm not a firebrand. But I tell you what – we shall have a lot more trouble out there by and by, for want of sorting it out now, while they're still off balance. I was talking to Charles Gordon the other day – he's on a couple of the same committees as me – and he says things are as bad as they can be in the Egyptian Sudan.'

'He served out there, didn't he?'

'No-one knows it better. He brought order to a wide area and got rid of most of the slave trade – or at least suppressed it. But since he left, things have gone to the bad. Now there's a native madman who calls himself the Messiah who's been raising revolt, and the misgovernment is so appalling they're flocking to his cause. It's the kind of thing that ought to be nipped in the bud, and I've tried to speak up in Cabinet about it, but Gladstone just harrumphs and my-boys me, and the rest of them hope that if they don't look at the problem it will somehow go away.'

'Poor Tommy! Who would have thought a cabinet post would bring you so much grief?'

On her return from the trip to Maidenhead, Venetia found herself so busy that she was unable to see much of Ivo; and Ivo, while reaffirming that he was a town bird and not a country man, said that as she wasn't likely to miss him, he would accept an invitation from an old friend to go and stay on his estate in Hampshire for a few weeks.

'He's rather a gymnastic sort of fellow, always riding and hunting and shooting – standing up to his waist in fast rivers tormenting fish with a bit of feather, that sort of thing. But he's a good sort, and he's been asking me for years, and I have word that his house is comfortable and his cook first-rate. So as you haven't a minute to spare for me . . .'

Venetia smiled. 'Not a minute or a second. Go, with my blessing. How long will you be away?'

'Three or four weeks, I expect.'

'So long?' she said, a little dismayed.

'Charles is a very sociable chap, so there'll be lots going on. And lots of company. He always gathers quite a party through September and October.'

Venetia had a moment of pique that he should be invited without her – time was when she'd have been a prize for any party to boast – but it was over on the instant. She had so much to do, and those parties had never been as much fun as they were supposed to be. One day, when they were married, she and Ivo would be asked together – and then they'd probably refuse to go!

'I shall miss you,' she said, and he stepped close and ran his hands up her arms.

'Oh, but think how glad we'll be when we see each other again!' he murmured.

She was at first so busy that she had no time to miss him, except at night in the moments before sleep claimed her. Then a cold snap at the end of September killed off some of the fevers that had been plaguing the mean streets, and she became a little less busy – enough so to be disappointed that Ivo wrote that he was not coming back to London for a week or two more. He had his friend and their party had been invited to someone else's estate in the north for the shooting, and he thought he might go and find out for himself what it was that so many of his sex saw in the sport.

Some of the families began to come back to Town, and Venetia's cousin Lord Batchworth took a house for himself and his sister Anne.

'William pretends it's for my sake,' Anne said, when she called on Venetia soon after their arrival. 'He says I need more exposure to the world of fashion in order to catch a husband – the shame of having me nineteen and still unwed being something no brother could stand! But the fact of the matter is that he's in love himself, and yearns to snare his beloved and carry her back to Grasscroft.'

'Why does he need to snare her? Doesn't she care for him?' Venetia asked.

'He's too shy to ask, the poor boy! Imagine, Venetia, almost thirty and he can't bring himself to propose to her, the booby! It's not as if she's a green girl – the lady in question is Hatterel's widow, Miss Ferguson that was, and she's almost as old as that herself.'

'I remember her – a very handsome woman. Wasn't there a child?' Venetia asked.

'Yes, a little boy, quite a dear, though I don't care much for children as a rule. He'll come in for his father's estate, so he wouldn't be a burden on William – not that William would care. He's in head-and-ears over her. If he doesn't speak soon, I shall have to do it myself to put him out of his misery.'

'And what about you?'

'About me? And matrimony, do you mean? Oh, I'm not looking for a husband yet.'

'Have you any young men in tow?'

'The usual half-dozen,' Anne said. 'I like them in quantity – saves them from thinking themselves too particular.' She gave Venetia a sidelong look. 'Speaking of being particular, I heard the oddest thing the other day.'

'What's that?'

'I heard it from Mary Somercott, who had it from Pauline Freshwater. I don't usually listen to that sort of thing, but it concerned you, dear Venetia, so I felt obliged to out of a sense of duty.'

Venetia felt herself blushing, and was angry at her own lack of control. Lord Freshwater was the Earl of Tonbridge's son – the Southports had known the Tonbridges all their lives – and his wife had been the very rich daughter of a manufacturer. Venetia saw how it might have happened: Lady Freshwater probably had acquaintances still among the set she grew up with. It was quite possible that she knew the Walcotts.

'No-one cares what Lady Freshwater says, surely?' she

managed to say in an even voice. 'She's known as a dedicated gossip.'

'And an outsider – quite.' Anne was looking thoughtful. 'I see from your face that I've touched a sensitive spot. I'm sorry to hurt you, but I thought you ought to know that things are being said.'

'What things, exactly?' Venetia asked.

'That you are having an affair with a young man and were seen by some friend of Lady Freshwater's disporting yourself – forgive me – at Maidenhead.'

Venetia forced herself to meet Anne's eyes. 'Is that so very terrible?'

'So there is a young man. Is he married?'

The abrupt question startled Venetia. 'No!' she said indignantly. 'Of course not!'

Anne shrugged. 'I dare say Mary Somercott is jealous – no-one ever wanted to disport themselves with *her*. She's trying to make it into a great scandal. But, Ven, if he's not married already, why not marry him? Gossip is stupid and decent people don't heed it, but it is unpleasant; and one's aim should always be to avoid unpleasantness.'

Venetia ignored the question. 'If it's scandal they want,' she said lightly, 'why don't they talk about my brother and sister instead? My poor little efforts can't compete with theirs.'

Anne allowed herself to be deflected. She laughed. 'My dear, they do talk, all the time! But, of course, Gussie and Southport are the Prince of Wales's friends, which makes them untouchable. The Freshwaters and Somercotts would *adore* to be part of his circle, but he's got more sense than to recruit them!'

CHAPTER NINETEEN

In September 1882, a meeting was held in Mrs Worsley's residence, Winthorpe Cottage – a misnomer, since it was a stout and four-square house at the far end of the village. The dining-room table had been removed, and rows of chairs introduced. Henrietta, as one of the leading ladies of the neighbourhood, had a place reserved for her in the front row. It was an honour she would gladly have forgone, except that she thought Elizabeth might like it. She had just had her tenth birthday, and was a gravely mature little girl, quite different from the heedless romp her mother had been at that age.

She seemed not to see much of her, these days, now that she was doing regular lessons. Mr Fortescue's partiality for his daughter did not diminish as she grew older. He had begun teaching her when she was four years old, at first just for an hour a day, increasing the time as she grew older. Now she went to him every day after breakfast, stayed until luncheon, and returned in the afternoon from three o'clock until five. At first Elizabeth had told her mother excitedly what she learned each day, but of late she seemed to think Mama wouldn't understand, and when asked would only say, 'Oh, it was mathematics this morning,' or Latin, or poetry, or botany; and if pressed for detail would fall back on, 'We went on with what we did last week.'

It seemed to Henrietta a heavy regime for so little a girl, and she wondered sometimes whether being with an old man for so much of her time was making Elizabeth abnormally solemn and grave. Yet the child went eagerly to her lessons, and seemed both healthy and contented. Henrietta made sure that she was out of doors every day between two and three, either walking or on horseback; and on Saturdays, when there were no lessons because Mr Fortescue had parish duties to perform, she tried always to be with Elizabeth, to take her out or play with her, to bring some variety and if possible fun into her young life.

She wouldn't have brought Elizabeth to the meeting, but that Mr Fortescue was unable to give his daughter her lessons that day, being otherwise engaged, and Henrietta had already agreed to go to the meeting and was looking forward to it. Mrs Worsley, a wealthy widow, had come to the village two years ago in 1880, and her coming had considerably enlivened village life. She was energetic, strong-minded, managing, and couldn't bear mental or physical idleness.

'She positively exhausts me,' Mary Compton had complained languidly after first meeting her. Henrietta, however, found her stimulating. Georgiana Worsley's interests were wide and varied, and as soon as she had settled into the cottage she began sounding out the village for like-minded ladies. Since then, there were all sorts of new societies, with meetings to go to every week, and there wasn't a lady of means in the neighbourhood who was not signed up for one thing or another.

Many were eager to join anything, just for the sake of sociability, for there had never been much to do in the village; but even the reluctant ones succumbed to Mrs Worsley in the end. She had an arsenal of weapons of persuasion, and if one failed she would switch to another. At the last resort she had a very grand way of saying, 'Everyone looks to you, dear Mrs So-and-so, to give the lead. If *you* are seen to interest yourself in this worthy cause, everyone else will follow.' It was a rare female who did not find this assessment of her influence too flattering to resist.

Henrietta involved herself in most of Mrs Worsley's activities. It made her days more interesting, and the sense of achievement gave a little more point to life than merely having survived another year. She had not seen Jerome since that Christmas of 1875: if he had visited Mary in that time she had not seen him and Mary had not said so. Mary never spoke of him to Henrietta, a kindness she was not sure whether she welcomed or not. Only once Miss Compton had broken her silence, in the early months of 1878, to tell Henrietta that he was to be married, to Miss Julia Winsham, the daughter of a colonel of the Guards, from Hampshire.

It ought to have settled her mind. Perhaps that was why Mary had done it. It meant he was out of reach for ever, and that she could put aside any lingering vestige of regret she might have had in the unplumbed depths of her mind. Miss Julia Winsham, from Hampshire. The words seemed to hold together always, an indissoluble whole; they lay across her life like a fallen tree blocking a road. What was she like, Miss Julia Winsham from Hampshire? Young, handsome, rich? Probably. Why should he take anything less? Did he love her? Henrietta hoped so. She hoped and hoped that they loved each other rapturously, and would be blissfully happy for ever and ever.

It was an ending, and having been thereby rescued from the sin of wishing, she schooled herself not to think of him. By day she managed pretty well, occupying herself with her household routines, her parish duties and her good works; but she could not govern her dreams. By night she dreamed, not often of him but of loss, and of trying to find something that was always just out of reach, out of sight. Her dreams were infused with sadness and longing, and she would wake sometimes with tears on her cheeks. On the few occasions she actually dreamed of him, she felt comforted through her sadness, but worried about the sin of it. She would go to church in the middle of the day, when it was empty, and pray for forgiveness. *I can't be held accountable for my dreams, can I?* she would ask; and in the wax-scented stillness, sometimes the answer would seem to be *yes*. But at other times she would seem to hear a sigh of understanding, like a hand resting in exculpation on her head. A loving touch, it was: she had seen Mr Fortescue rest his hand on Elizabeth's shining hair like that, had seen Elizabeth lift her eyes in trust and love at his touch. She longed for such comfort – real comfort in the real world. She had never known the loving touch of a father or a mother. All her life she seemed to have been without the things other people knew: a child without parents, a wife without a husband, a mother whose child was a little less her own with every passing week.

So Mrs Worsley came as a welcome distraction from the sameness of her days: her schemes were something new to think about, and at the very least meant that the ladies of the neighbourhood had the opportunity to meet each other without having to wait for someone to give an expensive dinner or party. And at best, Henrietta thought, they did achieve some good here and there.

Mrs Worsley's latest enterprise was to set up a branch of the Society for Women's Suffrage and, for a wonder, she had even persuaded Miss Compton to help.

'But I hate organising – and being organised,' Miss Compton had said wonderingly to Henrietta when confessing this departure. 'I loathe writing letters, politics bore me to death, and the very idea of a pamphlet is anathema.' Still, somehow or other Mrs Worsley had 'got at' Miss Compton: winkled her out, gingered her up, buckled her down, and actually got a surprising amount of work out of her. 'I don't know how she persuades me to do it,' Mary said.

'I don't think you are as lazy as you pretend to be,' Henrietta said.

'I assure you, the only thing I've ever exerted myself for is pleasure. I think she must be a witch. I'm going to take along a looking-glass to the meeting and see if she casts a reflection. I believe that's the infallible test.'

Henrietta had been looking forward particularly to this meeting. When she was very young, still a girl back on her father's estate, she had often pondered what a woman was *for*. The answer then, as now, had seemed to be to marry and have children. Yet it had never satisfied. She had had no education, but she was intelligent, with an enquiring mind. Since her marriage had fallen into its pattern of separation, she had undertaken a course of serious reading; and the more she fed her mind, the more it wanted, and the more puzzled she felt about the female condition. Why had God made it possible for a woman to wonder such things, if it was His will that she should live as women mostly did? She wanted to be persuaded one way or the other, to hear some argument which decided the matter, which would tell her whether to struggle or lie down. Perhaps those who agitated for the women's vote might have an answer for her of such unassailable logic it would finally satisfy.

At the meeting there was to be a guest speaker – someone, they had been assured, quite famous in the Movement, almost on a par with Mrs Fawcett herself. Henrietta liked the idea of the Movement. She had an image in her mind of women from every part of the country coming together, joining little local rivulets that ran into larger streams, which in turn joined great rivers, until the whole of womankind was flowing, sure and steady and strong, in one direction. To be swept up in that stream, she thought, would give comfort: ever since she had left childhood she had felt out of step with the world.

The speaker, a Mrs Pargeter, turned out to be a well-looking woman of about forty, very smartly dressed and with a hat that transfixed several of the less serious-minded in the audience for quite the first half-hour. Henrietta caught herself examining the hat and rebuked herself for frivolity, but Mrs Pargeter actually referred to her appearance in one part of her speech.

'It has been said,' she proclaimed, in her clear, ringing voice, 'that those females who *want* the vote also *want* all feminine virtues.' She waited for a little murmur of laughter to die down. 'It is true that there are some women suffragists who delight in being bold and mannish, careless and rude, in aping the worst part of the male sex in their desire to have a man's privileges. But I say to you, we should not go down that path.' She looked round at them sternly. 'No!' she cried, eliciting a guilty start from Regina Parke, who had been far away in thought, trying to memorise the sleeve detail on Mrs Pargeter's dress so that she could get her dressmaker to reproduce it.

'No,' Mrs Pargeter went on, 'we should not follow that sad example! For that is to give a weapon into the hands of our enemies, who wish to believe that the vote would destroy the virtues of womanhood. For that reason, too, we should not neglect the duties of our home life. It is not by being bad needlewomen and bad housekeepers that we will show ourselves worthy of the trust we claim. Quite the contrary! We must work with the grain of our times. It is the good housekeeper, it is the attractively dressed and well-mannered woman who is the more likely to achieve our great aim.'

The good housekeepers – they were more numerous in the audience than the attractively dressed – smirked a little, feeling they had been complimented, though not entirely sure how.

'And what is our great aim?' Mrs Pargeter went on, her bright eyes sweeping the upturned faces. 'Why, ladies, it is the vote, plain and simple! The vote, just as the men have it, and on the same terms! In the spirit of our great democratic age, our great liberal age, we must ask for nothing less. I give you an example. A woman householder – let us say, a respectable widow of means – requires some carpentry work performed in her house. She summons a carpenter, a simple artisan, and explains to him what she wants. She gives him, in fact, his orders. She inspects his work when it is done. It is she who decides whether it is satisfactory. It is she who pays him, or withholds the payment, and he accepts this power over him as right and reasonable. He treats her with subservience and respect. She is the mistress of the house, the employer, and he the humble employee. And yet, ladies, when the general election is called, the carpenter has the right to vote, and the woman, his employer, does not! I ask you, is this fair? Is this just? Is this—' she summoned up a great rumble in her voice like a roll of drums '—*democracy*?' There was a flutter of applause at this point.

It was a stirring speech. As it continued, Henrietta, glancing round, noted the ones who did not understand what it was all about, but were merely moved by her tones, as they were in church by a rousing sermon. Others were nodded quietly, agreeing with the sentiments, but probably, like Henrietta herself, not seeing what any of them could do about it.

'Our Government,' Mrs Pargeter said at last, 'is pledged to reform. Pledged to extend the franchise. You have all heard, I'm sure, of the agricultural vote? The agricultural worker has no vote, while his town-dwelling brother has. This, ladies, is perceived as unfair. An intolerable injustice. A potential cause of civil unrest. The present Government is pledged to enfranchise the countryman, so that all men are entitled equally to a say in the affairs of the nation. Yet this same Government, a government dedicated to fairness, to democracy, to liberal principles, is content to leave half the citizens of this country with no say at all in their own future! That is, need I explain, the female half! The Parliamentary Reform Bill, which this Government plans to introduce, will be our great opportunity. Every one of us must do everything she can to ensure that women are included in the changes to the franchise. The tide of history is in our favour. We must seize the moment, and ride on the flood to victory!'

When the speech was over, and the vote of thanks, the ladies rose from their chairs and passed eagerly into Mrs Worsley's drawing-room for the usual tea and cakes. Henrietta found herself standing near Mrs Pargeter, and as the bright eyes swept round and fixed on her enquiringly, she felt obliged to ask an intelligent question, for the honour of the village, if nothing else. She cleared her throat a little nervously, and asked what any of them could actually do.

'We can talk to our husbands, Mrs . . . ?'

'Fortescue,' Mrs Worsley supplied, at the speaker's elbow. 'Mrs Fortescue is our dear rector's wife.'

Mrs Pargeter raised her eyebrows. 'Oh! Yes, indeed, I have heard of Mr Fortescue, of course – his reputation as a scholar is universally known. And, in fact, Mr Pargeter has had the honour of some correspondence with him. So you are Mrs Fortescue?' She seemed to find it something of a surprise, but Henrietta was used to that: she was, after all, a great deal younger than her husband and had nothing about her that suggested great intellect, beauty, birth or wealth – nothing to tempt a great man to marry her.

'How wonderful it must be, to have privileged access to such a superior mind!' Mrs Pargeter went on. 'Well, my dear ma'am, you are in a position to do the Movement a great deal of good. If you can persuade your husband to take our part, his influence will be very great! Where men of scholarship and intellect lead, others must follow.'

'Persuade him?' Henrietta said doubtfully.

'Yes indeed! Talk to him. Argue the case. His great intellect will no doubt see the absolute logic of our position on the woman question. Get him to write letters. And write letters yourself, of course. A steady drip, drip of application and argument will, like water, eventually wear away a stone. Is this your little girl?'

'Yes, my daughter Elizabeth.'

'What a little love she is! And so well behaved. Well, my dear, did you understand what the meeting was about?'

Elizabeth, regarding her with the grave calm of a sage, said, 'I think so, ma'am.'

Mrs Pargeter smiled and laid a hand on Elizabeth's head. 'Votes for women, my child! Remember, when you are a grown-up lady, and have the right to vote, that it was people like your good mama who secured that right for you. Such a pretty child, Mrs Fortescue.'

'Thank you. But—'

Mrs Worsley interrupted, taking Mrs Pargeter's arm, 'I must introduce you to Mrs Antrobus – a lady of some influence in the neighbourhood. Do excuse us, dear Mrs Fortescue,' and steered the guest away.

Mary Compton joined Henrietta. 'I hear she lectures

all over the country, from London to Glasgow. We were lucky to get her – only Mrs Fawcett herself rates higher as a speaker. Mrs Worsley must have some influence in the Movement.'

'It all sounds so reasonable when one's listening to her,' Henrietta said. 'It lifts one up. But afterwards—'

'One deflates like a balloon?' Mary said. 'Yes, it's not as simple or as inevitable as she makes it seem. And I doubt her approach is the right one.'

'What do you mean?'

'We must be pragmatic: as she said, we must work with the grain. And I can't see there is any hope in the world of getting the vote for married women. But she insists it must be all or none. Far better to try to get it first for single and widowed women, where there is a chance, however small, of success. I don't know why she doesn't see that.'

'Because she is a married woman – and you, Mary dear, are single,' Henrietta said.

Mary laughed. 'Well, that may be true, but it doesn't alter the fact. Men regard the idea of a married woman's having a separate vote of her own as striking at the very heart of matrimony, patrimony and civilisation itself. They're not prepared to countenance it, and to my mind they never will.'

'But we have the secret ballot now,' Henrietta said.

'Would you be prepared to vote, even secretly, against your husband's known wishes? Or refuse to tell him how you had voted if he asked you directly? Exactly. So it would be better if we were to leave married women out of it for the present – with all due respect to you, my dear Mrs Fortescue.'

'Still, given that most of her audience here were married women, it might have made her speech fall rather flat if she'd said that,' Henrietta said shrewdly.

'True enough.' Mary took her elbow and turned her a little away from the rest of the company. 'Talking of married women,' she said in a low voice, 'I have something to tell you.'

There was such a world of meaning in her look that

Henrietta felt a coldness grip her scalp and run down her neck. 'No,' she said. 'I know what – who – you're going to speak about. Please don't.'

'My dear, you don't mean that,' Mary said. 'Oh, why were you so stubborn?' she cried suddenly, as though it had been surprised out of her. 'I know if I had ever had a man as much in love with me as he was with you, I'd have given up heaven and earth to be with him.'

'Please don't say that,' Henrietta begged miserably.

'I must! I've been silent all these years, but it burns in me intolerably. You have no idea how fortunate you are, and yet you threw it all away! No-one,' she added, in a tone Henrietta had not heard before, 'has ever loved me like that, and I don't suppose now that they ever will. Why did you let him go?'

'You know why.'

'Oh, yes, yes, you're a married woman, et cetera, et cetera! But that doesn't stop people. It never has, when real feelings are involved.'

'I made a vow,' Henrietta began.

'People don't regard that any more,' Mary said impatiently. 'The taking of a vow? Hocus-pocus. History, mystery, symbolism – a mere decoration, a meaningless flourish of civilisation!'

Henrietta was shocked. Mary had said provocative things on many occasions, but never so directly and angrily as this. She turned her head away. 'I can't listen to this. It's – it's sacrilegious and wrong. I wish you wouldn't say such things, Mary. I know you don't really mean them, but—'

'Don't I? Life is to be lived. The battle is to the strong. Tell me, why are you trying to get the vote for women? Because you're not prepared to accept the status quo meekly, just because a lot of old men have arranged it that way to suit themselves! And your particular old man—'

Henrietta turned back to her fiercely. 'Stop it! Not another word, or you'll lose my friendship! I shall be sorry I ever had anything to do with the Movement if it means women have to become like that.'

Mary met her eyes without embarrassment, seeming unmoved by the rebuke. There was something else in the depths of them, something like pity, which Henrietta didn't want to know about.

'He and Julia have separated,' she said, and though she spoke quietly, Henrietta felt as though the words had been shouted aloud, halting all other conversation in its stride. 'Their marriage was a mistake – on both sides – as anyone could have told them at the time, if they had been willing to listen. He was as much a fool as you – and for the same reason.'

'Why are you telling me this?' Henrietta whispered desperately.

'She has gone back to her father's house. There will be some kind of settlement. As there were no children, it will not be difficult for terms to be agreed.'

Something was slipped into Henrietta's hand. She started and looked down, and saw Elizabeth gazing up at her, puzzled and perhaps a little anxious. Henrietta looked at her blankly for a moment, then shook herself back to normality.

'Poor little Lizzie, you must long to be going home! I shan't try your patience any longer.' She turned a social face to Mary, not meeting her eyes. 'I must make my goodbyes. Where is Mrs Worsley, I wonder? Oh, there she is. Goodbye, Mary. Come, Lizzie, darling.'

She would not think of him, she *would* not. Clutching Elizabeth's hand like a lifeline, she made her escape.

There was a carriage in the sweep when she arrived home at the rectory.

'Is that Dr Mansur's?' she asked Andrews. Mansur was an old friend of the rector, and often called in a social way, but usually he stayed several hours when he came. 'Why wasn't it put away? Is he on his way somewhere?'

'I doubt he won't be staying long, ma'am,' Andrews said, embarrassed.

'What do you mean?'

Andrews looked as though he would sooner not answer.

'It's not by way of being a social call.' An insistent look from his mistress produced confession. 'Doctor was called in to the master.'

'Why? What is it? Is he ill?' Henrietta asked, alarmed.

The butler's eyes begged. 'He wouldn't like me to say, ma'am. Only he was taken bad so sudden this time, and I was that worried, I sent for Dr Mansur myself.'

'I don't understand. You mean this has happened before?'

'Not like this,' Andrews said evasively. 'Not sudden, as you might say.'

'Tell me plainly,' Henrietta said impatiently, 'is the master ill?'

'I can't exactly say, ma'am.' Andrews looked wretched. 'No-one's meant to know. Oh, please, don't say anything when you see him. He'll guess it was me told you.'

'You haven't told me anything,' Henrietta said, with some truth. 'Don't worry, I won't get you into trouble.' Andrews took this as his dismissal and hurried away before she could ask any further questions.

Old habit prevented her from sending a message or going herself at once to seek out her husband. The rule of the house was that he was never to be disturbed, except in case of emergency. Was this an emergency? She had no way of knowing. But she would find out, she supposed, at six o'clock: that was the hour at which Elizabeth would be brought down to see him in the drawing-room, since she had not been with him that day.

He was a little late, and Elizabeth was already there when he entered the room. Henrietta examined him with more attention than usual. She had grown accustomed to the appearance of him – hardly really looked at him any more on the occasions when they met. Now she saw how old he had become, how deeply lined his face. He was immaculately dressed as always, but didn't his clothes hang a little loosely on him? There was a greyness to his face, a pinched look she had not noticed before; and once she saw his mouth tighten and his eyes close for an instant as though he had suffered a spasm of pain.

Yet he behaved absolutely as usual, greeted her with neutral courtesy, sat down in his usual chair and called his daughter to him. Elizabeth went to him to be kissed and, standing before him, was soon deep in conversation with him, talking in the free-flowing way of those who are truly intimate. Henrietta watched them together, taking no part in the scene, not listening to what was being said, only to the tone of it. It struck her suddenly as strange when he invited Elizabeth to sit on his lap, and put his arms round her while their talk continued. She had seen it a hundred times before, but now it seemed remarkable that to Elizabeth he was not the dour rector, the terrifying intellectual, the stern master of the house whose wrath was to be avoided; to her he was just Papa, whom she loved and towards whom his few and rare smiles were directed. She had never had a harsh word from him in all her ten years on earth.

The servant came for Elizabeth on the half-hour, and the rector at once rose and took his leave to dress, giving Henrietta no chance to talk to him. They met again at dinner, but though there were no guests that evening, they shared the table with Mr Catchpole, so privacy was again denied. Henrietta, sipping her soup, wondered impatiently whether Catchpole were in on the secret, and listening to their conversation with more than usual interest, decided he was not.

When the plates had been changed, a silence fell. Henrietta, watching her husband's face for more signs of pain, suddenly found he was looking at her with a raised eyebrow.

'Well, Mrs Fortescue,' he said, 'have you had an interesting day? Tell me what you have been doing.' She hesitated, and he added, in something between a request and a command, 'My thoughts are heavy and in need of diversion. Pray give yourself the trouble of amusing me a little.'

She was moved to pity for him. 'Yes, I have had an interesting day,' she said brightly. 'This morning I rode out with Elizabeth as far as Top Woods, and came back round by Harper's Row. I stopped in on the Tomlinsons for a moment – he is no better, I'm afraid.' She realised that if her husband were ill, this was not a cheerful subject, and hurried on. 'And this afternoon I went to a meeting at Mrs Worsley's.'

'Indeed?' he said.

Anxious to divert him, she added some detail. 'There was a guest speaker today, who claimed acquaintance with you, sir – or, at least, she said her husband knew you. I wonder if the name is familiar to you? It was Pargeter.'

The rector's fork was arrested half-way to his mouth. 'Pargeter, did you say? Pargeter?' His brows were drawn in a tremendous frown, and her heart misgave. 'What is his Christian name?'

'I don't know,' Henrietta said nervously. 'She didn't tell me. She only said he had had a correspondence with you.'

The fork was put down, and, it seemed by a great effort, the rector turned to Catchpole and said, 'We must go over the parish accounts tomorrow – remind me to find a time for you to bring them to me. I think you said the returns are all in?'

Catchpole replied, and the conversation continued on those lines. Henrietta thought she had simply lost his interest – it had happened before, though he was not usually quite so abrupt – and went on with her meal in silence. But when Catchpole had withdrawn and the dessert was on the table, Fortescue fixed her with an awful eye.

'I would not speak in front of an inferior, but now that we are alone, let me understand you. You have had dealings with the wife of that Pargeter who has had the impertinence to canvass me on the subject of women's rights?'

'I didn't know until she told me so that her husband had written to you,' Henrietta said. 'She said he admires you very much.'

'Did she? Does he? And do you imagine for a moment that I can experience any gratification from the admiration of such people?'

'Really – I know nothing about them,' she faltered. 'I have never seen her before today. But I thought—'

'You *thought*?'

'I assumed she was respectable. She seemed so. Indeed, I wouldn't have—'

'Be so good as to tell me,' he interrupted her icily, 'what was the nature of this meeting at which you encountered Pargeter's wife.'

She swallowed. 'It was – at Mrs Worsley's.'

'So I understand. But I did not ask you where it was. What was the purpose of the meeting? What was the subject on which this woman addressed you?'

Henrietta knew a storm was coming, but she could not refuse a direct question. 'It – it was – the franchise. Votes for women.'

'*Votes for women?*' He glared at her. 'How dare you? *How dare you*, madam, attend such a meeting? Have you learned nothing in all the years you have been my wife? Have you listened to no single word I have spoken to you, here at home or from the pulpit? So openly to oppose my views – have you no thought for my position?'

Henrietta felt blanched by his withering scorn, as though a freezing wind were stripping her skin. 'I didn't know that you disapproved,' she said faintly.

'How could you not know?' he raged. 'You are the wife of a minister of the Church of England! It reflects upon *me*, madam, that you should espouse such a vulgar and ignorant heresy, as though I had taught you nothing better!'

'Heresy? But I didn't—' she gasped.

'God Himself has ordained the condition of woman,' he thundered. 'He has decreed that she shall be inferior, dependent, obedient to her earthly master in all things! And are you – you, a pitiful, ignorant female – to rewrite His laws? Do you presume to know better than your Creator? Do you set up your opinions against mine, who have been placed in authority over you by His divine will?'

Henrietta had nothing more to say. She wilted in her

seat, head bent to his furious gaze. The silence crashed around her like thunder rolling about the hills.

'I am appalled – ashamed by your behaviour,' he said at last. 'You have brought disrepute upon me, upon my name and my standing in the neighbourhood. You will never, *never* do such a thing again! You will go to no more meetings, Mrs Fortescue, that I promise you!' She glanced up at that moment, and saw something else occur to him. 'Where,' he asked awfully, 'was Elizabeth while you were at the meeting?'

'She was with me,' she said, in a small, helpless voice.

'With you? *With you?*' He stopped with a gasp as a spasm came over him.

She jumped to her feet, knocking over her water glass. 'What is it? Are you ill?'

'Sit down!' he said, faintly but fiercely. 'I have not finished.' He reached for his own glass with a hand that she could see was shaking, even the length of the table away. He sipped and put the glass down. His face looked horribly grey. 'Since you cannot be trusted to exercise your judgement in these matters, it seems I must curtail your activities. You will not take Elizabeth out of this house without my express permission. You will not speak to her at any time of any of these vulgar and seditious ideas. You are forbidden henceforth to attend public meetings of any sort. Mrs Worsley is obviously an evil influence, and I shall call upon her and tell her so. I had no idea that she had the effrontery to conduct such a campaign in my own parish, but I shall tell her, and all those who—' He broke off with a gasp and doubled over.

Henrietta went to him, though he waved her back with one blind hand; fell to her knees beside him. 'Oh, please, tell me what is wrong. Shall I send for the doctor? Shall I call Mansur again?'

'No!' he managed to croak, still bent over. 'Be still!'

'But I must get help for you!'

'*Be still!*' She waited, her hands twitching with the desire to touch him, though she dared not. At last he straightened up, composing his expression into something like normality, though his face was drained and exhausted, his lips blue. 'Some water,' he said, with difficulty. She handed him his glass and he sipped again, slowly.

When he put the glass down she said quietly, 'I am your wife. I have the right to know.'

He met her eyes, but his expression was a perfect blank. 'I was a little unwell. It has passed. It is nothing. You will not mention the subject again, if you please.'

'But—'

'If you please!' He stood up, turning away. 'Goodnight, Mrs Fortescue.'

He was at the door, leaving her, shutting her out like a stranger. That, perhaps, was all she was to him; but he was the only thing in the world she had to love, besides Elizabeth. Like someone in perfect darkness, she needed to touch something or she would lose herself. Desperately, she cried, 'Edgar!'

She had never used his name before: it sounded shocking on the naked air. It seemed to shock him, too, for he stopped and turned, and in place of the blank there was a man looking back at her, an old man tired to death.

'If you please, my dear,' he said, really quite gently. They stood looking at each other for a moment, locked in the situation. Then he said, 'I appreciate your concern for me, but it is needless.' He drew a breath – almost a sigh. 'I shall be going to Richmond the day after tomorrow. I shall stay two weeks at least.'

'It isn't your time to visit your other parish,' she said in surprise.

What gentleness there had been was gone on the instant. 'I am not required to answer to you for my movements.' He looked at her thoughtfully for a moment. 'I shall take Elizabeth with me. Be sure that her nurse packs her trunk tomorrow in readiness.'

Henrietta felt as though he had slapped her. Her eyes filled with tears. 'Please don't take Elizabeth,' she begged.

'I promise I shan't do anything you don't like, but please don't take her away from me.'

'Let us not have an emotional outburst,' he said shortly. 'Control yourself, Mrs Fortescue.'

She was so used to obeying him that she made a great effort to choke back her tears; but she couldn't quite remain silent. 'You're doing it to punish me,' she said miserably.

'My daughter must be protected at all costs,' he said. Another spasm crossed his face and he turned away hurriedly and left her.

CHAPTER TWENTY

A stone begins to roll down a mountainside. At first, one hand could stop it; but it gathers speed, and by the time it reaches the bottom it has the power to pierce a man's skull. Who can tell at which point in its descent it became unstoppable?

At the end of the hunting season of 1882, George gave in to the combined pleadings of the bank and Atterwith, and with a heavy heart sold the pack. It was a sad moment, and George, who had bred most of the hounds himself and knew them all like brothers, said a long goodbye to each one individually, sitting on the benches with the smiling faces and waving sterns all around him, as they jostled to put their paws up on his knees for their turn to be made much of. They went to good homes, he made sure of that. The one or two older ones whose hunting life was coming to an end he knocked on the head himself, rather than sell them where they might not be properly treated.

He cried a great deal when he had to put the old hounds down. After that, it was not so hard to part with most of his hunters, for they were all fit and in the prime of life, and they fetched such good prices he could be sure they would be well cared for. The sum of money raised by the sale of pack and hunters, although considerable, somehow just disappeared. Of course, he had a lot of debts – Atterwith didn't need to tell him that. And, of course, having borrowed so much he had to pay interest on the loans, which added to the debt. But all the same, he would have thought that having given up what amounted to half his life (he would hunt next winter as someone else's guest – a poor shadow of what should have been) the great hole of his indebtedness ought to have been plugged. But for all the difference he could see, it had been like throwing a spoonful of sand down a mineshaft. His sacrifice had been wasted.

'You've had my hunt – now leave me alone,' was his cry when Atterwith came to him for more economies. 'You made me sell my hounds, but I might have kept them for all the good it did.'

In vain Atterwith told him that simply paying the interest on the loans required much of what income the estate was still generating; in vain he pointed out that money was haemorrhaging out of the racing stables. George had made his sacrifice and he wasn't going to make another. Atterwith had felt a huge relief when he had finally persuaded his master to sell the hunt, but he saw now it was no triumph but the final tragedy, the thing that convinced George he need do no more.

They were still in mourning (mourning for a child was crape for nine months and black for three) and there was no entertaining – even had Alfreda been in any mood for company. That ought to have reduced expenses somewhat; but the stone was gathering momentum. Some tradesmen were asking for payment, or not extending the existing credit; and some new purchases had to be made with cash, in spite of anything George could do with haughty looks and expressions of astonished pain. The March quarter bill for the servants' wages emptied the coffers, and there was talk in the servants' hall that the next quarter wouldn't be paid, or at least not in full. People began to leave. Fanie was the first to go, but it was doubtful whether Alfreda noticed her absence. It was long since she had dressed formally, and Bittle attended her all the time now. George would have been happy to get rid of Fanie long since and save on her large salary, but he would not have dared send her away without Alfreda's orders.

John the footman left, securing a good place as butler to the new Mrs Havergill, where he would work alongside Fanie. After that there was a slow but steady falling away of servants, which did not impinge on George, since he didn't know their names anyway, until Mrs Holicar required an interview of him and told him she was presenting her notice.

George was shaken. 'Not you, Holi!' he said. 'Why, you've been here for ever!'

'It breaks my heart to go, sir, but it would break my heart even more to stay. Things are not right in this house, sir, and you ought to know it, begging your pardon.'

He frowned. 'We've had a very sad blow, as you know very well. But we'll come through in time. Your mistress will be very upset and hurt that you should think of going at a time like this.'

'My mistress won't even know I've gone,' Mrs Holicar said, surprising both of them with her boldness. 'Don't you see, I've even had to come to you to give my notice because she won't see me? I remember how things were before the mistress came to this house, and they're going back the same way again. I don't want to be here to see it.'

'It seems to me,' George said loftily, 'that we ought to have been able to expect a little more loyalty from someone we've cherished under our roof all these years. However, if your mind's made up . . .'

Mrs Holicar's eyes filled with tears. 'I'm not a young woman. I have to think of myself, too.'

'Then there's nothing more to say. We shall have to look about for a replacement for you.'

Their eyes met, and his slid away first.

'Begging your pardon, sir,' she said quietly, 'but there are rumours going about that nobody will get paid next quarter. I don't believe it,' she added quickly, 'and that's not why I'm leaving. But servants will talk, and I doubt you'll get anyone from outside to replace me – not anyone I'd like to see in this position.'

379

George was uncomfortable. 'Yes, well, there's no need for you to worry about that,' he said coolly.

'But I worry all the same,' she said, 'and if I were you, sir, I'd think about promoting Alice – Alice Bone, the head housemaid. She's young, but she's a good girl, and honest, and she knows most of the work. If you liked, I could instruct her in my duties before I leave.'

George's cheeks were redder even than usual, and he looked away. 'Yes, well, that will be for Mrs Morland to decide. You can go now, Holicar. I shall be sorry to see you leave – but I must say I feel disappointed in you.'

He couldn't get Alfreda to interest herself in the staff position. The news that Mrs Holicar was leaving left her unmoved – George wondered if she even heard him. Bittle got her dressed and downstairs every day after breakfast, where she sat in the small parlour for a few hours, and sometimes went for a solitary walk round the moat or through the Italian garden. George never saw her eat: she did not take any of her meals with him. He wondered how much of the delicate dishes Mrs Pender prepared and Bittle carried up on a tray to Alfreda's room actually found their way into her mouth, for she was getting very thin. She had always been slender, but now she was skeletal; and dressed in the plain, high-necked, unfurbished black that Bittle fastened her into each morning, with her hair concealed under a plain cap, she looked old, very old.

George was beginning to think that she was getting a little odd. She hardly responded when he talked to her, and often said things he didn't understand, as if she was talking to herself, carrying on a train of thought which was sometimes inward and sometimes spoken, like a stream running now above and now below ground. Her eyes seemed always fixed on something else, invisible to him. She had fits of terrible weeping, especially when she played the piano – which she did less often these days – and her temper was uncertain, making her more of a tinder-box than ever; but most of all she seemed absorbed to the point of mania with the memorial she was having built to James's memory. Many of her walks were taken with the purpose of selecting the site, and the only people she always spoke sense to were the architect, stonemason, carpenter, sculptor and master builder she was employing to realise her vision.

Every now and then, bills came relating to the memorial, and he paid them almost without looking. He didn't like to think about his boy being dead; and certainly it would have seemed churlish in the extreme to object to any expense involved in the scheme. He could imagine how Alfreda would have flown at him if he suggested things were getting out of hand – she already looked at him with a brooding resentment that told him she blamed him for James's death. But as the year broadened, and the June quarter bills approached, and George knew they could not be met as well as paying for Alfreda's folly, he decided something had to be done.

This time he didn't approach anyone in York. He remembered what Mrs Holicar had said: servants *would* talk, and probably it was all round the city now that Morland Place was in a tight hole. He went to Leeds, where the Morland name, his best clothing and a magnificence of manner he knew well how to assume, secured him another loan. The lender, however, named a very high rate of interest, and as George opened his mouth to protest, met his eye with a very canny look, which said that was the price of asking no questions. George signed meekly. The immediate problem was eased. Alfreda finally chose her site, on a slight rise in open ground opposite the brood mares' paddock, and the builders, reassured they would be paid, began digging the foundations.

All was well until Atterwith found out about the loan. He came to George to remonstrate, not angrily this time, but wearily.

'I won't be lectured,' George said, eyeing him sidelong. 'Damnit, man, who is master here? I think you forget your place sometimes.'

'I wish I might forget it,' Atterwith said, 'just for a few hours each night, but I can't. It follows me into my dreams. It comes between me and my vittles. I took care of this estate for your father, and it's a trust that means more to me than I can easily express. But how can I carry it out if you continually thwart me and do things behind my back?'

'Behind your back? I don't think I like your attitude! Morland Place is mine—'

'It won't be for much longer, if you carry on like this,' Atterwith said, trying to rouse himself to sternness.

'Oh, you said that last year,' said George.

'And you ignored me then, as I see you mean to ignore me now.'

'I think you're getting too old for this position,' George said kindly. 'You're tired, old fellow. Isn't it all getting a bit much for you?'

'Yes,' said Atterwith. He stood silent for a moment, staring sightlessly at the floor, his shoulders sagging. 'Yes, it is,' he said at last, raising his head. 'So I must tender my resignation sir, forthwith.'

George was startled. 'What – you? Go? But where would you go, man? You haven't any family, have you?'

'I'd like to go straight away,' Atterwith said, ignoring the question. 'I will forfeit a month's wages in lieu of warning, if that suits you.'

'Oh, do as you please,' George said. 'I'm sure we'll manage without you.' He was hurt at another defection, more ingratitude from an underling he'd cherished; and it would be good to be spared the old man's constant nagging, which was getting on his nerves more and more these days. But as Atterwith turned away without another word, a pang of regret softened him, and he said hesitantly, 'Erm – I say, you will be all right? I mean, where will you go?'

'I have a little saved,' Atterwith said. 'I shall go back to Lastingham, up on the moors, where I was born. I thought I might open a public house. I should like the company.'

'Oh,' said George. His softness had been wasted. It didn't sound as if Atterwith needed any sympathy, or as if he was sorry to leave at all. 'Well, good luck to it,' he said, and it was half meant, and half petulant.

Alfreda wasn't as pleased as he thought she'd be when he told her Atterwith was leaving. In fact, all she said was, 'Indeed?' and went on poring over the latest architect's drawing.

'May I see?' George asked, curious at last. He supposed if he was going to have to ride past the thing every day he ought to be prepared for what it would look like.

'See what?' Alfreda said, in a startled tone.

'The plans,' he said. She looked up, tightening her hands on the drawing as if he meant to take it away, and gave him a strange and glittering look which – frankly – he thought made her appear a bit mad. 'You've altered them quite a bit since the beginning, haven't you?'

'He's put in the new finials,' she said. 'I told him the scale but he didn't see at first. The pitch of the roof has to complement them.'

'Oh, it has a roof, has it?' he asked, at a loss.

'Well, you wouldn't have him out in all weathers, would you?' she said, a trifle indignantly.

'I don't know,' he said bewildered. 'I don't know what it is you plan – I've never seen it. May I see the drawing now?'

'You won't understand,' she said. 'I don't want you looking at it and making criticisms.'

'Well, I promise I won't,' he said. 'It's your idea. I shan't interfere.'

Reluctantly she yielded the drawing to him. 'Not a word,' she warned. 'I won't have it. It is to be exactly as I decide. I won't have him begrudged his memorial.'

George turned the drawing the right way up and spread it on the table. It looked strangely familiar, a square building like a summer-house, a tall pointed roof on four corners topped with long, tapering finials, each side an elaborately carved Gothic arch, sheltering a statue on a plinth, steps going up to it from each direction. It was grand and much decorated and oddly unsuitable to a ten-year-old boy. Then as he stared, seeking for something to say, he realised why he recognised it.

'It's the Albert Memorial,' he said. The memorial to the Prince Consort, designed by Sir Gilbert Scott, which had been erected on the site of the Crystal Palace in Hyde Park: he remembered now the illustrations of it which had been in all the picture papers at the time of its unveiling some years ago. He looked from the drawing to his wife, and could not fathom her. Had she asked the architect to copy it, or did she think it was her own idea?

'It's beautiful, isn't it?' she said, a shadow of anxiety in her eyes. 'It will be a fitting monument to him. The statue – I'm having him seated, reading a book, with his chin in his hand.'

'What – which book?' George asked, his mouth a little dry. That was how the Prince was depicted, too.

'The book of animals he liked so much. You'll be able to read the words on the page – he's even going to carve a picture on one of them. The other sculptor was no good at all. I had to dismiss him. But the new one is good. I've told him the face must be perfect – perfect! Like an angel. He swears it will be. And lifelike.'

'Lifelike,' George echoed. 'Well – well, that'll be nice.' He was not very good at understanding architects' drawings, but he was gradually working his way through this one. The only thing was, he seemed to have got the figures wrong. 'I don't understand this bit. The statue seems to be too big. I mean, the little chap was only up to my chest, more or less. This seems to be—'

'Ten feet, including the plinth,' she said dreamily. 'You'll be able to see it for miles, on that high ground. Wherever you are, you'll see the tip of the roof point, at least.'

Ah yes, now he had fathomed the notation. He stared. 'Alfreda, my love, this is going to be fifty feet high!'

Her eyes filled abruptly with tears, her lips quivered, and her fists balled. 'You swore you wouldn't criticise! You promised!'

'Yes, but—'

'You begrudge him! You begrudge him! He's my son, and I won't have you interfere!'

'I don't begrudge anything, of course I don't, but don't you think—'

She snatched the drawing away and clutched it to her. 'Leave me alone! Go away! I hate you! I don't want you near me!'

Bittle came in, and cast a resentful look at him. 'Best you go away, sir,' she said. 'You're only upsetting her.'

'I don't mean to upset you,' George addressed his wife. 'Don't cry, Alfreda. It will be beautiful, I'm sure. You shall have it just as you like, I promise.'

But she would not be calmed until he had left the room, and so he went, his brow furrowed, a new worry on his shoulders. Quite apart from the inappropriateness of the memorial and what it said about the state of Alfreda's mind, there was the question of what it would cost. A marble statue of that size would cost a fortune, leave aside the rest of the building. He wondered if Atterwith had any idea what she was up to. He had better talk to him, and see if any estimate of the cost had been forthcoming. And then he remembered that Atterwith was leaving. Life, he thought, with a sigh, was getting very difficult.

The harvest was better that year, but the price of wheat was down again, to thirty-eight shillings; and on one of the farms a plague of septic abortion rushed through the cattle and not a single calf survived. On the home farm his best milker died of milk fever, and the stirks that had been separated to be fattened for market got wooden-tongue.

With Atterwith gone, he had to take care of a great many more things himself, and he realised as he went round the farms what a lot of unpleasantness the steward had spared him in the past, acting as the filter between him and the tenants' discontent. Life, George thought, was becoming less and less comfortable. Now *he* had to look at all the bills that came in, and realise that he couldn't pay them; and find excuses for the creditors; and juggle the account books; and talk to the servants, too, for Alfreda wouldn't do it and Mrs Holicar wasn't there to do it. There didn't seem to be any fun in life any more, George thought – no parties or visitors or jollity, no hunting with his own pack to look forward to, his meals taken alone. Thank heaven Mrs Pender wasn't among the servants who had left. But it was all rather grim, and he'd have abandoned his own table and gone into York to eat, were it not that he was afraid of the looks and questions he might have to face. But a man must have some company, and from time to time he slipped out and across the fields with a dog or two at his heels and spent an evening in the Hare and Heather, where the labouring classes were quite willing to pretend he was one of them for the sake of a round or two of drinks. George had never been much of a drinker – hadn't the head for it – and a quart of old ale was enough to banish his cares temporarily, along with his sense of balance and power of lucid speech.

But the thing that seemed to dominate those summer and early autumn days of 1882 – like a spike driven through memory to pin it to one particular spot in reality – was the Memorial. From the moment he understood the scale of the project, it acquired a capital letter in his head. He did not remonstrate, afraid of his wife's temper and for her fragile equilibrium, but he watched almost heart in mouth as the reality unfolded little by little. She added things as she went along, and as long as they were paid, the builders and other artisans shrugged and did as they were told. The strong resemblance to the Albert Memorial was diluted a little as time went on and more and different details were added, but it grew more strange for the same reason.

It emerged that Alfreda planned a service of dedication for the Memorial on the anniversary of James's death, and as she became more anxious over whether it would be finished in time, her temper grew shorter. When Father Roding saw fit to protest to her, quite gently, that there was perhaps something a little idolatrous in the importance she was investing in the Memorial and that a service of remembrance in the chapel would be more appropriate to Christian feeling, she lost her temper and screamed at him, grew red in the face and almost choked with fury.

It hardly surprised George, though it made him sigh, when Roding came to him afterwards and told him he felt obliged to resign his post in the household. He explained his reasons at length, and with elaborate circumlocutions designed to avoid openly blackguarding the mistress. George listened in silence, feeling weary and put-upon.

'I feel somewhat superfluous here anyway,' Roding said at last, when George still made no comment. 'The tragic death of my pupil leaves me with too much time on my hands. Much as I hate to abandon this little flock at a time of sadness—'

'Oh, for goodness sake, man, go, and spare me the pi-jaw!' George interrupted crossly. Was there no-one in the world who felt they owed a little loyalty to George Morland? Was there no-one who felt he needed just a touch of consideration?

So now there was no more daily worship in the chapel. George had to read morning and evening prayers himself, or the servants would have descended into atheism and barbarity. Despite the absence of a chaplain, he noticed, out of the corner of his mind, that the chapel was kept burnished and sweet, the sanctuary lamp alight, the candles replenished and flowers always on the two altars; but it never occurred to him to wonder who did it.

In London, the bright, cold weather brought fog in its train. First there was the warning of the mistiness in the mornings and the vivid sunsets at night; then one day the capital woke up to find the sun missing, and the grey, gritty, sulphur-smelling blanket tight down over everything. In the strange half-darkness of the streets, sounds seemed oddly muffled, and it was impossible to pinpoint their direction. This made trying to cross roads even more dangerous than usual. Vehicles would loom suddenly out of nothing, right on top of you, and accidents were frequent. Sometimes, standing on the kerb as though on the bank of a river, there would be nothing to tell what was out there but a rumble of wheels and the sad, hollow cough of an invisible cab horse.

The gas lamps burned all day, vehicles carried their night lights, and the traffic crawled cautiously over the wet, slippery cobbles. Noon was like midnight, and there were frequent collisions. In the worst places, like the corner of Piccadilly Circus and Shaftesbury Avenue, policemen stood with flaming torches to wave the traffic on, for it was impossible having left the confines of one street to find the opening of the next. Pedestrians felt their way like blind men along the railings, or along the kerbside from lamp-post to lamp-post, muffled up like conspirators, scarves wrapped round their mouths and noses to keep out the wet, filthy murk.

When she set out to visit Ivo on the evening of the third day of the fog, Venetia preferred to walk, rather than trust herself to a cab horse just as blind as she was. At least, she thought, as she groped her way through the mysterious streets, she had no need to fear being recognised as she approached Ivo's house, for it was not possible to see more than a foot in front of her face. The light from a gas lamp served only to illuminate the swirl of fog around it, like steam round a kettle. If it hadn't been that she had known these streets all her life, she would have been afraid of getting lost – indeed, on her rounds this morning she had twice been stopped by strangers with the simple question, 'Where am I?'

It made it all the more like home-coming when she was admitted by Gethers to the house in Eaton Place, though it was alarming to see the fog swirling in with her as she turned to watch the butler shut the door with almost panicky haste. He pulled a curtain over the door before he turned to her to take her coat, hat and muffler. 'I beg your pardon, ma'am, but I was anxious to keep it out if at all possible.'

'Yes, it's horrid stuff, isn't it?' Venetia said. 'Sometimes when the fog comes down I wonder what would happen if it never lifted again. We'd all die, I suppose. Not a pleasant thought.'

Gethers rolled his eyes slightly as though he would have been happier not to have it voiced. 'The master is waiting for you in the drawing-room, madam,' he said.

'Thank you. I'll see myself up.'

Gethers let her go. She liked to go up alone, for if the man was with her, it meant a delay of sometimes several seconds before she and Ivo could fling themselves into each other's arms – and today was the first time she had seen him since he came back from the country. He heard her coming up the stairs and was in the doorway as she reached it, and lifted her off her feet, to carry her inside. Then they stood for a long moment, Ivo holding her face in his two hands while they kissed and kissed.

'Oh, I'm so glad to see you!' she cried breathlessly, as soon as she could.

'My darling!' he said. 'God, you look wonderful! I've missed you! Come, I must take you upstairs this instant.'

'No supper?' she teased.

'Supper can wait,' he growled. 'I can't.' And she laughed and put her hand in his willingly. She couldn't wait for him, either.

Some time later she lay in his bed, in his arms, watching, fascinated, as the thin wreaths of fog crept in through previously unperceived gaps around the window-frames.

'It's almost frightening,' she said, in a voice of utter contentment. 'Like a stealthy creep, creeping of a murderer into your house, where you always thought you were safe.'

'You don't sound frightened,' he said, resting his chin on the top of her head. Her back was to his front, his arms round her. 'In fact you sound disgustingly smug. And it isn't a murderer – only a jolly old London Particular.'

'Particular is right – full of particles,' she said.

'How scientific!'

'And it is a murderer. I've had two patients die already, and if it goes on much longer there'll be others. We need air to breathe, you know. Are you so devoted to your old London now?'

'Always,' he said comfortably.

'Then you shouldn't have stayed away so long in the country,' she said.

'Ah, well, I had a particular – that word again! – reason for doing so.' She waited, but he didn't tell her what the reason was. 'And what has my dear doctor been doing – apart from killing her patients?'

It was time to talk to him, though she was unaccountably nervous about doing so. She gathered her breath and her courage and said, 'Something rather unpleasant happened.'

'Oh?'

'To do with us.'

'I hope you don't want me to fight a duel with anyone,' he said, sounding only lazily amused, 'because I have to tell you I proved myself the world's worst shot last week. All the other fellows were knee-deep in fallen birds and I didn't manage to hit so much as a tree.'

She turned to him so that she could see his face. 'No, love, don't joke me. This is serious.'

He made a grimace of mock alarm. 'Don't tell me so!'

'We were seen together at Maidenhead,' she said. 'Someone who knows me saw us, and the word has spread.'

'What can they say about us that isn't true?'

'But you don't understand! The word has gone round that we're having an affair – oh, they make it sound so sordid! – and this morning I had a note from one of my patients saying that she would not require my services any longer.'

'Did she say it was because of me?'

'No – but I know that's what it was. She's a friend of the person who saw us, and she's a high stickler. She'd never have anyone in – in my position in her house. Especially as I attend her children. That's the thing, you see,' she added, seeing he was still not worried. 'Most of my paying clients are women and children. That's why I have to be careful.'

'Well, it's only one old harridan, so why should you worry?' Ivo said. 'It's a pity, but it's not the end of the world.'

'But I'm afraid she won't be the last.' Venetia wondered about the Walcotts, too. They hadn't said they no longer wanted her, but she hadn't heard from them since Maidenhead, and usually she was called to one of the little ones about once a fortnight. 'These things get about,' she said. 'There's no way to stop gossip once it starts. That's why I was always so careful about not being seen coming here. Oh, I wish we had never gone to Maidenhead! It was a wretched mistake.'

She seemed to have offended him. He turned away from her, over onto his back, and folded his arms under his head. 'I'm sorry you feel like that,' he said. 'I enjoyed every minute. But nobody forced you to go.'

'Ivo, please don't be like that with me. This is too important.'

'I wasn't aware I was being "like" anything in particular. In any case, what do you want me to do about it? I can't persuade the woman to take you back.'

'Perhaps not. But we can prevent any more patients leaving me. Stop the gossip – kill it.'

'How?' he asked, evincing no interest in the problem.

It was no good, she was going to have to say it, embarrassing as it was for her. 'By announcing our engagement. Being together at Maidenhead will be forgiven us once it's known we are to marry – and I think we ought to marry quite soon. After all, there's nothing to wait for, is there?'

Her heart beat thunderously in her ears when she had said it, and there was an appalling moment's silence before he answered; yet a moment later she'd have given anything for the silence to have gone on for ever. For what he said was, 'My dear girl, marry? Us? What is this?'

'Why – why, aren't we to marry, then?' she stumbled.

He turned his head and fixed her with a not unkind

391

eye. 'It was never something I considered. I thought you were quite happy with the arrangement. You've never mentioned marriage before, and I'm quite sure I never suggested it to you.'

'You didn't,' she acknowledged, in agony.

'Well, then,' he said. He seemed not upset by the conversation at all; in her shock and chagrin, she missed the tension of his body and the wariness of his eye.

'But, Ivo—' She forced herself to go on, though the shame was as bad as the pain now. 'We are in love. I wouldn't have become your – your mistress if it had been otherwise. And that's what lovers do – they get married. I've given you my honour. You surely don't mean to—' She couldn't go on.

'Oh, Venetia,' he said, 'why must you spoil things with these questions? My love, if you've made a mistake, I'm sorry, but it was never my intention to marry you. You came to me freely and without conditions, and given that you were not a young girl I assumed you knew how the game was played.'

'Game!'

'Yes, and a very delightful game, don't you find it so? You always seemed to before. I have never had a woman who gave herself so readily to passion. You are an unending delight to me.'

'Then why—?'

He pushed himself up on one elbow and stroked the hair from her face. 'Darling, don't make me say things that will hurt you,' he said tenderly. 'You are a wonderful mistress, but, frankly, you are not the sort of woman I could marry. A female who works for a living – who has a profession? And a doctor, of all things! It's hardly decent – a woman who examines people's bodies, cuts them up. Ugh!'

'It is important work,' she said, in a small voice.

'Perhaps, but why must you do it? Really, love, do use your common sense. Can you see yourself carrying on your profession from this house? Can you imagine patients coming here to consult you under the gaze of my

392

high-nosed neighbours? Can you see me as "the doctor's husband"? No, it's too much! You must see it.' He was laughing now – gently, but it hurt her just as much.

She pulled her face away from his hands. 'So what is to happen to us, then?'

'Nothing,' he said simply. 'We go on like this for as long as it suits us both – as long as it gives us both pleasure. You're a grown woman, Dr Fleet, you've taken control of your life, you can choose what to do with your own body. I love making love with you, I've told you that. I can't get enough of you. But this—' He patted the bed. 'This is all there is. Take it or leave it.'

In her mind she heard Ophelia's piteous cry, *Then I was the more deceived!* But she had not been – or, if so, she had deceived herself. He had never mentioned love or marriage. She had gone to his bed, as he said, without conditions, trusting that he felt and meant what she felt and meant. What a fool she was! In spite of all her knowledge of bodies, she knew nothing of people.

He put an arm across her body, used the side of his thumb to wipe a trace of tears from under her eye, leaned down to kiss the end of her nose and her unresisting mouth. 'Oh, darling, don't cry. Is it as bad as all that? You're no worse off than you were five minutes ago. Let's enjoy what we have while we can. *I* don't want us to part.'

She dragged a huge, quivering sigh up from the soles of her feet, and a great weariness seemed to settle on her. He had not tricked her, she had tricked herself. He was what he had always been: attractive, amusing – light. Really, she had always known that, but she had let her physical passion for him, and her desire to be loved and approved, conceal the knowledge. What was between them was not love, but lust.

And he was right, she was a professional woman, and as such was unmarriageable. Given that, she might as well enjoy what she *could* have, might she not? She turned over to face him and slid her hands under the sheet. 'Well, then,' she said lightly, 'we had better not waste any more time. Kiss me, lover.'

Their bodies caught fire from each other as always, but this time it was wilder than anything he had ever known before, and he cried out with passion that was as close to love as anything he had ever felt. Afterwards he fell asleep in the easy way men have, and she lay watching the fog creep in like slow poison, and tried not to think of anything at all.

CHAPTER TWENTY-ONE

As October and the anniversary of James's death approached, Alfreda grew more tense, nervous and depressed. It seemed doubtful to George that the monument would be finished in time, but that didn't seem to be what was troubling her. In fact, he was beginning rather to wonder if she knew what was going on at all. She no longer, as far as he could discover, went to visit the building site, and, as the workmen told him when they came to him with complaints or problems, she would never see them now.

What would happen when the day came, George could not guess. If the Memorial wasn't finished, he hoped that perhaps she would satisfy herself with prayers in the chapel. He could get the village priest in to conduct a proper service, if she liked. What he hoped was that when the mourning was over, they would be able to get back to normal. He had lost his son, and he would never forget him, but he was still young and he wanted a return to their previous happy life. He wanted to entertain and visit and have friends like everyone else. They had financial problems, of course, but they would be got over. The winter racing season offered opportunities to make money – he had an absolute certainty for the October meeting at Newmarket – and there were three and four-year-olds ready to sell. Alfreda didn't like the idea of him being a horse-coper, but after all, they must sell something to live, and he still didn't see that horses were any different from sheep or wheat in that respect.

One day at the end of September George came riding home on the track that went past the Memorial. It was late afternoon, the weather had turned suddenly cold, and his horse, Oliver – a nice youngster he was hoping to sell as a hunter once he'd had him out a few times – was putting his feet down with a will, keen to get back to his warm stable. The leaves had been holding on well until recently, but the sudden cold had stripped the trees, and the bare branch-ends against the grey sky gave the day a wintry feel. George realised suddenly that he could see Oliver's breath faintly clouding the air – a sure sign that summer was really over.

As they came over the rise and the Memorial have into view, Oliver slowed his busy trot, and began to peep and dither, shaking his head and mouthing his bit as if he was thinking of bolting. His ears were going back and forth, and George soothed his neck automatically. It was not the first time he had had this reaction, nor the first horse who had objected to passing the building. It was well known that horses could see ghosts, but how could the Memorial be haunted? There had been nothing on the site before construction started, and no horse had shied at the open field. Perhaps it was because it was new; or just something about the look of it. Horses were odd creatures, and one never knew how they saw things.

He shortened rein and dug his heels in. 'Come on, you old fool,' he said. 'Trot on!' But as Oliver made reluctant progress, his ears sharply focused, George thought that there *was* something a little uncanny about the building with dusk coming on. The statue was not yet in place, but the white plinth glowed eerily in the low light, and the scaffolding sticking up against the sky somehow reminded one of a gallows.

Naturally, he thought, with an inward snort of annoyance, there was no-one working on the damn' thing—

Oliver suddenly gave a huge leap up and sideways, almost unseating George, and then crouched on his hocks ready to flee, quivering all over, boggling and snorting at the Memorial. George had only just recovered from that shock when his heart gave another painful bound as he saw what had startled the horse. He laughed, shakily.

'It's only a workman, you idiot,' he told Oliver. The horse snorted again in horror, his ears so pricked they were almost crossed, and took a step backwards. 'Come on out,' he shouted to the man. 'Don't lurk there frightening my horse into fits.'

'Beg pardon, sir,' the man said. 'It's Arkwright, the carpenter, sir.'

Oliver quivered a long moment more until the man had advanced clear of the building's influence, then relaxed in that exaggerated way horses have when danger disappears. He sneezed, shook his head until his ears rattled and his bridle clinked, then loosened the rein with a series of gentle tugs until he could get his head down to nose at the grass.

'Are you the only one here?' George asked.

'That's right, sir. I was just finishing off a bit of carving, but it's getting a bit dark to be up the scaffolding, especially as I'm on my own. My boy's gone home, d'ye see?' He gave George a rueful look. 'He doesn't like to be here when it starts getting dark, and short of tying him up, I can't stop him slipping away. It does have a queer sort of look to it in this light, don't you think?'

'Lots of things look queer at dusk,' George said impatiently.

The carpenter was not snubbed. 'True enough, sir,' he said. 'But a lot of the men think the place is unchancy – begging your pardon, sir. It doesn't bother me. I don't mind ghosts, never have. But some of them are real old women. Cullen, the stonemason, now—'

'The place isn't haunted,' George said sharply. 'How could it be? It was just a field before.'

Arkwright shrugged. 'As to how, sir, I couldn't pretend to tell you. But there were a lot of battles fought round here back in civil-war times. Who knows what might have happened on this spot, that was forgotten and asleep until we came and stirred it up?'

'I don't give a dam about your goose histories,' George

snapped, feeling a cold shiver down his back. 'What I care about is that there seems to be no progress being made on this building, and with the finishing date coming up.'

Arkwright shrugged. 'I'm doing my part, sir, as far as I can. But when the plans keep changing and no-one will give proper instructions, you hardly need ghosts to hold things up. Now we've had word that the roof is to be changed, but nobody will say what the changes are, so we can't get on.'

'Who said the roof is to be changed?' George asked impatiently.

'A message came from the house yesterday, sir. Hold off the roof until new orders.'

'Very well,' George said. 'I will try to find out what's wanted. If you all start again tomorrow, will it be finished in time?'

Arkwright scratched his head. 'Depends how different the new orders are, sir. But if nothing changes too much, we might make it all right.'

George gave him a curt nod, pulled Oliver's head up and rode away. When he reached home, Goole came into the hall to meet him. George had been just slightly surprised that Goole had not left when Mrs Holicar had; but perhaps he was too comfortable to want to change. Without visitors coming to stay, there wasn't much for Goole to do. In fact, now he came to look at him, wasn't there a hint of red about the butler's nose and of wateriness about his eyes? George was not an imaginative man, but it didn't take much to realise that the servant who had the cellar keys and nothing to do was facing great temptation, especially when he had a private room of his own in which to sit away from prying eyes.

'A letter came for you, sir,' Goole said, coming forward to take George's hat and crop.

'A letter? Why didn't you give it to me this morning?'

'It only came this afternoon, sir, by special delivery,' Goole said.

Now he was close up, George sniffed hard, to see if he could catch any aroma of drink about him. Goole watched him with hangdog eyes. He was a cadaverous-looking man, and had always had a short way with lower servants and a venomous tongue to go with it; but in the last few months the heart had gone out of him. With the shrinking of staff numbers his authority was being diminished, and it was plain that the master was on the rocks and the house going to the dogs. But he couldn't summon the energy to extricate himself. It was like sitting by the fire late at night when you're out of coal: gradually the flames sink and the cold creeps up, but the longer you sit there, the less you can bring yourself to leave the last pathetic puddle of warmth and venture out into the freezing spaces beyond. Mrs Holicar had up and gone when she saw the bucket was empty, while her blood was still hot; Goole had left it too late, and though it was apparent to him that he was butler of very little any more, he was now too paralysed by the cold to get up.

'Is Madam in her room?' George asked. He couldn't *smell* drink, but he had his suspicions.

'I believe so, sir.'

George turned away, and then turned back to say, with extraordinary cunning, 'I think I'll have some port after dinner tonight. You'd better bring me the cellar book so I can see what we've got.' He watched Goole carefully for a start of guilt or a look of consciousness, but Goole only asked when he would like to see it. 'In half an hour, when I come down again. Bring the keys, as well. I might inspect the cellar – haven't done it for a while.'

In fact he had *never* done it. 'Very good, sir,' Goole said gloomily, thinking this was one more sign of the slippage of things; and George, translating his gloom as guilt, took himself off feeling satisfied with his own subtlety. No butler was a match for *him*, by Jove!

He slit the envelope as he walked up the stairs, and when he got to the landing outside Alfreda's bedroom he paused to take out the letter. *Geo Crowdie, Purveyor of Fine Art and Architectural Supplies.* What the dickens was this all about? Oh, Lord, it was something to do with the Memorial. Shouldn't it have gone to Alfreda?

He read down the page, and his eyes bulged. A moment later he banged on Alfreda's door and let himself in so precipitously, without waiting to be asked, that he almost flattened Bittle against the wall.

Alfreda was sitting by the fire with the plans spread out across her knees. She seemed to be mouthing something to herself as she pored over them, and didn't look up at his entrance. *She looks*, an alarmed small voice said in George's head, *quite mad*.

But his indignation carried him forward. 'What the deuce have you been up to now, Mrs Morland?' he demanded. 'Leave us, Bittle. I have just got this letter – look at it!' He shook the page under Alfreda's nose. 'Gold leaf? *Gold leaf?* What on earth possessed you to order the stuff – and this much of it? Good God, woman – Bittle, I told you to get out!'

'I'm not leaving her,' Bittle hissed, advancing crablike across the room. 'Not with you shouting at her like that.'

'I'm not shouting,' George shouted, 'but if I was, haven't I the right?' He turned back to his wife, who was looking up at him with mild surprise, as if she had only just noticed him. 'What on earth did you think you were doing? It's lucky for you this Crowdie fellow wouldn't give you the damn stuff on credit! He's sent me this letter asking for payment in advance – and I'm not surprised. It's ruinous! What the devil did you want it for?'

'For the Memorial,' she said. 'What else? I'm having the crockets and finials and the frieze on the baldaquin gilded, and a golden orb and needle on the roof pinnacle. Lots of gold. It will shine beautifully when the sun strikes it,' she added dreamily. 'You'll be able to see it from miles away, glinting like a semaphore.'

'No,' said George.

She looked at him, surprised out of her dream. 'No? Did you say no?'

'I said it and I meant it. Enough is enough. Have you any idea what gold leaf costs?'

'The Albert Memorial is decorated with gold leaf,'

she said, with dangerous quietness. 'And it looks *beautiful.*'

'The Albert Memorial wouldn't even have been finished if the Government hadn't paid fifty thousand pounds towards it!'

'And what's fifty thousand pounds, when it's for someone you love?' she demanded.

'It's fifty thousand more than I've got!' George shouted. 'No, it's worse than that, because I'm already in debt over this damned monument of yours.'

Her eyes filled with tears, but they were tears of anger as much as sorrow. 'How dare you use that language to me? How dare you speak like that about my son's Memorial?'

George moderated his voice. 'I'm sorry. I didn't mean to swear – but, really, Mrs Morland, you must see that this has all got out of hand. And two thousand pounds for gold leaf—'

'I will have it!' she cried, coming to her feet. The plans slid off her lap and into the hearth. 'I will have my monument! He had so little of life, he must be properly remembered.'

'Alfreda, please—'

'You're against me, like all the rest! I've heard them talking – seen them muttering behind my back, as if I were some madwoman in the street. But I'm no ordinary person, I'm a Turlingham! The last of the Turlinghams! And my son was a Turlingham too, by blood. He'd have been master of this house and everything in it, and who knows what besides? If he is not to have his inheritance, he must have this!'

'You don't seem to—'

'You never loved him!' she screeched, panting with sorrow. 'If you had, you wouldn't begrudge him his monument! You took him away from me and put him down in that dark place all alone, but I'm going to make him a place up in the sunlight where he—'

One corner of the plans had got too close to the fire bars, and, having scorched, now caught fire. Alfreda saw

401

it, broke off in mid-sentence and snatched the paper up. The flame, encouraged by the movement, licked up the paper. Alfreda screamed in fear and fury; Bittle shrieked too and grabbed her mistress as if to pull her away; George shouted at Alfreda to drop it, and when she didn't, grabbed at it himself, smacking at her hands when she wouldn't let go. Then the flames reached her hands and she screamed on a different note; the flaming paper fell to the ground and George jumped on it and stamped it out in a mad, grim dance.

In a moment it was over, and there was nothing but a scattering of charred fragments on the carpet and the smell of scorched paper and singed hair.

'Are you hurt?' George asked. 'Did you burn yourself?' Bittle was trying to catch her mistress's hands to examine them, making little moaning noises; but Alfreda kept pulling them away, and finally pushed Bittle so hard she overbalanced and took two unintended steps backwards.

'You burnt the plans! You did it deliberately!' Alfreda hissed, glaring at George with such molten fury that he was almost afraid. 'I hate you! Get out of my sight!'

But, afraid or not, he had his responsibilities. He stepped closer, took one of her wrists in an iron grasp, and despite her struggles, forced open the clenched fingers with his other hand. Alfreda cried with anger and began beating him with the other hand; he caught that and examined it likewise. Then he said to Bittle, 'They look a little red, but not too bad. Put some ointment or soothing oil on them, and if they are not better by tomorrow morning send for the doctor.' And to Alfreda, 'I'm sorry about the plans, but it was an accident. There must be other copies, however. It won't make any difference to the building.'

But Alfreda stared at him with wide, tragic eyes, as though all hope was gone. 'It will never be finished now,' she said.

'You're a little upset,' George said awkwardly. 'I'll leave you in peace. Let Bittle dress your hands and give you some brandy for the shock.'

Alfreda said nothing, but she subsided into a chair on Bittle's urging, so he bowed and left her. He was shaken by the incident, and thought he might take his brandy advice himself.

Old habits died hard, and even when Alfreda was not likely to come downstairs, George did not feel comfortable about smoking in any part of the house she used, so after dinner he retired to the billiards room, of which one end was laid out like a parlour, with a big fireplace and comfortable chairs. There he sat with his dogs all round him and smoked a cigar, stared into the fire and tried to think what he had ever done in his life to deserve all this trouble. Even when the clock told him it was past his usual bedtime, for once he was wide awake. He threw the cigar stub into the fire and decided to shove the balls about for a while in the hope that it would make him sleepy. The great mass of dogs, toasting their bellies at the fire, didn't move when he got up, but Maggie, his pointer bitch, padded at his heels wherever he went, following him up and down and around like a toy on a string as he circled the table. Gradually a peace descended on him. There was something very soporific about billiards. The silence was broken only by the click of ivory on ivory, and of Maggie's nails on the wooden floor, by the small conversation of the fire and the occasional snore or groan of a sleeping dog.

He was just about ready to go to bed when the door opened. Maggie growled a warning, and Bittle came in. George's heart sank, then sank further as he saw her wild expression.

'She's gone!'

'What?'

'She's *gone*!' Bittle repeated impatiently. 'I just went in to settle her for the night and she wasn't in her room. She's left the house!'

George shook his head as if there were water in his ears. 'Are you sure?'

'Of course I'm sure! I put her to bed with her supper

tray and then she sent me away. That was eight o'clock, and it's after ten now. Her supper's not been eaten and she's not there!' George only stared at her, and Bittle clenched her fists with frustration. 'For God's sake, go after her! It's bitter cold out there and I don't know what she's wearing.'

'But – but where—'

'You *know* where!' Bittle almost screamed.

It sank in at last. George shut his mouth and went.

Fortunately there was a quarter moon, and the sky was clear. It was very cold, with that glitter in the air that tells of frost falling. Out in the yard he hesitated. Now was the moment when he regretted the changes they had made to Morland Place, for in the old days his riding horses would have been stabled here, instead of out at the new block, inconveniently far away. Damnit! All there was in the stall here was Peel, the whiskery old grey cob that was used to go for the post. Speed was important. Would it be quicker to run to the stables for his own horse, or take the slow old cob that was here? He decided on the cob. In a frenzy of impatience he fetched the bridle and went and woke the animal up, bridled it, fumbling maddeningly with the buckles, which seemed deliberately to thwart him, then led Peel nodding and clopping out into the yard. He didn't bother with the saddle, but vaulted onto the bare back, only to realise a moment later, as he reached the barbican, that he would have to dismount to open the outer door.

At last he was out into the moonlit, freezing night, vaulted up again, kicked the old pensioner into a trot and then a canter. Peel, startled out of a deep and peaceful sleep, began to catch the scent of urgency, and laid himself out at his best speed. It was agony to George: the old horse had a backbone like an unsheathed knife, and he couldn't help thinking what all that white hair was doing to his trousers. Peel soon slowed, however, unable to keep up the pace; George tried to keep him cantering, which was slightly less uncomfortable, but it was a dot-and-carry-one pace as the horse fell into a trot every few strides and had to be kicked on.

Everything looked strange in the faint moonlight, and George was glad of Maggie's shadow streaking along beside him: a dog was always reassuring company. They came to the fork of the track and George urged Peel to the right and up the slope towards the mares' paddock. The incline slowed him almost at once to a shamble; and when the monument came in sight, the horse fell into a reluctant walk, and finally stopped, trembling and staring. George kicked him, drummed him with both legs together, but his sides had set to concrete and his hairy hoofs were rooted in the earth.

'Oh, God damn and blast you!' George cried, and slithered down. 'If you won't go on, then stand. Stand!' He dropped the rein and stumbled forward over the cold, tussocky grass with Maggie pressed against his legs. She whined softly and he felt her reluctance. 'What is it?' he said. 'Can you see something?' The monument was a jumble of shadow and light, looking quite unreal, roughly sketched in with charcoal on a flat background. The marble plinth gleamed whitely like something lurking inside. Maggie stopped and his pace carried him on past her. His leg felt cold without her. She whined again and he stopped and looked back, and then forward. There *was* something there. The white was not just marble. There was something on top of the plinth. Oh, dear Lord! Then the dog suddenly unfroze and ran forward, and he knew what it was.

He thought at first she was dead, she was so cold; lying on top of the plinth, her legs slightly drawn up, her head pillowed on her arms, she looked as though she had lain down there to sleep. Her eyes were half open but she stared at nothing and she didn't seem to be breathing. But when he gathered her into his arms with a cry of pain, he felt her take a small, shallow breath. 'Alfreda,' he said, and balancing her against his knee, he tried to rub some warmth into her hands. 'Alfreda, please!' She slid sideways and he had to grab to stop her head striking the marble. She was so limp! Was she going to die? He shook her in anguish. 'Alfreda, don't leave me! Please don't leave me!'

Maggie barked, upset by his voice, and it brought him to his senses. He must get her home. He couldn't hope to warm her here. He struggled out of his jacket and put it round her. How long had she been lying here? Bittle had left her alone for two hours. How long would it take her to walk up here? Half an hour? Oh, God, she was so cold! But light, he discovered as he staggered to his feet with her in his arms: light as a starveling bird.

Peel was still standing there, thank God! He walked towards him, but his white shirt and the bundle he carried must have made him look strange, for the horse, facing him four-square, jerked his head up and snorted. 'Steady, old boy. It's only me. Steady, Peel!' But Peel knew a ghost when he saw one. With a grunt of fear, he laid his ears back, swung stiffly round on his hocks, and was cantering away down the hill with a surprising turn of speed. 'No!' George cried in despair, and 'Come back! Whoa! Coo-up, horse!'

But Peel was facing in the right direction, and there wasn't a blandishment in the vocabulary that would have made him turn. There was nothing George could do but follow, carrying his wife, holding her as close to him as he could to try to give her his body's warmth. It was not long before he discovered that she was not as light as he had thought. He stumbled over the uneven ground, catching his toes in long tussocks that were growing crisp with frost. The sky was powdered with a glitter of stars, but the moon had set, and Morland Place seemed vanished for ever in the darkness. But Maggie knew the way home: thank God for Maggie. She ran just ahead of him, and he kept his eyes fixed on her, on the glimmer of white in her liver-and-white coat.

Alfreda lay in her bed, staring at the wall. The strange unreality in which she had existed for the past months had dissolved, and there was nothing any more to shield her from the pain. Her son was dead. Ever since that moment when she had lifted him from the grass and felt the terrible limpness of death, she had wanted to die. She had prayed for it – *you have taken my child, take me too* – until she realised that the God who had done that to her was not a God for granting mercies. No mother should have to witness her child's death, or see the flowering of his bright blood in his hair, on his cheek, on the uncaring grass. She turned from God, who should have saved her boy but had looked away.

She didn't really blame George for James's death. It had been an accident, she knew that. But she hated him all the same, for being alive. *He* should have been the one to die. Why should he have life when her son had not? Why should he move, breathe, speak when her boy was mute and cold? If there was only so much room under the bright day, it should have been for James. She would willingly have died to keep him safe. She could not bear to be near George, in whose weather-coarsened red face she could trace a haunting likeness to the delicate features of the child. She could not bear his clumsy, inarticulate sorrow.

The Memorial had been a madness, she saw now: almost a deliberate one, a way to fix her mind on something else, to beguile grief, as one might distract a wolf by throwing things for it to run after. But sooner or later the wolf learns the trick, and closes in for the real meat. If the Memorial had ever been finished, what then? That was why she kept changing it, frantically throwing more and more elaborate lures to keep grief away from her heart, on which it yearned to gnaw. The Memorial would never be finished now. The wolf was on her breast, tearing into her. Only death could save her; and death was not far off.

She drifted a little, remembering her life. So much sorrow, so much hardship: her father's ruin and her mother's death, and the years and years of grinding poverty and humiliation as a 'poor relation', tolerated for the sake of an impatient and imperfect charity. But she had held on, had kept her pride, had struggled – oh, how she had struggled! – to pull herself out of the mire, to drag herself back up to the station in life to which she was born, to which she was entitled. And for what? If she had known how it would end, she might have saved herself the excoriating effort. She married George – a mere bucolic farmer if it had not been for his wealth – and re-created him as a gentleman; reformed his household, worked unstintingly to make it beautiful and elegant, and to assemble about them the sort of social circle she – and he as her husband – deserved. She bore him a child in peril of her own life. She made him what he was, a man of fashion and society, welcomed everywhere, whose domestic style matched his fortune, with an heir to inherit after him.

And what had been her reward? Her ill health, the pain and discomfort she endured, she made nothing of. She accepted that as she had accepted poverty – with a furious pride. But first her brother had been killed, her darling Kit, the only treasure of her heart before there had been James, the love she had grown up with. Kit and Kitten they had been in nursery days: the prettiest children in the county, back in those happy times at Turl Magna, before Papa's bankruptcy and death. One of her pleasures in George's fortune had been to see that enough of it went Kit's way. And then, in the prime of life, he had been killed in a vulgar, senseless accident.

She had been able to endure that only because she had James; and now James was gone, and there was nothing to live for. Fiercely as she had denied it to herself, she knew George was heading for bankruptcy in his turn. It was the shadow in the corner she would never look at, the thing so terrible to contemplate she could only ignore it and hope it would go away. With James gone, there was nothing else to look at. Even if she could have faced life without him, she could not go through it all again, the bankruptcy and shame and necessitude. It was like history repeating itself: it was a recurring nightmare, and the only way out of it was just to stop. Death beckoned her like peace. Perhaps she would find James and Kit there, on the other side of that barrier; or perhaps she would find oblivion. Either would be a blessing compared with life; and the barrier was growing thinner, more transparent all the time.

The doctor did all he could. He was an elderly gentleman, whose medicine pre-dated what he called 'the fads and fashions of the fifties', and there were many in York who preferred the 'tried and tested' ways of his youth and theirs. Certainly his fees were reassuringly high – and he was too much of a gentleman to require payment on the spot, or even to mention his bill at all, for which George was grateful.

But in spite of all the physician's efforts – he even bled Alfreda, saying as he applied the leeches that 'it was surprising how often some of these old remedies worked wonders'. But no wonders were worked. Pneumonia set in, and Alfreda went down before it without a struggle.

'She doesn't want to live,' Bittle said starkly to George, as he hovered in anguish at the bedside. Bittle was always there, never slept as far as he could tell, though there was nothing, really, to do for Alfreda. Sometimes George wanted to send her away, felt he was being excluded, but in pity he let her be. She had nursed Alfreda from babyhood, and there was nothing else in her life. George was finding it very difficult to believe that his wife was going to die. He presented his mind with this certain fact first thing in the morning when he woke, and at regular intervals through the day, and his mind looked at it, acknowledged it, then simply refused to come to grips with it. There always had been Alfreda – the time before her was as misty and unreal as a history lesson to him – and therefore there always must be.

She died on the day before the anniversary of James's death, just before three in the afternoon. The doctor had given them ample warning it was coming. 'She's sinking,' he said. 'It won't be long.' So George was there at the bedside. He heard her shallow, slow breaths, and wondered at each one if it would be the last. But when the last one came he knew that it was, for the inhalation had a little hitch in it, like the last hiccup of a child who has been

409

crying and is finally falling asleep; and the exhalation went on too long, fading into nothing.

Yet he waited and waited for the next breath, and even when he knew she had stopped breathing, he could not convince his mind that she was dead. This could not be the last word; this could not be irreversible. A child wakes again from sleep. Somehow Alfreda would resume what she had given up. Bittle was crying, kneeling by the bed with her face buried in the counterpane, and he wished she would go away because she was distracting him, making too much noise, so that he couldn't listen for the breathing to start again. And he had a horrid superstitious fear that if Alfreda, in that vestibule just beyond the world where she must be waiting, heard Bittle's extravagant grief, she might decide that it really was all up, and not try to come back. She might think it was impossible after all, and go the other way.

CHAPTER TWENTY-TWO

It was a particularly unlucky chance, Venetia thought, that of all people she should have been seen at Maidenhead by Mrs Walcott, who happened to be a friend of Lady Freshwater. In normal circumstances the worlds of the Upper Five and the middling sort of commercial people did not intersect. But Viscount Freshwater's second marriage had perhaps been contracted too soon after the untimely death of his adored first wife, Lady Cordelia Stratford (who had been not only a distant cousin of Venetia's but a close friend, too).

Freshwater had fallen for Pauline Stacton's youth and prettiness at a time when his judgement was impaired by grief. He married her against the advice of those closest to him and, once he had recovered his equilibrium, discovered he had nothing in common with his wife, and little esteem for her either. She was a silly, vacuous, self-regarding, uneducated girl, who had grown used to being adored for her looks, and when she found herself no longer the centre of everyone's attention grew shrill and resentful.

Venetia had sometimes felt sorry for Lady Freshwater, and considered her husband at fault for not helping her more, and for letting his indifference to her show. But the fact remained that, finding she did not fit in with her husband's set, she turned for friendship to that other sphere in which she had grown up, and took to promulgating spiteful gossip about those who had rejected her.

Mrs Walcott did not know that Dr Fleet was born

Lady Venetia Fleetwood, but Lady Freshwater did. Dr Fleet's misbehaviour would have lost her the Walcotts as patients, but Mrs Walcott would probably not have spread the news, not being, herself, a great one for gossip. However, in confiding it to her friend Lady Freshwater she received a new light on the business that made it much more fascinating, especially given the notorious behaviour of the Duke of Southport and his sister Lady Augusta Vibart, which was always in the papers. A private sin suddenly became the paradigm of upper-class vice, and it would have been asking too much of human nature for Mrs Walcott not to talk about it. Lady Freshwater, of course, could not have asked for better material than the transgression of one whose tribe had rejected her.

So from this unfortunate intersection of two worlds, the gossip flew like wildfire through both. Mrs Walcott satisfied herself with simply not calling for Dr Fleet again, but Mrs Walter Simpson, to whom she confided the news, had at once penned the indignant letter that had been Venetia's first warning of how things were going. After that, slowly but inexorably, word spread. Ivo Jennings was named, and those who knew where he lived now began to remember that they had seen Dr Fleet in the vicinity suspiciously often. Others remembered the times they had seen Mr Jennings entering the doctor's house in Welbeck Street. More and more patients fell away. Some wrote an angry dismissal, some with an excuse, others simply did not call again. Venetia hardly noticed at first, for her dispensary patients were as numerous as ever. But when she came to make out her bills, she discovered the gaps; and discovered, too, the fall in her income.

The winter was a hard one, and there was a lot of sickness, and despite the absentee patients, she was kept busy. But when spring came the gossip sprang up more vigorously like new grass. She was still visiting Ivo, he still called for her at Welbeck Street to take her to the opera or the theatre, and there was ample opportunity for people to see them together and make much of little. One day Mrs Chedzoy crossed Bond Street to avoid her; another day she saw herself pointed out by young Mr Llewellyn to a friend, and the two of them whispered and stared after her the length of the street.

She shrugged off these things, hurtful though they were. The first real pain came with her rejection by Mrs Anderson, who told her one day that she could no longer ask her to perform operations for her at the New Hospital.

'I am very, very sorry,' she said, her tired face creased with anxiety. Quite apart from the usual occupations of her busy life, Mrs Anderson had a new worry just then. The Dean of the London School of Medicine for Women, Mr Norton, had decided to resign, and a new dean must be chosen. Naturally, Sophia Jex-Blake would expect to be appointed, since she had almost single-handedly set up the school; but her 'difficult' personality and the notoriety of her past would almost certainly cause problems for the school. Mrs Anderson had been asked if she would be willing to take the position. It was more work than she really wanted, and she disliked very much to hurt Miss Jex-Blake's feelings; but for the sake of the school's welfare, and for the fragile progress of the women's Cause, she felt she had no choice but to accept.

So there could not have been a worse time for the gossip about Venetia to have come to her ears. 'You know that I regard you as a very fine surgeon – one of the best I have ever known,' she said, 'but the welfare of the hospital *must* come first with me. I have always said that as pioneers we must be utterly scrupulous in our behaviour, much more so than any man. The whole world watches us, and you know how many of the male sex long for us to show a weakness they can exploit to condemn us. The future of women in medicine – yes, and in other fields – depends on how we are perceived. That's why I cannot allow any breath of scandal to touch my hospital. Anyone who works there must be above reproach.'

Venetia felt the words like searing irons to her soul. To be rebuked and rejected by this woman, of all people!

'You think it so important, then, this gossip?' she managed to say.

Mrs Anderson looked grave. 'I have no wish to judge you. But you knew from the beginning what was required, what sacrifices you would have to make. The scandal now surrounding you reflects on us all, and on the London School. You were a prominent graduate: there must be many who feel you have let them down.'

Venetia turned her head away to hide the tears. 'I see,' she said. 'Who will do the surgery instead of me?'

'I shall have to do it myself until I can find a replacement. One of the students, Mary Scharlieb, shows great promise. She graduates this year. If I can persuade her not to go back to India . . .' She was deep in thought for a moment, then recollected herself, and stood up to go. 'We shall overcome the problem somehow. I take my leave of you, Miss Fleet. I am very sorry it should have come to this.'

When she had gone, Venetia went to her room for privacy and indulged in a storm of tears. She so much needed comfort, but Ivo was out of Town for the week – surprisingly, since this was the beginning of the Season. His proclaimed love of London life notwithstanding, he had gone to stay with the same friend in the country, and so was out of reach. Even Miss Ulverston was out – at this very moment, the Prime Minister was preparing his Reform Bill for presentation in the next session, and every hand was needed for the campaign to have women's suffrage included.

Well, when it came to comfort, she thought, rousing herself and wiping her face, there was one obvious source. The next morning, having rearranged her appointments, she went down to Ravendene to visit her mother.

A kinder old age had overtaken Charlotte: at sixty she was going through a period of remission in her illness, and, seeming at peace with the world now, she pottered about her house and garden, visited some of her old tenants, wrote letters, read books. She wanted no more exciting occupations: it was enough for her to wake in the morning to a world without pain, to limbs that would carry her and eyes that could bear the light of day.

She greeted her daughter with warmth and calm affection, and seeing she had troubles to tell, took her out into the garden. 'I had old Stebbins make me a bower seat, just where the morning sun falls,' she said. It was something like a hall porter's chair, made of woven willow, and wide enough for two.

Venetia sat beside her under the high hood and lifted her face to the sun. 'You're right, it's delightful,' she said.

'And I've planted all the sweet-smelling things around – lavender and camomile and thyme. Not much to smell at this time of year, of course, but later it will be lovely, and full of bees.' For a moment Charlotte watched a wren running along the top of the wall, ducking in and out of the creeper; then she said, 'What is it, then, darling?'

Venetia had not meant to tell her. She had never spoken to anyone about Ivo, and she did not want to upset her mother's hard-won peace; but the quiet question and the receptive face broke down her reserve. Keeping her voice quiet and even, she told everything. 'I always knew,' she concluded, 'that being a doctor would involve struggle and even sacrifice, but this – this seems so unfair.'

Charlotte sighed. 'Yes, it always was unfair. The very fact that you couldn't be a doctor just by virtue of your sex . . .' She reflected a moment. 'I think now that I was wrong to oppose you. I ought to have supported you more. But your father – well, he's dead now, so anything I say can't hurt him. He would never have accepted it. He had very rigid ideas about women, and it bent his nature as far as it would go to accept *my* differences. Yours were just too much.'

'You'd have thought that he'd have got into practice with you and found me easier,' Venetia said, with a painful smile.

'Ah, but you see, you were his daughter. You were part of him. It was as if his own hand had struck him. And, you know, you were always his favourite child. I think if it had been Olivia or Augusta he might not have minded so much, but he couldn't let you go without pain.'

'I suppose that's why he cut me out of his will,' Venetia said, with a little residue of resentment.

'Oh dear, poor Venetia. But they say struggle refines the soul. You are a much stronger person than if you had had everything your own way.'

'Yes, but now it's all going against me. And what offends me most is that Harry and Gussie do much worse things, and nobody censures them.'

'Don't they?' Charlotte turned to look at her. 'I think perhaps that's too general a statement. It's a matter of class, really.'

'Do you think so?' Venetia said, surprised.

'Oh, not theirs – I mean the class of the disapprovers. The lower classes always love a reprobate. Their own lives are irregular in the extreme, and they admire a person with spirit and good humour and don't worry about their virtue. Look how they adore the Prince of Wales and don't much care about the Queen.'

'Yes, I suppose that's true,' Venetia said.

'And then the upper classes expect a certain amount of misbehaviour,' Charlotte went on. 'Arranged marriages give rise to it: if the couple aren't in love, it is only reasonable that once the nursery is supplied they should find happiness away from each other. As long as they are discreet and appearances are kept up – I don't suppose any of our own set have condemned you?'

'I wouldn't know about that,' Venetia said, a little stiffly.

Charlotte nodded. 'But the middling sort – the middle classes as people call them now – ah, that's another matter. They want to go up and are afraid of going down. They see the vice and squalor and idleness at the bottom, and believe that only strict virtue and hard work can stop them slipping back.'

Venetia smiled. 'And they see the vice and idleness at the top and resent it. Yes, I see. I must be uniquely abhorrent to them!'

'Well, I'm glad you have retained your sense of humour,' Charlotte said. 'When you come up against something you can't change, the only thing to do is laugh at it.'

Venetia turned to look at her mother. 'Were you ever tempted?' she asked abruptly.

'Tempted?'

'You know – to go astray. Was there ever another man?'

Charlotte stared out at the garden. 'Just once,' she said. 'I loved your father – he was the only man I ever loved – but we didn't always have an easy life. And there was a time when he and I were estranged. I was very unhappy, and someone offered me comfort.'

'Was it Sir Frederick Friedman?' Venetia asked.

Charlotte looked at her, surprised and a little dismayed. 'However did you know that?'

'Oh, I sort of guessed. Something he said to me once . . . And he was a very handsome man. Even when I knew him. He had lovely eyes.'

'Yes,' said Charlotte.

'And did you?' Venetia asked after a moment.

'Did I stray? No. In the end I couldn't do it. But I was tempted. It wasn't just that he was attractive and loved me. It was that . . .' She paused, searching for words. 'I suppose he was of my own kind. He was like me. Though I was born a countess in my own right, I didn't live that kind of life until I was grown-up, and in a way I could never quite get used to it. I was out of my place. It was always an act of will for your father and me to love each other. It was always hard – though, of course, the more satisfying for that when we got it right.'

There was a silence, and after a while Charlotte turned to look at Venetia, wondering why she hadn't spoken, and found her frowning with thought. 'What is it, darling?'

'What you just said, Mama. That's what I'm lonely for – people of my own sort. Ivo isn't – I've just realised it. He thinks differently from me, and expects different things, and I'll never really know what he's thinking and feeling. What I miss is being with people who know the same things that I know, the same people and the same jokes, people who have the same memories.'

'You were always bound to be out of your place as a doctor,' Charlotte said. 'That's one of the reasons I thought it would not make you happy.'

'Yes,' Venetia said thoughtfully. 'You were right. I suppose if I had thought about it at all, I would have thought I could have two lives, a professional one in one class, and a private one amongst my own sort. But it can't be done.'

'No, I don't think it can,' Charlotte said carefully.

'So I have to learn to accept that I am a doctor and nothing else,' Venetia said. She was silent a moment, and then gave a little snort of laughter. 'And I've been feeling sorry for Lady Freshwater!'

The visit did her a great deal of good, and she went back to London feeling more settled in her mind. But as night closed in and the empty house closed round her, her great loneliness rose up again. It was all very well to speak bravely about acceptance when she was sitting at her mother's side; and being a doctor was enough when she was *being* a doctor; but there was all the rest of the time to get through, when she ached for someone to talk to, and for a man's warm arms around her.

So when Ivo came back to Town a few days later, she went to him.

'My darling doctor, how I've missed you!' he cried gleefully, swinging her off her feet.

'I've missed you, too,' she said, and they kissed, twining their arms about each other. The familiar heat burned up in her, the passion he awoke that demanded satisfaction. We must find some way to be together, she thought. If this is all there is for me, still I must have it. If we were more discreet, made sure we weren't seen, perhaps . . . ?

He released her at last, and instead of going upstairs, led her to the sofa and obliged her to sit down. He was in high good humour. 'I have some champagne here, nicely chilled, just waiting for you. I sent Gethers out for ice specially. We must have some first.'

He opened the bottle, poured two tall glasses and handed her one; took his to the piano, drank deeply, and set it on the top as he began to play. His hands flew over the ivory, and a tumble of music fell into the room, tunes migrating through the keys, overlapping and blending into one another. And while he played, he talked.

'Music, music. It is to me what I suppose medicine is to you, except that I have no need to make my living at it, thank God. Should I care to give concerts? I wonder. There would be the excitement, the applause. But most of the people in the audience would be fools, because that's what most people are, and would I like to play to fools? Would I enjoy their praise, knowing they would praise anything done in front of them if they had dined well enough beforehand? London audiences are the worst of all. You've seen how they talk all through everything. I like playing to you, though. You really listen. I can almost see you *eating* the music – you have a very expressive face, my love, did you know that? I can read you like a particularly clear book. You could never follow a career as a conspirator. Oh, what is this I'm playing? Do you recognise it? Go away, Mendelssohn, leave my head and my fingers. Let me have Mozart, Mozart!'

She said nothing, seeing it was her part to listen and admire. He threw out brilliant flashes of what she recognised as one of the piano *concerti*, and then released his bass hand to lift his champagne glass to his lips, while his tenor hand tinkled up and down something that was almost a tune, but not quite.

'More champagne!' he cried, putting the glass down again, and began playing two-handed. She got up and took the bottle to him to fill his glass, and as she was about to move away he twisted out an arm and drew her down beside him, kissed her, and said, 'Champagne and you – what a way to celebrate!'

'Celebrate? What are you celebrating?' she asked.

'Oh, Mendelssohn, are you back again?' he said, as a familiar tune shaped itself under his fingers. 'I can see you will have to have your way with me. Well, Doctor, do you recognise it? Yes, I see you do!'

'The Wedding March,' she said, and her heart tripped as a terrible hope welled up in her.

'From *A Midsummer Night's Dream*,' he confirmed. 'From which, and the champagne, you conclude the nature of my good news! Yes, I am to be married. I know, you never thought it possible that I would willingly put my head in the noose! You thought I would have to be tricked into it. But I assure you I have gone as meekly as a lamb to be shorn. Well, Dr Fleet, have you no congratulations for me?'

She felt as if she had swallowed something unchewed – her own heart, perhaps. 'Of course, I congratulate you most heartily. What is the fortunate female's name?' she said, making herself smile. She must not give herself away. She must not make a fool of herself. He had told her he would not marry her and she had stayed with him on that basis. He must not be allowed to mock or pity her.

'It is Miss Eddowes. Amelia Eddowes. Don't you think Amelia the most beautiful name in existence?' The music changed to something running and lyrical, like water. 'She's the daughter of Eddowes' Bank, from which you might conclude that this is a marriage of business rather than pleasure, but you would be wrong, Dr Fleet, as wrong as can be. It is a love match, pure and simple – and simply fortunate that her father and I are in the same interest.'

She had to say something. 'I didn't think you were *interested* in banking.'

'I think I might be from now on, especially when I have a quiverful of little half-Eddoweses to plan for.' He slipped into Beethoven, the slow march from *Eroica*. 'When Papa Eddowes goes to meet his maker, Amelia will inherit all, and her children after her. And all that besides, she is a perfect angel. It was love at first sight. I met her at Charles's last year. He invited me specifically to fall in love with her, the cunning devil – said he knew we would suit, and he was right. She is,' the music became lyrical again, 'young, beautiful and good. What more can a man ask?'

She *had* to get up, get away from his side. She tried to do it gracefully, made going back to her glass the excuse, poured more champagne into it and lifted it to him, saying, 'To your happiness, then.' Young, beautiful and good: when she was thirty-three, and had never been a beauty – and as for *good*, was she not a fallen woman? Oh, God, the pain was so bad!

The music stopped abruptly and he crossed the room like a whirlwind and took her in his arms before she could speak or move. 'Yes, my happiness!' he said, squeezing her tightly against him. 'How glad I am that you're here to celebrate with me. Lovely Venetia!' He pressed his lips down on hers, and the lonely, hurt part of her yearned towards him, longed for him, wanted to yield and be possessed and held. But her conscious mind held back, protested: how could she take a hurt to him to be soothed, when he was the one hurting her? And so she pulled back, hardened her lips against his, and at last he released her and stood looking quizzically at her.

'What is it? Aren't we going to bed?'

'No, of course not,' she said, as calmly as she could.

'Haven't I just said how glad I am you're here? What, no kisses for the almost-married man, is that it?'

She had never liked his humour less. She wanted to respond as lightly, so that he should think she didn't care, but she couldn't raise her leaden spirits that high. 'You belong to Miss Eddowes now. I had better not poach on her estate. Goodnight, Ivo. I wish you happy – you and your wife.'

She thought she was doing quite well, but there was a satirical gleam in his eye that she did not trust.

'My darling, that sounds so horribly final. But there's no need for us to part, you know. I won't be able to see you here once I'm married but there are plenty of other places we can meet. Why should we deny ourselves the pleasure we make so excellently together?'

She didn't say, *You talk of loving Miss Eddowes and yet*

you would so lightly betray her with me? She thought it, but she knew it would only make him laugh. Instead she said, 'Ah, but, my dear, it wouldn't be a pleasure to me.' That was quite good in the circumstances, she thought.

'What? You mean to leave me for ever?' he cried dramatically. 'How can you do it? In fact, *can* you do it? I think not. Come, kiss me, and let's to bed.'

'Goodnight, Ivo,' she said, and left him. She was trembling all over, and she knew that as soon as she reached her cold, empty home she would regret it, and long like an idiot to be back with him, in his arms, in his bed, for the sake of the meagre warmth that was her only portion. But she held firm and left him, and was proud of herself for doing it. She hoped she had at least surprised him, and that he would admire her for her resolve. But afterwards, when she thought about it – and knew she was doomed to think about it over and over, perhaps for the rest of her life – she remembered how he had said she had an expressive face and that he could read her like a book. The thought came to her, depressing in its likelihood, that he had wanted to be rid of her, and had manipulated the whole situation so that she would leave him, to save him the unpleasant duty of casting her off and the fear that she might make a nuisance of herself. This way she kept her dignity, and that same dignity would require she never troubled him – or the future Mrs Jennings – again.

Once Alfreda had been laid to rest beside her brother in the crypt – the village priest being summoned for the duty then hastily dismissed again – George abandoned the house. He could not bear to be in it: it was her place, created by her, loved by her, every inch redolent of his loss. He took his dogs and went out, and tramped the fields and woods all day. Sometimes he took a gun, and shot things for the pot, more out of habit than for either necessity or sport. He did not hunt that season. He couldn't bear the idea of meeting other people and having to listen to their expressions of regret. He couldn't bear the thought of talking to anyone about it.

Despite the fact that he had not invited anyone to the interment or informed anyone of his wife's death, the word got about, and a few calls of condolence were made. Teddy came out of brotherly concern; one or two people came from the goodness of their hearts or from respect to the family left over from the old days. Morland Place had not entertained since the little boy died in that tragic accident, and the new friends had all fallen away. But whoever called, they were met by Goole at the door with the same message: the master was not at home. Teddy, being family, enquired a little further. The master, Goole told him, was quite literally not at home; and when Teddy proposed to wait, Goole rolled his eyes a little and said he had no idea when the master might return, but he was certain he would not see him, he never saw anyone.

Teddy cast a curious eye around the hall, but things seemed in good case. There was a fire burning in the great fireplace, the floor was clean and the furniture dusted and polished. Moreover, if Goole was still here, the rumours of trouble must have been exaggerated. 'Very well,' he said. 'You'll tell your master I called? And that I will come at any time should he wish to see me.'

'I'll tell him, sir,' Goole said, with a faint, dubious emphasis on 'tell'.

Teddy reached into his pocket for a coin, which he slipped with practised discretion into Goole's palm. 'If he's in trouble, Goole, you will send for me?'

The coin disappeared and Goole bowed assent. It depended, he thought, on your definition of trouble.

Christmas came, and there was no celebration. More than that, the quarter day brought no wages. The staff was already reduced to a level that would have made Mrs Morland shudder (when she had been in her right mind) but this was the final blow. Goole assembled them on Christmas morning, distributed what little was in the household petty cash and said anyone who wanted to work for the future hope of payment when things got better was welcome to stay. By Twelfth Night they were down to four. Mrs Pender, the cook, stayed because she was comfortable, the work was no longer arduous, and, since the home farm supplied it, there was still plenty of food. Old Aggie stayed because she had nowhere else to go, and at her age any change was likely to be for the worse. Goole stayed because now he had come so far he was not going to leave without some recompense. And Alice stayed because she loved the master.

George, sadly, was hardly aware she existed. He roamed the estate, avoiding everyone, and when he was forced by cold, hunger or exhaustion to come indoors, he penetrated only as far as the gentlemen's wing, where Alfreda had never been. Goole brought him his meals here, and he sat before the fire afterwards, surrounded by dogs, drinking wine, port or brandy, or sometimes all three. He had never been a great drinker, but now he had discovered that enough wine anaesthetised his feelings of loss, bewilderment and fear; and a little more brought a dead sleep without dreams.

Afraid to leave the master in an armchair all night, and unwilling either to stay up tending the fire or carry him upstairs to bed, Goole ordered Alice to make up a bed on the sofa in the smoking-room next door, and thereafter with her help carried the master through there when he had drunk enough to sleep. After a few weeks, the rearrangement was completed by bringing down a glass and wash-stand; and Goole, who had been valeting his master since Hayter left, shaved and dressed him in his new makeshift bedroom so that he never had to enter the house proper at all.

Winter, the dead season, on the whole had been kind to George. Provided he avoided the area of the abandoned Memorial, he could wander all day on his own land without being reminded of his loss. But when spring came, the pain returned. The frozen grip on the earth loosened, the softer air brought all the smells of nature leaping to the nose, keen and tantalising; the grass began to grow again, new shoots began to push up from the soil and break from bare branches; the fields began to be whitened with lambs, the most poignant of reminders of the pitiless, wonderful force of life.

All of it reminded him that there was no new life in his house. His dear son was dead; his wife too – and she had left him willingly, perhaps even of her own accord, caring too little for him to make life worth living, if *he* was all there was in it. And, as if released by the warming of the year, another disaster struck: foot-and-mouth disease, beginning in the south, hopped north from cattle-market to cattle-market and arrived at last at Morland Place. The deadly disease rampaged through the stock, doing to the cattle what liver rot had done to the sheep years before. As the stock died, news of the disaster spread, creditors lost their nerve, and the bills flooded in.

Finally the stone which had been tumbling down the mountainside struck the bottom with a blow like a meteorite. Two of the three banks called in their loans; and when George ignored their letters, sober but determined gentlemen in frock coats called at Morland Place and, in spite of anything Goole could do, cornered George, confronted him, and forced him to listen.

His privacy, his solitude, his escape – all were cut off. Reality had to be faced. They were sorry to intrude upon him in his state of mourning, said these sober gentlemen, but things had come to such a pass they could no longer be ignored. They were unwilling to proceed against him in court: the Morland name was an old one; they had known his father, and their fathers had known *his* father. Bankruptcy or prison, those frightful stigmas, were unthinkable. The alternative was for an agent appointed by them to oversee the sale of everything that could be sold, the proceeds to be applied to his debts.

They were being very kind to him, undertaking considerable work on his behalf rather than see him broken and humiliated by the actions of the law; but George was unable to appreciate it. He only wanted to be left alone. Do as you please, he told them; I don't care. But it was impossible for him to go on ignoring the situation, when everywhere he turned he found strangers with pencils and small books noting down his possessions and their value.

The horses were the first to go. The racehorses, his remaining hunters, the stallions and brood mares; the four-year-olds that would have been sold this spring anyway; the three-year-olds that were only half trained; the two-year-olds and yearlings that were his bright-eyed hope. Some went privately, some were sent to sales in other parts of the country where a better price might be obtained; the rest were put up together, the stud stables at Twelvetrees turned for the purpose into a market for two days, advertisements in the newspapers bringing buyers from all over the country and elsewhere.

George kept away, an undirected bitterness in his heart. They were taking his horses, he cried inwardly, without any clear idea of who 'they' were, knowing only that it was the worst thing you could do to a man. The sale brought Teddy to Morland Place again, worried about his brother, fearing it meant the worst. George saw him this time, but only so that he could keep him at a distance. 'The sale?' he said. 'I've decided to get out of racehorses, that's all. I've got a new scheme up my sleeve – something much more interesting, I promise you.'

Teddy eyed his brother anxiously. He *looked* all right: neat, clean, shaven, properly dressed – not pale or wild or dishevelled. He didn't look as if he had lost weight or taken to the bottle. Yet there were all these rumours flying about, and the undeniable fact that the sale was being organised by one of York's leading banking houses. And George wouldn't meet his eye. *What* was going on?

'Georgie, old fellow, are you in trouble?' he asked bluntly. 'You would tell me, wouldn't you? I know we haven't been particularly close all these years, but I am your brother and if there's anything—'

'Oh, don't talk rot! Of course I'm not in trouble,' George said airily. 'What trouble could I possibly be in?'

'The financial sort. I hear rumours—'

'Yes, well, you shouldn't listen to gossip,' George said loftily. 'And if you really want to do something for me, you might deny the rumours when you hear them. If it's not you spreading them in the first place, that is.'

Teddy flushed angrily. 'That's a rotten thing to say.'

'Is it? I know nothing about you, you see. All I know is that you never liked my wife; and all your life you've been jealous of me. Perhaps your jealousy is at the bottom of this. You never came near us all those years—'

'I was never invited!' Teddy said hotly.

'But now as soon as you think there's something wrong, you come here to gloat. Well, I'm sorry to disappoint you, but there's nothing to gloat about. Everything is as fine as could be, and I don't need your help, now or ever.'

'Good,' said Teddy. 'I'm sorry I offered it. I shan't do so again.' He began to turn away.

'I know what's behind this,' George called after him. 'You're wishing you hadn't swapped that land of yours for those rubbishing factories. Well, that was business, fair and proper, and there's no going back on it. If you want to be a landed gentleman, you're going to have to buy a piece of land. Not that owning land can make everyone a gentleman!'

Teddy walked away without comment, and George felt he had struck a good blow. That would teach him to come gloating and sneering. Teddy was definitely one of 'them' – a group that was coming to comprise pretty much the whole world.

Teddy shrugged off his brother's insults, and told himself that they discharged him from any duty of caring about George or his plight. Underneath, of course, he did worry still, but he reasoned that if George would not let him help, there was nothing he could do about it. He would keep an eye on the situation from a distance, but he wasn't going to put himself in the way of gratuitous insults.

But when the excitement of battle had faded, at the end of that day which saw his horses gone and his brother gone, George felt very alone. He picked at the supper Goole brought to the billiards room on a tray, but drank deeply of the claret, and the wine made him feel restless. He had a sudden revulsion for his surroundings. He had been confined to this room for months now, and just at the moment he hated every familiar inch of it. He broached the second bottle Goole had thoughtfully provided, and walked about the room. Despite the dogs, it seemed a solitary confinement. How dare They shut him up here like a prisoner? He was master of Morland Place, wasn't he? They had better learn that, if they had forgotten. He was his father's eldest son, and everything – the name, the house, the chattels, the land, the stock – was rightfully his. How dare those vultures come picking over his possessions as though he were a corpse?

Taking the bottle and glass with him, he went through the connecting door into the main part of the house. Only the passage lamps were burning, turned down low. Alfreda had agonised long about having gas laid on: on the one hand, she had felt instinctively that it was somehow vulgar; on the other, the cost involved in having a private pipe laid to the house was so high that it made it terribly desirable as a proof of how rich they were. In the end, other plans had ousted that one, and there was no gas, only lamps downstairs and candles in the bedrooms. George had never really cared either way, but now seeing his house by low lamp-light he was glad that it looked as it always had. Not just his house, but his home. But, Lord, how empty it was! His whole life suddenly seemed a procession of people leaving him: his mother, his father, his sisters and brothers, his child, his wife! Self-pity overcame him and he emptied his glass, decided it was slowing him down and put it aside in favour of drinking from the bottle. And now They were even trying to take his home from him. An end to Morlands at Morland Place? It would be the end of history, the end of civilisation.

He wandered from room to room, Maggie padding at his heels with an anxious air, unable to settle, driven out of each by the emptiness, which seemed paradoxically almost like a forbidding presence. Finally he went into the chapel. He had not been here since Alfreda's interment.

It felt cold, but only with the usual cold of an unheated church; it smelt familiarly of damp and furniture polish and the ghost of incense and wax; it was lit dimly by the glow of the sanctuary lamp, burning at the far end. Everything here spoke of continuity, and he felt obscurely comforted. He walked down the central aisle and sat down in a pew near the front, still absently tilting the bottle to his lips from time to time, staring at the flame of the sanctuary lamp and the flowers on the altar. The smell of candle wax was not so very old, he thought. Someone must come in here and light candles from time to time.

He had no idea how long he had been sitting, but his feet had got very cold, the bottle was empty, and he had grown too numb to get up. Then he became aware that someone was coming down the chapel towards him. He heard a soft footfall, a faint rustling, almost too quiet to be heard. The hair rose on the back of his neck as he became irrationally convinced it was a ghost: who else, after all, could it be? He was alone in the house; the servants had gone to bed.

With an enormous effort he turned his head, though he was so reluctant to see what was behind him it was like trying to turn a tap that had rusted shut. He glimpsed a moving light and a white shape, and his mind screamed; and then he realised a ghost would not need to carry a candle and forced himself to turn all the way round and look properly.

'It's you!' he gasped with relief. 'What are you doing here?'

Alice, with a bed gown over her nightdress, stopped before him, holding the candle away so that she could see his face. 'I heard you moving around. Are you all right, sir?'

She looked very pretty in the candlelight, her hair loose down her back. Here was company, he thought, and company of the right sort – someone who treated him with the respect due to the master of Morland Place. He pictured her rising from her bed and coming downstairs, driven by anxiety for him. Devoted to her duty! It did not occur to him, in his fuddled state, to wonder how she could have heard him from the servants' rooms in the attic, or why, if she had already gone to bed, her hair was loose. He pictured her bed as a downy nest, a soft and tumbled place, warm with the delicious heat of her body.

'I'm cold,' he said. 'I want to go to bed.'

She crouched down beside him, and laid a tentative hand on his knee. He could feel the heat of her, like the warmth of a fire: alive in this cold darkness. 'Shall I help you?' she asked. He stared at her a long moment, reading the offer – practically the request – in her eyes. Well, why not, after all? Who had more right? Who deserved comfort more?

'Little Alice,' he said fondly. 'I'm glad you're here. Help me to my bed.' He stood up and she stood with him, and put herself under his arm to support him, holding the candle before them. 'We don't need that,' he said, and blew it out. The scent of hot wax smoke reminded him. 'It's you who takes care of the chapel, isn't it? You keep it clean and fill the lamp and light candles?'

'It's the heart of the house,' she said. 'I was afraid if it wasn't looked after it would be – like the house dying.'

He chuckled, pulling her against him, feeling the warm softness of her body through her thin clothing. 'Foolish little Alice! *I* am the heart of the house. Let's go to bed.'

And so it was on the sofa of the smoking-room that Alice finally reached the place she'd been longing for for almost nine years. She gave herself, the unstinting handmaid, for love; and when George fell instantly asleep afterwards, that was her reward – to have been the one to bring him comfort and respite.

CHAPTER TWENTY-THREE

One day in the summer of 1883 Henrietta had been visiting her sister: Regina had not long been delivered of her fifth child, and summoned Henrietta most days to relieve the tedium of her confinement. Henrietta liked visiting the Red House. There was always an atmosphere of cheer, the noise and bustle of family life. Perry was just the same genial, sociable man his father had been, and he loved Regina and his children. Given the Parke philoprogenitive nature, it seemed odd that the twins, Amy and Patsy, had not married. They had had offers, and had appeared to consider them – though sometimes with a faintly amused air – but had always concluded that marrying would not add to their happiness more than it took away.

Luckily the fortune they inherited from their mother provided an ample income, and Perry urged them always to consider his house their home. The twins spent their time travelling and painting, returned several times a year to the Red House to rest, unpack their paintings and see their family. They loved Perry's children, and the children thought 'the aunts' the most romantic figures, besides being the purveyors of fabulously exciting presents. After a few weeks, restlessness would set in and the twins would be off again, travelling all over the world, sometimes to remote and even dangerous places: two neat, tough little English ladies setting up their easels before pyramids and temples, in deserts and jungles, by rivers, on mountain tops, beside distant oceans. Wild animals did not frighten them, nor half-naked tribesmen embarrass them; they would not be cheated in the souk or cozened in the bazaar; but they were generous with tips and little presents, and always willing to advise the native mothers on hygiene and the proper arrangement of drains and middens.

Perry worried about them constantly, and still hoped, every time they came home, that they would stay, get married and settle nearby; but they were as happy in their way as he was in his, and he tried to be content for them. Henrietta envied them: to travel the world and see its wonders – and especially to do so with someone you loved and trusted and who was perfectly companionable! It was company she missed the most. Regina was taken up with her children and husband, Mr Fortescue and Elizabeth were taken up with each other, she rarely saw or heard from Teddy these days, and there had been a coolness between her and Mary since last year. She kept house, performed her parish work and her good deeds, and in her unoccupied moments she read, sewed, or went for solitary rides. She would be thirty this September, and there seemed no reason that her life would ever change again. The passionate years of youth were over, and the best that could be hoped for from now on was comfort and peace of mind.

She arrived home to find Elizabeth sitting in the drawing-room reading a book. 'Shouldn't you be at your lessons?' she asked.

'Papa sent me in here,' Elizabeth said. 'He wants to see you. I was to ask you to go to the library as soon as you came in.'

Henrietta felt immediate alarm. Mr Fortescue was such a creature of habit, any departure was worrying. 'Is Papa unwell?' she asked her daughter.

'I don't know,' Elizabeth said simply. 'He didn't say.'

Henrietta refrained from asking if he looked ill. It wasn't that Elizabeth was unnoticing, but she remembered from her own childhood that when you were eleven, grown-ups seemed to live in a separate world where other rules applied. The question would merely have puzzled her.

But while Henrietta was hesitating, Elizabeth volunteered, 'He has been a bit different lately, though.'

'Different?'

'Well,' she frowned with thought, 'he doesn't talk to me the way he used to. And when I do my lessons, he doesn't stay with me.'

'What do you mean?'

'He used to be in the library with me all the time. Even when I was doing a piece of work on my own he would sit with me and do his own work. Now he doesn't even teach me, not really. He just gives me a piece of work to do, and goes away and doesn't come back until it's time for me to stop. I did two pieces of work last week that he hasn't even marked. And then today he came back early and told me to take my book to the drawing-room and send you to him as soon as you came in.'

Henrietta could see that Elizabeth was puzzled, though not yet worried; and not wishing to alarm her, she smiled and said, 'Then I had better go at once. I mustn't keep Papa waiting.'

As she walked through the house towards the library she reflected. Since that time last year when she had seen Mansur's carriage at the door, she had not been aware of any visit by the doctor, and had assumed that the indisposition, whatever it was, had gone away. It was true that Mr Fortescue had handed over more and more of his parish and priestly duties to Catchpole: he took a service only about once a month now, but when he did so, he spoke as vigorously as ever. He did not look any different to her – though when you see a person every day, it is hard to notice changes in them, especially if they are gradual. At all events, she had stopped worrying about him; but she wondered now whether the illness, whatever it was, had returned. It was not like him to absent himself from Elizabeth's company, or to be careless about her work; and it was perfectly possible for him to visit Mansur, rather than have him come here.

She tapped at the library door, and at his quiet, 'Come in,' entered, and walked across to his desk. He was writing, and did not look up at once, giving her the opportunity to study him. His hair had retreated further, she could see that now; and he was perhaps a little more cadaverous, a little greyer in the face. But on the whole she thought there was no great change in him. Certainly when he finally looked up it was with as sharp an eye and unyielding a face as ever.

'Lizzie said you wanted me.'

He studied her with his usual dispassion, which had always made it impossible to tell what he was thinking. Yet what he said was the last thing she would have expected.

'It has occurred to me that your life is rather monotonous, and that you are perhaps in need of a change of scene.' She was too surprised to speak, and he went on, 'The human spirit needs rest and refreshment even as the body does. It is my wish that you should take a holiday.'

They had been married for twelve years without his ever considering this necessary before. But old habit prevented her from expressing pointless wonder. Instead she said, 'Where do you want me to go?'

He had his answers ready. 'You should go to the sea side. The sea air is considered particularly therapeutic. Whitby is a quiet, respectable place, I understand. You may take Elizabeth with you. She has never seen the sea.'

She returned his stare, trying to understand. 'And you?' she asked at last. 'Will you be coming too?'

His eyes moved away from hers, the only evidence that he was not entirely at ease. 'No. I have a great deal to do.'

'You always have a great deal to do,' she replied.

That roused him. 'Don't be impertinent. I have important work and do not wish to be disturbed by you or Elizabeth. A holiday by the sea side will do you both good.'

She couldn't fathom what was going on. His mask was

434

too perfect. The idea that either of them might disturb him at his work was nonsense – they were too well trained, and he had never found it difficult to ignore them before.

On the face of it, it was a kindness he was doing her; but why should he hide behind a false excuse? And kindness to her had not been his most notable trait; it was many years since he had wanted her near him, or found any pleasure in her company. It must be that she was being sent away for some reason: perhaps she had displeased him more than usual. But, then, why was he letting her take Elizabeth? And again, why the excuse? She didn't understand; and what she didn't understand, she didn't like. But probably she hadn't any choice in the matter.

'Is it an order?' she asked at last.

'An order?' He seemed surprised. 'No, it is my recommendation. My sincere advice.'

'You had better make it an order,' she said, 'so that there's no misunderstanding.'

He looked at her a little oddly, and she had the obscure feeling that she had hurt him somehow, though she couldn't think how. 'Go to Whitby,' he said at last. 'Leave tomorrow morning. Take Elizabeth. Remain until I send for you to come home.' He paused a moment, and then added, 'I hope that you have – a pleasant time.'

'Thank you,' she said, her puzzlement clear in her voice, both at the instruction and this last unexpected sentiment.

But before she could ask anything else, he said, 'Leave me now,' and began writing again to indicate that the interview was terminated.

It was breezy in Whitby, but in sheltered spots the sun was warm and fell like a benison from a sky of aching blue, across which large clouds bowled like laundry blown from the line. The sea sparkled, a million diamonds scattered over the dark blue, rocking waves; flecks of white here and there mirrored the white gulls wheeling above. The air was exhilarating, with that combination of tar and seaweed and salt-bleached wood, which once smelt is never forgotten.

He had said Elizabeth had never seen the sea – but Henrietta had never seen it, either. She felt she had never been so alive before. She had been thinking about freedom, about travel, envying the Misses Parke – and now, against all expectation, here she was! It wasn't Petra or Tashkent, but to her it was as exotic as any far-flung place because it was new, and different, and above all it was here and now!

Elizabeth was enchanted by the sea. 'It *talks*, Mama,' she cried the first day, standing on the lower rail and leaning over the upper so that she could gaze at the waves breaking on the shingle. 'A whoosh and then a clatter and then a gurgle. I do like the gurgle! And those *birds*! They sound so sad. But aren't they white? How do they keep so clean?'

'I don't know. Doesn't the wind smell nice? Look, Lizzie, at that boat out there! Wouldn't you like to be on it?'

The boarding-house Mr Fortescue had chosen for them was small and plain, though comfortable, and the owner was a respectable widow recommended to him by the local parish priest. Henrietta had wondered, learning this, whether Mrs Evesham was the extension of her husband's control, ordered to report any breach of decorum to the vicar, who would report it to the rector. But when she met her, Mrs Evesham seemed a pleasant and unsuspicious woman. In any case, Henrietta and Elizabeth spent most of their time out of doors, where, illusion or not, there was a sense of absolute freedom.

It was good to have time alone with Elizabeth, talking to her without restraint, listening to her, sharing with her the discovery of a new world. Her daughter, of course, was far more educated that Henrietta, and her erudition, and the long hours she had spent with her father, had made her solemn and quiet. Henrietta remembered the freedom of her own childhood, and wanted Elizabeth to taste a little of it too; but she had no experience of running about and getting grubby and untidy. At first Henrietta could hardly get her to leave her side, or make her understand that she might make a noise if she wanted.

Fortunately the other guests at the boarding-house were a Mrs James, a bank manager's wife from York, and her two daughters, who were about Elizabeth's age. Sarah and Anne had been to the seaside before, and knew exactly what to do on a beach. After an initial shyness, the girls made friends, and Elizabeth began to learn that there were other pleasures in life besides construing Virgil. Henrietta was happy to see them play together. Mrs James was a woman of few words, who would sit in the shelter of a breakwater knitting by the hour together without wanting conversation, which made her very restful company.

A week passed with amazing speed, and after the first two days, the relaxing qualities of the air and light operated on Henrietta so that she stopped wondering why Mr Fortescue had sent her here – almost stopped thinking entirely. On this breezy, bright day a week later they had come out early and walked and gazed and exclaimed, until they had discovered themselves unbearably hungry and repaired to the tea-room to recruit their strength.

Afterwards they went down onto the beach. Mrs James had taken the girls to visit relatives, and there happened to be no-one else around, so they had it to themselves. Elizabeth took off her boots and stockings and paddled in the breaking surf, holding up her skirts and looking back often at her mother to make sure she was sharing the moment. Henrietta would have expected her to shriek at the cold roughness of the water, but she was silent with rapture, her mouth open wide in soundless delight.

'Don't you long to do the same? How can you bear not to take off your shoes and join her?' The voice at her shoulder was so familiar and so unexpected that, for a moment, she thought she had imagined it: she didn't want to turn round in case she had.

She turned. It was Jerome: his tanned face, so handsome, but marked with lines of sadness now; his bright blue eyes, narrowed against the dazzle of the day; his dark hair lifted by the sea breeze, madly ruffled. Her heart seemed to stop; time hung suspended. How could it be him? How could he suddenly appear at her side in this obscure place?

'"Speak, I charge thee speak,"' he said, gently teasing. '"Am I thy father's spirit doomed for a certain term to walk the night?"'

'Is it really you?' she asked.

'Yes, poor bewildered child, I'm not a ghost. Here, touch me, if you like.' He held out his hand, but she didn't take it, so he lifted it before her eyes and turned it back and forth. 'Flesh and blood – you see?'

'I see,' she said, but she could still hardly believe it. It was more than eight years since she had last seen him; she had never thought to see him again. But here he was, smiling at her – the old, sidelong smile, but without its mocking, challenging edge. He had changed in the years between. He looked a little rueful, a little unsure of himself; there was wariness in his eyes and the tense line of his shoulders, as though he had taken a fall or two and been surprised by how hard the earth could be.

'You don't look as though you saw,' he said. 'You are as white and staring as Hamlet. I'm almost sorry now I crept up on you, but I couldn't resist it when I saw you standing there. And please don't tell me that great girl prancing in the waves is your little baby daughter!'

He was talking to give her time to adjust to the shock, she realised. It had been a shock: she felt that airy sensation in her chest.

'What are you doing here?' she asked at last.

'I came to see you,' he said.

The only sense she could make of that was that he had been sent with a message. 'Is something wrong? Has something happened?'

'Oh, Lord, I've alarmed you again! No, all is well, as far as I know. Give me your hand. Dear me, it's like a block of ice.'

His was warm and alive, the fingers strong, the palm hard from riding. At the touch of it, such a hot flood of love and joy rushed through her, such relief at being with him again, that she could only stand motionless and let it have its way with her. Her helpless dreams had given her only the pale shadow of what she felt now; for one thing, her dreams could not re-create the living look of him, or the expression in his eyes, which told her what he must be reading in her face.

It lasted only an instant. She remembered who she was and where, and was shocked with herself for revealing so much, and in a public place. She withdrew her hand and looked down, conducting a brief, fierce struggle with her feelings; and then, trying to sound neutral, said, 'But how did you know I was here?'

'Mary told me, of course.'

'Oh,' she said. At the mention of Mary's name, she became suddenly calm. It was a word to disperse magic, reminding her of everything that was worldly: her position, his, the impossibility of anything ever existing between them. She thrust down the uprushing spring of love for him that had taken her so unawares. *Be still*, she told her heart. *This is not for you.* When she lifted her eyes again, she was ready for him – ready to withstand him. 'Perhaps you were just passing through,' she suggested, as much for her own benefit as to him.

He did not take the offered escape. 'Whitby isn't on the way to anywhere,' he pointed out. 'Pleasant place, isn't it?'

'I can't imagine it's the sort of place to appeal to you.'

'Oddly enough, you're wrong about that,' he said. 'I spent many happy childhood days here, and it's a place that holds my affection. But why don't you believe I've come here to see you?'

It was not a question she could possibly answer. She searched his face. Had he come to tempt her to wrongdoing? No, it was absurd to think that, absurd and conceited. Besides, his manner was so different now.

'Will you walk with me a little?' he asked. He saw the refusal forming and hurried on, 'Just a walk along the sea front here, what could be wrong with that? As a friend.'

'A friend?'

'Are we not friends? I thought we were,' he said. 'Must all honest, innocent feeling be crushed by stifling convention?'

She could not bear his sadness. The care-for-nothing impudence that had been his hallmark was gone, and though she never would have thought she could miss it, she found she wanted him to be invulnerable, to have everything, never to suffer, not to be like the rest of humanity.

'If I thought we could be friends—' she began.

'That can never change,' he said. 'Did you think so? Come, walk with me.'

Elizabeth, down by the water, was looking at them. Henrietta waved to the child, and made a pantomime so that she would understand. 'I must stay in sight of her,' she said to Jerome.

'Of course,' he said. 'We'll go just to the point and back. I can't believe she's grown so much. How old is she now?'

'Nearly eleven.'

He turned and she turned with him, and they walked slowly, side by side but not touching. Yet she could feel the heat of his body as though he were a fire. She could almost feel his thoughts, like a humming of electricity in the wafer of air between them. And this after – how long?

'Almost her whole life,' she said aloud.

He understood her. 'So much must have changed for you.'

'No, I don't think so,' she said. 'A woman's life is not a thing of change and movement.'

'You mean *yours* is not. You can't speak for others.'

'I should think I could for all married women, at least.'

'It must depend on the husband,' he said.

'Well, you can't speak for others either. If I am only one wife, you are only one husband.'

He laughed. 'How I've missed your refreshing mind!

Tell me all the news of home. How's my old friend Ginger?'

'She's dead,' Henrietta said, wishing he had begun somewhere else. 'She went lame half-way through the hunting season a few years ago, and the vet said she'd sprained her back and would never be sound again, so it was the kindest thing. You were right about her, you see. You always said she was no good.'

'I'm sorry. I'd have been glad to be wrong about that. Tell me some happier news. How is your sister?'

She looked at him suspiciously. 'If you've seen Mary, you must have had all the news.'

'What makes you think I've seen her?'

'You said she told you—'

'In a letter. She wrote to me that you had come to Whitby without your husband and I came straight here.'

They were on dangerous ground again. 'You shouldn't have. What good could it do?' she asked.

'I don't know. I didn't calculate, precisely. I simply had to see you, and took the chance.'

She said nothing. They reached the end of the walk and stopped, and he turned to face her. 'I've missed you,' he said, 'but in a strange way I've never felt separate from you. I know you so well, you see. You were always there, like a part of me.' He made a gesture, laying his flat palms together and then hinging them open like a book. 'Like the two halves of a walnut when you shell it – not the same, but complementary. I knew when I first met you – knew it without knowing it, if you understand me.'

She nodded reluctantly. 'I understand – but it's wrong. I mustn't—'

'Mustn't what?'

She wouldn't elaborate. That would be to play his game. 'It's no good. Nothing's any good,' she said unhappily.

'There's this,' he said. 'We can be friends. We needn't be cut off entirely from each other, need we? It wouldn't be wrong to behave like friends, since that's what we are.' He was serious, and there was a quietness about him that

441

had never been there before. He was chastened – ready to compromise with life. He had grown up, she thought; but she had too.

'I don't know,' she said. 'I don't know if it's possible.'

'We can see,' he said. 'Let's try to be friends while you're here. Then we'll know.'

Elizabeth waved to them, a small figure on the beach, dark bunchy skirts tucked up, pale thin legs like primrose stalks. Henrietta waved back and began walking, and, satisfied, Elizabeth bent again to pick up another interesting stone.

'She'll be worn out this evening with all the fresh air,' Jerome said. 'She'll sleep like a log.'

'Yes,' Henrietta said, smiling fondly at her child.

'Come and dine with me,' he said.

She looked at him, shocked; but, revealingly, what she said was not 'No,' it was 'Where?'

'At my hotel.'

'It's not respectable,' she said.

He gave a shout of laughter. 'My hotel? It's the soul of respectability! You can't imagine a more dull and solid place.'

'I mean, it isn't respectable for a lady to dine out,' she said, blushing. 'What would people say?'

He sobered. 'No, you're right,' he said. 'We mustn't do anything precipitate. We must proceed with great caution. Any sudden move may startle.'

'What do you mean?'

'Nothing, nothing at all. I won't ask you to dine with me, then. But you will let me join you and Elizabeth day by day, so that I can show you how safe and good friendship can be?'

Elizabeth was running towards them now, slithering and scattering pebbles, waving her hand. 'Look what I've found!' she cried, her voice tiny and far off in the resounding air, full of the boom and pull of the sea. 'Look, isn't it beautiful!'

'Yes, darling,' she called back automatically.

'I'll take that as my answer too,' Jerome said, with a small smile.

The second week passed quickly. Henrietta had never been so happy. The place itself was a delight – the magic of the sea renewed itself every morning when she first set eyes on it, and wove itself into her dreams at night, as she lay with her window open, listening to its hushed rocking sound far below. Elizabeth loved it too. She ran about in such mad delight that her mother felt if she had lifted her arms she might have flown, buoyed by rapture into the breezy sky. There was freedom for the child such as she had never known at home, in the formality of the rector's house, the restraint of the rector's village. She seemed positively to grow, straightening and stretching, her thin white legs becoming strong. Henrietta ought to have worried about freckles and sunburn, but she could not bear to hamper the child's pleasure, and reasoned that a little brownness would wear off before she was eighteen. With her face growing tan and her hair silver, Elizabeth paddled and played, searched for crabs, collected shells and seaweed, made friends with other small biologists on the beach, ate hugely at mealtimes, and slept hugely at night.

And while Elizabeth played, Henrietta and Jerome talked. It was a bliss she could hardly have conceived of, to have such full and unfettered conversation with someone who seemed to understand everything before she said it, who seemed to know all her thoughts and disapprove of none of them. He did not again touch on their feelings for each other, which made it seem safe, and assuaged her conscience. It was just friendship after all, she told herself, and what could be the harm in that? After the first two days they would sometimes not talk, sitting silently for long periods, and that was good too, and in a strange way no different from talking. There was a freedom with him that she had not known with anyone before: not even with another woman.

'It's like being on my own,' she said once, 'but better.'

'I should hope so,' he said.

'Not just better because of the company,' she explained, 'but because I *know* everything I know, so I know what I'm going to say and think. But I can't anticipate you – or not always.'

'And you are a constant delight to me. Your mind is so original – I could never have invented you.'

At the end of the second week the fine weather broke and there was rain. Jerome sent a note to say that he was going away on business for two days, but would present himself, with her permission, on his return. Henrietta's disappointment was acute. The thought of two whole days without his company made the day outside seem darker and wetter. But confined indoors, Elizabeth grew fretful, and Henrietta set herself to entertain her child, playing spillikins with her, teaching her card games, singing songs and showing her how to draw.

The rain passed, and with the fine weather Jerome returned, all smiles, and called on them. He had come back to Whitby with a hired phaeton and horse, and proposed to take them out for drives.

'It would be a pity for Lizzie to be here and not see something of the countryside,' he said. Elizabeth was so pleased with the idea that Henrietta could only thank him for his kindness. The expeditions were a great success. Jerome pointed out things of interest to Elizabeth, told her the history of every place they visited, chatted and told her stories, even let her hold the reins and taught her to drive. From what she had known of him before, Henrietta would not have imagined he could be so patient with a child. She saw with gratitude how he treated Elizabeth as an equal, and how she responded to him; a real affection was growing between them, which Henrietta saw, with some surprise, satisfied him as much as her.

At the end of the week he asked Henrietta, 'Will you come for a drive with me tomorrow – just you on your own?'

Henrietta looked at him doubtfully. 'I couldn't leave Lizzie.'

'Oh, I think you could. She'd love to play all day on the beach with those two little friends of her, and I'm sure their mother, Mrs Whatyemaycall . . .'

'Mrs James?'

'Yes. Mrs James would take care of her, wouldn't she?'

'I expect so, but—'

'Let her have a few hours of freedom from you.'

'From me?'

'A parent is always hampering, however much loved. Don't you remember from your own childhood?'

'I had a very different sort of childhood,' Henrietta said. But she had an imagination, and believed he was right; and so she allowed herself to be persuaded. Elizabeth's excitement at the idea of being away from her mother was almost insulting, and Mrs James said it wasn't the least trouble in the world to look after her for a day, so it was easily settled.

As he drove them up out of the town and into the open country, her own doubts about the propriety of being alone with him ought to have raised their heads, but a week in his company had accustomed her to it, and familiarity had bred unwariness. They went by narrow lanes, through overhanging woods, climbing up towards the moors. Sometimes there was a glimpse of the winding course of the river Esk, sometimes a house half hidden in the trees; a man with a long staff and a dog at his heels, stepping back to let them by; a field with a pond in it and a dozen grey geese, raising their wings and their orange bills and rattling out an alarm. Everything was interesting to Henrietta; the simplest thing seemed invested with new significance, sharply drawn on her eye and mind.

And then they were out onto the moors, and it was like being at the top of the world, for there was nothing higher than them, only the rolling vastness of the land and the sky all around them. The moors stretched, gently billowing like a shaken eiderdown, brown and green and purple, for miles and miles and miles. Sometimes there was bog-grass – unnatural, vivid emerald green – and little rills, running between black lips of peat; sometimes acres of bracken, secretly rustling. Now and then there was a stunted thorn tree, or a milestone, or a rocky outcrop for a landmark. There were sheep about, grazing or lying down out of the wind, sometimes even resting in the middle of the road, getting up at the last minute and flouncing away in a panic. There were grouse, calling from behind rocks, and crows, and small birds flying out from the heather in sudden flocks like thrown-away tea-leaves; and once she saw a fox, trotting purposefully along a sheep-trod. He stopped and looked at them, then went on, too far off to worry about them.

They hardly talked as they drove. Henrietta was simply enjoying the novelty. Jerome seemed sunk in his thoughts; but when she glanced at him his face was serene so she decided they were not unhappy. At last he turned off the road onto a narrower track through deep bracken. After a hundred yards the track petered out and they were on the edge of a steep slope down into a dry valley. Jerome stopped and put on the brake. The horse sneezed mightily and rubbed its nose on its knee with a prolonged jingling of harness, but when it had finished, there was absolute stillness.

The sun fell hot and clean through the clear air. Below them the valley bent away to the right, a cleft full of dark curling trees, falling to yield at last into a misty blue vista of open country and distant hills. The stillness resolved itself into a tapestry of tiny sounds: the sigh of the wind, the faint rustling of the bracken, a thin trickle of water running somewhere out of sight. Far, far away a crow cawed, a tiny scratch of sound on a backcloth of silence; and then the horse sighed deeply and cocked one hind foot, settling itself.

'Is this it?' she asked.

'This is it.'

'This is what you wanted to show me?'

'Wasn't it worth the drive? Come, let's get down. There's a convenient rock just along there.'

He jumped her down and led her a few yards to the left,

along the valley edge. Here the bracken ended and there was a natural turf lawn out of which a knob of grey rock protruded. They sat down side by side on the turf, their backs supported by the rock, facing the curving valley.

'Oh, this is wonderful,' Henrietta said. 'Smell the air! It's so clean, as if it's never been used before.'

'The moors are the most beautiful place on earth,' Jerome said. 'They're the last place God made before he retired to bed on Sabbath eve.' She laughed, and he said, 'I mean it. That's why God feels so close here. He's just on the other side of the sky – and on the moors, the sky is near enough to touch.'

'I thought you didn't believe in God,' she said teasingly.

'Oh, I believe in God all right. I just don't believe in the Church.'

'We mustn't talk about that,' she said quickly. 'I don't want anything to spoil this place for me. It's like a place out of time.'

'That's just what it is,' he said. She looked at him curiously, and he was staring away down the valley, his face content.

'How do you know about it?' she asked.

'I used to come here as a boy. Most of this land was part of my father's estate. It's been sold now, all but a little cottage just out of sight over there, and a few acres around it.'

'You have a cottage here?'

'It's usually rented out. People like to come here for holidays – walkers and artists and botanists and the like. And people who want to step out of time for a little while.' He looked at her. 'People like us.'

She grew nervous. 'Don't,' she said.

'I must,' he said. 'This is our chance to talk about all the other things we haven't said. You're safe here. It's a magic place, and what's said here doesn't count.' He held up the crossed fingers of childhood games. '*Fen larks.*' Still she looked at him, troubled. 'Tell me about your life,' he said. 'I promise it will never be spoken of outside this place. But I want to know. If we are friends, you can tell me.'

The longing to talk was strong in her; and so she told him. He listened with great pain, now understanding fully the terrible sterility of her life with Fortescue, which he had only guessed at before. 'Do you love him?' he asked at last. 'You can't love him.'

'I don't know,' she said. 'I don't know how you tell.'

'If you loved him, you would know it,' he said.

Her intellect protested. 'How can you say that? It's absurd.'

'No, it's not. I'll tell you how it is. You are in a crowded street, looking for a friend. You think you see him, you call and begin to wave, and he turns, and you see it's not him after all. And then a while later you see your friend and know him at once and run towards him; and then you wonder how you could ever possibly have mistaken the stranger for him.'

The question that had been uppermost in her mind ever since he came to Whitby burst from her then. 'Why did you marry?'

He examined the tone of her voice. '*Did* you mind? I thought you didn't care.'

'I cared,' she said. 'Why did you do it?'

'I was angry.'

'With me?' She asked it tentatively, not to put herself forward.

'With the situation.' He shrugged. 'A very bad reason for marrying, I know – and in my own defence I can only say that she had a bad reason too. She wanted to get away from her mother, and I had sufficient money to make her comfortable. So we made a beggars' bargain.'

Henrietta stirred. 'I don't want you to tell me bad things about her.'

'I won't. I don't hate her. We parted by common consent – it was what we both wanted. We never loved each other, that's all. We should never have married, and we both acknowledge it. It's all over and done with now.'

'It will never be done with,' she said sadly. 'You are

married, I am married, and there's nothing to be done about it.'

He gave her a faint, painful smile. 'Now you know a little how I always felt. From the first moment I saw you, I hated it – *hated* it – that you belonged to someone else. I still can't bear to think of you with that – with him,' he corrected himself hastily. 'And yet you are lucky to have Elizabeth,' he went on. 'I've never had a child. It seems such a waste now.'

'You are so good with her,' Henrietta said. 'I love to see you together.'

Jerome took her hand, folded it in his two, and she was so absorbed by the remoteness of the place that she let him.

'*We* should be together,' he said. 'We belong together.'

'Yes,' she said. 'But I don't understand why.'

'Did you ever feel like that about him?' She shook her head, a little guiltily. 'Even at the beginning?'

'I admired him. I even adored him, I suppose. He was so far above me, like a – a god on earth,'

Jerome suppressed a smile. 'Was that all?'

'All? How much more should there be?'

'Oh, a great deal more that I can see he has never taught you. For that you should have come to me.'

She felt herself blushing. 'You mean the – the bedroom thing?'

'That's part of it.'

She thought of the strange scenes the rector had acted out with her in the darkness of the bedchamber. Perhaps they were not normal? But they were not for Jerome to know. She said only, 'I don't see how that can be so important.'

'It's different when it's with someone you really love. Someone you love as I love you. Don't you feel it?' He lifted her hand to his lips and kissed the fingers one by one. 'Don't you feel how it could be? You're trembling – that can't be cold.'

'I'm not—' she began, without an idea what she was trying to say.

'Do you love me? Say you love me. Say it.'

'I can't say it. It's wrong,' she said.

'How can you be so sure? Everything in life seems so uncertain to me. The only thing I'm sure of is that I love you.'

She met his eyes, and her stomach clenched, the hair on her scalp seemed to lift – a strange, atavistic reaction to him that excited and frightened her.

'Come with me to the cottage,' he said. 'Let me show you. It's empty – there's no-one to see or know.'

'That's why you went away for two days?'

'That, and to hire the phaeton to bring you here.'

'You meant to have me, then?'

'I meant you to have me,' he said. 'I always did.'

A huge, stinging emptiness was inside her, seemed to be expanding, an aching hunger that demanded to be fed or she would die. She wanted him, she was aware, in a way she had never felt for anyone else. Was this the uniqueness he had spoken about? She wanted everything, all he had to give: she wanted to *know*. He had brought her to this safe place, out of the world, so that she could ask the question and be given the answer. *What am I for? What is love for? What is it I've been searching for and never found?*

It was she who made the next move, chose it in the full knowledge of wrongdoing. She must have this, though she paid for it afterwards. She put herself into his arms, her arms went round him, her mouth yielded, she was kissing and being kissed with a huge, flowering hunger that wiped out thought, shame or doubt. They were kissing each other, touching faces, hands, heads, with great tenderness; she felt his vulnerability, and it touched her unbearably. This was no heartless trick for self-gratification: it mattered desperately to him that she should return his feelings. His love made him weak as it made her strong. *That* was when she believed; and that was when she understood what she wanted to happen. She wanted to take him inside her, to be pierced and made whole, to be one flesh: she hungered for it as a dying man hungers for the light. Yes, she saw now that the strange

450

act would have power if it was between people who loved as she loved him, and he loved her.

And in the same moment she knew she could not do it. Because it was important, it mattered – a synonymy she wondered he had not seen for himself. He felt the change in her, lifted his lips from hers; his expression was almost bruised as she gently detached herself from his arms.

'I can't,' she said.

He looked at her carefully, wondering if she still didn't understand. 'This is not,' he said, 'a casual, unimportant thing. I am not trifling with you. I want you to leave him and come and live with me.'

She sighed, as though dragging in a breath from under a great stone weighting her. 'This is a place out of time. I'm glad you brought me here. I never knew before what love was, or why it was supposed to be so wonderful. All those things I read in books, like Paris and Helen and Antony and Cleopatra – I understand now.' Her voice ran out.

'"But",' he said. 'You are going to say "but".'

'But I must go back,' she said. 'We mustn't see each other again.'

'You can't mean that,' he said, putting his arms round her again. 'Not now you know.'

Unconsciously she leaned into the embrace, not away from it. 'It will be so much harder for me now I know. But nothing has changed. I am a married woman. I made a vow, and I have to keep it.'

'That old man doesn't want you. He doesn't love you. Who would care if you broke your vow?'

'*I* would care. Please,' she went on, stopping him from answering, 'don't say things that I shan't like to think of afterwards. Mary says things sometimes – about vows and God; she doesn't mean them, I'm sure, but – when she says them, sometimes I almost don't like *her*.'

'Darling—'

'All my life I've wondered what God wanted me for, and still I don't understand, but if I stopped trying to find out there would be no point to life at all. It's the only way

451

I know to carry on. It will break my heart to be without you—' She couldn't speak for a moment. 'But I can't turn away from God, and that's what it would mean, to leave my husband and abandon the duty I took up, for the joy of being with you.'

'You choose duty over joy?'

'There's no other choice,' she said. Her throat so tight with tears it ached unbearably.

He let her go then. 'I honour you,' he said. 'But I'm quite, quite sure you're wrong. You're so much younger than me. Can't you accept that I must know better? I've thought about it carefully over the years, I promise you. I didn't leave Julia lightly. But living with her was a desert, a place where nothing grew, not even dutifulness, not even love of God. My soul was withering and dying. Don't condemn us both to that. That would be to waste everything good between us. Can that be what God wants?'

She didn't answer; and that was his answer.

The sun had moved round, and one side of the valley was deep in violet shadow. 'We should get back,' he said at last.

'Yes,' she said. Elizabeth would be waiting.

They didn't speak on the drive back. Her eyes were heavy with tears she was trying not to cry. When he came to the place where the road bent down towards the little town, the last place on the windy tops, he stopped the horse and turned towards her. 'A moment here to say goodbye,' he said. 'We can't do it properly down below.'

He took her face in both his hands and kissed it, eyes and cheeks and lips, and her lips clung to his forlornly.

'Oh, my love,' he said, 'don't go back. Come and live with me, and let's be happy.' She began to shake her head and he went on quickly, 'Think of what your life will be, and mine, if we part. Come to me and I will take care of you always, I promise.'

'I can't,' she said, and now the tears slipped over.

'Is it your last word?' She nodded, and he looked suddenly grey, as though in pain. 'Then there's an end,' he said.

'What will you do?' she asked.

'Go abroad,' he said at last. 'Go to the devil. I can't stay here. I'll go abroad and try and find a place where I'm not reminded of you. Africa, perhaps. Some hellish place. Who cares?' He released her, turning away, taking up the reins, his expression hard.

He drove slowly down into the town while she tried to compose herself. When he reached the boarding-house he stopped a few doors further on, for discretion's sake.

Through the agony in her throat, she said, 'I will love you always. I'll never forget you. I will see your face every time I close my eyes.' She began gathering her skirts to descend.

He reached out suddenly and caught her wrist in a grip so hard it hurt her. 'I can't believe you will do it,' he said. She shuddered with the pain but made no sound. He approached his face to hers, looking fiercely into her eyes. 'Listen! You know where I lodge. Tomorrow you will send me word, and I'll come to you.' He released her wrist, and she rubbed it slowly, gazing at him with a troubled look. 'I'll wait for your decision. If you don't send to me tomorrow, I'll go abroad, and you'll never see me again.'

She mustn't start crying again, she mustn't. She wanted to say goodbye, but she knew if she opened her mouth the tears would come. So she leaned over and laid her lips a moment against his cheek, then climbed down from the phaeton and walked away.

Somehow she managed to get up to her room without being seen, and sat down on her bed, staring blankly at nothing, desperately trying to summon the strength to face Elizabeth and the world. Another few minutes, and she would go down. She was still sitting there with that desperate stare when there was a knock on the door. When she didn't answer, it opened.

It was Betsy, Mrs Evesham's maid. 'Oh, there you are,

ma'am. I'm sorry, I didn't hear if you said, "Come in."
Only, Cook said she thought she saw you go upstairs.'

'What is it, Betsy?' Henrietta said at last. Her voice
sounded light and dry as a seed husk, empty and unimportant.

'There's a letter come for you, ma'am, just this minute.
I thought I'd better bring it straight up, in case it was
important.'

'Thank you,' she said automatically, taking it. She
opened it and unfolded the sheet, but it was a while
before her numbed brain could take in the words. Betsy,
waiting to be dismissed, had given up and was heading
for the door by the time Henrietta understood what she
was reading.

'Betsy!' she said sharply, and the maid, turning back,
saw Mrs Fortescue's face was white and grim. Bad news,
she thought, with unconscious relish. Bad news from
home.

'Yes, ma'am?'

'Is Mrs James in the house, and my daughter?'

'Oh, yes, ma'am. They're downstairs in the parlour.'

'We must leave at once,' Henrietta said, already on her
feet and looking round her. 'We have to go home. Run
and tell Miss Elizabeth to come upstairs at once, while I
start packing. And please tell Mrs Evesham and ask her
to send for a cab to take us to the station.'

CHAPTER TWENTY-FOUR

It was very late when she arrived at Swale House. Although they were in the long days of summer, the light was fading from the sky, and the station cab crawled its way through the dusk of the deep, winding lanes as though in fear of some speeding vehicle round every bend. Elizabeth had slept the last half-hour on the train and was asleep again now, a dead weight across Henrietta's lap. She envied her that child's ability to abandon consciousness so utterly and anywhere.

Despite the noise the cab must have made over the gravel sweep, no-one came out to greet her as they drew up before the door. The house was in darkness, but there was a gleam of light where the library shutters did not quite meet: he was still reading there, and the servants would not have gone to bed. She woke Elizabeth and helped her out, shivering and blinking from her sleep, while the cab driver, rather ungraciously, lifted down the bags and went to ring the doorbell. He relieved his feelings at having to do these things himself by pulling long and hard, and listening with satisfaction to the minor tocsin he had set up deep within the house.

At last a lamp glow showed at the fanlight, and there were sounds of unlocking. The driver abandoned his fares with unseemly haste – a lone female and a child arriving late at an unprepared house could only mean trouble and he wanted no part of it – and drove off. The door opened only a crack, and the white whiskery face of Allen, the manservant, peered suspiciously out, with a lamp held high to illuminate the arrivals.

'It's Mrs Fortescue, Allen. Open the door,' Henrietta said. Allen swung the door a little further back, revealing that he was holding a stout poker defensively in his other hand; but, amazingly, he did not step aside to let her in.

'We weren't expecting you, ma'am,' he said.

'Well, I'm here,' she said impatiently.

'Master didn't say anything,' he objected. His eyes were watery and Henrietta remembered that he sometimes drank, especially in the evenings. 'There's no bed made up. Were you wanting to stay?'

'Of course I'm staying,' she snapped. 'Do you think I'm going to go to an hotel? Open the door and let me in this minute.'

He admitted her at last into the oak-panelled hall, which was always cold, even in the middle of summer, and smelt faintly of damp. Allen's wife, the housekeeper, was standing forbiddingly at the foot of the stairs, her hands folded over her stomach, her heavy dark face a scowl of disapprobation. She disliked Henrietta, had disapproved of the rector marrying at all, let alone such a young girl. Running the house as a domestic tyrant, and for her own benefit for most of the year, she resisted anything that interrupted her routine. Mr Fortescue came to Swale House only a few times a year, his parish in Richmond being run for the rest of the time by the vicar; and since spending his honeymoon here twelve years ago, he had brought Henrietta with him only once. Mrs Allen felt outraged at being presented with her not only without warning but at this time of the night.

Henrietta remembered her first visit to Swale House, and how afraid she had been of everyone and everything. Mrs Allen had done nothing to make a timid young bride welcome. Now, in the silence punctuated only by the heavy ticking of the long-case clock, Henrietta felt Elizabeth shiver and sway against her with weariness, and was angry on her child's behalf more than her own.

'Bring the bags in, Allen,' she said to the dithering old man.

'We weren't expecting visitors,' Mrs Allen said, her chest swelling with indignation. 'There's no rooms ready.'

'Then you'd better get busy,' Henrietta said. 'Have beds made up in my old room and the one next door – Miss Elizabeth will want to be near me in a strange house. You had better light fires, too – those rooms will be damp – and put in warming pans, since the sheets won't be aired.'

'You come here at this time of night and with no servants neither,' Mrs Allen said angrily, 'and expect me to run around after you?'

'Certainly I expect it. And I do not expect to be answered back. What servants are in the house apart from you and Allen?'

Mrs Allen stared in wonder at this newly assertive mistress. 'Just Tina, the housemaid – and Polly the kitchen-maid's not gone home yet.'

'Very well. Have Tina get Miss Elizabeth's room ready first. It's long past her bedtime. But you must give her something to eat – bread and milk will do – and wash her hands and face before she goes to bed.'

'Nay, I don't look after children,' Mrs Allen interrupted, her face mottling. 'I've not come to that.'

'So much the better. Tina can take care of Miss Elizabeth and you can make up the bed and fire, and Polly can help you. Hurry up – don't just stand there.'

'I don't take orders from you,' Mrs Allen said, beside herself now.

'You had better, or you'll find yourself without a place tomorrow,' Henrietta said. She kept her voice low and pleasant, but her expression was adamant. Allen threw his wife an anxious look and Mrs Allen wavered.

'Master wouldn't turn me off on your say-so.'

'Are you willing to risk your place on it?' Henrietta said. 'Come, no more unseemly bickering. This child needs her bed, and I must go and see my husband.'

Now Allen was moved to protest, though in his case

457

it was a reaction to sacrilege rather than any hostility to Henrietta. 'What, disturb Master?' he gasped, the lantern wavering wildly in his hand, sending bat-shadows swooping about the hall. 'In his library?'

Henrietta smiled wearily. 'Just as you say. No, you needn't announce me. You had better carry coals up to the bedrooms. Mrs Allen, call Tina and let her take Miss Elizabeth into the kitchen for her supper while you get the rooms ready.' She bent to kiss her daughter, who had been listening without comprehension to the exchanges, still only half awake. 'Be a good girl, Lizzie, and I'll come and see you when you're in bed. I must go and see Papa.'

Elizabeth's face lit. 'Can I see Papa? I want to tell him about the boats.'

'Not tonight, it's too late. You can tell him tomorrow.'

For all her bravado, it took courage for Henrietta to do the next thing. All her married life, her husband's study had been sacrosanct – and she was at Swale House against his orders. But she squared her shoulders and walked down the passage to the library, listened a moment, scratched at the door and went in.

There was a fire in the grate, which made the room warmer and more cheerful than anywhere else in the house. In the yellow lamplight, there was an autumnal mellowness to the colours, the brown leather and dark wood, the deep red carpet and curtains. The leather-topped desk was covered in books and pages of the rector's small, difficult handwriting, but Mr Fortescue was not at the desk. He was sitting in the big wing-backed armchair by the fireside; beside him on a small table was a decanter and glass, and the firelight glinted in the depths of the wine, turning it to dark ruby. His hands were resting on the chair arms, and he was staring into the flames. He did not stir or look up as Henrietta came in. How could he not have heard the commotion of her arrival? As she crossed the room uncertainly towards him, she was seized with the terrible thought that he was dead, had died in his chair with his eyes open.

'Sir. Mr Fortescue,' she said, and when he still didn't stir, 'Edgar?' He moved then – *thank God*, she thought. He sighed, as though coming back from a great distance, and looked up, a frown between his brows as if he didn't know who she was. 'It's me – Henrietta. Your wife.'

'You?' he said faintly. 'Good God, what are you doing here?'

She crouched down impulsively, to be on a level with him. His eyes followed her down and fixed on her face, still frowning. She thought perhaps he had been asleep with his eyes open and was confused, as one could be on waking. 'I came to be with you,' she said. 'I'm here, and I shan't go away again.'

He examined her for a long moment. 'Did you not receive my letter?'

'Of course I did. That's what brought me here.'

'My letter specifically told you to go home to Bishop Winthorpe, and to stay there.'

She smiled, a little waveringly, for she was not used to defying him. 'Yes, I know, but I chose otherwise. I wanted to be with you.' He looked as if he did not understand, and she sought words to reach him. 'It is my duty as your wife.'

He shook his head slightly. 'My letter absolved you from that. You are young. There is no need for you to watch me dying. It will not be a pleasant thing to witness.'

'How can you think I care for that? If you are ill, more than ever my place is at your side.'

'There is nothing you can do,' he said. 'Mansur gives me no hope. It is a matter of time, only.'

'There's a great deal I can do,' she urged. She wished she might take hold of his hand, but did not dare. 'I can make you comfortable – fetch and carry for you – read to you when you are tired. You should not be dependent on servants at such a time – and what servants!' she added in a low tone.

'It will not be for long,' he said bleakly.

'You mustn't say so,' she said, tears rising. He seemed

459

so alone, so devoid of all warmth and human contact, unable even to reach out for it at such a time. No-one ought to die like that. Indeed, no-one ought to live like that. Though he had rejected her, she was his wife, and perhaps the blame was partly hers, for allowing herself to be rejected. 'Mansur is not God, he can't tell you or anyone when they will die. You have good work still to do, and though I am only an ignorant female, I can help you to do it. I can minister to you, and make you easier. How could you try to keep me away at such a time?'

He looked unsettled; his eyes moved away from her face. 'I – I wanted to spare you,' he said, and it was the gentlest thing he had said to her for a long time.

She responded with warmth. 'But it is my pleasure, as well as my duty.'

'Your pleasure?' His eyes returned to her. He seemed amazed.

'My pleasure to be of use to you. Don't send me away.' He didn't answer, seemed to be examining her face as if he had never seen it before. She brought out the clinching argument. 'Besides, you need Elizabeth. How could you think of staying here and never seeing her again?'

His gaze sharpened as he caught her meaning. 'You brought Elizabeth here?'

'Yes, of course – and before you tell me I shouldn't have, reflect that she loves you as much as you love her, and it would be a cruelty to her to abandon her as you proposed to do.'

'Abandon her? What language is this?'

'You meant to come here alone and stay here until you died, without ever seeing her again, without even saying goodbye. What would she have thought? She would have felt abandoned.'

'She's too young to witness an old man's dissolution,' he said bitterly.

'You aren't an old man to her, you are her papa,' Henrietta said. 'And she and I are going to stay here with you. I'm sorry to have to defy you, husband, but so it is. Now I'm going up to say goodnight to Lizzie, and then I shall come back and see you comfortable. I dare say you haven't had any supper?'

'I don't know. No, perhaps not,' he said, watching her with a dazed expression.

'Then I shall make you some and bring it here on a tray. I'm hungry too. If you will allow, I'll eat here with you – this is the only fire in the house. Such a damp house – I don't know why you chose it. Perhaps you might think of going home, now that you know I am not going to leave you.'

'There's a change in you,' he said. 'I can't account for it, but something has come over you. You are so firm and outspoken.'

'It's a long time since we have spoken together,' Henrietta said. 'Perhaps we will have time now, and you will get to know me a little better.'

'I know that you are self-willed and disobedient,' he said. But he raised no further argument to her presence, and watched in silence as she made up the fire. When she reached the door on her way out he said, 'What room have you ordered for Elizabeth?'

'The one next to mine,' she said.

'See that it is thoroughly aired tomorrow,' he said, and went back to his contemplation of the flames. Satisfied with her progress, Henrietta left him.

With Ivo gone from her life, Venetia set about rebuilding her career. She had made a mistake, made a fool of herself, and perhaps her troubles were the punishment for wrong-doing – who could tell? At least, unlike many poor fools who had done no worse and no better, she had another life to retreat to and important work to do.

She could not hope to regain the patients she had lost, but by dressing soberly and behaving impeccably she hoped to stop the rot. There were still very few female doctors in London, far fewer than the demand for their services, so she hoped to gain new patients to replace the Walcotts of her world. And Miss Ulverston did what she could by letting it be known in a few select, indiscreet places that Dr Fleet had ended her liaison and rejoined the ranks of the virtuous.

But it was not easy. The unfortunate revelation that she had been born Lady Venetia Fleetwood was leaking out along with the rest of the gossip, and the behaviour of her brother and sister was often in the news. The Duke of Southport was having an affair with an actress, Alicia Booth – 'The Kentish Songbird' – and playing host to the most raffish of the Prince of Wales's set; Lady Augusta Vibart was appearing in plays herself, and was reputed to be the Prince's mistress. Not surprising, then, said gossip, that their sister the doctor should behave so scandalously. Venetia discovered all over again that while Harry and Gussie's behaviour was noted with tolerance, amusement, or even in some circles admiration, her own poor peccadillo was another matter. It was as if the duke and his younger sister inhabited a world of make-believe where criticism was pointless and irrelevant: Venetia, living in the real world, had to behave.

But slowly, slowly, she began to claw her way back. New patients did come. Some, unhappily, came for the chance to see the wicked duke's daughter turned doctor, as if expecting her to have horns and a tail, or to be wreathed in the garlands of Sodom and Gomorrah. Some came from the snobbish desire to be treated by the sister of a duke who was a close friend of the Prince. But Venetia exercised her hard-learned patience, and told herself that if their ills were real, they deserved to be treated like anyone else.

She missed her surgical work, and feared her skills would grow rusty; but she still had a lot of police work, and was involved with the preparation of the Criminal Law Amendment Bill, which had been presented as a result of the Lords' Select Committee to which she had given evidence. The main provisions of the Bill were to raise the age of consent to sixteen, and that of procurement for immoral purposes to twenty-one, and to make it illegal to solicit or attempt to procure any woman to leave the United Kingdom for the purpose of entering a brothel. The Bill had been presented that year and passed in the Lords, but had been thrown out by the Commons, and work was now going on to re-present it next year.

So she kept herself busy, and tried to be content. Marcus was a great comfort to her in those months, visiting infrequently, but giving her a feeling of belonging somewhere. His interest in her was unemphatic but unshakeable; he regarded the censure of her in certain quarters as foolish and unimportant – 'Just what that sort of person would say'; and as he had sadly washed his hands of Harry and Gussie, he regarded their antics with robust indifference.

So it was particularly hard for her to learn that she must lose him. The troubles in Egypt had developed as many had predicted. The native who was calling himself the Messiah – Mahdi in his own language – had virtually driven the khedive out of his territory of the Sudan, and the khedive had finally sent an army under the command of a British officer, Hicks Pasha, to crush the rebels. But Hicks and his army had been defeated and cut to pieces in November, and Gladstone's government had been faced with the problem it had tried to avoid: whether to mount a full expedition to retake the Sudan, or to abandon it and redraw the Egyptian border at Wady Halfa.

'Cabinet can't make its mind up,' Marcus told her. 'Gladstone don't feel much like fighting the khedive's battles for him, but a lot of the ministers think this Mahdi fellow is a threat to world peace. And there's the question of what to do about our garrisons. We've got a chap at Suakim, by the Red Sea, and he can be got out by the Navy, but there's a lot of inland garrisons around Khartoum. So they've decided to send Gordon out there to see what's the best way of withdrawing. And I'm going with him as liaison.'

His expression warned her that this was an honour. 'Oh, Marcus, I'm so pleased for you,' she said. 'They must think very highly of you.'

'Well,' he said, with a modest smirk, 'it *is* rather gratifying. Apparently Gordon himself asked for me –

Tommy Weston mentioned my name to him, so I suppose I've him to thank – and of course the Queen's fearfully interested in the whole thing. She thinks the world of Gordon.'

'What's he like?' Venetia asked.

'Oh, he's as brave as a lion – tremendous hero, never known what it is to be defeated. Rum sort of cove, though – bit of an eccentric, likes to go his own way to work. Impossible as a subordinate, of course, but just what you want in a leader in an unpredictable situation. Has *ideas*.' Marcus pondered this odd trait in silence for a moment. 'They're giving him wide powers, which is just what he likes – he'll be a sort of governor-general. Just as well, I suppose, since nobody knows quite what we'll find when we get there.'

'And when do you go?'

'Pretty soon. January, I shouldn't wonder,' Marcus said.

'I shall miss you,' Venetia said. 'You're all the family I've got now.'

He blinked a little, and patted her shoulder. 'Ditto, ditto. Like a couple of old cats by the fireside, ain't we? But I don't expect I'll be gone more than a couple of years, and you'll be too busy to notice.'

'I'll notice,' she said.

He cleared his throat. 'This business of yours – damned foolishness. Don't let it upset you, hey?'

'I'm trying.'

'Good girl. And go and see Mama while I'm away.'

'Is that for her sake, or for mine?'

'A little of each.'

Marcus and the General set off on the 18th of January 1884 for Cairo. Venetia fulfilled her brother's parting injunction in February by going down to Ravendene to see her mother. She found her looking well and strong, the remission of her illness still holding. They had a comfortable luncheon together, talking with that increase of intimacy that had come with Venetia's greater age, which had brought them somehow to a level with each other. Venetia was still struggling to regain the position she had lost, but spoke hopefully.

'Things are getting better. I am always pleasantly surprised to discover that there are lots of people who haven't heard of my disgrace.'

'Memory for gossip is usually blessedly short,' Charlotte said. 'I remember I was the talk of the drawing-rooms once when I jilted your father and ran away to the country, but a year later I doubt if I could have found anyone who even remembered it.'

'You jilted Papa? But how . . .'

'Oh, it's a long story,' Charlotte smiled, 'and not much worth the telling. It was only delaying the inevitable, but I was full of pride and the juice of youth in those days. When I think now of all the time I wasted when I could have been with him! But there, young people always think they're immortal.'

'You must miss him dreadfully,' Venetia said shyly.

'Of course I do. But one of the few graces about growing old is being able to bear things better. I'm not desperately unhappy, darling, so don't fret about me.'

'You seem content,' Venetia said doubtfully.

'Oh, I am. Norton and I rub along very well. We've plenty to talk about, and I've my garden to tend while she tends me. But,' she roused herself, 'I mustn't forget: I have some business to attend to in Town, and I wondered if you would have me to stay for a day or two. I've never seen your little house and I've a mind to. Would it be inconvenient?'

'No, of course not!' Venetia said eagerly. 'I'd be delighted to have you. I long to show you everything – my consulting-room, my dispensary – and if you'd like to visit my free dispensary, I'd welcome your advice on how it might be improved. You have so much experience in that field. In fact, if you should think of coming back to London permanently . . .'

Charlotte laughed. 'Oh, darling, I'm very flattered, but I don't think I could live in Town any more. I'm a country girl by upbringing, you know. I need green around me.

No, just a few days while I conduct my business, and then I'll leave you in peace.'

Henrietta had thought the rector might go home to Bishop Winthorpe once he knew that she was going to stay with him, but he didn't; and any hope she may have had that his nature would undergo a sudden change was dashed. He remained aloof, expressing no warmth towards her or pleasure at her presence, and kept himself mostly to his library, where he seemed to be engaged in some urgent work.

Henrietta settled in to Swale House as best she could, taking up the reins of government, and if Mrs Allen fought a grim rearguard action, at least it gave her something to think about during the first difficult weeks. She engaged more servants and had the house cleaned properly, and insisted that fires were lit and kept burning in the principal rooms to combat the damp chill that prevailed even in the middle of summer. Mrs Allen then played into her hands by stating categorically that she couldn't cook for all these extra mouths, giving Henrietta the excuse to send home for Mr Fortescue's cook. Mrs Allen's efforts, Henrietta considered, might do well enough for a fit and healthy person who was not too fussy about food, but it needed a master chef to tempt the appetite of a dying man.

By making the house more comfortable and the food more palatable, Henrietta hoped to prove her worth to her husband, but he showed no sign of noticing at first. He did not even seem to notice Elizabeth, and it was left to Henrietta to guide her studies and order her days as best she could. Then one day when they were at breakfast (the rector took his alone and much earlier) a message was sent that he wished to see his daughter in his room at ten. She went, knocked, and was admitted; Henrietta waited for her – loitered all morning around the hall – but she did not come out until lunch-time. Henrietta pounced.

'What did Papa want?'

'He's teaching me again,' Elizabeth said, with a glad

466

look. 'He's set me to work on comparing a Greek translation of some of the Old Testament books with the
Hebrew.'

'I'm glad, darling,' Henrietta said, happy that contact
had been made. 'How did Papa seem to you?'

'Oh, he was just as he used to be,' Elizabeth said. 'We
talked a lot.'

'What about? Did he ask you about Whitby?'

Elizabeth laughed. 'Oh, Mama, he wouldn't be interested in that. I don't suppose he even remembers I've
been there.'

A new pattern was established. Mr Fortescue taught
Elizabeth in the morning, going on with his work in the
same room. In the afternoon he worked alone and she
was her mother's property: Henrietta ensured she went
out of doors for a good part of it. But he took his meals in
the library, the food being carried in on a tray. Henrietta
spent her evenings alone.

The leaves began to turn, the mists clung to the Swale
valley, and out on the high dales the heather rolled out
a purple carpet. The days shortened, and there was a
smell on the wind of winter coming, something that said,
'Hurry and finish what you're doing, and get inside before
the cold and the dark come.' Elizabeth grew quiet, and
Henrietta thought she was affected by the melancholy of
autumn, but one day she said, 'I think Papa's worried
about something. I wish you would ask him, Mama.
Couldn't you?'

'He's so fond of you,' Henrietta said. 'He'd surely tell
you if you asked.'

'But I'm only a child,' she said, with that clear certainty
of hers, and Henrietta acknowledged the point. She had
come here to serve: she must not hold back from fear or
false pride or habit. That evening, when his dinner tray
was prepared, she took it out of the servant's hands.

'I'll take it in. Open the door for me, and close it
behind me.'

He was at his desk, writing. His hand seemed to jerk
and stutter over the pages as if in frantic haste. He did

not look up. 'Put it down and go,' he said. She looked round, saw the small table near the fire, deposited her burden, and went back to stand before him again.

'Leave me,' he said, still without looking up. His hasty pen caught in the paper and spluttered and he made a sound under his breath which, in an ordinary mortal, she would have thought was a curse. 'Why will you not go?' he cried out in a rising voice, as if the blot had been her fault.

'Because I wish to see you eat,' she said. His head jerked up at the sound of her voice, and she drew a sharp breath. His face was haggard, and the sidelong light from the fire and the lamp on his desk emphasised the bones and hollows, so that he looked like a death's head.

'I cannot eat. I have no time,' he said, and he sounded driven.

It was such a departure from his usual composure that she said, 'What is it? Is there something I can do? Let me help you.'

'You can't help me,' he said starkly. She stood still, looking at him steadily. 'Mend the lamp, then, if you must be busy. It's so dark I can barely see the page.'

It was not. She looked at the lamp, and then at him, and the eyes staring from those deep sockets were the eyes of a prisoner pleading for release. 'Did Mansur say this might happen?' she asked softly.

For a long moment she thought he might go on denying it, but he took a small, shuddering breath and said, 'He was not specific. All powers would gradually fail, he said.'

'How much can you see?'

'Things that are close, if the light is good enough. You are just a shape.'

She was trembling inside at this sudden surrender of his. She could see that it was a relief to him to tell her, but she was still on a knife's edge: a wrong word or movement from her would make him retreat, and she would never be let near again. She thought frantically.

'Well, then,' she said, in a matter-of-fact tone, 'we must

make more light. Three lamps, arranged around you, will give better illumination. And a screen across the back of your desk would help by reflecting it. A light colour would be better. There's one in one of the spare rooms, covered with ivory damask – that would do.'

'A screen,' he said blankly. Was he wondering why he hadn't thought of it, or ridiculing her contrivance?

'I'll see to it,' she said. 'But for now, won't you come and eat before it gets cold?'

'I cannot eat,' he said. 'I have no time.'

'You must stop in any case while I fetch the lamps,' she said. 'A few minutes – a half-hour—'

I have no time!' he cried again. 'I must complete this work before—' He couldn't seem to finish, and to her horror he put his hands up to his face as if he meant to cover it and weep. But there were no tears. He dug his knuckles into his cheeks and dragged down on them; he stared at her in naked fear. 'I don't want to die,' he whispered. 'I'm afraid.'

Her heart lurched. Down at her sides, her fingers dug into her palms to keep her still and with the appearance of calm. 'It's natural to be afraid,' she said.

'You don't understand,' he said. 'I am a minister of the Church. I ought to welcome death. But I don't. I'm afraid of dying.' He closed his eyes, and now she saw a glimmer of tears under his lids. His voice as the merest thread. 'I'm so ashamed.'

She had to move. She went to him, knelt at his side, dared to take one of his hands. It was clenched rigidly, and she had to tease out the fingers one by one against resistance before she could hold it properly. She understood that it was terrible that his faith should have been found wanting; or was it only a lack of faith in the kindness of God – he who had had so little kindness for anyone? 'Why should you be?' she said. 'God made us as we are, and He made us to love life. Even an innocent child is afraid of the dark. Don't be ashamed. God understands.'

He stared at her for a long time, his face unreadable. Then he said, 'Why are you here?'

'You know why,' she said.

An expression of bitterness crossed his face. 'It was weakness,' he said, 'and weakness is always punished. That part of me – I knew it was there. I should have rooted it out. The pleasures of the senses – fine food, wine, poetry – the beauty of words on the tongue, the pride of intellect. He set the trap and baited it – but why? He was testing me, I suppose. I mistook His purpose. I thought you were something above the earth, delicate airy, all intellect and spirit. Dear God!'

He thrust her hand from him as if he had just noticed he was holding something repulsive. Henrietta knelt, bearing the lash of his words.

'I should have known it was defilement. My work suffered. I was dragged down from the upper air, down to earth. Woman is dust, and all she touches becomes dust. And yet, out of that vilest of communions came Elizabeth – and she is pure. Yes, still! I wanted to save her. I must save her! But there's no time, no time – and my work! I must finish my work.'

Henrietta dragged up a voice from the ashes of her love for him. 'Let me help you,' she said.

'You? How can you help?'

'I can read to you. I can write to your dictation. I can look things up for you, take notes.' She saw the furious refusal on his lips and said, 'Lizzie and I can both help. She can do the more difficult things, and leave the simple tasks to me.' He was thinking about it, doubtful, baffled by her introduction of his daughter to the argument. She injected a note of sternness to her voice. 'Your work is too important for you to allow your pride to intervene. You must let us both help. You owe it to God to finish the task, whatever it takes.'

'Yes,' he said at last, 'you are right. How can it be that you are right?'

'Have you taught me nothing?' she said. He accepted that. What was good in her must come from him. 'Come to the fire now and eat. You must keep up your strength for the work in hand.'

He did what she suggested.

So as autumn advanced into winter, the household became concentrated in that one room. The fire was kept bright, and the three of them worked together. There was, she saw, a companionship between father and daughter, and she was glad of the comfort it gave both, and would not allow herself to be jealous. He explained things to Elizabeth, trusted her with tasks; to Henrietta he gave only the simple and mechanical jobs. She absented herself from time to time to see to the house and their comfort, and often she felt they hardly noticed whether she was there or not.

She didn't understand what his work was, only that it was a collection of corrections and commentaries on the Holy Writ. She asked Elizabeth once if she understood it all, and Elizabeth said, 'No, only bits of it,' then frowned as if something troubled her. The first snows came, and soon the hard Dales winter set in, piling up outside the door in glittering cruel brightness, beating at the shutters at night, trying to get in.

He was failing, Henrietta could see that, though she thought Elizabeth hadn't noticed yet. He could not write now – the pen would not stay straight in his fingers – and could hardly read. He had little strength, could hardly get up from his chair. Leaving the room to go up to bed was a hardship: Allen had to help him, and it took sometimes half an hour just to get up to his room. That he was in pain she guessed, though he would never admit or show it. But he held on with all the grim tenacity of his mind, engaging them all in his battle: and as they came to the darkest days of the year, it was clear that the battle was not to finish his work, but simply to stay alive.

January came, and one morning Allen appeared before Henrietta to say that he didn't think the master could get up, and would she come and see. She went with him. She had never been to his room before. It was well-furnished with handsome, heavy, plain pieces in the style of a hundred years back, things that had been purchased thoughtfully, placed with care, then left. He had not seen any reason to change them. Yes, the room was like him, she thought. Having fixed an opinion, he would not even notice its existence again. What madness had made him marry her? He had stepped so far out of himself to do it, he had never been able to get all the way back. No wonder he blamed her for everything.

He was propped up in the high bed under a surprising counterpane of purple and gold brocade, a grim figure, hardly more than bones clothed in rage. She did not make the mistake of asking him how he was or whether he wanted help to get up. She simply said briskly, 'You have a good fire in here. No reason to disturb your thoughts by going downstairs. Lizzie and I will bring your work up and sit here with you.'

But he said, 'No. Only you. No Elizabeth.'

It was too immodest, she thought, for his daughter to see him in bed. And then, more kindly, she thought, No, he does not want her to see him like this; he does not want her to suffer.

So it was Henrietta alone who sat with him through the last days. Sometimes he commanded her to take dictation, and she would write what he said faithfully, to the last word. But when she read it back to him, it seemed to bewilder him. 'Are you sure you have it right?' he would say, and she would say, gently, 'Yes.' He was like a man trying to unravel tangled wool in the dark. He would start again and again, trying different directions, and never get to where he thought he was going. At the end, his mind, the only thing he had ever really valued, betrayed him.

Silence came at the end. He no longer dictated, only lay with gritted teeth, holding on to life. Sometimes he asked her to read to him, but she did not think he heard much. She asked once or twice if Elizabeth could come to him – the child asked every day – but he always refused. No, no Elizabeth.

The day came when it seemed all he could do to breathe. There was snow outside, almost a blizzard, which made it as dark as dusk. Henrietta had lamps lit all round the room and the fire was made up bright and high. She sat by the bedside, a book in her lap, but she wasn't reading. Her mind was drifting back over her life, touching here and there, as someone walking round the house might touch this or that ornament or piece of furniture, not really seeing it, but comforted by its existence. She must have dozed a little, perhaps only for a few moments, but she woke with a start to the sound of his voice.

'All my work, come to nothing,' he said. 'I will have to leave her with you, and what will become of her?'

'I'll look after her,' Henrietta said. 'Of course I will. She's my daughter too.'

He shook his head a little, as if defeated. 'It's inevitable.' He swallowed, struggling between breath and speech. 'I thought – it would – be different.' A pause. 'She – was so perfect – when she was born. I wanted – to keep her perfect.' Another pause. 'But I can't save her. She'll grow up to be a woman.' He closed his eyes. 'Defiled.'

Henrietta felt an awful pity for him, tormented as he was even at a time like this. 'She's a good girl, a lovely girl. She always be good and lovely. But no human being is perfect.'

He did not answer her, only lay with closed eyes, shaking his head slowly with grief.

The day closed in, and real dusk fell. He did not speak, and his breathing grew more shallow and irregular. Henrietta was suddenly frightened. He was going to die, and she was not ready for it, for the guilt, for the responsibility. Allen came in to make up the fire and when she beckoned he shuffled over to look at the master.

'He's sinking,' he said.

'Should we call the doctor?' Henrietta asked, desperate for guidance.

'No use,' Allen said, shaking his head.

'A priest then – the vicar?'

Allen continued shaking. 'Not unless Master says so.

That's for him to say.' He shuffled out, leaving her alone.

She stood up and leaned over her husband. 'Mr Fortescue. Edgar.' She even shook him a little, and his eyes opened, looked at her, seemed to know her. 'Do you want me to send for a priest?' He looked without answering. Perhaps he couldn't speak. She fumbled for his hand and folded her fingers round his icy ones. 'Squeeze my hand if you mean yes. Shall I send for the vicar? Do you want to make your peace with God?'

There was no response from the fingers; he did not speak. But still he looked at her with those hollow, faintly glittering eyes, stared into her from that remote place where he lived and she could not reach him.

'I'm afraid!' She gave him his own words back now, feeling almost faint with fear. She didn't want to be here with this dying man. She thought for an instant, like something illuminated by lightning and then lost, of the fields and woods of her home. 'Oh, why did you ever marry me?' she cried in desperate sorrow. Something seemed to happen in the black depths of his eyes, and his lips drew back in a grin. He was mocking her! She dropped his hand in sudden horror, her heart contracting; but no, he was not, of course – he was struggling for breath. And then she saw him die. It was a terrible thing, to see that instant when life turned into death, to see how small and unimportant and irrevocable it was. Just a flicker between a living being and an inanimate shell, a flicker anyone might have missed, but there was no going back after it. She sat staring at him. There ought to be some great transformation, a beam of light, a trumpet, an angel of fire, a chariot bearing the triumphant soul up to heaven – something to mark the passing, something! But there was not. He was gone, that was all.

CHAPTER TWENTY-FIVE

Henrietta did not return to Bishop Winthorpe immediately. She did not want to submit herself or Elizabeth to the rigours of mourning. Here at Swale House they were unknown, and the rector had been a respected public figure rather than a loved friend. Visits of mere form could be intercepted by the servants without offending anyone, but in Bishop Winthorpe they would be expected to receive people personally, to listen, to talk, to be consoled, to be looked at.

Mr Herbert, the vicar, was a kindly soul – a little threadbare and greatly overworked, but happy in his small house under the shadow of the church tower with his wife and numerous children. Henrietta was glad to have him come to call, and handed the problem of the burial over to him. Mr Fortescue had left no instructions and had no relatives other than his wife and child, and since Henrietta had no preference, Mr Herbert proposed that the funeral should take place here, where he could oversee matters for her. Henrietta thought of the rage of Mr Catchpole at being thus circumvented; she thought of the pomp, ceremony, and funeral feast that would be required of a Bishop Winthorpe funeral. Both considerations made her accept Mr Herbert's offer with gratitude.

So all was done quietly and seemly. Widows did not attend funerals in any case, and she kept Elizabeth at home with her, so the coffin was attended from the house only by Mr and Mrs Herbert and their family and the Swale House servants, and there was no feast afterwards.

Allen reported to Henrietta the next day that it had been 'done very nice': Mr Herbert had 'spoke beautiful' and a suitably large number of the local congregation had attended out of respect. Mrs Allen, however, was furious with Henrietta at what she regarded as the 'slight' on the rector of not 'having people back' and would not talk to her for several days – very much a benefit as far as Henrietta was concerned.

She and Elizabeth had an enormous task, in any case, in sorting out the rector's papers. The difficult, time-consuming, and yet tedious nature of it was just what they needed in the days after his death: matters dry and academic were healing to overwrought emotions. From the rector's desk the papers soon spread over the whole library floor, and she and Elizabeth sat amongst them or shuffled on their knees from heap to heap, trying to assemble his last great opus into some kind of order. Outside, frozen January turned to dark, wet February, and the sound of rain lashing the window-panes was their constant companion.

Henrietta began to wonder long before Elizabeth first expressed a doubt. She had not been formally educated, but she had a quick mind and common sense. She sorted and worried, created ever more separate piles under new headings, and noticed that Elizabeth's eager activities had gradually slowed under the weight of a puzzled frown.

At last one day Henrietta said, 'Lizzie, I wonder—' just as Lizzie began to say, 'Mama, do you think—'

They looked at each other. 'What were you going to say?' Henrietta encouraged her daughter. 'Don't be afraid. You can say anything to me.'

Lizzie bit her lip. 'Well, I may be wrong. I'm not as clever as Papa. Perhaps I don't understand, but . . .'

'But? You're wondering whether Papa's last work is really quite right?'

A look of relief lightened her face. 'Did you think so too? I was afraid I was being disloyal, but – but the more I read, the more I think a lot of it's – well – nonsense.'

'I don't think you're disloyal at all,' Henrietta said

quickly. 'Remember that Papa was ill for a long time at the end, and it might well have affected his mind. I don't understand much of his academic work, of course, but this,' she waved a hand round the densely written sheets, notebooks and odd scraps, 'is very muddled, and some if it seems like sheer babble.'

Elizabeth's eyes filled with tears. 'Oh, poor Papa! Do you think he knew? It would be so awful to try to think and not be able to – to know you were writing nonsense.' Henrietta passed her handkerchief over. 'But probably it's us,' she suggested hopefully when she had blown her nose. 'Papa was very, very clever. Perhaps it's just too brilliant for us to understand.'

'The only thing I can think to do is to bundle it all up and send it to one of his colleagues at the University, and see what he makes of it.'

They stared at each other while this suggestion was evaluated. Then Elizabeth said slowly, 'But if it *is* nonsense, it would expose Papa so dreadfully.'

'Yes,' said Henrietta. 'I was just thinking that.'

'He would hate Professor Marriott or Mr Sayers to think he'd done bad work.'

'And those Oxford dons are such terrible gossips, and so spiteful about each other. When I first married Papa and he used to invite them to dinner, I would sit and wonder that they could be so cruel about their absent colleagues. Worse than women by far.'

'But if we don't show it to anyone, what should we do with it?' Elizabeth asked anxiously.

Henrietta thought of asking her how sure she was that the work was not good. But that was unfair. The decision must not be put onto Elizabeth's shoulders, to haunt her with doubts and guilt for the rest of her life.

'I think we should put it all away carefully in boxes. And then some time in the future, when all the people Papa knew at Oxford have gone, it could be shown to someone who could judge it disinterestedly. Then if it is nonsense, no-one he would mind about would know.'

A huge relief spread across her daughter's face. 'Yes,

that's just what we should do,' she said, and began instantly to gather papers together. As Henrietta tied them into bundles, she thought of the years and years of effort that he had put into desiccating the sappy greenness out of life. She would be glad never to see the black, crabbed writing again. Once it was all stored away, she might manage quite effectively to forget that it had ever existed.

While the sorting had been going on, Henrietta had had other business to attend to. Because her husband had been such a prominent figure in Bishop Winthorpe, his attorney had been quite willing to travel to Richmond with his Will and other papers to attend her there, rather than expecting her to come to him. So there had been long sessions with him in the drawing-room, and a different but equally obscure language – the legal one – to master.

There were generous pensions to the servants, some of whom had served Fortescue's father before him; a very large sum of money to both his churches to provide memorials for him; a large bequest to an Oxford theological college to provide the Fortescue Scholarship; and another to his *alma mater* for an annual lecture on a topic of classical scholarship, the Fortescue Lecture. This last had the unexpected addition of a fine dinner to be provided after the lecture for all dons from his own college who attended it – a surprisingly practical but cynical measure to ensure the lecture survived in the calendar. It was clear that Mr Fortescue had intended to be remembered, and it both amused and saddened Henrietta, for it seemed a conceit undermined by fear and a lack of self-confidence. Added to the sad muddle of his last work, it gave her the unwelcome picture of a man tormented with the fear that he had, after all, only a second-rate mind. She would have preferred to remember him as arrogant with cause.

The consequence of all these bequests, however, was serious for her.

'Once they have been accounted for,' the lawyer, Mr

Eagleton, explained, 'the residue of the estate is to be divided between you and your daughter, two-thirds being put into trust for Miss Fortescue until the age of twenty-one, and one third to go to you as your jointure.'

Henrietta nodded. She had come to him without dowry, and had no reason to expect great generosity from him; and he had loved Elizabeth above anyone.

'However,' Eagleton said, with a worried look, 'the late rector's income has diminished over the past ten years – the agricultural slump, as you know.'

Henrietta knew. She had been dealing with the resultant hardship amongst the labouring classes every day.

'Because his rents have fallen so severely, he has been withdrawing assets from the funds for the normal expenses of daily life, and there is insufficient liquidity to pay the bequests in the Will,' said Eagleton. 'Insufficient by a very long shortfall, I'm sorry to say. The result is that property will have to be sold. I can realise the amounts required in no other way. And, of course, land prices have been depressed by the same slump which had caused the problem.'

Henrietta tried to get to grips with this. 'The bequests have to be paid, of course.'

'They take first call on the estate, since it is the residue which is to be distributed to you and your daughter. Had the late rector specified a particular sum to you, that would have taken precedence, but as it is . . .' He let the sentence hang.

'What will have to be sold?' Henrietta asked.

'Almost everything. I have made a list of the more obvious assets – the livings, the two houses, the farms and sundry small dwellings. And then there are the more personal effects – furniture, books, china and so on. I need to go through everything with you to determine if there are things for which you have a preference, and then, of course, I will come to them last and only at need.'

Henrietta considered her life as it had been, and as it might be. As the rector's wife she had lived in a large house with a numerous staff, but that had been for his

479

benefit rather than hers. A neat, small house was all she needed, with two or three in help: she and Elizabeth could be comfortable together without much more.

'I don't think there's anything that I particularly want to keep,' she said. 'And my daughter and I can live in quite a small way.'

'I'm afraid you may have to,' said Eagleton. 'Remember that your daughter's fortune will be locked up until her majority, unless the trustees feel able to advance anything for her needs. I am one of the trustees, and would certainly recommend flexibility, given the circumstances, but I cannot speak for the other two, of course, and they may overrule me.'

'So I shall have to keep Lizzie on my one third?' Henrietta said. He assented. 'How small is a small way?' she asked. He hesitated, and she read the warning in that. 'What about my horse?'

'It *may* be possible for you to afford a horse,' he said, but Henrietta could see Starlight's fate in his eyes.

Elizabeth was not downcast by the change in their fortunes. She seemed, with the resilience of youth, to see it rather as an adventure. 'It would be lovely to live in a small house. Or a cottage? Oh, Mama, do let it be a cottage! With a cat and a dog. Think how snug and nice!'

Henrietta knew perfectly well the picture-book illustration Elizabeth was imagining, of roses and hollyhocks and contented hens scratching round the door. Her own experience, from visiting the poor, was rather different. To her 'cottage' meant low, dark, damp and insanitary; but she supposed there might be cottages and cottages.

Elizabeth had another idea. 'Does it have to be in Bishop Winthorpe?'

'I suppose not, except that's where our friends and relatives are. Why?'

'I was thinking,' she said, with shining eyes, 'that we might go and live by the sea.'

The words brought Whitby vividly before Henrietta's

inner eye; and with Whitby came Jerome. She had deliberately banished him from her mind all these months, for to allow herself to think about him while she was with her dying husband would have been horribly disloyal, besides painful to her. But now he surprised her, ambushing her from the dark corner of memory, and such an agony of longing overcame her that she felt quite weak for a moment and had to hold on to the back of a chair. Where was he now, she wondered. Gone abroad? He had said he would go to Africa – or to the devil, which was much the same thing. Had he waited the next day for her message? Had he enquired after her and found her gone, and taken that as his answer? Gone not only from Whitby but from Bishop Winthorpe: well, that must have seemed conclusive. She would never see him again, but, dear God, how she loved him! She closed her eyes a moment and let the pain loose, until the flood abated and she was able to gain control of herself again. If she was to get by, and give Elizabeth the happy life she deserved, she must never think of him. She must pack her memories of him away as firmly as she had the rector's last work.

'It might be a good idea to leave Bishop Winthorpe for a new place,' she said at last. 'And it could well be by the sea. But not Whitby, I think.'

They had to go back, of course, if for nothing else to settle affairs and oversee the sale of the rector's goods and chattels. Perry and Regina were anxious they should stay at the Red House, and Henrietta was glad to accept, preferring not to go back to the rectory, which had always been his rather than hers. She had to endure a number of visits of form, expressions of sympathy, some of them genuine, and a great deal of curiosity, most of it impertinent and some of it angry, as to why she had buried the rector in his other parish. The good people of Bishop Winthorpe had loved him so, she was to understand, and had looked forward – if the expression might be permitted – to a very grand funeral indeed. The parishioners had heard of the memorial bequest, and were divided between the peeved, who thought that as he had neglected them by dying elsewhere, they should neglect him and erect something chastening; and the faithful, who wanted the memorial to be as grand as could possibly be contrived, expressing their taste and superior piety, and also heaping coals of fire on his widow's head.

Perry diverted as much spleen as possible from his sister-in-law, and surrounded her and Elizabeth with his children, which in his mind was the greatest treat in the world. He had Starlight and Elizabeth's pony Apple brought over to the Red House stables and encouraged them to go riding every day, and ordered from his cook every delicacy he thought might please them. Henrietta found his simple kindness comforting, and as always the house struck her as being full of life and warmth.

She had written to Teddy telling him of her husband's death, and he visited her at the Red House to express his condolences. She hadn't seen him for a couple of years and was surprised at how fat he had grown. He puffed as he walked and sat down with the air of deserving it, though he had only come from his carriage into the drawing-room.

'Well, Hen, you're looking better than I expected, all things considered. It's a sad thing about Fortescue, but always to be expected when you married a man so much older than yourself. What was his age? I never did know.'

Henrietta had only discovered it herself when the death certificate was given. 'He was fifty-four.'

'Hm. Not so very old. But he was one of those lean, dry fellows that quarrels with his food, wasn't he? Never trust a poor doer. Now I,' he slapped his girth as one might slap the rump of a fine horse, 'like to keep a little flesh between me and the world. For insurance, you see.'

Henrietta saw. 'You look as if you dine well,' she said. meekly.

'No sense in being uncomfortable. I think of poor little Manny, y'know. Nothing but skin and bones when he died.' He shook his head sadly, and was glad when

482

Elizabeth came in to divert him from this sad train of thought. 'Why, is this my little niece? Good Lord, how you've grown! Come and give me a kiss and tell me what you've been up to.'

Elizabeth was soon followed by the other children, and then Regina, and there was no more sad talk. It was not until Henrietta was walking with Teddy back to his carriage that he reverted to the subject of the rector's death.

'What do you mean to do now, Hen?' he asked. 'You won't want to stay on in that great house all alone, I suppose?'

'I shan't be able to anyway,' she said, and explained the situation.

Teddy listened with concern. 'That's bad! A fellow ought to take care of his wife and family. I suppose his mind was on higher things, but even so . . .' He pondered a moment. 'Look here, you always were my favourite sister, and I can't see you in trouble. If things come to the worst, you can come to me. I only have a bachelor household, as you know, and it may not be very comfortable for you; and as for Lizzie – well, but I suppose you'd manage all right. You might send her to school, of course.'

She noted his increasingly furrowed brow, and smiled inwardly. His basic generosity had made the offer, but the thought of having a woman and child cluttering up his comfortable life troubled him dreadfully. 'It's kind of you, Ted, but I don't think it will come to that. There'll be something left to live on, I'm sure, and Lizzie and I don't need very much. And if all else failed, Perry and Regina would give us a bed here.'

His brow cleared. 'Well, you know, I was wondering about that. There's nothing I'd like better than to make a home for you, but it would suit Lizzie better to be with other children, wouldn't it?'

She hugged his arm and he squeezed back. 'You're a good old thing,' she said, 'and I appreciate the offer, but we shan't starve. How are things at Morland Place, by the way? I wrote to Georgie when Alfreda died, but he didn't reply, of course.'

'Well, it's rather rummy,' Teddy said. 'Old Georgie had been outrunning the tallyman for some time, you know, and when she died a lot of bills came in and the banks foreclosed. He's had to sell all his horses, his stock, and the outlying farms into the bargain to pay them off.'

'Oh, Teddy, no!'

'I don't know how bad things are, to tell you the truth. You know George – wouldn't tell you if you asked, and I'm not keen to have my nose bitten off so I don't ask. Haven't seen him around York for quite a while, though. Suppose he's sitting at home and retrenching.'

'But how much land did he sell?'

'I don't know for sure. I saw some of the notices up – the last two he bought, Manor Farm and Glebe, and Thickpenny, I think it was.'

'He's sold Thickpenny?'

Teddy looked distracted. 'I think that was it. There may have been others. I don't look at land sale notices as a rule – not my field of interest – just happened to notice the other two. He's not bankrupt, that I *do* know, because I'd have seen his name in the paper if he'd been declared; but the exact state of things I can't tell you.'

Henrietta got the impression that Teddy didn't notice very much at all any more, apart from what was on his dinner table. There was no point in asking him any more questions; and even if George was in trouble, there was nothing she could do about it. But it was sad to think of Morland Place in trouble. She thought of how Alfreda had brought it up from shabbiness to glory – and spent a fortune in the process. Perhaps that was the problem. *Folie de grandeur*, Jerome had called it. But she mustn't think of Jerome.

'I do feel sorry for poor old Georgie, though,' Teddy said. 'First his little boy in that terrible accident, and now his wife. I never liked Alfreda, but he was devoted to her. It's a sad business.'

It was a generous summing up, Henrietta thought, considering how little he had to thank either for. She squeezed his arm again, then raised herself on tiptoe to kiss his cheek. 'You're a decent old stick, aren't you?' she said.

'Soft!' he said, but he looked pleased.

The only chill note at the Red House was Mary. Though she had greeted Henrietta with courtesy and expressed the usual sympathies, she seemed a good deal more silent and less forthcoming than usual, and looked at her with a brooding coldness only Henrietta was meant to notice.

There was something on her mind, and Henrietta was afraid she was only waiting to catch her alone to express it. The moment came when she had been ten days at the Red House. She had gone to a meeting of the committee considering the form the rector's memorial should take: she had put in a word for a bell, feeling it would be a lasting memorial and bring more pleasure to people than the vast marble construction, like a cross between a fireplace and a bedstead, that had been mooted for the wall of the south aisle. Having presided over another complete failure to decide, she went up to the rectory to see to one or two things. As she walked back down the lane to the village, she found Mary leaning on a stile, evidently waiting for her.

'So, Mrs Fortescue,' she said, her eyes hard. 'A moment alone to say a few things that have been on my mind.'

Henrietta stopped. 'Oh, Mary, must you?'

'Yes, I must. Do you really think I have the desire to spare you? Because of you, I have lost my brother – my only brother, the one person in the world I loved.'

'Lost?' Henrietta faltered.

'Ah, that touches a nerve! The more wicked of you, then, to send him away, if you cared for him so much! But no, I suspect you care for nothing but your precious *respectability*!' She spat the word contemptuously. 'And what has it got you? The rector's dead and you are done up. You'll be a poor widow now, and how will that warm you in your old age? Well, it serves you right!'

'I don't understand why you're so angry with me,' Henrietta said.

'He loved you,' Mary cried. 'He would have taken care of you, been faithful to you for ever. You don't know how rare love like that is in a man, especially a man like Jerome. I never knew him care so much for a woman – my God, he loved you more than me, his own sister! But you threw it away. You rejected him, drove him from the country. He's gone to Africa, and he'll die there, and I'll never see him again – all because of your stupid pride!'

'He's not – you haven't heard that he's—'

'I haven't heard from him at all, and I don't expect I will. It's a wild, dangerous place, and there are more ways for a man to die out there than you can imagine. And he was mad with grief at losing you. *Why* were you so arrogant? If you cared for him, why wouldn't you go to him?'

'I was a married woman,' Henrietta cried, provoked into defending herself, though she knew it was pointless and that Mary's anger was misfounded and wrong. 'I had no choice.'

'You *chose* all right – chose stupid propriety over the happiness, the *life* of the best man—' She choked a little. 'You selfish, wicked woman! You stole my brother from me, and I'll never forgive you, never!'

For a moment Henrietta thought she was going to hit her, but Mary bit her lip and turned away, walking rapidly down the lane away from the village. Henrietta went sadly on her way. The incident had shaken and upset her, and she even wondered for a moment whether Mary was perhaps right, whether she had been wrong. But no, that was madness. Mary's argument, her moral sense, was warped with selfishness. Mary did not know, of course, about the rector's letter, but that made no difference. It had spurred Henrietta into action, but her decision would have been the same without it.

But the unhappy meeting crystallised Henrietta's decision

to leave the village. She must set about looking for a suitable place elsewhere, as soon as the probate was through. She had thought it would be difficult to live here with Mary to remind her of Jerome, looking so much like him as she did; it would be impossible now, knowing how Mary felt about her. The difficulty was that given the state of the rector's affairs, probate would probably take a year, or perhaps more. Perhaps she might end up with Teddy after all, poor fellow.

On a windy, rainy April day Venetia had just crossed Victoria Street into Princes Street when her umbrella clashed with that of someone coming out of HM Stationery Office.

'I beg your pardon, ma'am. Unforgivably clumsy of me,' the gentleman said at once.

He was hurrying on when she said, 'I know that voice.' He paused, they both swung their umbrellas up out of the way, and she was face to face with Lord Hazelmere. He'd grown a large moustache and side whiskers, and between them, his hat pulled low and the muffler wound high round his chin, there was not much face to be seen. Had she not heard his voice, she might not even have recognised him. But the eyes were the same, though older, and marked with the lines of age and experience.

'It is you,' she said.

'It's you, too,' he said foolishly. 'What are you doing in this neighbourhood? Oh,' he recollected, 'I suppose you've been to the Westminster Hospital.'

It was a fair guess, since it was right next door to the Stationery Office, and she had been coming from that direction. 'No,' she said, 'as a matter of fact I've been to see a patient in the Peabody Buildings, just off Old Pye Street. A very good sort of man – an omnibus driver who was kicked by one of his horses. Quite an interesting fracture of the femur – interesting to me, that is, not to him, poor fellow. All he wants is to get back to work, of course.' She realised that she was gabbling – proof of how discomposed she was. She stopped and looked at him in silence for a moment. He didn't seem eager to end the encounter, though the brisk breeze was blowing rain full in his face, making him squint.

'So you're keeping busy,' he said at last.

'Yes, always busy. And you?'

'Oh, yes, I'm busy too. Government business, and one or two other things. Keeps me occupied.' Another silence. 'How are you? Are you well? You look – very well.'

'Thank you, I'm never ill. You – I heard—' This was delicate. She did not want him to think she was impertinent, or gloating. 'My brother, Marcus, said that your affairs were . . . not in the best of ways.'

He didn't seem offended. 'Yes, I was hit rather hard by the slump,' he said. 'I had to sell the estate – Father hadn't left it in too good heart, and there was nothing *but* the land. Those of us who had other sorts of investment managed rather better. But things weren't as bad as first seemed, and there was something left over to invest. I'm comfortable enough. I live in London permanently now, you know.'

'So Marcus said.'

'He went to Egypt, didn't he?'

'Yes, with General Gordon.'

'Have you had any news? Things seem to be getting a bit hot out there.'

Venetia shook her head. 'They're in Khartoum, and the lines of communication keep being cut. It's very worrying.'

Though General Gordon had gone to Egypt with orders to arrange the evacuation of the garrisons, he had barely arrived before he began trying to persuade the Government to reverse the order and try to retain control of the territory. In February he had conceived a plan to enlist a local pasha, Zobeir, to hold Khartoum and the Nile Valley against the Mahdi, but after long dithering the Government had finally decided against it. Zobeir was a former slave-trader – Gordon had actually fought against him years before and admired his warlike qualities – and the cabinet felt it would be against public sentiment to employ such a man on Her Majesty's business.

'I'm sorry,' Hazelmere said. 'I hope they're not in immediate danger?'

'I'm afraid they may be. Baring seems to think so, and I heard yesterday that Wolseley urged Mr Gladstone to make immediate preparations for a military expedition to get them back.'

'They ought to know.'

'The trouble is, of course, that General Gordon considers it would be a disgrace to abandon the garrisons, and he hasn't a particle of fear, so he won't withdraw however bad things get. But Mr Gladstone won't make up his mind, and delay could be dangerous. If the Mahdi reaches Berber they'll be cut off from the Nile, and I don't know how else relief can reach them.'

'You obviously know a lot about it. I'm afraid my geography isn't so good.'

'Tommy Weston's in the cabinet,' Venetia said. 'He keeps me informed.'

'Yes, of course. Good old Tommy. He'll add his weight to the argument.'

Venetia knew that he already had, for he had reported to her, somewhat ruefully, that Gladstone wouldn't think about anything but his precious Reform Bill, on which his mind was fixed like a tram on rails. The Reform Bill was dear to Tommy's heart, too, which made it hard for him to badger the old man.

'The comfort is that Gordon's a consummate soldier,' she said, passing on Tommy's words to her. 'And nobody knows the Sudan better.'

'True,' said Hazelmere. A gust blew rain into his face like a handful of needles. 'Well, I mustn't keep you standing here,' he said.

They looked at each other, not knowing how to end the encounter. 'It was nice to see you again,' Venetia said at last.

'And you too,' he said. He looked as though he were trying to think of a way to say something else, something

489

difficult, and not managing it. At last he raised his hand to his hat. 'Goodbye, then.' And so they parted, walking off in opposite directions through the increasing rain.

When she reached home, Venetia found a letter waiting for her from her mother.

My darling girl,

You will have wondered, I'm sure, what business brought me to London on all those occasions over the last year, but of course you were too polite and too well brought-up to ask! I would not have kept it secret from you except that I was not confident of success and did not want to raise your hopes only to have to dash them. But now your patience and tact shall be rewarded. I write to tell you that my business was with the Southport Hospital. I know how much you have missed being able to practise surgery at the New Hospital, and though it is to be hoped that Dr Anderson will change her mind and reinstate you, I did not see why you should depend so wholly on her when I must have some influence still over the hospital I founded and financed for so long. Well, the deed is done, and I hope you will not feel insulted that it took so much persuasion on my part! You are a sensible woman and know that you must deal with situations as they are, and prejudices still run very high in the medical profession. But you will soon receive a letter from the Board inviting you to take up a surgical position at the Southport. I expect they will begin by confining you to surgery on female patients, but it is a start, isn't it, my Venetia? Your own skill and wit will enable you to build on that. Ideas *are* changing, and you will help to change them. In case you are wondering, I only had to pledge them a bequest in my Will in exchange for this favour. I will leave you to determine, by interaction of your vanity and your knowledge of the world, how generous the bequest had to be!

Ever your devoted and admiring,
Mama

Venetia read and re-read the letter. She was to practise surgery again! Dearest, wonderful Mama had won her the privilege! And how careful she was in her letter to warn Venetia not to turn down the post out of stiff-necked pride. Yes, she knew her daughter: it might well have crossed her mind that if the favour had to be purchased, rather than coming as a tribute to her skills, she should throw it back in their faces. Would she have, though? Probably not, now. She had learned to keep her temper, and she was older and wiser. And – funniest, saddest thing of all – darling Mama had not told her how much money it had cost to buy the place for her, in case she thought it was too little (surely she was worth more than that?) or too much (why should they need bribing so heavily to take her on?).

Wiping a tear from her eye, she went to find paper and pen to write a letter of thanks to her kind, tactful mother.

As summer came, the excitement of Miss Ulverston and all the friends of the Cause rose to a fever pitch. The Reform Bill was to come on in June, and the movement had obtained pledges from sufficient Liberal Members to get the women's amendment, to be presented by Mr Woodall, through with a comfortable majority.

But in the event it was not to be. Though he had not publicly expressed an antipathy to the female franchise, Gladstone now came out against it. He declared that Woodall's amendment would 'overweight the ship', and warned that if it were passed he would drop the whole Bill and abandon it. The whips were out, and over a hundred of the Members pledged to support the amendment voted against it. It was defeated by a large majority.

Miss Ulverston could not stop crying for two days. Tommy came to see Venetia, sighed and shook his head, and said that it had been their last chance. Once the

491

rural householders had the vote, bringing the electorate to about five million – about two in three of all males – there would be nothing more to do, and no more Reform Bills would be introduced. To bring a Bill purely to enfranchise women was beyond the realms of fantasy.

'There's the deuce of a row going on,' Tommy confided. 'Dilke, Fawcett and Courtney all abstained in protest – walked out of the House before the division. They couldn't vote against, of course, being under the whip, but abstaining's almost as bad, especially as Dilke's in the Cabinet.

'Mrs Fawcett made a very witty remark about it,' Tommy went on. 'She said that Gladstone's remark about "overweighting the ship" was unfortunate, because the tradition of seamanship is "save the women first", whereas Gladstone's instinctive reaction seemed to be "throw them overboard".'

'I suppose Fawcett and the others will lose their positions?' Venetia said.

'No, they'll be lucky this time,' Tommy said. 'We've had a meeting about it, and the old man thinks it would damage public confidence to chuck three fellows out when there's a crisis brewing in Egypt.'

'Oh, he realises that, does he?' Venetia said, with some heat. 'I should have thought "brewing" was the wrong tense. The Mahdi's taken Berber and Khartoum is cut off, and Mr Gladstone only thinks that trouble is "brewing"?'

Tommy spread his hands. 'I'm doing all I can, but you know what a one-track mind he has. And the rest of the cabinet is not helping. Harcourt, Granville and Northbrook are all against sending an expedition, and while the argument goes back and forth like a shuttlecock, nothing happens.'

As he was leaving, Tommy laid a hand on her arm and said, 'But at least things are coming right for you at last. I hear you've taken up your position at the Southport.'

'Yes, and it's very odd to walk in there and see Mama's portrait over the fireplace in the main hall, and the plaque of dedication with her name on it by the front door.'

'Do they know who you are?'

'Some do and some don't. Those who do don't mention it, though. I think they want it to be felt that they exercised their minds freely and are above being bribed – which is what it came down to. But some of the medical staff wanted me. Four of them have sidled up to tell me they welcome my presence. And there's been no shortage of patients wanting my services.'

'Good. I'm sure you'll win them all over in the long run,' Tommy said. He hesitated a moment, and then said, 'Have you seen Hazelmere at all?'

She was surprised. 'I bumped into him in the street – oh – back in April, it must have been, but I haven't seen him since.'

'I see him in the club from time to time. And in the House,' Tommy said.

Venetia waited for more, but nothing was forthcoming. 'So why did you mention him?'

'Oh, I just wondered if you'd seen him,' said Tommy vaguely, and took his leave.

CHAPTER TWENTY-SIX

All through the summer of 1884 the Cabinet dithered about the situation in the Sudan, and the Prime Minister continued to occupy himself with other matters and assert that there was no need for an expedition. A former colleague, Forster – he of the Education Bill – remarked despairingly to Tommy Weston that Gladstone could persuade most people of most things and himself of almost anything.

It was not until August that Sir Garnet Wolseley was finally given the order to go to the relief of Khartoum. It took a couple of months to assemble and transport the troops and equipment to Cairo and then to Wady Halfa, and the Army did not set out up the Nile until the 5th of October. It was all uncharted and hostile territory, eight hundred and fifty miles along the great river, which wound in two giant curves like a letter S. The Army had to fight every inch of the way. Back in England daily reports appeared in the papers, and were consumed with unprecedented interest by a population that had dedicated itself to the cause of the gallant General Gordon and his beleaguered force.

In the interests of urgency, an advance column was to cut across the second bend of the river. A picked force under Sir Herbert Stewart set out across a hundred and fifty miles of the Bayuda desert, and in January 1885 won a desperate victory against the wild, knife-wielding Dervishes at Abu Klea, still a week's march from Khartoum. On the 21st of January this advance force reached the river again and met four steamboats, which Gordon had sent down from Khartoum in a desperate plea for help. But Stewart was dead from his wounds, and his inexperienced successor delayed three days before starting up the river. They reached Khartoum on the 28th of January, only to find that it had been stormed just two days earlier, and Gordon, his staff, and most of the garrison were dead.

In England there was a public storm of grief, and fury at the Government, particularly the Prime Minister. Their delay had caused the tragedy: Gordon's heroic blood was on Gladstone's head. There was a vote of censure in the Commons, which was only defeated by fourteen votes. The Queen sent a telegram *en clair* to Gladstone blaming him for the disaster; Gladstone was furious, taking the view that this represented a public vote of no confidence, and threatened to resign in protest at her interference, which would have caused a constitutional crisis. But the discretion of the Post Office prevented the telegram's contents becoming generally known, and he remained in office, though swearing he would never set foot in Windsor again.

Venetia heard both sides of this story, the one from Olivia and the other from Tommy. It was a minor distraction from her great sorrow at losing her brother, whom she had come, though late, to know and love. Marcus's body was sent home for burial. The first plan was for a family funeral down at Ravendene. This was what Charlotte wanted, and she wrote to Harry to say that Venetia must be included in the plans. Harry wrote back to say he would not countenance Venetia's presence for an instant; and while this correspondence was going on it transpired that Harry was intending to bring the lovely Miss Booth with him, at which the dowager duchess declared that if the actress was at Ravendene, she would not attend the funeral at all.

Unfortunately the argument somehow got into the papers, much to the amusement of the reading public and the distress of all concerned. Tommy Weston stepped in to mediate, and at last it was agreed Marcus should be given a military funeral by his regiment, which would mean that no women of any sort would be present, and buried in the regimental churchyard. Harry attended as head of the family and Tommy represented the absent women, and so it was done. In the middle of it all the troops were brought home and the Queen reviewed them, and the sight of the horrible gashes the men bore reminded everyone in a graphic way of exactly how General Gordon and the others had died.

Two things happened as a result of Marcus's death, which comforted Venetia. The first was a letter of condolence from Mrs Anderson. Her sister Millicent's husband, Henry Fawcett, had died suddenly the previous November, and she and Millicent had always been very close. Shortly afterwards her husband's father had died, and her beloved daughter had fallen seriously ill. 'All these terrible events serve to put other matters into perspective,' she wrote. Her daughter was now convalescing and she and her husband were taking their two children on a six-month holiday in Australia. 'As you know I have always undertaken the surgery at the New Hospital myself, and I am very reluctant to have any male doctor brought in to take my place while I'm abroad.' The only other women whose surgical skills she admired, Mary Scharlieb, was abroad; she would be grateful therefore if Venetia would undertake the surgical cases at the New on the same basis as she had before until her return.

Venetia was amused by the letter. Mrs Anderson was always practical and often blunt. No doubt she knew that Venetia had given up her shocking liaison and was working her way back to respectability; but the inference was that had Dr Scharlieb been available, Dr Fleet would not have been troubled. Not the pinnacle of tact; still, it was wonderful to be received back into the fold. It had reflected badly on Venetia that the head of the famously close-knit community of women practitioners had rejected her.

The other thing that brought her comfort was a visit

from Lord Hazelmere. He called one evening in April when she was not at her best, having had rather too busy a day. As well as her usual rounds she had had to fit in some work for the Criminal Law Amendment Bill – which had been defeated for a second time in 1884 and was to be brought again this year – and she'd been called to attend two emergencies, which had thrown out her plans and resulted in her missing both breakfast and luncheon.

She had just got home, tired and hungry, and remembered that it was the cook's evening off, which meant she would have to dine on cold meat, when the doorbell rang. Her first reaction was a scowl and a curse at being disturbed again. When the maid brought up Hazelmere's card she almost said she was not at home, but changed her mind and told Lotty to admit him; and then rushed to the glass over the chimney to see what she looked like. The reflection was not reassuring. Her hair was coming down, her face was white and tired, she had a smut on her cheek, and she was wearing one of her least becoming coat and skirt 'uniforms', of a thick dull purple bombazine, which made her look at least fifty, as she told herself, scrubbing at her cheek with a handkerchief. And then she thought, My dear girl, why are you worrying about how you look? She didn't really want to give herself an answer, so she pushed a few pins back into place in a rather futile gesture and turned to face the door with her hands clasped before her in what she hoped was a serene pose.

Hazelmere came in looking diffident, hat in hand, his head slightly ducked in the unsure manner of a man who feared he might have plates shied at him. 'I beg your pardon – I hope I don't intrude. If this is not a convenient time, please say so, and I'll take myself off at once.'

Venetia realised she was still scowling, and adjusted her expression hastily. 'Oh – no – not at all. Please come in. I was afraid when I heard the bell that it was a call-out, and I've had such a day I felt I couldn't bear to see another patient.'

'You look tired,' he said frankly. 'I shan't stay more than a moment.'

'No, please, do sit down,' Venetia said, waving a hand, and sat herself quickly so that he would have to. She was pining for company – particularly company of the old sort. With Marcus gone, the only person ever likely to visit her now was Tommy.

Hazelmere compromised by perching on the very edge of the sofa. 'I am so sorry about Marcus's death. I know what a blow it must have been for you.'

'Thank you. Yes, it was.'

'I hope you don't think me lax in waiting so long to call. I thought of coming sooner, but I didn't suppose you would want strangers intruding on you just at first, and a letter is somehow so cold.'

'Come, you're hardly a stranger,' she protested.

He looked at her gravely. 'You are very kind. But it's a long time since you and I were . . .' He didn't seem to know what word to choose. 'So much has happened since then.'

'Yes,' said Venetia. 'Sometimes I feel as if I'm living in a different world.'

'Everything's changing,' Hazelmere said. 'And I believe change will become even more rapid soon. When we look back, I think you and I will see that we have lived through a great upheaval. We'll hardly recognise the world as the one we were born in.'

He said it with such regret that Venetia was hurt. She thought she knew what he was thinking: that here she was, an unmarried woman living away from home, pursuing a career which ought to have been reserved for the male of the species. But the changes she had seen were good for her, and weren't happening half rapidly enough. Still she only operated on female patients, and the Hospital for Women in Soho Square wouldn't allow a female practitioner of any sort through the door. The women's suffrage amendment had been thrown out by the Government, little girls of thirteen were considered old enough to consent to sex, three-quarters of poor families lived in a single room, and the Royal Commission which had been set up to investigate the housing conditions of the poor had been unable to appoint Miss Octavia Hill because the Home Secretary said a woman couldn't be a commissioner.

So she said briskly, 'Yes, well, that's all to the good, isn't it? I don't look upon the past with any great affection, I assure you. As far as I'm concerned, the present is in every way preferable.'

'I see,' said Hazelmere. He seemed to sigh a little, and stood up. 'I really mustn't intrude on you any longer. I only came to express my most sincere condolences. I'll take my leave now – after your busy day you must long for a little solitude.'

She stood too, and rang for Lotty. 'Thank you for calling,' she said, thinking perhaps she had been a little brusque. Because she was tired and unhappy she had spoken more sharply than she meant to, and it occurred to her that in saying she had no affection for the past, she was consigning his former friendship to oblivion. 'It was kind of you to take the trouble,' she said, trying to inject a warmer note into her voice.

'It was no trouble,' he said. Lotty opened the door and stood waiting. 'I hope,' he added, hesitated, and went on, 'I hope you will always regard me as a friend. If there is anything I can do for you at any time . . .'

She saw the interest in Lotty's eyes at these softer words, and was embarrassed. 'Oh, thank you!' she said quickly. 'But I'm quite comfortable.'

He bowed. 'I'm glad to know it. Goodnight.' And he went, leaving Venetia to curse her awkwardness, which she was afraid would make him think her hard and ungracious.

A year after the rector's death the slow-grinding wheels of probate still had not disgorged a final settlement for Henrietta and her daughter, and the business of setting up the funds for the Fortescue Scholarship and the Fortescue Lecture was so complicated that Henrietta feared there would be nothing left once the lawyers had taken their handsome fees: it was rumoured that Mrs Eagleton had been to York to look at models for a new carriage.

On the positive side, her situation at the Red House had stabilised. Perry had said many times and with obvious sincerity that he was happy for them to stay as long as they liked. Henrietta tried to make herself useful by taking over the running of the house from Regina, who was both idle and muddled, besides being tired from the effects of constant childbirth – she was pregnant again with her sixth. Henrietta had had hard training at the rectory, and was able not only to get things running more smoothly, which pleased everyone and made the servants less irritable, but also eliminated a lot of waste, which she hoped compensated for the extra expense of her and Elizabeth.

The problem of Mary also sorted itself out. Since neither of them wanted a public scene, they treated each other with courtesy, if with coolness, when they met. Henrietta's mourning enabled her to avoid many of the social gatherings at which Mary might be present, and Mary herself, missing her brother and brooding over what might have happened to him, went out less often. Perry, who liked everyone to be jolly, did notice something, and asked Henrietta once, 'Is there a quarrel between you and Mary?' but when Henrietta said unemphatically, 'No, I don't think so. Why should there be?' he let it pass.

Perhaps more astutely, Amy, on the twins' next visit home, said to Henrietta, 'I think poor Aunt Mary really misses Jerome. I wish we could find out where he is.'

And Patsy said, 'I think she's bored without him, too. I wonder if she'd like to come with us on one of our trips.'

It proved a great tonic to Mary to have something else to think about, and a trial run to Switzerland proved so successful that in the spring of 1885 the three ladies set off together on a journey to India, which was to last several months. So there was no reason for Henrietta to think of leaving Bishop Winthorpe at all.

Yet she felt restless, as if her life had been put into suspension, and she was waiting for some signal to take it up and start again. It was perhaps understandable while she had been in mourning, but now that was over, what more would ever change? She was a widow with a child to bring up; and when the child was grown and gone, she would be a widow and nothing else. She had nothing to aim for, nothing to work towards, and in that, surely, she was no different from most people, who lived their days out one by one and all the same. Why, then, did she feel that her life here was a temporary measure? Why could she not accept this as the pattern for the rest of her existence?

Perhaps, she thought, she just needed a change; and this feeling, together with a natural curiosity, led her one day to ask Regina for the use of a carriage and have herself driven to Morland Place. It was wonderful and painful to come gradually in sight of more and more familiar landmarks, until she was driving past fields and trees of which she had once known every inch. But there were signs everywhere that trouble had overtaken her childhood home. The home pastures were empty of stock, the fields unsown, the hedges untended and ragged; there were no people about either – had things got so bad? When she reached the new stable block, which had been built to replace the home stables and the hunt kennels, she stopped the carriage and got out, to stare in wonder.

It was a most handsomely built, spacious stable yard, everything fine about it, even to the arch over the entrance, topped with a little square turret housing a clock, and finished with a weather-vane. The clock had stopped at twenty past eight, and paint was peeling off the weather boards. She walked in under the arch and stared around at the silent stables. There wasn't a soul about, and even the smell of horses had gone. It must have been empty for a long time. She looked in through a door that was standing half open, having fallen off its top hinge. Inside were saddle-horses and bridle hooks all round the walls, some with brass name-plates above them, but there were no saddles or bridles. There was nothing in the room at all but a lot of dry, dead leaves that had blown into the corner, and a sheet of newspaper screwed up into a ball, which somebody seemed to have used to wipe mud off something. She picked it up – the mud was quite dry – and teased it open. The date at the top was the 14th of May 1883.

She went back to the carriage and said she would walk up to the house and that it could follow her. She walked past the old barns and pig-houses and found them empty too, except for a few stray chickens scratching about. She walked on and came to the barbican, found the main gate standing open and no gateman on duty. She was beginning to feel nervous: the silence was unnatural. Where was everybody? Was Morland Place completely deserted? What had happened to George? She entered the courtyard and stopped dead with surprise. She ought to have been prepared for the differences, but in her mind the house had remained as it had always looked, and the reality was a shock. The new wings seemed to dwarf the face of the old house in the centre with its worn stone panel over the great door. The house had a look of sleep about it. There was no movement or sound: it lay enchanted like Sleeping Beauty's palace waiting for the prince.

The silence lasted only an instant longer. From out of the main door shot a huge dog, which flung itself at her, barking furiously. Her heart leaped in panic for a moment, but she had been brought up with dogs and knew better than to run or flinch. She stood still and faced it, and said, 'Down, sir!' in as commanding a voice as she could muster.

It ran round her, still barking, but not trying to bite her. She smiled and said, 'Come here, then, good boy. Come then, good old boy,' in as beguiling a voice as she could. It stopped barking and inched forward, craning its neck to sniff at her warily, and then a hesitant swinging of the tail began.

Someone came out of the main door of the house.

She straightened, expecting it to be George, but it was a woman.

'Come off it, dog!' she said, wiping her hands on her apron, and the animal left Henrietta and ran to her. She was hard to categorise: tall, strong-looking, in her middle twenties, quite attractive except that she looked worn and anxious. Henrietta would have put her down at once as a servant by her apron, her bare forearms and her hair tumbling untidily from its moorings; but the dress she was wearing was of silk, not a servant's dress, and she had called the dog with familiarity and even authority.

'Hello,' Henrietta said. 'Where is everybody?'

'Who are you?' the woman said.

Henrietta raised her eyebrows at this form of address, but she was, after all, on foot and a stranger. 'I'm Mrs Fortescue, Mr Morland's sister. I've come to visit him – Mr George Morland. Is he at home?'

The woman shook her head in a distracted way. 'No, he's out somewhere. He didn't say you were coming.'

'He didn't know. I came on an impulse. Who are you?'

'Alice. Alice Bone. I'm – I was housemaid here. Now I'm housekeeper, sort of.' The woman blushed at Henrietta's look, and began trying to push bits of her hair back up.

'I see,' Henrietta said, though she didn't. What was going on? Had George gone away and a family of gypsies taken over the house? 'Is there someone else here I can talk to? The butler, perhaps, or the steward?'

'There's only me,' she said. 'Everyone else left, apart from Aggie in the kitchen.' She gave Henrietta a piteous look and tears rushed to her eyes. 'I do my best but there's too much to do. I look after him, but I can't keep everything the way it was.'

Henrietta stepped forward and laid a hand on Alice's arm. 'I'm sure you do what you can. May I come in? Where is my brother, do you know?'

Inside, the hall was bare – the furniture had all gone, and the paintings from the walls – and there was no fire in the hearth. Henrietta took a deep breath to steady herself. 'Has he sold everything? All the furniture?'

'Not all,' said Alice, 'but a lot. They keep coming, you see. There's a loan from years back, the one Mr Atterwith left because of, because he didn't know about it, and the – interest, is it called?, keeps building up. So they come and take something to make up for it.' She swallowed and sniffed. 'It breaks his heart. I think that's why he stays out of the way. He goes out all day, most days, and only comes home at night.'

'Alice, this is terrible. He's all alone here apart from you?'

'And Aggie in the kitchen, like I said. She's a bit simple, but a good soul, and she helps me cook and clean. But the house is too big. I can't manage it all.'

'I should think you couldn't!'

'There used to be so many of us – more than thirty when I first came, indoors alone. But it's all gone to rack now.'

'But where *is* he?'

Alice spread her hands helplessly. 'I don't know. He just goes off, doesn't tell me where. He walks about, I think. Takes a gun sometimes and brings back a rabbit or something. He comes back when it gets dark. He doesn't like being out in the dark. Says it's unchancy.' She gave a little shiver. 'There's ghosts in this house, did you know?'

'Yes, I've always heard it, though I've never seen any. I was brought up here, you know.'

Alice could not be interested in anyone else's story. It was so long since she had had anyone to talk to, she wanted only to tell. '*He* sees them. All sorts. He hardly goes in the rest of the house now, only the chapel sometimes. He hasn't been upstairs for months. I don't bother with upstairs any more. It's all I can do to keep the gentlemen's wing clean. That's where we live now.' She seemed to remember some old law of hospitality and said in a social voice, 'I'm sure if he'd known you were coming he'd have stayed in for you. I'd – I'd offer you

504

some refreshments but he has the wine all locked up and keeps the key about him. I could make you a cup of tea, perhaps?'

Henrietta, taking account of the dress, the housewifely offer, that tell-tale 'we', was beginning to add some things together. 'No, thank you. Tell me, is it really bad? Is there no money? Do you get enough to eat?'

'Oh, we don't go hungry,' Alice said, as if the question surprised her. 'There's the orchard and kitchen garden, and the farms send up things, milk and eggs and such, and George – Mr Morland, the master – shoots stuff for the pot. And there's lots in the still-room yet, and the cellar – he found out before Mr Goole took the lot and threw him out. That's why he keeps it locked now. Mr Goole hadn't had his wages, you see, so he was taking the wine instead and selling it. Not that I think it's right,' she added quickly. 'I'm only saying that was why.'

She spoke in an odd mixture of the proprietorial and the humble, and looked at Henrietta a little awkwardly, as if she didn't know how to address her, whether to curtsy and say 'ma'am' or treat her as an equal.

'Who tends the kitchen garden? Surely not you?'

'No, some of the men come up from Woodhouse Farm. They take most of the stuff for tending it, and leave us some, and bring us other things, flour and meat and such. We're all right,' she concluded, with a sudden access of dignity.

'That's a nice dress, Alice,' Henrietta said gently.

She blushed scarlet. 'It was one of the mistress's,' she acknowledged, but put her head up. 'He gave it me. I didn't take it, if that's what you think.'

'I didn't think that.' Their eyes met and a great deal was exchanged, woman to woman. 'I'm sure you take good care of him, and if that's what pleases you both, it's none of my business. I just wanted to know that he was all right, that was all.'

'Well, he is,' she said, still defiantly. The dog had come to nudge up under her hand, sensing emotions in the air. She stroked the big, rough head and scratched automatically behind its ears, a practised gesture that told Henrietta more than words.

'I'll go, then,' she said.

'You're welcome to stay.'

But Henrietta had no wish to confront her brother in his shame; and there was nothing she could do for him anyway. She shook her head. 'When my brother comes home, you'll tell him I called? And that I send my love.'

Alice nodded. 'All right.' She waited until Henrietta had reached the door before she called, 'I say!' Henrietta turned enquiringly. Alice hesitated a moment and then said, all in a rush, 'We're having a baby. I mean I am.' Her eyes were bright and defiant, but her cheeks were red.

Henrietta nodded slowly. 'I wish you well,' she said, and went away, leaving Alice with the dog, alone in the middle of the empty great hall – where Henrietta had danced once, long ago, and first caught the eye of Mr Fortescue. How the wheel turns, she thought sadly.

In June 1885 the Government was defeated over beer tax, when the Parnellites decided to vote with the Tories. Gladstone resigned, aware that the real cause of his defeat was his unpopularity over the massacre at Khartoum. Something of a crisis ensued. The work on the electoral rolls following the previous year's Reform Act had not been completed, and it would be impossible to hold a general election until the end of the year. Moreover, the Queen was on holiday in Balmoral and refused to return to Windsor because it was Ascot week, and the crowds and noise, she said, would be unendurable.

The situation was resolved by Lord Salisbury's agreeing to form an interim government and the Queen's agreeing to come to Osborne, going on to Windsor the following week when Ascot would be over.

Tommy called on Venetia and said ruefully, 'Well, so ends my first taste of government – with a farce!'

'Oh, poor Tommy!'

'Never mind, we'll come about again. I don't believe

the Old Man means to be out of office for long. Did you know the Queen offered him an earldom?'

'No! I thought she hated him so?'

'I think it was the euphoria of relief at being rid of him that prompted it! But the point is that the Old Man refused it, saying he felt his destiny lies in the Commons. So he means to come back. And since Salisbury's going to be too busy from now on for the Housing Commission, he's asked me if I'll serve, which is just up my street. So I shall be both busy and useful. What more can a man ask?'

'Or woman, for that matter,' Venetia said.

'By the by, talking of woman,' he said, eyeing her curiously, 'aren't you a bit tough on poor Hazelmere?'

Venetia raised her eyebrows. 'What on earth are you talking about? I haven't seen him for weeks.'

'Exactly. He came to condole with you and you bit his head off. Was it that you were too grief-stricken to be kind?'

'What nonsense. Has he said I was unkind?'

'Oh, now, don't starch up at me! He didn't say a word, but he's been drooping around like a kicked puppy, and I wheedled out of him that you'd said something pretty snubbing.'

'I had no idea that there was anything to snub,' Venetia said. 'Lord Hazelmere and I have had nothing to do with each other for years. He doesn't approve of my being a doctor, as you know very well. In fact, he doesn't approve of anything about me. I'm "one of these modern women", as far as he's concerned.'

'Oh, I see,' Tommy said, 'I'm sorry I put my nose in.'

'So I should think,' Venetia said. 'Well, why are you looking at me like that?'

'I was just wondering why the subject makes you so cross. No, please don't answer me! My hide isn't thick enough. I cry pax and drop the subject. So, Salisbury's to double in the Foreign Department and we shall have Cross as Home Secretary again. Who do you think will get the Board of Trade?'

One evening a few days later Venetia was coming home from visiting patients and saw quite a queue of people outside the dispensary, waiting for it to open. Amongst them she saw Mrs Phillips, a consumptive patient of hers, with her son Sam, a merry little devil of five whom she always had to bring with her when she visited the dispensary for fear of what he might get up to without her. As a consequence Venetia and Sam had built up quite a friendship over the months.

Sam now spotted her as she waited to cross Welbeck Street, and with a shriek of delight he waved, tugged his hand free from his mother's and ran to meet her. A gig had just come round the corner from Barrett Street and was picking up speed and the child, his eyes fixed on Venetia, ran straight into it. The horse reared back, its iron-shod hoofss skidding on the cobbles. There was a shout from the driver, a scream from Mrs Phillips, and a composite splurge of outcry from various onlookers as the child seemed to disappear under the horse's hoofs. Venetia was there in an instant, grabbing the noseband of the still plunging horse, saying, 'Ho, ho, steady,' in a soothing voice, as she tried to see what had become of Sam. He was curled on the ground under the horse, and she could see blood. A horny working hand joined hers on the harness and a voice said, 'I've got him, miss. You see to the kid.' She let go and crouched, perilously close to the tramping hoofs, got hold of Sam's jacket and pulled him to her, backed a step and scooped him up into her arms. He was limp, and heavier than he looked.

The horse had stopped plunging but was shifting its feet and trembling, probably more frightened by the noise and milling of the crowd than it had been by the original incident. 'I couldn't help it! He run straight at me,' the driver was saying. The traffic had stopped all around, and further down the street, where they couldn't see the reason, drivers were shouting impatiently and those who had horns were using them.

A voice beside Venetia said, 'Here, let me take him, poor little fellow.' In the tension of the moment it did not seem strange that it should be Lord Hazelmere. 'You go ahead and make way.'

She passed the child over. 'My bag!' she cried, looking round.

'Here y'are, miss. I got it!' A helpful onlooker passed it over, and she led the way through the traffic across the road, Hazelmere behind her. People were craning out of windows, out of carriages, gathering on the pavements, eager for a bit of excitement in their lives. Mrs Phillips was hovering in front of her, her weak, white face whiter than ever now, her fingers fluttering about her mouth. 'Is he dead?'

The crowd picked up the word and passed it back eagerly. 'He's dead! Dead! Poor little feller's dead!'

Venetia thrust her way to the steps down to the basement dispensary. 'He's not dead. Make way, please. Only Mrs Phillips to come down for the moment. The dispensary will be opening a little late today.'

Inside the dispensary it was always rather dark, because of its subterranean position, and Venetia led the way to the back room, where she did the treatments, and told Hazelmere to put the child on the table while she lit the gas. Sam was stirring now and muttering. She took off her jacket and made an examination. He looked a frightening sight to begin with, his face a sheet of blood, and blood in his hair, and Mrs Phillips was making horrified moaning noises behind her hands, which ceased blessedly when her overtaxed heart and lungs gave up on the situation and she fainted. Venetia met Hazelmere's eyes and divined his question. 'No, no, leave her. She's in the best position. The blood will come back to her head now she's horizontal. Can you turn his head this way and just hold it still. There, there, now, Sammy, it's all right. It's Dr Fleet. You've had a bit of a bump.'

'A bit?' Hazelmere questioned, in a horrified murmur.

'Looks worse than it is,' Venetia said, after a moment. Some of the blood was coming from Sam's nose, and when that was wiped away and accounted for, there was only a gash across the boy's forehead, presumably from

509

a flying hoof, which though long and copiously bleeding, was quite shallow. Venetia felt about the injury delicately. 'You're lucky,' she informed her patient. 'Nothing broken. That horse could have stoved your head in with one kick. Don't you know better than to run out into the road?'

The boy smiled weakly. 'Yes, miss.'

'Well, don't do it again! A great boy like you getting himself knocked down. I'd have been ashamed not to know better at your age. How old are you – six, seven?'

'Five,' Sam said, immensely gratified. Venetia knew, of course, but flattering Sam kept his mind off his troubles. 'Nearly six, though.'

'If you want to get to be six, you keep on the pavements. Is your head aching?'

'A bit,' Sam admitted.

'It's going to ache a lot more by and by, and you're going to have a big lump there tomorrow to show your brothers and sisters. And probably a scar to show your friends for the rest of your life. I suppose that's what you did it for, hey?'

A grin slithered across his grimy face. 'No, miss, 'twas an accident.'

'Well, now you'll have to pay for it. I'm going to have to stitch up this cut of yours, and you're going to have to show me what a brave soldier you can be.'

'I ain't afraid, miss.'

'Doctor!' Mrs Phillips corrected him in a hiss. She had staggered to her feet and was putting herself to rights in the background. 'It's Doctor, not miss!'

'All right, Mrs Phillips. I don't think there's any great harm done. I'm going to stitch the cut, and then you can take him home.' When this was done, and a bandage wound round his head, which would surely gratify him the next day, Venetia lifted him down from the table. He was quiet now, the headache beginning to take hold. 'Put him to bed and keep the others away from him,' she told Mrs Phillips. 'He's had quite a bang on the head, and I expect he'll fall asleep soon and probably sleep for quite a while – twelve or fourteen hours. Try and keep him quiet tomorrow, and I'll call in to see if he's all right.'

When she had departed, Venetia washed her hands and wiped the blood from the table, then turned to find Hazelmere watching her. She felt embarrassed and defensive. He had seen her doing those things he abhorred, and now would surely come the lecture. But he was not looking at her with distaste. She wasn't sure what it was, but it was not horror or disgust.

'You've got blood on your shirt,' she said.

'You've got blood on you too.'

'I'm used to it,' she said. 'I'm sorry you got mixed up in all this. But thank you for your help.'

'I'm glad I could be of use,' he said. They looked at each other awkwardly for a moment. Behind him, through the window of the other room, she could see the dispensary people waiting. 'Venetia,' he said, 'I'm not sure how to say this. I don't want to sound patronising. But what you did just now—'

'It was nothing. Just a simple stitching job.'

'No, it wasn't nothing. I'm sure you do lots of things much more skilled. But you were – so professional. Stitching the cut as if it was a piece of linen rather than human flesh. The way you dealt with the child, so he shouldn't be afraid. How firmly you advised the mother. Everything done so well – so neatly.'

She cocked her head a little. 'So unwomanly?'

'No, I wasn't going to say that. What you did was to create order out of chaos, to relieve suffering and put things right. That's a good thing for anyone to do, whatever their sex. Good and honourable. I honour you – that's what I'm trying to say.'

'Thank you,' she said awkwardly. Somebody tapped urgently on the dispensary window and she felt an irritation at being interrupted just now. 'I ought to open up,' she said. He did not jump at the excuse to go, so she said, 'You should try to get the blood out of your shirt before it sets. Perhaps you'd like to go upstairs to my house and

511

have my maid do it for you. It will be much less trouble if you rinse it out right away.'

'Well, yes, thank you – if you don't mind.'

'Not at all.'

'Perhaps,' he said hesitantly. 'I could wait upstairs until you've finished here. I'd like to talk to you.'

She felt herself blushing. 'That would be – nice.' She dragged her eyes away from his. 'No need to go out into the street again. Go through the door there and up the stairs. And tell Lotty *cold* water, remember!' she called after him. He smiled a private smile and left her.

While she worked, everything else went out of her mind, and when she had finished and closed the dispensary door, the fact that Hazelmere was waiting upstairs for her came back as a delightful shock. What he had said – *order out of chaos, I honour you*; the look in his eyes; his willingness – no, his eagerness to wait and talk to her; it all signified a change of heart. What had Tommy hinted? That she had hurt him by snubbing him? Well, she responded robustly, hadn't he hurt her a great deal more? But that was her old combative, defensive self retorting. She was grown-up now, she had no need to hit out: she knew her worth and had proved it. She would go upstairs and be serene and gracious and show Lord Hazelmere that she didn't depend on *his* good opinion to bolster her own.

In this confused frame of mind she mounted tensely, a little grubby and dishevelled and with Sam's blood dried on her shirt, to the drawing-room, to find Hazelmere sitting reading the newspaper with every appearance of ease. It made her heart jump a little to see him sitting there as if he lived here. He looked up as she came in and smiled such a warm smile of welcome that her jumping heart had no time to settle down.

'How tired you must be! I hope I'm not adding to your burdens by being here?'

'You mean I look like a shipwrecked mariner and that this sort of work is too hard for a female?' she retorted.

512

Even as she heard herself, she cursed. Why couldn't she talk to him like a normal human being?

But he didn't take offence. He had stood up, and now made a little spreading gesture of his hands, still smiling, and said, 'Dear, prickly Venetia! I don't doubt that I deserve every sharp word for being such a prig in the past, but do you think we could possibly call pax now? I'd like to convince you that I really have had a change of heart – or I should say a change of opinion, because my heart is yours just as it always has been.'

Venetia stood stranded in the middle of her own drawing-room and her own ungraciousness. She didn't know what to say or do, and if Hazelmere did not take the lead she would be stuck here forever, until the world turned to coal.

'I meant what I said down there, you know,' he went on. 'I do honour you. What you do is valuable and important, and I was blinkered fool to think that such intelligence and talent as yours should be harnessed to the mere business of housekeeping.'

'All this, because of a little stitching job?' she said, bewildered.

'No, because of everything you do. It's been coming on a long time,' he said reasonably, 'but it takes a while to overcome the prejudices of a lifetime. You could blame my upbringing, if you were minded to be generous. Or the tide of history.'

'And when did this sea change begin?' she asked warily.

'Probably the moment I realised I'd lost you. One of us had to be wrong, and since I was the one doing all the suffering, I supposed it was me. But I had a great deal of conceit to overcome first.'

She couldn't resist his wry contrition. 'Oh, Beauty,' she said, trying not to smile.

'Yes, that old name! I was spoilt, that's what it was. Beauty Winchmore, the darling of the Blues! Lord, what a pompous ass I was!'

'No, never pompous,' she protested wickedly.

'But an ass?' he said, coming a step closer.

'Definitely an ass,' she agreed, taking one of her own, just to help him along. 'Particularly an ass not to let me know much sooner how your state of mind was coming along. I had no idea, you see.'

'I had none either,' he said. 'I thought you still hated me.'

'You didn't ask.'

'It's not the sort of thing one can ask easily.'

'No, I suppose not.'

'But I did try – when I came to see you a few weeks ago. And you said—'

'Oh, don't remind me. It was a chapter of misunderstandings. But to what do we owe this *éclaircissement*?'

'Tommy Weston. He told me I was mistaken and that you still had feelings for me, so I finally decided to come and see you again. I was lingering about outside your house trying to pluck up courage to ring the bell when you came home, and that young limb of Satan intervened.'

'Oh, good Lord, I'd completely forgotten to wonder what you were doing on the scene,' said Venetia. 'But don't curse poor little Sam. He did us a favour, really.'

'Us? I like that word. Is there an "us", dearest Venetia?' He was close enough now to take hold of her hands, and he could feel her trembling through them.

She looked at him searchingly. 'I don't know. That depends on you. I am what I am, Beauty – can you live with that?'

'I can not only live with it, and be proud of it, I can even help. It seems to me that you have far too much to do and need an assistant.'

'I really could do with an assistant in the dispensary,' she admitted. 'It doesn't have to be a fully trained doctor, but *some* training is necessary. I'm not sure you—'

'Not me, idiot!' he grinned. 'But it occurred to me that if we pooled our resources, enough economy would result for you to be able to afford to pay for an assistant.'

'Oh,' she said innocently. 'I see. Pooled our resources – in what way?'

'Well, if we lived together, that would save one whole set of household bills.'

'Lived together where? Here, or in your house?' she asked suspiciously.

He cleared that one neatly. 'This seems a perfectly nice house, but it shall be as you please. But we'd have to get married, to keep it respectable.'

'Then you'd be the doctor's husband,' she pointed out.

'And you'd be the doctor's husband's wife.'

She smiled. His face was only inches from hers now. 'What makes you think I want to marry you?'

'This,' he said, and kissed her.

The kissing went on for a long time. Lotty came in, started, smirked, and backed out again, all without either of them knowing it. Lord Hazelmere, in a daze of bliss, felt his beloved's pent-up passion and thought that they probably ought to get married very soon. God bless Tommy Weston, he thought – which was an example of his deep compatibility with Venetia, because that's just what she was thinking at the same time.

CHAPTER TWENTY-SEVEN

One morning in July 1885, Jeb Walton and his son Davy, from Huntsham Farm, were coming down a track on the far side of Harewood Whin. Davy caught his father's arm, halting him in mid-grumble about the rain, which hadn't stopped for days, and said, 'What's that?'

They both peered through the teeming rain towards the beck. There was something lying on the bank.

'Someone's coat, is it?' Jeb said uncertainly. 'It's not a sheep, anyroad.'

Then the thing moved and they heard a sharp, imperious bark. Their own dogs, who had been standing patiently, ears down, waiting to go on, lifted their heads and growled a warning. They were upwind of the beck and caught no scent.

'Best go and see what's up,' Jeb said, just a touch reluctantly. Water was dripping off the end of his nose.

The dogs raced ahead, barking, and the men hurried after. A liver-and-white pointer lying on the bank turned her head to them and barked again. 'That's Master Morland's bitch!' Jeb exclaimed.

'Why don't she get up?'

'Mebbe she's hurt.'

But when they got closer they saw what she was guarding. There was a torn place on the bank where the slippery turf had been ripped from the mud like the pelt being skinned off a dead rabbit, and George Morland himself was lying half in and half out of the beck, one leg bent under him at an unnatural angle. They could see his gun, lying on the stones under the water. The bitch had couched up as close to him as she could get, and growled a warning when they came near.

Jeb held out a soothing hand. 'There, old girl, good old girl. Peace now. I won't hurt thee.'

'Is he dead? I can't see him breathing.'

'I don't know. He's terrible cold. Here, help me pull him out o' the watter.'

'What about that leg? It looks queer.'

'Brokken, I reckon,' Jeb said. 'But we can't leave him there. The watter's icy.'

'I'll get in the beck, then, and lift from that end.'

'Easy, now – handsomely!'

The master was a big man, and inertia made him heavier. It was a struggle for the two men to lift him, and the bank was slippery. In spite of their care they jolted and bumped him, and perhaps the pain from the broken leg was sufficient to bring him half-way to consciousness, for he groaned and muttered.

'Well, at least we know he's still alive,' Jeb said. 'Thank God!'

But once they had him out and lying on the grass, he seemed to go off again. 'Eh, but he's awful cold,' said Jeb. 'We've got to get him home.'

'We'll never carry him that far,' Davy said. 'Not the weight he is, and you with your back.'

'We'll have to get help, then.'

Davy met his eyes across the silent body. 'I'll go, Dad. I'm quicker on my legs than you.'

This was true, though Jeb didn't relish the thought of being left alone with the body in the rain. Still, there was no help for it. 'All right. Give me your coat first. I'll put mine over him an' all. Get as many men as you can – and bring a hurdle or some'at to carry him on. And tell Mother to send one o' kids for a doctor.'

'Right!' Davy said, and set off at a run. The rain was so heavy he disappeared from view in just a few yards.

'Dark as Newgate Knocker,' Jeb grumbled to himself; and then met the beseeching eyes of the pointer bitch.

Realising there was someone worse off than himself, he caressed her cold, wet ears and said kindly, 'Eh, th'art a good lass to stop by him. Poor old girl! Won't be long now.'

But it seemed a very long time before they finally got the master back to the farm, out of the rain and onto the sofa before the fire, which Mrs Walton had hastily kindled in the parlour; and in all that time he had not stirred again.

'He's cold as stone,' Mrs Walton marvelled, as she hurried up with a towel to dry as much of him as possible. 'How long had he been in that beck?'

'No knowing. Could be all night for all we know,' Jeb said. 'Is doctor coming?'

'I sent Patrick for Dr Whetmore. Eh, look at that poor benighted dog! Our Phil, take the poor creature to the kitchen fire and give it a rub with a sack or some'at.'

Dr Whetmore arrived at last, a trace of egg on his moustache showing that he had obeyed the summons without delay. He agreed the leg was broken, sighed and tutted over it, and said, 'Perhaps it's a good job he is unconscious, or straightening it would be very painful for him. You made a fine mess of it, I must say.'

'It were hard getting him out of the beck,' Walton protested in his own defence. 'Bank were right slippery, and it's steep just there.'

'I suppose that's how he went in?' Whetmore said, straightening the leg carefully.

'It looked as if he slipped. There were a great gout torn out of bank.'

Whetmore had noticed something else. 'He's had a bit to drink by the smell of his breath.'

Jeb exchanged a glance with his wife and stepped closer, lowering his voice. 'I have heard tell that master drinks a bit now. No wonder, with all the trouble he's seen lately. But . . .' He let the sentence hang.

'He'll have more trouble after this,' Whetmore said, shaking his head. 'I doubt if this leg will ever be sound again. Hand me that splint, will you? I suppose he slipped

518

and went down the bank, and then, what with the broken leg and the drink, couldn't get himself out again. Has someone gone up the house to let them know?'

Walton sent his son Joe, who returned at last with the news that there was no-one there but the old woman in the kitchen, who said that Alice Bone had gone the morning previously to visit her mother, who was ill. The master, she said, was in his quarters as far as she knew. It took Joe some time to persuade her that he wasn't. She never disturbed him before he rang for her, she said, and she wasn't surprised that he hadn't rung because he drank heavily in the evenings and often didn't wake until noon. Eventually a cautious visit to the master's room convinced her of the truth.

Joe, a bright boy, thought to ask her where Alice's mother lived, but the old woman did not know, and couldn't say when she would be coming back. By the time he got back to the farm the doctor had finished with the splinting, and they had managed to get the wet clothes off and put George into a warm, dry nightshirt, but still he was unconscious, cold to the touch and breathing very shallowly.

'Someone ought to come,' Whetmore said, frowning. 'You'd better send a message to his brother, Mr Edward Morland.'

Teddy came as soon as he had the message, and listened in silence as Whetmore explained the situation. 'He had his gun with him, so one must suppose he came out early this morning – he'd hardly go shooting in the dark. But he might well still have been fuddled from the drink, went too near the edge or perhaps overbalanced, and then couldn't get himself out.'

Teddy nodded, dry-mouthed. 'He never had a head for it,' he said. 'I didn't know things had got so bad, though. What – what's going to happen to him?'

Whetmore shook his head. 'He could have been in the water for hours, and in any case it's been raining like the dickens. He was wet through when Walton found him, and he's got so cold that he's sunk into a kind of coma. If we can't get him out of it, I'm afraid he will die.'

Teddy swallowed. 'Would it be better to take him home? Or to my house? I'd be happy to do anything I can, if—'

'Better not to move him,' Whetmore said. 'What we need is to get him warm. Later, if he recovers consciousness, he'll have to be nursed until the leg heals, and then it may be better then for you to take him.'

Teddy noticed that Whetmore said *if* and not *when*. He stayed at hand all day while the Huntsham women did everything they could think of, keeping up the fire, piling on blankets, administering hot bottles; even Mrs Walton's boiling stone was called into service, wrapped in a cloth and put against his feet. At noon the Huntsham labourers came in for their dinner, and gathered in a hushed and respectful group at the door, until Mrs Walton drove them off for dripping rain on her parlour floor. She told her eldest daughter to get their dinner on the table so that they could go back to work, and they ate in subdued silence, asking for the bread to be passed in a whisper, as if any sound might disturb the balance of the struggle going on in the next room.

In the afternoon Alice arrived, having returned from her mother's house and received a garbled message from Aggie. She struggled through the rain to Huntsham Farm, running where the path was good enough, and came in wet through and breathless, her wide eyes darting round the assembled faces for information. Teddy silently made space for her and she flung herself down beside the couch, white and silent, and took his hand, chafing it between hers. Teddy had expected hysterics, and respected her more for keeping control of herself, though it must have been plain to her, as it was to him, that his brother was close to death. His body was still cold to the touch, and his face seemed to have sunk, taking on a marbled look so unlike his normal rubicund health it was pitiful.

About an hour or so later Maggie, who had crept

back to his side, suddenly threw back her head and began to howl. Whetmore stepped across and felt for George's pulse. After a long moment he shook his head gravely. Alice put her arm over the dog to comfort it. She bent her head, and slow tears began to seep from her eyes.

'Without ever regaining consciousness,' Teddy told Henrietta, the next day. 'I don't know why that makes it seem worse, but somehow it does.'

'It's as if he died alone,' Henrietta said, understanding.

'Yes, perhaps that's it. Though he had his – well, housekeeper, whatever you want to call her, with him.' He reflected that she seemed to love old Georgie all right. Maybe the only person left who did, since he'd driven his brothers and sisters away. Alice had wept almost silently, but desperately, for hours after he died; the Huntsham women, who had been disposed to resent her, were won to her side by her obvious desolation.

'She blames herself,' Teddy went on. The steady July rain was falling outside the long windows of the Red House morning-room. They were alone there, the family having given them privacy. 'She said she shouldn't have left him alone.'

'That's foolish,' Henrietta said. But, poor Alice, she could imagine how she would have felt in her position! 'He was a grown man, after all.'

'And her mother was ill,' Teddy agreed. 'But it seems he's been drinking heavily for months. I suppose something like this was almost bound to happen. I wish I'd known how bad things had got. But he'd never let anyone help. Last time I saw him he bit my head off for asking if he was all right. Still, I'd have tried to do something. Family is family, when all's said.'

Henrietta stared out at nothing. The rain had obscured everything into a uniform greyness beyond the window.

Teddy cleared his throat carefully. 'She's with child,' he mentioned. 'Alice, I mean.'

'Yes, I know,' Henrietta said. She looked up. 'Don't blame him, Teddy. He took comfort where he could, and she did the same. They weren't hurting anyone.'

'I wasn't blaming him,' he said. 'It makes it awkward, though. Something must be done for her.'

'Yes,' said Henrietta.

'I've left her at Morland Place for the time being. Well, someone has to take care of it.'

'Yes.'

'Is that all you can say?'

'Teddy, I can't help you,' she said. She was too stunned by the news to give advice. George had been only four years older than her, and had always been so strong and healthy, of all of them the most vigorous and full of life. How the ranks were thinning! 'Is there any money at all?' she asked, after a moment.

'I don't know yet. I have to see the lawyers tomorrow. I expect it will take months to sort it all out. But it doesn't look good. He's been over head and ears in debt for years. You think she ought to be paid something, then?'

'If she's carrying Georgie's child, he had a responsibility to provide for it. But the question won't arise if there's no money.'

Teddy walked about a bit, working up to some confession. His bulk crossed back and forth between Henrietta and the dim rain-light from the window. 'The thing is,' he said awkwardly, 'Georgie and I did a trade a long time ago, my land for his factories. You know Father left me a piece of land out at Moon's Rush?'

'Yes, of course.'

'Well, it wasn't very good land, but Georgie wanted it and he didn't care about the factories. But the factories are doing rather well, now, whereas the land, well, you know how it is with farm land these days.'

'Yes, I see,' Henrietta said.

'So I have money and George ended up with none.'

'But, Teddy, you can't feel guilty about that. The trade was made freely, wasn't it? And besides, George's financial troubles were mostly his own fault. He and Alfreda spent and spent. And the part that wasn't his fault was the fault of the agricultural slump.'

'Yes, I know all that, really, but – well, you know how it is.'

'Yes, I know.' They were silent. Then she said, 'Do you remember, when we were children, how you and I used to stick together? All we had in common was that we weren't Georgie. He was special and apart because he was the heir.' Teddy nodded. He sat down beside her, to be close, for comfort on this grey, dark day. After a while she said, 'Will it come to you, now, Morland Place and everything?'

'I suppose so. There's no-one else, is there?'

'Not that there's much left. When I went there a few weeks ago it was all so forlorn. No stock grazing, no horses, the fields not cultivated, the house stripped.'

'And then there are the unpaid debts,' Teddy said gloomily.

'There was a bank loan outstanding, too, wasn't there? Alice told me.'

'Was there? It doesn't surprise me.'

'Will everything have to be sold to clear the debts?' Henrietta asked unhappily. 'I'd hate to think of strangers taking over Morland Place. Our family's been there for centuries.'

'I don't know,' Teddy said. 'I just don't know, Hen. Maybe it won't come to that. Something might be left when everything's paid off. I shan't know until I see the solicitor. But we have to bury him first.'

'Yes, of course,' Henrietta said. 'I'm sorry. I shouldn't be thinking of money at a time like this.'

'It's all poor old Georgie ever thought about,' Teddy said. 'But I often wonder what he would have turned out like if he hadn't married Alfreda. She was a bad influence on him.' Yet he had really loved her, Teddy marvelled. When she died he went to pieces, despite the fact that he was still young and could have married again and had more children. Well, as the common people said, there's nowt queerer than folks. 'You'll come, won't you?' he asked.

'To the funeral? Of course. At Morland Place, I suppose?'

'Yes, he ought to have that, at least.' He frowned. 'It ought to be done as soon as possible, I think.' He met her enquiring look, and said, 'If the bank loan is secured on the house and it can't be paid, there may be some question about who it actually belongs to now. If the bank seizes it, they might not allow the funeral to go ahead.'

Henrietta looked shocked. 'What an awful thing! Oh, Teddy, we can't let that happen! Whatever he did, he was Master of Morland Place. Let's get it done quickly, then.'

So George Morland was laid to rest in the crypt under the chapel with the bones of his ancestors. His brother attended, and his two sisters and their families, as well as Alice Bone, carrying his unborn child – a good send-off for any man, especially one who had cared so little for any of them when he was alive.

The bank in Leeds called in its loan at once: in default of payment, Morland Place was forfeit. The terms of George's Will made Teddy his heir in the case of his dying without a surviving child, but it was clear that everything would have to be sold to cover the great mass of debts, and it seemed likely that Teddy would inherit nothing but the name and a few personal items once the dust had settled. George had been teetering on the brink of bankruptcy ever since his wife's death.

It was also clear that Morland Place must have a caretaker for the time being, and Teddy asked the solicitor to persuade the bank to employ Alice Bone in that capacity, for she was anxious to stay there, and would need money to buy things for the baby when it came. The solicitor was able to tell the bank with absolute truth that Alice had been housekeeper for years and had taken good care of things and they agreed to keep her on; and so the immediate problem was solved.

In the weeks that followed, Henrietta found herself growing increasingly restless and unhappy. A wet July and August gave way to a warm and sunny September, so she was not confined to the house as before, but even walking and riding did not use her up or calm her. Her life seemed to her both monotonous and uncertain. The twins and Mary were still away, having decided to sail back from India the long way, round the Cape, and spend some time in South Africa. Regina was pregnant again, and the early stages always made her sleepy and indolent, so she was little company; while Elizabeth was being taught by the Parke governess and so was not Henrietta's province any more. The new incumbent of the rectory had met Elizabeth and been impressed by her intelligence. He was a more flexibly minded man who saw nothing against the education of females, and had offered to give her the more advanced lessons that Miss Bell could not provide, so she went up to her old home several afternoons a week to continue with her Latin, Greek and mathematics.

And Perry, of course, had his horses, dogs and estate, and all the other businesses that kept men occupied and happy. It seemed to Henrietta that everyone had something to do and a role to play except her. Running Perry's house was not like having a household of her own, and she had no parish duties now. No work to do, no company, no friendship, no home of her own; and, it seemed increasingly likely, no future income. Mr Fortescue's fortune, such as it remained, was disappearing into the hungry mouth of the law, and it looked as if there would be nothing left for her and Elizabeth. They would be dependent on charity for the necessities of life.

And now Morland Place was to be sold, too; a stranger would buy it and call it his own, perhaps even change the name. The idea hurt her more than she could have anticipated. When she had left it to marry she had known it would never be her home again, but there had been a comfort in knowing that it was *there*, just as it had always been. It was absurd, of course, to think that it would be any less there with a Smith, Brown or Robinson in

525

possession, but the heart and anchor of the family, as it had been through hundreds of years, it would be no more. No more Morlands at Morland Place. A piece of herself would die when it came under the hammer. She dreaded the visit or letter from Teddy that would tell her the date of the sale; it all added to her restless unhappiness.

One day she went up to the church to arrange the flowers – a job she had begged from the new rector's wife, Mrs Chase, who had perceived Henrietta's unhappiness and yielded it up from compassion. Henrietta made it last as long as possible, concentrating her whole mind on the act of artistic creation so that for a while her restlessness was shut out. When it was done, she sat down in one of the front pews to try to let the beauty and quiet of the church seep into her.

The air was cool and still, with a faint smell of wax and turpentine, and just a hint of the white roses she had used in the vase at the base of the pulpit. The sunlight was coming in through the south aisle windows in dramatic beams, like so many fingers of God pointing out details of the interior: the brass of the eagle lectern, the poppy-head pew end, the memorial on the wall to Sir Joseph Steed, who had been squire before the Parkes came, and had gone to join his maker in 1723, leaving behind a wife and three children who apparently missed him so much they hurried after him, and all joined him on the memorial within ten years.

In the quiet, surrounded by the soaring architecture, it was easy to believe in the goodness of God. So it was during service, listening to the melting cadences of Cranmer's – surely divinely inspired – prose, or to the heavenly harmonies of the choir: the glory of music meeting, as it rolled off the curves and angles of arches and hammer beams, the exquisite certitude of mathematics. She had fallen in love with Mr Fortescue's voice when he preached at her brother's wedding so long ago (*oh, poor Georgie!*), and had believed he was a divine messenger, sent to call her to the fate God had chosen for her. All her life she had wondered what a woman was for, what

God expected of her. As a child she had wanted to be *good*, but there had been no-one who could tell her what that involved. Then God had sent Mr Fortescue, and she had done her best to be what he wanted, obedient, quiet, useful; to subdue the urges and longings he disapproved of, to confine her limbs and mind within the narrow frame he permitted.

Well, having entered the contract, made the vow, she had kept her part of the bargain; but now what was left for her? Mr Fortescue was gone, and though she had done everything she was supposed to do throughout their marriage, he had left her in penury, turned out of her home, without an income, having seen her very china and linen sold to pay for the perpetuating of his memory. How was that fair? If this was the reward for good behaviour, how could disobedience and wilfulness have been punished? And if her marriage to Mr Fortescue was God's will, what did He want for her now?

She sent the question upwards, imagined it spiralling, gently up the beams of sunlight like a dust mote. *What am I to do, God? Is this all there is for me?* She was young still, her mind was vigorous; she was strong and energetic. There was passion in her, and love, and a desire to give. *Send me a sign, God,* she begged. *Tell me it wasn't all for nothing, that you noticed, that you're still listening. Tell me what to do next.*

The sunlight hung moveless on the air, painting bars of blue shadow below the lintels. Outside in the chestnut trees a wood pigeon burbled his song. The saints looked down impassively from the stained glass of the north aisle windows, and Sir Joseph and Lady Steed knelt nose to nose above their marble tablet, absorbed in communal prayer. If God was listening, He was keeping His counsel. Henrietta sighed and stood up, picked up her basket, and turned to go.

She had left the west door open on the sunny afternoon, and when she was half-way down the aisle someone appeared in the doorway, a dark silhouette against the bright day; a man's shape, hatless. She walked on a few

527

paces more, unconcerned; and then he came on through the door and into the church, and they both stopped. The hair seemed to rise all over her scalp: it prickled like an army of ants and sent a shiver down her spine. She wanted to speak, but her lips were dry and her tongue seemed paralysed.

He saw her bewildered state, and thought perhaps she did not recognise him. 'Henrietta?' he said. She didn't move, and he started towards her again, instinctively spreading his hands in a little, open gesture, to show he meant no harm.

She could see him properly now. He was leaner, and very brown; more lined, too, either by the harshness of the weather or his experiences, she didn't know which. But still his face seemed to burn like a lamp, to her, as though he carried his own personal sun inside him.

'Is it really you?' she said at last.

He had reached a point a few paces from her and stood still. 'It's me,' he said.

'I can't believe it.'

He saw she literally couldn't. 'It's me. Poor bewildered thing, it is me! I came back.' He looked her over hungrily. 'You're still in black.'

'My brother died. George. In July.'

'I'm sorry. I didn't know.'

'No, how could you?'

A bar of sunlight was touching her head, showing all the little unruly hairs that curled upwards from her sleek crown, invisible except in silhouette. It would be illuminating, he knew, the three little curls at the nape of her neck, which would never grow long enough to be caught up. The thought of those curls and that nape made him shiver. He wanted so badly to kiss them, he could see himself doing it, as if watching a ghost. He remembered, as he had remembered nightly in the shrilling darkness, under the hot white stars of the African midnight, the feeling of her skin under his lips, the scent of her hair. He had dreamed and longed for her, hopeless of forgetting, no matter how far he wandered.

'What are you doing here?' she asked at last.

'I came back for you,' he said. 'I know your husband died – I'm sorry for your loss.'

'Thank you. It was a long time ago,' she said. It seemed so to her. Her married life was as strange as another world.

The thing he asked next had an air of blurting itself out almost despite him. 'You're not married? You haven't married again?'

'No,' she said; and it was so much in the tone of 'of course not' that he smiled, almost laughed.

'I was afraid you might have,' he said, and his relaxation was palpable.

'What about you?' she asked tentatively.

'Julia and I are divorced. It was all arranged quite amicably.' He looked at her quizzically, unable to fathom her thoughts.

'How did you know—' she began, and stopped, unsure how to phrase it.

'About you? It was simple. I met my sister and the Parke twins in Cape Town, and they told me.'

'*Did* you? What a strange coincidence!'

'Not nearly as strange as you might think. There are so few English people in Cape Town that it's impossible not to meet each other. And there are so few civilised places in Africa it's almost impossible not to be in Cape Town.'

It was something of his old manner, and she found herself smiling. 'So they told you I was a widow – what then?'

'What then, she asks. I came hurrying back, that's what then – as fast as the horses of Poseidon would carry me. You're young, beautiful, infinitely desirable – I was afraid someone would snap you up before I had a chance to make my bid. Why haven't they? The men of Bishop Winthorpe must be blockheads. The men of all England, indeed!'

'Jerome!'

'Ah, she speaks my name! It's not a dream, then. But come, come outside – I can't talk to you properly in here. Somehow one always feels one ought to whisper, and whispered eloquence is a contradiction in terms.'

He offered her his arm, and though she didn't take it, she fell in beside him and let him lead her out of the church into the sunshine. Now close beside him, and with the light full on him, she could see how much he had been worn by the weather, his travels, his unhappiness, whichever it was. Experience was graven into his face; the hair at his temples was threaded with silver. And she loved him more for it. She wouldn't have thought it possible, but she loved him more than ever.

'I'm sorry about your brother,' he said. 'How did it happen?'

She told him. 'It was odd that he died of being out in the cold too long, when that was how his wife died, too,' she concluded. 'I think he really did love her.'

'Even to his securing a matching death?' Jerome said. 'Is that the ultimate proof, then? Will it take that to convince you?' She stopped, and he turned to face her. 'I love you,' he said. 'Do you know it? I hope you do. I think you must admit it has stood the test of time, at least. And you're free now – no blame can be attached to you. You did your duty by him – I've heard all about it. I honour you for that.' She didn't speak, and he added, 'If it helps, I should tell you that in my frantic wanderings I've had time to think about things, and I believe now you were right.'

'Do you? Do you really?'

'Don't sound so surprised. It is possible for me to think an unselfish thought from time to time,' he said, gently teasing. 'You were right to keep your promise. And now you're free. Will you accept my love now? You won't still hold me off?'

Henrietta looked at him in an agony of doubt. She wanted more than anything on earth to be held in his arms, to go to him and never be more than a breath away, ever again. But she asked, 'What about your promise?'

His sadness had taught him patience. 'What about it, love? She has released me from it, as I have released her.

No harm has been done to anyone, no-one has been deceived or deserted. I've done my duty as you have done yours – now we can please ourselves.'

'In the eyes of the Church,' she said, though the words had to be dragged out of her, 'you are still married.'

He read past the words into her eyes, into her heart. If he could find an honourable way out for her, she would take it.

'The Church is only human,' he said. 'A collection of faulty, stumbling men. Look now, the Church has always remarried divorced people. In the old days, when it took an Act of Parliament to be divorced, only the wealthiest could do it, and they did it solely in order to be remarried. It was the only reason they spent the money. Now, if the Church can do it for the rich, it can't be an absolute, can it? It's not a matter of theology, but of convenience.'

She was still troubled. 'One can always argue away scruples,' she began.

'I have no scruples in this case. I believe with all my heart and my best conscience that I am free for you. Can't you respect that and accept it?'

She was silent a long moment. What God hath united, let no man put asunder, she thought: but were God and the Church one and the same? She knew he didn't think so, and she wondered herself, now. God's laws were immutable, but man's were open to interpretation. Which was marriage? God's law or man's?

Well, she had made a promise to God, and she had kept it, and that was all over now. Death had released her. She was free to make her own choice of what happened next. She had asked for a sign, after all – and here he was. And perhaps it was not possible for mortal man to be absolutely right about anything. Only God was perfect. If she was wrong, she was grown-up enough now to take responsibility for that.

She was silent for so long he misgave. Had he got it wrong again? She saw his anxiety and doubt, and was moved by the enormous courage it must have taken to present himself again after she had rejected him, risking himself so generously, exposing his vulnerable heart for her to break again. She put down her basket and held out her two hands.

'I accept it,' she said. 'I love you. I'm free to choose now.'

He took her hands, used them to draw her to him. 'And what do you choose?'

'I choose you.'

Then he folded her in his arms. He had often dreamed of this moment, and in his dreams he had kissed her passionately, as wildly as she had kissed him back. But in the event, all they did was to stand quietly, arms around each other, her face against his shoulder and his resting against her hair; pressed together in grateful silence like two people whom an avalanche has passed by and left, miraculously, alive.

DYNASTY 1:
THE FOUNDING
Cynthia Harrod-Eagles

Set in the years 1434 to 1486, the first glorious
volume of the Dynasty series is an enthralling historical
novel with the Wars of the Roses as its background. Power
and prestige are the burning ambitions of domineering, dour
Edward Morland, rich sheep-farmer and landowner, as he
sets out to arrange a marriage that will secure his empire's
future. And Robert, his son, more poet than soldier, idolises
his proud young bride, Eleanor, ward of the
influential Beaufort family.

Used to gentility and grace, Eleanor is outraged at
having to marry the son of a Yorkshire sheep-farmer, but she
must obey despite her consuming secret passion for Richard,
Duke of York. Times creates a bond, both passionate and
tender, between the apparently ill-matched husband and wife;
for Eleanor's warmth and her love for life are as great as her
rigid sense of justice. This remarkable woman is at the centre
of a pageant which blazes with colour and life.

Robert and Eleanor's marriage is the founding
of the Morland Dynasty. Life holds for them prosperity
and success – all too often mingled with tragedy as they are
embroiled in the civil strife which has divided families and
sets neighbour against neighbour.

978-0-7515-0382-1

DYNASTY 21: THE OUTCAST

Cynthia Harrod-Eagles

England in 1857 is stable and prosperous. Benedict
Morland seems settled into a comfortable routine of
estate matters and civic interests. But his orderly life
is shaken when a mysterious orphaned boy arrives on
his doorstep. No one – least of all his wife Sibella – can
understand why Bendy should take Lennox Mynott into
his household.

In London, Charlotte's stepfather persuades her to
support the new Divorce Bill, which serves only to
deepen the rift with her husband, Oliver. Should she
accept the comfort she is offered from an unexpected
source, and give up all hope of reconciliation with the
man she still loves?

Forced to remove Lennox from Morland Place, Benedict
takes him to America to join his daughter Mary at
Twelvetrees Plantation. As Lennox, an outcast no
longer, finds a new life, a family, and a cause to fight
for, Benedict becomes enamoured of the Southern
way of life, just as bitter civil war is about to destroy
it for ever . . .

978-0-7515-2317-1